sweet bird of prey

sweet bird of prey

Janice Pettit-Brundage

Sisu Books

Sparrowbush, New York

ISBN 978-0-9842283-9-3

Cover by Lisa Helder

Published by Sisu Books
www.sisubooks.com

P.O. Box 421
Sparrowbush, New York 12780

info@sisubooks.com

To my brother, Phillip Charles,
who gave me this story.
To the little boy who encouraged me to seek
The Truth.

I unconditionally love you!

thanks and acknowledgements

Special thanks and recognition to the following beautiful people:

Mom and Dad- we went through this journey together and came out better people.

My husband, Frank- your encouragement and gentle support is greatly appreciated. You have given me what I value most- freedom to walk my own journey. Much love to you.

Leslie Pasquini-Clifton, Charlotte and Frank Brundage, Michael Pettit, Moira Santiago-Brookshire, Lisa Pasquini-Helder, Lisa Hopp, Wendy Affron, and Kathy O'Neill. Thanks to my MSMC, Gator, and Pfeiffer friends. Thanks to The Hudson Valley Writers Association for your passion and creativity.

Thanks to The American Foundation of Suicide Prevention.

Special thanks to The Center for Being, Knowing, and Doing. Thank you for making this book more than words. It is filled with purpose because of all of you.

And finally, to anyone who has lost someone to suicide- this book is especially for you. We may never fully understand, and the truth is that we do not need to. All we need to do is journey through our lives with forgiveness in our hearts and unconditional love in our souls.

Much love. Namaste. God Bless.

independence day

September 6, 1988 was the morning I entered eighth grade. That day, I was secretly giddy because my psycho brother had moved to Florida. My older brother, Phillip, presented a strange situation. A situation that haunted my princess dreams at night and granted me blissful denial during the day. On that glorious September morning, I could finally savor the sweet taste of freedom. During the walk to school, the fragrance from the early morning grass along with the melodies from the delicate sparrows seemed to guarantee that my life was going in the right direction. Both liberation and independence led each confident stride as I made my way to my new homeroom. While Ms. Wolinski took roll, I daydreamed about the possibilities of a perfect, valley girl life without him: good-bye panic, good-bye humiliation, and good-bye fatty Phil. It was my chance. It was my first opportunity to simply be Shannon and not Phillip's little sister. My weirdo, butt-head brother was (gulp) gone.

While nervously thumping my legs under the desk and biting the skin around my nails, I ignored the possibility that my thoughts might be shallow and selfish. With that problem, that stupid situation thousands of miles away, I could focus on the important stuff: the stuff that revolved around Seventeen magazine, boys, or mastering the art of eyeliner application. Freedom from him allowed me to come home to a peaceful house and carelessly walk though the dimly lit halls without any vile harassment. Phillip used to call me 'a snob', or was it 'a stuck-up snob?' Who cares? His behavior over the past fourteen years gave me valid reasons to back up superficial beliefs. If only we could find some common ground. Something. Anything that could mend our deteriorated relationship.

It was difficult to ignore our sibling connection because we looked so much alike, and yet we were so different. On a typical Friday night, I was perched on the cold, metal bleachers wearing a royal blue and white Gator sweatshirt. My friends and I supported the varsity football team, made fun of the bleached blonde cheerleaders, and used any opportunity to flirt with boys. On a typical Friday night, Phillip wore his green army jacket over a dingy Metallica t-shirt. He inhaled tiny puffs from his roach clips with his druggie friends. He drank Old Milwaukee's Best while thrashing his head to Mega-Death, defying gravity by keeping his cigarette tucked behind his ear. He signified everything my friends and I hated about high school. He was one of them and my need to distance myself from him became a full-time job.

I didn't always feel that way. There was a time in a galaxy far, far away when Phillip and I were inseparable. He was my Luke Skywalker and I was his Princess Leia. I loved him. Put simply, I adored him. The idea that Phillip was my every reason to wake up in the morning seemed unbelievable. Of course, we had our share of fights, but I never considered him a full-blown terminal disease until I was twelve years old. Throughout my school years, Phillip was a sharp needle piercing my side that I never picked out until he was sitting in front of me in homeroom. That funny, freckle-faced kid was gone and I was content living my life as if I never knew him (mainly because I had no other choice.)

Phillip failed seventh grade, so we shared the same homeroom. On my first day, I stared at his greasy locks and almost barfed from the smell of stale cigarettes emanating off his dingy clothes that totally reeked. Why couldn't we just get along like normal people? Why couldn't he have cool friends? Why couldn't Phillip be like everyone else? If only he played football, or hung out with the popular guys, or dressed like the kids in the Gap commercials, or listened to music that didn't sound like someone was being murdered. Unfortunately, it was more complicated. Phillip was complicated. He drained me. I was exhausted from all the years of keeping his dark secrets and listening to confessions that always left me confused and helpless. I stewed quietly in my seat, crossed my arms, bit the inside of my lip, and reviewed all the shady stuff between us. It was then that I realized that didn't like him at all. Actually, I hated him.

My inner rage wasn't his entire fault, but I blamed most of it on him. I could sum up seventh grade with two words: it sucked. Seventh grade really sucked. For me, it was a combination of random things; random things that really sucked. I had to change for the first time in front of girls who wore black thongs, dabbed perfume behind their ears, and wore lacey bras big enough to hold C cups. I wore my grandma, Jockey-striped underwear that came in a pack of three that I had to strategically roll down, so the elastic would not peek out my shorts. The summer before seventh grade, Mom purchased my first bra at Kmart in the junior department. Instead of wearing black, lacy bras that I saw in the locker room, I wore a white razorback sports bra with thick elastic straps. My brother, who could detect my weaknesses like a canine, called me a carpenter's dream.

I also hated the greasy, stale food that the lunch ladies served us with a side of sass. Not only was the food putrid, but the humidity from the cafeteria combined with fruit flies circling the bananas made them beyond edible. Being a seventh grader meant that we were the last to eat. We were the last link on the social food chain, so we had to endure the raunchy smell of tuna salad that sat around unrefrigerated for four hours. Food wasn't the only issue. The worst, and highly overlooked, part of lunch was the vicious mixture of insecure boys and insecure girls. It could be classified as a perfect storm of insecurity. Insecurities that would no doubt follow most of us beyond adulthood, perhaps even in death.

I could never decide who was worse: the girls or the boys. The boys incessantly tried to impress each other by farting, calling each other fags, making perverted comments to innocent girls. Of course, they enjoyed making fun of the fat kid who sat alone as he nervously ate his slop. Boys were blatant. They hid nothing; in fact, they made it their number one priority to stand out amongst the sea of adolescent boys, trying to disguise their general lack of confidence by making fun of the fat kid in the corner. I saw right through it. The girls, my outward allies, were probably worse than the boys. Girls did the same stuff (with the exception of farting for pure attention) but girls did it in their own catty, malicious way. Instead of yelling down the hallway so everyone could hear them, girls simply whispered nasty stuff behind your back. Thirteen-year-old girls are certified professionals at gossip. Gossip was the class that every girl took and every girl aced easily. Junior high was the hell on earth where a girl would call you a slut behind your back and tell you that she was your friend to your face. To make matters worse, girl on girl gossip was totally accepted, if not encouraged.

Fortunately for me, seventh grade was nothing more than a distant memory clouded by the stench of oily French-fries, Aqua Net high hair, and skin-tight, acid wash jeans. My hopes of becoming a new Shannon Bennet kept me up at night with dreamy visions of being *that girl*. Everyone wants to be that girl; the girl who looked like a peppermint gum commercial, the girl who had clever answers to everything, the girl who was free from any dirt-bag association. The endless possibilities danced around my head at night and managed to waltz into my daydreams. I was finally free. The embarrassment of my brother would no longer lurk in the halls of Gateway, or in my teacher's sympathetic faces, or even in the confused looks of those who could not associate the two of us as brother and sister.

My brother was living his new life in Florida and I was rebuilding my new life in south Jersey. For the first time in fifteen years, he reclaimed his relationship with his long lost, dead-beat dad. Regrettably, his dead-beat dad was also my dead-beat dad. I have never met him. The only evidence of his existence or physical resemblance to my brother or I was captured in an old Polaroid from 1976. I joked that I could only pick him out of a criminal line up if he was standing next to a group of Japanese men. I should mention that I am German. In my eyes, he was the dispensable sperm donor who bolted when Phillip and I were babies.

Phillip always had a false heroic version of his father - or fairytale. He thought that our absent father was locked up in a dungeon with a fire-breathing dragon guarding the door. Phillip assumed that there had to be some inexplicable reason why our father was missing for so many years. I, however, figured out that there were not any dragons or mythological explanations; he was simply a dead-beat. My brother filled himself with aspirations of salvaging their long lost father-son relationship. Phillip's desire to be his father's son would finally become a reality in April of 1988. Fifteen New Year's resolutions made, fifteen Christmas mornings came and went, and fifteen birthday cakes were wished upon before my brother finally met his mysterious dad.

I was fortunate enough to have a best friend by my side throughout the years. Her name was Elizabeth Joanne Bastini. Lizzie was the youngest of three sisters. Lizzie was Catholic and a hard-core Italian. All of those things intrigued me because I had no sense of religion, no sisters, and my light complexion and freckles were a dead give away to my German/Irish background.

Lizzie became my best friend when I was five. She never had to worry about being embarrassed in public by her brother or her brother shouting to everyone that she wore a Barbie doll bra. She was lucky enough to have two popular older sisters and, by that genetic association, she was instantly cool. I, however, had to defend my honor when people asked, "You're Phillip's sister? Hmmm? Phillip? Wiezer?"

At our sixth grade graduation, we both wore pink and we both had incredibly bad hair. I, regrettably, admit we were sporting typical eighties mullets. Lizzie held her ceremonial royal blue and white carnations, while I leaned in close pretending to smell them. That day, Mr. Knauss and Mr. Owens, the only male teachers in our school, took turns addressing the departing class of 1987. I suppose the idea was to inspire us with last minute words of wisdom or memorable clichés before we took our long journey two miles down the street to high school.

Mr. Knauss, my sixth grade teacher, severely disappointed me with his commencement speech. I expected something profound or philosophical to lead me in the right direction. Instead, he cleared his turkey gizzard throat, pressed his bottle-cap glasses to his large, bushy unibrow, and declared, "Right now, you are a big fish in a little pond. Next year, you will be a little fish in a big pond."

I listened to him with my head sideways, my palm propping up my cheek, wondering if he gave the same advice every year. I expected a better ending. His analogies about "fish" and "ponds" were completely unacceptable, not to mention juvenile. That sophisticated, old man enlightened us with lectures about the Titanic and civil rights. That man taught us about the history of Philadelphia and introduced us to the ideas of communism, socialism, and capitalism. All of which were probably not suitable for our eleven year old mentality. Mr. Knauss was the first teacher who spoke about social issues and allowed us to give an actual opinion in class. Nevertheless, that bull-crap line about "fish" and "ponds" was an extreme disappointment.

Unfortunately, Mr. Knauss had a reputation throughout the years of being the weird, creepy old man; the old man who possibly lived with his mother or possibly owned five cats. His name circulating around the playground was "Boogie-Man." I was never sure if that name stuck because he picked his nose or because he lived in a haunted house in West Deptford (allegedly.) His knowledgeable lectures were suited for an audience much older and wiser than bucked-toothed, sixth grade brats. To me, his tweed jackets adorned with brown leather patches on his elbow and his white skunk stripes on the side of his head made him more interesting than weird.

Mr. Knauss was obsessed with the Civil War. I got the impression that he was one of those cheesy guys who attended or engaged in Civil War reenactments in local parks during the weekends. I was certain that he spent hours researching that war, that time, and anything to do with the 1860s. I imagined him taking tiny sips of whisky, sitting in his creaking rocking chair for hours on chilly nights while he pondered the many battles fought on American soil. His love for the only war fought on our homeland sparked a new love within me. Although, I would never admit it, I stored all my hand written notes regarding the civil war in a blue spiral notebook. From time to time, I would read it for my own enjoyment- minus the whisky and rocking chair.

Mr. Owens, Lizzie's sixth grade teacher, was undeniably the cooler teacher. When you are in sixth grade, cooler will always beat smarter. Mr. Owens possessed both charm and humor. He often whistled show tunes when he strutted down the hallways. Perhaps it was his skintight, polyester pants or his tight, curly afro that caught our attention, but I thought it had something to do with his insane whistling skills.

The departing sixth grade class perked up at their desks anticipating an intense farewell speech by Mr. Owens. We waited anxiously; we waited for our super-cool hero to expel the secrets to surviving seventh grade. He sauntered slowly to the front of the classroom, afro swaying while the zipper of his skintight pants held on for dear life. He surmised that we were still children and that it was time to start adopting the morals, values, and responsibilities held by adults. Just as he is finished his remarks about commitments and accountability, Todd McManus ripped the loudest fart ever, right behind me. After Mr. Owens inspected the area and caught a glimpse of Todd, he scoffed, ignoring the disturbance. When he picked up his speech from where he left off, all I could think about was

Todd's fart. Why was that so funny? It always amazed me that any dull moment became hilarious when someone farted. I straightened my back, pressed it against the hard seat while laughing inside at Todd's shenanigans. Todd leaned toward me and whispered in my ear, "Was that you? Did ya have beans last night?"

I turned around to face him, rolled my eyes, and calmly recited, "Those who blame it... must claim it." I heard my brother say that. I shook my head, trying to act like I was totally grossed out, (but I wasn't) and whispered, "You smelly... gross... never take a shower... degenerate."

"Degenerate? What's a degenerate?" He asked.

With the final dismissal bell and our summer freedom only two minutes away, Mr. Owens began laying it on pretty thick. He sternly, but gently, warned, "You will find that you will go different directions at Gateway and some of the friends you have now may not be your friends in high school. And... that is ok." Mr. Owens nodded his head as he agreed with his own statement. It seemed like all adults had an uncontrollable need to nod their heads when they are trying to make a point. After an extended pause and awkward silence, he added, "You will all create your own paths and choose different directions. Value each other, be nice to one another, and never forget who you are." He held his hand up to his chest and proclaimed, "By sheer numbers, there is a good possibility that one of you will not make it all the way to twelfth grade."

His statement caught me off guard because I was still thinking about Todd McManus. Why would he say that? Wasn't he supposed to perpetuate the idea that life was going to be wonderful? I thought that all of us would live happily ever after with a white picket fence, 2.5 kids, and a black Labrador retriever. I twisted my body toward Todd, wanting to know if he was the slightest bit worried or alarmed by Mr. Owens's statement. I gathered that he was not interested at all when I noticed him scribbling all over his yearbook. He drew mustaches and devil horns on the black and white class pictures.

I nudged him with my elbow and eagerly inquired, "Todd, did you hear that?" There was a hint of anxiety hidden in my voice that I tried to disguise. I nudged again, "Hey, Todd? You might not see me at high school graduation. Hey! Psst!"

Todd looked to me with a big grin and said, "Yeah, if I'm lucky."

With dry sarcasm, I blankly glared at him and flatly whined, "Ha-ha."

When I turned back to face Mr. Owens, I remembered why Todd was not interested in hearing about death. Todd was one of the few kids in my school who understood what death was like, unlike the rest of us who just passively talked about the possibility. Todd's dad died of a heart attack when he was in third grade. Every single sixth grader knew that his dad died and every single one of us avoided talking about it. In fact, Todd and I sat next to each other for a full year and during that time, he mentioned his dad only once. One day, he said, "My dad has been gone for three years and I feel like it just happened yesterday." I wanted to tell him that I was sorry about his father, but I just nodded my head with sympathetic agreement and slowly turned around.

The only thing good about seventh grade was my locker partner, Justine Turner. Justine flashed me an overly happy smile when she heard her name matched with mine. I was both relieved and skeptical. Anyone who smiled that big or that often made me nervous. I listened to Justine gab cheerfully like a valley girl hopped up on Sugar Smacks. The entire time she spoke to me, I stared at her deep dimples and painted smile. Justine bobbed her head and used her hands to emphasize every other word. She seemed so happy. Why was she so happy? I wish I could be that happy. Justine was a cute Wenonah girl. Wenonah was the town next to mine where lawyers, doctors, and expensive she-she salons were located. Justine played that part of a preppie lawyers' daughter perfectly and I imagined that she went to those she-she salons. Her long ponytail swayed back and forth whenever she moved her head. She asked me if I liked The Cure and I debated on whether to tell her that I hated them or loved them. So, I just said, "They're alright." I was just glad the girl who wore the shirt with the small alligator was my locker partner, instead of the girl who wore the glittered pastel unicorn. Big difference.

On the way back to my desk, after receiving my combination lock from my homeroom teacher, Phillip took advantage of our unfortunate situation. He called out, "Hey, Shannon… we're missing some toilet paper at home. Did you stuff your bra, again?" After his crude comment, he scanned his new classroom hoping that someone would find him amusing. The response, thankfully, was a mixture of curious glances along with nervous disinterest. Throughout my entire life, I have endured embarrassing comments and nasty jokes by Phillip. I knew I was an easy target to him. However, after thirteen long years of living with my brother, I had some insight into his weaknesses, and his biggest weakness was painfully obvious. Phillip's Achilles heal: his chunky body was always exposed for all to see.

I calmly strolled back to my seat, pretending that his antics did not bother me, but, naturally, they did. I flopped down on the hard seat and hissed at him from behind.

"Shut-up! You big, fat loser!" I studied my new locker combination, and then added, "If you weren't such a fugly-ugly, fat lard, you wouldn't be in this homeroom, and I wouldn't have to smell your horrible body odor! God! You are such a skuzzy... ugly... smelly... jerk-off!" After I settled down from my attack, my face turned red with embarrassment. I looked around and noticed that not only were all my new classmates staring at us, but my new homeroom teacher also looked on with repulsion. I sunk down in my seat and blamed Phillip for making me look like an idiot. It appeared our ugly relationship would reveal itself much sooner than I had anticipated.

The kids in my class eagerly sat on the edge of their seats, waiting for Phillip's rebuttal. Phillip gave up in defeat. He clicked his teeth and muttered, "Whatever." I won the first of many battles. The only way to defeat him was by never backing down or giving in. Phillip had an uncanny sixth sense that gave him the ability to detect a person's most guarded weaknesses. He was like a hound dog that could sniff out hidden vulnerabilities from miles away.

Phillip's attempt to impress the kids in our new classroom would be tougher than he thought. I knew my brother, and I knew that he would spend all of his energy getting their attention, somehow. My brother had an insatiable need for desperate disciples to laugh at all his stupid jokes. I watched him gather blind followers throughout the years. His followers were the delinquents that needed someone like Phillip to entertain them. It did not matter who laughed at his jokes, just as long as someone laughed with him, instead of at him. Unfortunately, his desire to be accepted would come at my expense.

Mrs. DeStephano, our homeroom teacher, observed the two of us from her desk. Her interest made me feel like some kind of social experiment. Her inquisitive stares were all too familiar and I was quite used to the undesired negative attention. I played with my Trapper-Keeper, checking the contents inside repeatedly in order to appear busy. I opened and closed the bulky Velcro notebook several times to avoid the eyes that burned holes in my back. Sometimes, I felt like Phillip's only purpose in life was to make me feel as bad as he did about himself. It wasn't my fault he failed. It wasn't my fault he was fat. Most of all, it wasn't my fault that he acted like a total retard; so why did I feel like it was my fault? Somewhere deep inside me, I knew I shared some responsibility for him. I was supposed to look after him, guard him, and protect him; instead, I blamed him, hated him, and shunned him away. Even at thirteen, I knew my brother was not normal, but I ignored it- just like everyone else.

Seventh grade was off to a terrible start. I cursed at him under my breath and wished that I was an only child. I spent a lot of my time visualizing how wonderful my life would be without him. I sat behind him as he made jokes, imitated cartoon characters, and harmonized to the human beat box by the Fat Boys. Within minutes, everyone congregated around him, soaking up all of his corny jokes, practically begging him for more. I rolled my eyes, shook my head, and scoffed every time I heard one of his recited lines. If they only knew what he was really like- then they would understand why I was so mean to him.

Unfortunately, Phillip and I shared the same last name. I hated my last name. I hated looking at it, writing it, or being associated with it. I hated having a last name that held no meaning or significance to me. Wiezer was a painful reminder of my sperm donor, dead-beat father who left us before I was even born. When mom remarried, she took on the last name Bennet, which left Phillip and I with a family name and heritage riddled with white-trash drunks. A family tree that sprouted one bad apple after the next. Phillip and I were the latest rotten seeds that promised more disappointment. History had a way of repeating itself and I was determined to be the first Wiezer to finish school or graduate college. Actually, the family had set the bar pretty low, so just staying sober seemed like a victory.

It seemed ironic and somewhat abusive to have a name of someone that you have never met. My biological father and I never shared one conversation in thirteen years. He didn't know me at all. He didn't know that I liked peanut butter and banana sandwiches. He wasn't there to see my first missing tooth. He didn't know that I was scared of gorillas. In fact, he spelled my name wrong when he mentioned me in a letter addressed to my mother. Yet, I had his last name; that declared me his property. My birth name, Wiezer, was in capital letters on the back of my soccer uniform, on my birth certificate, and on every one of my official documentations. To make matters worse, I had to explain to everyone why my mother and I had different last names. What was a kid supposed to say? "My dad split." Or, "When my dad found out my mom was pregnant with me, he bolted." Or, "My father didn't want me." Each answer was true. Instead, I said, "My mom and dad got divorced and now my mom is remarried." That answer was also true.

Ever since I could remember, Phillip was proud to have his father's name. The name was the one and only tangible bond that tied them together. Phillip and I also shared the same last name, so we had permission to discuss and theorize about our absent father. We instinctively knew we were never supposed to ask questions about him to anyone who did not share our last name. Our biological father was a mysterious man who freely roamed the earth. He was a desperate man who left the three of us behind to fend for ourselves. Mom never talked about him, so we never asked. We had a new father. A father that took care of us, fed us, housed us, and loved us. I often felt that bringing up the subject meant that I was somehow disloyal to my new dad. Phillip, however, wanted to know more about the man who claimed to be his father on his birth certificate. Back then, my older brother often sought help from the only person who could possibly help him- me.

Phillip and I always hid our discussions regarding our missing father. We only felt comfortable talking about the situation when we were in each other's presence. Even though the topic was obvious, we often danced around it because it was too complex for either one of us to understand. The pieces of the puzzle didn't seem to fit. We made up our own stories about him and rationalized the reasons why he left us behind. Any made up reason was agreeable to me, but Phillip could never come to grips that his own flesh and blood had abandoned him. It was evident that Phillip held the weight of his father's disappearance upon his tiny shoulders, while I blissfully denied that I cared.

"Where do you think he is?" Phillip asked, as he held his beat up Death Star spaceship in the air.

I could not remember the date, or the exact time, or the condition of the weather, but I could always remember the feeling in the pit of my stomach whenever my brother asked about him. Our conversations about our father were never serious; in fact, the mood was often ordinary or intentionally riddled with distractions to keep our minds preoccupied if the subject became too deep.

My face was flush after he posed the question. I knew who he was asking about, but I played dumb. I placed Princess Leia by my side and coyly inquired, "Who?" I searched the *Star Wars*-littered floor and found Han Solo. I held the miniature figurine in my scrawny fingers and announced, "Here he is... Han Solo. You want him?"

Phillip did not respond. He didn't bother to raise his head or shrug his shoulders to acknowledge my gesture. After a couple nervous moments of fidgeting with his action figures, he shook his head in disappointment. I knew why. I knew that I was the only one who would understand why his question needed an answer. Phillip expected more from me. His question about our father required an answer that would ultimately absolve him from any responsibility. Phillip wanted to hear that it wasn't his fault.

"No! Not stupid Han Solo... you dummy!" He clicked his teeth and let out a deep sigh. He finally looked me in the eyes and whispered, "Phil. Phillip Weizer. My dad. Your dad. Our dad. Duh?" His eyes softened as the words awkwardly came out of his mouth. Then he asked, "Do you think he's in Florida?"

Funny, I never connected the word dad with Phil Weizer. Hearing that name and 'our dad' in the same sentence made me very uncomfortable.

I hesitated a little bit, and then muttered, "Him." I narrowed my eyes and gazed at the ceiling.

Maybe my hesitation was partly due to my temporary belief that Phillip might actually need me. When we were kids, nothing made my self-esteem skyrocket like the acceptance of my older brother.

At that moment, I wished I could give him exactly what he wanted. I wanted to give him the truth. The only facts that I could give him were the facts that he already knew: Our dad left us. I didn't know where he was and I was not supposed to care. Any response to his question would simply be assumptions or possibilities. All I had to do was make the assumptions look encouraging. I shrugged my shoulders and thoughtfully said, "Well, maybe he's in Florida. I mean, that's what Mom said. She said he lives in Florida. Well, that and he was a truck driver or something." That was true. That was all I really knew about him.

I could tell by Phillip's blank expression that he was hoping for more information. His thirst for knowledge from me gave me a sense of superiority. For once, I was in control and I liked that feeling.

Phillip's head went down. Then, he quickly looked up and curiously asked, "Don't you ever wonder about him?" It was a question that was really a statement in disguise.

"No!" I emphatically responded. I lied. I had to lie. If I told him that I thought about my biological dad, then I would betray my stepdad. I was lucky to have a new dad, lucky to be loved, lucky to have a stranger take my biological father's place. So, admitting that I sometimes thought about him made me feel disloyal.

Phillip placed his Luke Skywalker in fighting position to distract him from the tension that was building in the room. "What if he is not such a bad guy? I mean, you never know. He might be okay. Mom married him, right?" Phillip glanced curiously in my direction. His facial expression told me that I was supposed to agree.

Phillip's theory about our mother was very subjective. It was clear that my mom had no other choice but to marry him. She was poor, alone, 16 years old, and scared to death. My brother never knew the power he had over me and the mere suggestion that our father might be a decent man caught me off guard. A decent man doesn't leave his family behind.

"Phillip!" I barked.

My brother quickly turned in my direction. His face reflected a mixture of sadness and interest.

"He's gone. He is not here. Right?" I tried to sound sincere, but it came out demanding instead. I tried again. "I don't know where he is and if I think about it... it makes me, uh, I guess, it makes me mad. You know?" The conversation wasn't supposed to be about my feelings, but they crept their way out of the darkness and into the light.

Phillip coughed. He looked sideways and slowly repeated, "Mad?" He cleared his throat and then admitted, "I guess I get mad sometimes. Uhh, I just think that..." He tossed his toys in a small pile while shrugging his shoulders and continued, "I just, I don't know how to say it."

"Say what?"

"I just think that, like, maybe it was my fault. You know?" Phillip began rattling off all the reasons why he was to blame. They were all stupid reasons, but in his mind, he believed every single one. He came at the wrong time. He cost them too much money. He wasn't smart enough. Each reason was more ridiculous than the last.

"Yeah, but, it's not your fault. That's just a stupid thing to say."

The truth was simple: I blamed myself. I was the one who was unwanted. I found out that my dad left when I was born, not when Phillip was born. It was easy to deflect my issues in order to console my tormented brother.

"Phillip," I began, "He's a loser. We're better off without him. I mean, if he really wanted to see us, don't you think that he would have, like, called or something?"

Phillip looked at me with a new intensity. I must have said something profound.

I repeated, "Loser."

Phillip sighed and shook his head with agreement.

"I guess," he replied.

As I sat in my seat behind my brother, I angrily recounted the abuse he advertently and inadvertently put me through. Mrs. DeStephano diligently took attendance and when she called Phillip's name, her glare was an indication that they were not strangers. When she called my name, she pronounced the 'a' in Shannon very short. I hated when people did that. She sounded like one of those people from up-state New York. I cringed at the sound of her enunciation of my name. Most people made that mistake and most times, I corrected them. However, since I was already under the microscope, I decided to sit quietly and let it pass, realizing that I will probably be called that everyday for the rest of the year.

"Shannon Wiezer?" She frantically searched the room to catch a glimpse of my face. She wanted to look me over, just like every other teacher I have ever had in the past.

Without looking her directly in the eyes, I dropped my head to review my new schedule. I could feel her staring at me. I was the weirdo's sister, so people would study me like a new species at the zoo.

That feeling was nothing new, but it certainly never became old. When I was small, I was confused by all the negative attention. Children have an uncanny intuition that can sense emotions, so even though I wasn't sure why Phillip was bad, I understood the uncomfortable butterflies that fluttered around my stomach.

I guess my first recollection of those nervous butterflies was in first grade. Mrs. Melindo was my teacher and she had the privilege of having my brother in her class the previous year. Mrs. Melindo never knew the impact that she made on a windy November morning. The class lesson was just starting. I recall it being very early in the day. My first grade teacher stretched her long stick with the white rubber on the end, pointing out the alphabet letters strung above of the black board. I could not sit still. I could not endure the monotony of singing the alphabet one more time. Back then, they called it "fidgety" or "hyper"; today, they might call it Attention Deficit Disorder. It takes a whole team of doctors, teachers, and therapists to classify kids with this disorder. Perhaps, they should label it boredom disorder. The class chanted another tedious rendition of the ABCs, while my mind shifted from one random thought to the next random thought. My thoughts became acting out, and my acting out resulted in a couple of ignored warnings from my teacher. Mrs. Melindo shot me that face; the face that meant, "You better shut the hell up."

Mrs. Melindo placed her stubby hands on her plump hips. I wasn't sure if she was annoyed with me or if she was on the verge of cracking a smile. After she hobbled over to me with her enormous cankles and grabbed my arm, I knew which direction she was heading. She led me into the hallway by pressing her fingers in the skin of my arm, using minor pressure when she held my arm high to direct me outside the classroom. I stood in front of her and held my breath as she leaned in close to me. I literally held my breath because I could smell her coffee breath and her nasty, stale cigarette stench. Her big bowling ball brown eyes began to narrow when she began to chastise my inappropriate behavior. She leaned over and waved her miniature sausage fingers in my face.

My heart began beating fast at the sight of her nostrils flaring in anger. She barked, "Shannon. What has gotten into you today? You are being very rude!" Then, she finally closed the door, leaving us alone in the spooky, dimly lit hallway.

I stood mere inches from her disapproving eyes, inching and squirming backwards to avoid her rancid breath. Mrs. Melindo continued her line of rehearsed questions, never allowing me to answer anything before she asked another. "Do you think you are funny? Do you want to be out in the hallway? Are you happy with your behavior today?" Every time I opened my mouth to answer, I was dealt another blow of the remnants of her menthol Virginia Slims.

I kept my mouth and nasal passages shut and let her proceed. Mrs. Melindo took a step back and looked me up and down. Her voice changed from condescending to sarcastic. She coyly asked, "You know what? You know who you remind me of right now?"

That was a weird question to ask.

She smirked, shook her head methodically, and stated, "You are acting just like your brother. Do you know that? Is that who you want to be like? Your brother?" She crossed her arms and rapidly tapped her Barney Rubble foot. She cocked her head to the side when she muttered, "Just like him."

Judging by her accusations, I knew what I was supposed to say. I knew I was supposed to tell her that I did not want to be anything like Phillip. At that moment, I was confused. My stomach began fluttering the first of many nervous butterflies. If I just told her that I did not want to be like him, then the bad breath, the flaring nostrils, and the humiliation would end. But, at the time, I liked my brother, looked up to him, and wanted to be just like him, so the answer should have been... no. So, naturally I did what any six year old would do; I gave in and told her what she wanted to hear.

I put my head down, glanced down at my Buster Brown boots, and answered, "No."

I lied.

I scurried back to my seat, thankful that the humiliation was over. My entire first grade class watched my every move, wondering what happened in that hallway. When I sat in my chair, I put my head down on the hard desk. I hid my face and tried to pretend that the kids in my class were not there and that I was all alone. That unfamiliar feeling in the pit of my stomach made me feel weird about my brother. I kept my head down and wondered why he was so bad, and hated myself for betraying him.

Moments later, I turned my head sideways and caught a glimpse of the second graders going to art class. Phillip walked past and saw me looking into the hallway. He stopped walking when our eyes connected. He crossed his eyes and stuck out his tongue. I smiled. Then, he put two fingers in the air and mouthed the word, "peace." I smiled again.

I sat in my seat and wondered why I shouldn't be like him... he's funny.

i don't like mike

Walking into eighth grade offered both freedom and a new identity. I was officially Shannon Bennet. My step-dad adopted me in a tiny courthouse in the center of Woodbury. My biological father consented. The judge asked me three basic questions, Lizzie's mom testified as a witness, and then (Tada!) I was Shannon Bennet. Afterwards, we ate pancakes at the Colonial Diner. It was that easy.

A different last name gave me hope. My adopted name granted me independence along with concrete evidence that Phillip and I were not related. Phillip was probably bopping into his new homeroom, thousands of miles away, still cracking perverted 'Yo' Mama' jokes. Instead of staring into his straggly, brown hair, I saw Lizzie's bouncy ponytail swaying and enjoyed the flowery scent of Finesse that lingered wherever her hair moved. That moment, the moment I declared that I was my own person- that I was free- filled me with a newness that most people searched for an entire lifetime. As my homeroom teacher began to rattle off our last names, I folded my hands on my desk, held my breath, and anxiously waited to hear my new name called so everyone could hear.

Mrs. Wakowski, my eighth grade homeroom teacher, called out each name without taking one single breath. Without inhaling, she managed to take roll in a matter of seconds.

She called out, Abate... Albertson... Antonuchi... Bastina... Bennet?"

When my name was called, I was the only one who actually raised my hand *and* verbally responded. I beamed inside with pride as I assertively announced, "Present."

I began to blush when I thought about the gravity of what just occurred. Nobody knew. Nobody could ever understand why it was so refreshing to respond to my new last name. I smiled, and then quietly giggled when I heard the words of Martin Luther King, Jr., echo in my head, *free at last.* My warm and fuzzy feelings vanished as I, along with the rest of the class, gawked at skuzzy Jen Butler. Thankfully, her fugly-ugly face was virtually undetectable due to the enormous pink Hubba-Bubba bubble protruding from her black painted lips. Apparently, she mastered the ability to blow a bubble the size of a balloon and I was positive she worked on that useless skill all summer. She was such a loser.

The first dismissal bell rang, excusing us from one tiny classroom to our next tiny classroom. Like a herd of sheep, we methodically followed each other around the halls. My social studies class was literally forty steps away, so I took my time picking up my backpack and adjusting my new, pink, Polo-collared shirt. In junior high, it was common knowledge that showing up to class on time was a complete waste of our allotted four minutes of freedom. I greeted my salt and pepper haired teacher, Mr. Jenner, with a half smile. The kind of smile that implied, "I am here, but try to act like I am not here." Even though there were twenty-four seats open, I stood in the front of the room, examining each desk, so I could pick the perfect spot. Mr. Jenner watched me with slight amusement and returned my half smile with a cynical chuckle.

He cocked his head sideways and said, "You know, they're all the same price." He followed his statement with another chuckle. "Would you like the usher to accompany you to your seat?"

I politely nodded and immediately found a seat next to the wall. I loved sarcasm and I could sniff out sarcastic people miles away. My recipe for perfect sarcasm was: two parts intelligence, one part humor, perfect execution, and just a pinch of smart-ass. Two minutes later, the seats were stuffed with fresh meat. The second bell went off, warning the sheep to join their herd or forever be lost in the abyss of empty hallways. Mr. Jenner took roll and predictably explained the rules for his predictably lame eighth grade social studies class. His dry humor kept me interested. I liked him. Most teachers lacked a witty personality or they lost it somewhere over the years. Teaching immature, junior-high punks could suck the life out of anyone. His rules were basic, but I could tell that he was a teacher who would bend them sometimes.

He raised one finger to accentuate each of his rules. He stated, "No gum. No food. Get here on time. Don't talk unless you raise your hand. And, of course..." he moved his head back and forth, scanning each of us. "...No beer." He laughed and then dryly stated, "Just joking." Then, he darted his eyes playfully at Monty Bard.

Monty smirked and put his hands up to defend himself. "Hey man! I only touch the hard stuff."

As the class chimed in with their "oooohhhs and aaaahhhhs," I began to wonder how it was even possible for Monty to be in my grade, let alone high school. Monty was at least eighty years old (slight exaggeration) with a full-grown beard.

Later in class, Mr. Jenner was handing out our syllabus. I made believe that I had to scratch my shoulder, so I could peek at who was sitting behind me. Unfortunately, I saw Jen Butler's pale face staring out the window. Wow, Jen certainly changed over the summer. Within the span of two months, she transformed into a creepy goth. The only color Jen wore was black. She covered herself from her shoulders to shins with a long, black trench coat. Her short nails, over-sized cargo pants, and high top Dr. Martens were different shades of black. The only other color she wore on her skinny body besides black was a wispy streak of white hair that lined her mohawk. Jen's dark raccoon eyes gazed out the sunshiny window; she seemed so out of place. I stared her up and down with total disgust. My disapproval was mixed with fear because I knew she could seriously hurt me. What was up with the goth look? It was so hideous. Does she own a mirror? She was so freaking weird. My thoughts about her apparent attempts to terrify the general public were disrupted by the sound of Mr. Jenner's voice.

"Uhhh- hey you! Skunky! No gum in my classroom!" He picked up his green trashcan, extended his wrinkly pointer finger to Jen, and then to the trashcan.

Skunky! I loved it! Skunky! I laughed out loud. I shrunk in my seat and blushed with the realization that I was the only one who found it remotely funny. Perhaps the class remained silent for fear she might cast a spell on them, or make a voodoo doll and stick needles in it late at night. By that comment alone, I fell in love with Mr. Jenner. I began laughing inside, visualizing how hard it must have been to create such a pitiful look. The entire class held their breath, switching their glances back and forth between Jen and Mr. Jenner. We held our breath and curiously watched to see if the newly transformed goth girl conformed to rules and regulations.

Jen slowly rose from her chair. She managed to stand up while keeping her hands firmly pressed on the wooden desk. I could not take my eyes off her. She deliberately walked to the front of the room in super slow motion. Her scary eyes darted at Mr. Jenner as she defiantly blew another monstrous pink bubble. Instead of physically removing the slippery glob from her gross, black mouth, she narrowed one eye, sized up the green trashcan, and spit her pink gum from a remarkable two feet away. Bull's-eye! She hit her mark. Holy crap! That was amazing! Everyone hooted and hollered, clearly repulsed by her actions, but at the same time, we were completely entertained. I questioned if I could spit that far and hit my mark. I mean, it was quite a distance.

Mr. Jenner sat behind his desk with his hands folded on his lap. He shook his head and watched her strut back to her seat. My entire class seemed intrigued by Jen's performance. The dismissal bell saved Mr. Jenner from giving a standard teacher(ish) lecture. We bolted out the door before he could reprimand her. I even witnessed a boy from my class give her a thumbs-up sign.

With the departure of my brother, I assumed that people would be curious and ask questions about his absence. To prepare for all the awkward questions, I created fake conversations in my head. I practiced my rehearsed lines and thoroughly planned every response. It took six hours and fifteen minutes for someone to ask me about Phil Weizer. Ms. Franklin, my old math teacher in seventh grade, stopped me at my locker between seventh and eighth period. She hugged her books, placed her hand lightly on my shoulder, and tenderly asked, "How was your summer?"

Ms. Franklin was young, maybe five years out of college, and I always liked her because she seemed to like me. She had my brother in her class two years ago and, even though he was a royal pain in the butt, she seemed genuinely interested in him.

I nervously switched my backpack from one shoulder to the other. I was happy to see her. I actually missed her over the summer. I politely replied, "It was good."

"So?" She began, "Are you ready for field hockey this year?" Her perfect, white teeth were mesmerizing. I found it difficult to look away from her mouth.

I shrugged my shoulders as my official answer and, then, replied, "Yeah. I guess. I mean, we started practice, like, a week before school started and…" I switched my backpack again, "We have about thirty girls on the team."

She asked about my summer and I asked her about her summer, but we both knew that she really wanted to ask about Phillip. Eventually, our friendly talk changed from idle chitchat to matters that were more serious. Her voice became lower as if we were about to exchange secrets. Her voice reminded me of how old people talked when they discussed cancer. "So, how is your brother? Is he attending school in Florida?" Her brown eyes expressed both sympathy and concern.

By the look in her eyes and the sound of her voice, I knew my brother was the student who was talked about. (Not in a good way, either.) I stood with my backpack swinging by my feet and had a vision. I visualized the teachers, the faculty, the principle, and the entire school board having a wild party in the sacred teachers' lounge to celebrate his departure. I imagined the balloons swaying in the stuffy room, the half-eaten cake, the women letting their hair down, the men undoing their ties, and the music blasting as they merrily chanted, "Hey, hey! Goodbye!" Talking about him made me feel uncomfortable. I tried to remember how I practiced it. I had to sound happy. I had to make the situation look good. "He's good." I nervously smiled. "He calls home sometimes, and he wrote me three letters over the summer." I couldn't make eye contact with Ms. Franklin when the subject was about Phillip. "Umm, I think he goes to some kind of, like, technical school. I think it's a special school. You know? It's for kids who don't go to normal high school." My response came out more like a question than an answer. "I don't know. It's something like that. But, yeah, he's good."

Ms. Franklin smiled with the positive news. Before she left, I sarcastically added, "Well, he's only been in school for a week. So, just give him some time- he'll mess it up." Then, I quickly walked away. After my comment, I winced and thought: *awww, man! That was not what I rehearsed.*

Science was my last class of the day. Science was right after lunch, so I was severely crashing after inhaling French-fries and ice cream. To make matters worse, my science teacher was Mrs. DiCicca. The frail, delicate woman standing in the front of the classroom stuttered and repeated every other word. On top of that, she had a terrible blinking problem. I tried to count every time she blinked, but I gave up due to the mental exhaustion of just watching her. She was so skinny. Did she ever eat at Burger King? Instead of listening to her opening commentary, I stared her up and down and tried to figure out how much she weighed. My estimation was 99 pounds soaking wet. I laughed inside when I thought about her ordering a double cheeseburger from McDonalds. "Double, double. Cheese, cheese. Burger, burger. Please, please."

The seating chart was predetermined, which meant it was probably going to be in alphabetical order. Mrs. DiCicca called us out two by two, which sounded more like four by four. She directed us to our raised laboratory tables and announced that we would have our lab partner for the remainder of the year. I almost ran out of the room when she paired me up with Mike Drummond.

Mike slowly made his way over to our lab table, dragging his super-sized, untied high-top sneakers. His huge red and white Reeboks flopped off his heals when he walked over because his shoelaces were missing. He slithered into the seat next to me and crossed his arms awkwardly. When he sat down, I rolled my eyes and scoffed. Some people might have thought that I was acting like a total snob, but truthfully, I was acting like a total stuck-up, snob. Mike Drummond and I were from two entirely different planets. He was the scum that I picked off the bottom of my shoes. My reaction to him was quite normal; he was a dirt-bag and I was not. I clicked my teeth to make my displeasure known. Mike noticed my attitude. He peeked over at me and looked completely confused; perhaps it was his crossed-eyes that made him look that way. He nodded to me and timidly waved his hand, which I conveniently ignored.

Even though I never had a single conversation with him, I hated Mike Drummond. It wasn't because he was cross-eyed or because he wore untied high-tops. (That was only part of it.) Mike was one of the dirty losers that Phillip hung out with last year. Not only did I hate Mike, I hated anyone who looked like him, dressed like him, or associated with him. Mike, along with his crew of 'druggies,' were the freaks that my friends and I made fun of. Last year, my brother joined the coalition of scumbags and I blamed all of them for playing a part in his breakdown.

Druggies had a dress code. The worn-out, black concert tee-shirt seemed to be mandatory. The tee-shirts ranged from *Megadeth* to *Metallica* to *Pantera*, or any group that glorified the skull and crossbones. Druggies wore skin tight, acid-wash jeans, high-top sneakers, and a leather/jean jacket. Of course, their jackets were embroidered with a *Guns N' Roses* patch on the back. Naturally, the ensemble would not be complete without an outdated mullet haircut.

When Phillip began hanging out with the druggies, our sibling relationship went from bad to worse. Not only was his entire way of thinking completely different from mine, his physical appearance drastically differed from mine, as well. He grew his hair long, changed his music from rap to metal, and he became a professional chain smoker. His devotion to his new group of friends was permanent. His appearance hid what lurked deep inside and his change was not only cosmetic, it was socially noticeable. His transformation embarrassed me, and formally separated us into classifications of 'us' and 'them.' He was one of the losers who smoked cigarettes by the gate at the end of school grounds. After he puffed on his Camel, he poked fun at me when my friends and I walked by. He would say, "Look, it's my snobby sister and all her phony friends." Mike Drummond laughed along with my brother, so he was my sworn enemy.

We had the last five minutes of class to ourselves which made me wish that Mrs. DiCicca talked more about school policy, or our science syllabus; anything to avoid Mike Drummond. I turned my head when Mike began humming an unfamiliar tune. I rolled my eyes when he beat his fingers on the desk like a drum, and tried to appear busy by intensely studying my new science book. The explanation of condensation was more interesting than Mike.

Suddenly, Mike stopped tapping and looked over to me. He shouted, "Hey!" He pointed. "Aren't you, like, Wiezer's sister?"

I turned my head to respond. It was almost impossible to look directly at him because of his crazy eyes. I raised one eyebrow and methodically nodded my head. My casual nod served as my official response.

Mike tried to strike up a friendly conversation. "I knew it! Dude! How is that dude? You talked to him lately?" He asked, as his crossed-eyes danced with excitement. "Damn-how is he?" Mike laughed while cupping his hands over his mouth, trying to stop the hysterical laughter from coming out.

I understood his laugher because I heard it many times throughout my life. Mike was laughing because Phillip was funny; the official/unofficial class clown. He was the one who said the stuff you always wanted to say, but never did. He was the kid who did all the things that most people thought about doing, but never attempted.

I coolly responded, "Good. He's good."

Mike was clearly interested in my brother's new life. He leaned in toward me. His faded black t-shirt smelled like a cross between a wet-dog and an old ashtray. He eagerly asked, "Is he going to school and stuff?"

"Yeah." I moved back, trying to avoid any further conversation.

Mike pumped me for more information. "Cool. So, who does he live with? Is he coming home for Christmas? Do you have his number?"

Mike pulled out a piece of paper to take down Phillip's new phone number. Even if I had my brother's number memorized, Mike would be the last person on the planet to get his hands on those digits.

I hesitated, "Uh, he's living with his father. I really don't know when he's coming home."

He held the paper toward me and pleaded, "What about his number- you got it?"

"No."

"Do you think you can get it?"

"No."

Mike put the piece of paper down. "Um, is he coming home for Christmas?"

"No." I lied.

"Oh." Mike turned away and began drumming his fingers again. "Can you..." He clicked his teeth, sighed, and then lowered his voice. "Can you tell him I said hello?"

I looked at Mike, smirked, and simply replied, "Nope."

With Phillip gone, I was officially an only child. Things around our house were different since he left. Not good or bad- just different. We continued to do the same things, but there always seemed that something was a little off. After dinner, mom and dad sipped their coffee, casually smoked their cigarettes, and engaged in tedious adult conversation that was always about the price of gas or the weather. (Boring.) After dinner, Dad usually grilled me for any information about my day at school. I often wondered why he thought school was so interesting; didn't he go there like fifty years ago? Nevertheless, dad was relentless. His need to understand my world was totally annoying. I never asked my dad about work, or what he learned, or if his colleagues made honor roll.

After Dad mashed his cigarette butt in the ashtray, he began a long list of standard questions. His interrogation was so predictable that it often made me wonder if he had some sort of pamphlet that outlined the top ten questions to ask your kid. Maybe, it was titled, "*So, you have a teenage daughter.*"

He began, "So, Shan, tell me about your day. What happened? Did you learn anything? How are your classes?" I rolled my eyes as I took a block of Oreo ice cream out of the freezer. Was dad really expecting me to tell him the truth? "Come on, Shannon. What's shaking?" He pressed.

"Ewwwww! Dad! Did you really ask me *what's shaking*?" I blurted out. Maybe, he was going to start using words like: 'yo' or 'dude' or even worse, 'radical.'

Dad pleaded, "Oh come on, Shan! Just humor me, huh?"

As I strolled to the dinner table with a cold mug of ice cream in my hand, I quietly snickered as I thought about the latest gossip in school. Maybe I should tell him about ugly-skunky Jen and her amazing ability to spit Hubba-Bubba gum two feet into a trashcan. I could tell him about the new girl, Michelle Maicco, who transferred from Gloucester Catholic. Apparently, Michelle was kicked out (allegedly) for hooking up with her art teacher. (Gross.) I could tell him that Renee Oliver (repulsive) played *Seven Minutes in Heaven* with Ryan Buddington (hot.) Maybe Dad would find it interesting that the rumor going around eighth grade was that our reading teacher once posed for Playboy magazine. Everyone called her 'chick-chick' or was it, 'click-click?' I couldn't remember.

I chuckled after I plopped down in my seat, replaying all the latest stuff that happened at school. Instead of blabbing the gossip, I simply licked my spoon and replied, "Nothing happened. Nope. Boring."

"What about your classes?" He inquired.

I shrugged, "Good. They're good, I guess."

Then, I choked on my ice cream and pointed my finger up in the air with a hint of injustice. I rambled, "Oh, except for my stupid, reject math class. My hairy gorilla teacher spits when he talks, and has like, white crust around his mouth. Yuck!" I shivered with the thought. "The kids in my class are such retards. Then again, I'm pretty much retarded in math."

Dad narrowed his eyes, objecting to my use of the word *retard*. He tapped his knuckles on the table and rhetorically asked, "Don't you think that maybe the word *retard* is kind of, oh, I don't know? Offensive?"

I shrugged. "No. Everyone says that." I tried to rationalize my use of the word by adding, "It doesn't mean anything, like, bad. I mean, I'm not, like... whatever." I knew it was offensive.

Dad remarked, "I guess if you do better in math this year, then you won't have to be with the 'other kids' anymore." He quoted the words, 'other kids' with his fingers to accentuate his point.

Mom and dad sipped their coffee and began a monotonous conversation about repairing the garbage disposal; a conversation that they had at least one hundred times. *Just fix the stupid thing!* Dad's advice about doing better in school seemed familiar and as I ate my ice cream, I remembered why.

When Phillip entered seventh grade (the first time) he complained to Dad that the kids in his classes were not only stupid, but they might be 'special.' He asked Dad to move him to another class, so he could be with the smarter kids. Dad's recommendation was simple. He told him to work his way out of his classes and earn his way into the classes with smarter kids. Instead of working hard to move up levels, Phillip not only joined the special kids in his stupid classes, he became their leader. Ironically, those special kids went onto eighth grade while Phillip failed and joined me.

I guess I could compare my brother to Bart Simpson. He was the Bart Simpson of Gateway. His insatiable need for attention, any kind of attention, was more important to him than any harsh disciplinary repercussions. I called him, "The king of the jerks" and to my dismay, I think he liked that title. Funny, how things changed between us. Once upon a time, he was my king and I, his loyal subject.

It is hard to imagine it, but when we were little, Phillip was my leader- my hero. He chose what we were going to do and for what amount of time we would do it. Like a doting little sister, I adored my older brother and tried to emulate him by liking the same things that he liked. As a girl, I liked Barbie and princesses, but when I was around my brother, I preferred G.I. Joe and He-Man. My older brother ruled; he made all the vital decisions for me, and I willingly allowed it.

Phillip had a way, a very convincing way, of making me do whatever he wanted, or like whatever he liked. When I was a kid, my only job in life was to impress him, or to somehow make him need me, or want to be around me. I followed him around like a stray puppy. I crossed my fingers that he would allow me to play with him, go places with him, or hang out with his friends. I became jealous when Phillip would choose his friends over me and, sometimes, I stood by my bike outside of his friend's house and stared into the window, hoping that Phillip would let me come inside to play (Never happened.) On Saturday nights, I wanted to watch *Solid Gold*, but if Phillip was around, I settled for *Kung-Fu*. I never fought him either. I was submissive and allowed him to take control. Of course, that was many years ago. That seemed like an eternity ago.

I no longer looked up to my brother because I no longer knew him.

There was no question that Phillip and I were close as children. I always knew he was always a little bit odd, but I accepted him that way. Last year, Mom tried to convince me that being embarrassed by him was just a stage and that I would grow out of it. I no longer saw him as my heroic, funny, and strong older brother. Being near him or associated with him embarrassed me. He was a weirdo, a social scumbag, and with each passing day, his behavior became unpredictable. The things he used to say were simply odd, but then they turned kind of scary.

Before he left for Florida, he had an official diagnosis. It took a team of doctors, along with a three week hospitalization to tell us he was depressed. His depression was linked to other things, too. The doctors wrote up a summary about Phillip that indicated that he struggled with a dream disorder (night terrors) and oppositional defiant behavior. I guess that meant he didn't like people telling him what to do. I didn't need a team of doctors with a clinical background to tell me that he was sad, or that he hated authority. Phillip was lost somewhere in his own world. He shut us out. And as much as it hurt to admit it, none of us had the energy left to deal with him.

He scared me because I knew (although, I did not ever admit it or tell anyone) that he was doing drugs. Even though my generation grew up with D.A.R.E. counselors that came into our schools to educate us about the dangers of substance abuse, I could never figure out why people did drugs in the first place. Nancy Reagan along with countless celebrities advised us to "Just Say No!" The "One to Grow On" public service announcements that played during the cartoon breaks on Saturday mornings were just as phony. Their predictable skits never appealed to me or answered any of my questions. Prime time television shows fixed any drug or alcohol problem within a thirty minute span and had the nerve to call it groundbreaking material. They made it seem like someone was just going to randomly walk up to you wearing a black trench coat, dark sunglasses, and offer you some dope, or weed, or dust.

Drugs. Drugs were everywhere. They were in my medicine cabinet. They were lined on the shelves at the local department stores next to band-aids and toothbrushes. They all did the same thing. Drugs fixed something. I was never completely sure, but I figured that Phillip used his 'fix' to forget. My brother didn't need someone to approach him in a trench coat because he was the one who sought out that man with the dark sunglasses.

During my basic living skills class in seventh grade, my teacher wheeled in an oversized television on a cart, shoved in a VCR tape, and turned off the lights. The grainy video was about a high school boy who was popular, incredibly hot, and naturally athletic (Chiseled-six-pack-quarterback.) After losing a dramatic football game and being dumped by his beautifully busty girlfriend, he dabbled with angel dust because someone offered it to him at a party. By the end of the movie, the all-American boy was a total failure. Drugs ruined his life. Immediately following the movie, our teacher played us a song by Eric Clapton. She shook her head and blamed rock and roll music for sending us secret messages instructing us to use cocaine. Either way, education about drugs did not educate me, but rather instilled fear.

Unfortunately, my suspicions about Phillip became a reality the night I watched my brother's drug induced performance unravel before my eyes at the family dinner table. It was an Indian summer. That particular day, the day I saw Phillip stoned, was unseasonably warm considering it was late October. Even though the chances of Phillip joining us for dinner were slim to none, mom set the table for him- just in case. Fighting about whether or not he was home for dinner was a battle my parents decided to drop, although they expected me to be prompt everyday at five o'clock. I wasn't quite sure if my rules were different because I was a girl, or their expectations for me were higher. Either way, it totally sucked.

Lizzie ate over that day. We took turns poking fun at Mom's new hair color, which was unquestionably orange. Dad's mandatory routine questions about school or our friendly debates about morality and social injustices would be on hold as Lizzie and I tried to point out the difference between the colors orange and burgundy.

Lizzie and I ate baked potatoes and pork chops while taking playful cheap shots at Mom. We tried to convince her that she was completely delusional for thinking her hair was anything but the color orange.

I snorted, "Mom, your hair is orange. Totally orange."

Lizzie chimed in, sarcastically asking, "Did you actually pay someone to do that to you?"

Lizzie and my mom had the type of relationship that allowed her to ask questions like that.

Mom was starting to get defensive. She retorted, "Lizzie, it is *not* orange!"

Mom walked over to the refrigerator and retrieved an actual orange. She playfully pointed to the peel. "This!" Mom held up the round fruit. She stated, "This is orange!"

Both Lizzie and I laughed hysterically. I glanced over to my dad who was wisely staying out of the discussion. I asked, "Dad, don't you think it's orange?"

Dad diplomatically commented on her hair. "I think your mom's hair is really pretty." He smiled, looked over to my mother, and then shoved a pork chop in his mouth. Diplomatic, indeed.

Mom cocked her head sideways and smirked at us. She boasted, "See? See, you guys. He thinks it's pretty." She ran her fingers through her hair and smiled.

Lizzie instantly replied, "Yeah, but he didn't say it wasn't orange." Lizzie and I cackled.

After the laughter subsided, the four of us could hear a voice coming from the backyard. I immediately knew it was Phillip. We took turns looking at each other, trying to figure out why he was banging so hard on the back door. I jumped out of my chair, ran to the door, and saw his puffy, left cheek firmly pressed against the glass. He giggled like a little girl. His squinty, bloodshot eyes peeked at me through the window. When I saw his watery eyes, I was alarmed and wondered if he was crying. My empathy for him quickly diminished when he flashed me all of his teeth, exposed his pink gums, and then shot me the middle finger.

He shouted, "Let me in, you butt-head!" He banged on the door with his fists and chanted the words, "Butt-head! Butt-head! Butt-head!"

"You retard!" I punched the door in retaliation. "The door is unlocked. You are the dumbest human being in the entire universe! No wonder you failed seventh grade. I wish I could poke your ugly eyeballs out with a fork! Jerk!"

Everyone at the table shot me perplexed looks, wondering why I was so agitated. When Phillip arrived in the kitchen, he marched in slowly and imitated a hard-core rapper by pointing his fingers in every direction. He bopped his head and shoulders from side to side. He then proceeded to do the robot. His voice sounded like a digital recording when he said, "I am a robot! I am a robot! Red alert! Red alert! Danger!"

All of us were watching with mild amusement. He happily sung, "The steak! The steak is on fire! We don't need no water... let the mother-trucker burn." Then, he started performing like a street mime. He strategically placed his hands in the air as if he was stuck in an imaginary box. It was surprisingly professional.

After he unsuccessfully tried to free himself from his fake box, he reverted back to the angry rapper. He swiftly moved his head, snapped his chubby fingers, and belted out, "We don't need no water; let that mother-trucker burn."

I was furious when Dad ignored his animated display and invited Phillip to the dinner table. It was another reminder that my parents expected me to follow a different set of rules. Phillip walked to the table as if he was balancing himself on a tightrope by following a single line from a tile crack. His arms were stretched out on both sides of his body. He proudly patted himself on the back after he arrived safely to his assigned seat.

Phillip had the four of us completely hypnotized. We were so captivated by him that we decided to leave the orange hair debate for another day. Phillip sensed our curious stares and seemed pleased by all the attention. He timidly peeked at the food on his plate and then proceeded to have a full-blown conversation with his baked potato.

With his fork, he cautiously poked his baked potato. Next, he began sternly questioning the lifeless spud. "So, Mr. Potato... what do you wanna be when you grow up?" When he grinned, he looked like that striped cat from Alice in Wonderland. He gobbled his food, exuding tiny specks of butter and white bits of potato from his mouth. He proclaimed. "Too late! You're too late! Ha-ha! I have defeated you! No more Mr. Potato Head!"

We just stared. What else could we do? He followed his declaration by stating, "You are in my mouth. You were on my plate, but now, you are in my mouth. And next you will be in my stomach, and next…" My dad stopped him from going any further.

I looked over to Lizzie a few times and wondered what she was thinking. Her blank expression gave me a clue. His oddly entertaining exhibit became weird when he sat motionless for two consecutive minutes. He suddenly perked up when his chin hit his chest. After the realization that he was the object of our attention, he began hysterically laughing while keeping his eyes tightly closed. I will never forget that hideous laugh. It was disturbing to watch my brother and with every chuckle, I hated him a little bit more.

Dad slammed down his fork. "What's so funny?"

I looked toward my mother who appeared nervous. Phillip instantly stopped laughing. He smirked when he whispered, "A joke."

"A what?" Dad demanded.

Phillip, with his eyes still tightly shut, exhaled a deep breath, sighed, and then repeated, "A joke, man!"

"Well, if it is so funny, why don't you tell us? Come on." His tone indicated that it was an order, not a request.

"You won't get it!" He claimed with his eyes half opened. "You just won't get it, man."

Dad demanded, "Come on. Tell us."

Phillip raised one eyebrow to inspect his audience, and then playfully scoffed. "Okay, okay." He put his hands up to settle us down, trying to convey that he was only going to tell his joke because he was unfairly pressured. His eyes remained closed when he asked, "What do you get when you cross an elephant and a rhino?"

The four of us took turns looking at each other, shifting our stares from each other and then back to my brother. There was an awkward silence before my brother smiled again with bits of food falling out the sides of his mouth. Finally, he shouted, "Hell if I know!"

Phillip began hysterically laughing. He grabbed his stomach and shouted, "Oh, that's funny. Hell if I know! Hell if I know!"

The joke itself wasn't all that bad; it was his reaction that was disappointing. After he settled down, we watched Phillip take his napkin from the table and roll it up. I wasn't sure what he was doing with it, but it only took moments for all of us to understand. Phillip rolled up the napkin like a small joint. He put it to his mouth and, with a wicked grin, he said, "Anyone got a light?"

Dad barked, "Go to your room."

As my brother walked away, he turned around and looked directly at Dad. He remarked, "Hell if I know!" He bopped out of the kitchen and chanted, "The steak, the steak, the steak is on fire…"

Later that night, I overheard my dad on the phone requesting a drug test for his son.

shoulda. woulda. coulda.

Fourteen days. Everything seemed rather ordinary within a span of fourteen lousy days. The euphoric notion that my name would grant me some sort of magical life that gave me both popularity and happiness was simply just a notion. I wondered why a new name mattered so much. I was still the same. Lunch smelled the same. My classes blended into one boring block of time. Every girl in my class morphed into the same cookie cutter who conformed into a typical early nineties girl by accessorizing themselves with their oversized Swatches, teasing their bangs with Aquanet (slightly lower than the eighties), and slinking their skinny legs into puffy Z Cavarichi pants.

After science class, I usually walked to my locker with Tricia Warner. Tricia was a big blabber-mouth, who was either a certified compulsive liar or suffered from an undiagnosed borderline personality disorder. Either way, I liked her because she kept me amused with all her exaggerated fictional stories. Even if they were total lies, I got a kick out of her crazy fabrications.

Tricia and I grabbed our hockey bags before heading to the locker room. As we walked down the hallways, she nearly lost her breath when she asked if I heard about John

Riley. The only information I had regarding John Riley was that he was a junior, cute, played soccer, had a crew cut, and used to go out with Megan Budd. Tricia squealed and then followed her piglet impersonation with a long (way overextended) pause. Naturally, I knew anything that came out of her mouth would be petty gossip, so that is precisely why I gave her my full attention. In the world of eighth grade, gossip never needed validation or confirmation. If someone said anything, true or false, it was presumed factual. Tricia became very serious as if she was going to reveal the location of Jimmy Hoffa when she leaned in close to me.

"Shan, I heard that John Riley went to a party in Washington Township, and..." She stopped in the middle of the hallway, extended her freckly arms out in front of her body, and blabbed, "... and... he got totally wasted." She leaned in close to me again, so she could whisper what she probably told half the school already. "He totally hooked up with some slut from Washington Township. And... and, that's not it!"

I was interested. Very interested.

Tricia rolled her eyes, smirked wickedly, and whispered in my ear again, "The skank gave him herpes. Ewww! What a slutty skank!" She laughed wildly. Her laughter reminded me of *Cruella De Vil*. Instead of thinking about John Riley or that girl from Washington Township, I visualized Cruella cackling wickedly with a long cigarette in her hand.

Tricia confirmed her story by mentioning that John had a cold sore, so therefore he definitely had herpes and he would probably die. I dissected her made up story, then concluded that John Riley may have gone to a party in Washington Township, but everything else was totally bogus.

I bumped my shoulder into Tricia's shoulder and tentatively whispered in her ear, "How do you get herpes?"

Tricia pulled away with a playful grin. She soaked up my innocence while shaking her head in disbelief. She leaned back into my shoulder and, with her Juicy Fruit breath lingering in the air, she calmly explained that it was some kind of freaky disease that can't be cured. Tricia warned me that you could get it by kissing.

"Kissing?" I cocked my head sideways and then quietly repeated, "Kissing?"

Tricia began cackling. "Duh? Don't you know anything?"

We walked to the locker room and rambled on about how Washington Township girls were all easy, ugly sluts (also fictional.)

Field hockey practice in early September was hot; I mean, Africa hot. My summer tan was almost gone because my shin guards and shorts covered my bronzed legs during our long practices. My dark knees were the last bit of evidence left of my summertime Coppertone tan. Just like school, field hockey practice was boring. We followed the same routine everyday. It went something like this: jog, stretch, sprint, stick-work, and then repeat. After we had our water break, we scrimmaged for about an hour.

While we scrimmaged in the hazy September sun, the freshmen football team ran by us in two perfect, single file lines. The immature, yet mesmerizing macho boys ran by as they methodically chanted, "We are… Gateway! We are… Gateway! We are… Gateway!" The boys looked so masculine in their royal blue and white practice uniforms. I found football uniforms repulsive, but not quite as repulsive as wrestling singlets. I could not stomach the idea of watching two boys in singlets rolling around on a sweaty gym mat. (Eeeeww!) When the boys ran by us, the girls on my team began giggling, intentionally talking a little bit louder, and secretly competing for any sort of attention. The sight of football boys, or any boys, running near their turf overjoyed the girls on my team. I viewed the boys much differently than my teammates. Most of the guys on the football team were my friends, but when they ran together as a unit, a team, they were my sworn enemy. They represented a past riddled with bitterness along with a future that was never meant to be. I watched with mixed emotions, secretly wishing that my brother was chanting along with them.

With unexpected sadness, I watched the lines ease past me when I thought about that year Phillip played Pop Warner football. Phillip should have been running with them. He should have been wearing white nylon pants and a royal blue mesh jersey that had his name printed on the back in white capital letters. In a perfect world, Phillip would be a freshman, running laps, tackling his teammates, making perverted jokes, and soaking up the attention from the girls on my team. As the boys became two distant lines, the painful memory of Phillip's experience on that team made me curious about what could have been.

It was a very long time ago, maybe seven years, since my brother put on his football gear for his first and last Pop Warner football season. Phillip was one of the youngest kids on the team. That fall, I faithfully cheered for my older brother while I clung to my mom's leg. Most times, I played with my shaggy-haired Barbies underneath the bleachers, imitated the curly pigtail cheerleaders, and made dozens of trips to the concession stand for penny candy and watermelon Italian water ice. Although, I could only remember bits and pieces about his games, I would never forget what happened during a hot and humid fall day following a routine practice.

I dreaded going to his practices. It was more like torture or punishment to sit through an entire football practice. However, that boring afternoon changed my life, or more importantly, changed my view of my brother's life. That day, I waited for him after his practice was over while my dad pulled the car around to pick us up. I helped my brother pick up his helmet, over-sized shoulder pads, and red water jug. We started making our way towards the car, but turned around when we heard two voices singing in unison, "Tough enough to over stuff- 'cuz Phillip is fat enough." The two boys, who were much older, snickered as they continued to taunt Phillip by repeating the same childish lines.

There was no denying that he was fat enough. Ever since I could remember, my brother was overweight or labeled 'the fat kid.' Every class, every team, every school had their own fat kid to tease. Those poor kids were often tortured with jokes along with subtle innuendos or blatant offensive laughter. Phillip was one of those kids. It was the one physical trait that most, if not all kids, felt comfortable to make jokes about- cruel jokes. Making fun of them was so easy and so acceptable. Most kids teased my brother, poked fun at him, or simply hated him just because of his size.

I listened to the boys with apprehension that eventually turned into fear when I noticed that familiar look in Phillip's eyes. He was not going to back down. I understood that look because I saw it many times before. I watched Phillip defend himself in our neighborhood, at school, and, occasionally, in front of our own house, so I knew he was not going to give up and simply walk away. He and I both knew that winning the fight was not important. It was not the victory that he was interested in, but rather his need to stick up for himself- defend himself. My brother held a belief that if he walked away, then and only then would he suffer defeat.

My fear came to fruition as my brother turned away from me to confront his teammates. They continued to rattle off classic fat jokes while taking off their sweaty gear, playfully squirting cold water on each other. To them, my brother was just an easy target.

Phillip, who stood about a foot and half shorter than either boy, tried to make himself as tall as he possibly could by walking toward them with his shoulders pressed back. He shouted, "You got a problem? Jerks!"

From the bench, I watched both boys strut toward my brother with their shoulders pressed back just like him, only they were much taller. I called Phillip's name four times and each time, I yelled a little bit louder, but he ignored me.

The taller boy, who looked about fifteen years old, snidely retorted, "Yeah, Weizer, I got a problem. It's your ugly, fat-lard face."

The smaller boy got in on the action by adding, "Weizer, you're so fat... you got more chins than a Chinese phonebook!"

They both laughed while my brother stood alone and took their unified abuse.

I could not take my eyes off the oncoming disaster. It was like witnessing a car accident from start to finish.

Phillip's cheeks became red as he marched confidently toward the two strapping boys. I was never sure if it was because I was younger, a girl, or submissive, but I never, ever engaged in a fight, any fight... ever. My brother fought enough for the both of us. Phillip's response was generic and well-rehearsed. He challenged, "Why don't you pick on someone your own size?"

As I watched the reaction from the boys, it was obvious that they wanted Phillip to get angry all along. My brother took the bait. The smaller boy hocked a huge loogie that strategically landed on the tip of Phillip's white Puma cleats, then he smugly retorted, "I thought I was... you fatso!"

Phillip decided to dig up the mama jokes. I cocked my head sideways and knew he was going to tell the one about the strip club. He pointed his fingers and tried to sound tough when he recited, "Yo' mama is so fat... they pay her to get dressed at strip clubs!"

I called it.

The three of them went back and forth spewing childlike insults, calling each other every cliché schoolyard name. I continued to watch the inevitable unfold and could literally predict the words that came from Phillip's mouth. I sat on my hands while I watched from the bench, secretly crossing my fingers that Phillip would just walk away. My hopes were shattered when I saw my brother hurl his white helmet at the smaller boy, hitting him on his left shoulder. The boy winced in pain, lunged toward my brother and with one quick move, pinned Phillip down. The other boy did his part by holding Phillip's feet, making it impossible for him to move.

I sat on the bench and watched. I chewed nervously on my fingers, shifting my eyes back to the parking lot, hoping Dad was coming soon to break it up. I anxiously looked back to the small crowd of parents who did nothing to stop the fight. They carried on with their casual conversations; maybe they thought that my brother was simply playing.

Phillip was plastered on the ground, struggling to get control. The boy pushing his shoulders down ordered him to say uncle. He commanded, "Say uncle! Say uncle, you load!"

I was afraid to get up from the bench, so I just sat there and hoped Phillip did as they asked. I thought- *just say uncle*. I knew Phillip would never say that one word because that would signify his surrender. I also knew he would have preferred a broken nose or full body cast before he gave in.

As Phillip struggled to get loose, he made the most atrocious sounds. I could hear grunting, shrieking, and muffled coughing. Unfortunately, I never heard the word "uncle." The boys took turns pinching him, spitting on him, and calling him obscene names while my brother wiggled on the ground in an attempt to break free.

The sight of my dad coming to the scene was both comforting and terrifying. He was used to breaking up fights between my brother and other neighborhood children. Dad was equally calm and assertive when he threatened to call their parents. The two boys got up slowly, both sweaty and out of breath. They pushed Phillip one last time before casually walking away. I was relieved when my dad saved the day. However, my brother did not feel the same way.

Dad glared back at the parents- the parents who seemed to allow the fight to happen. "Yeah, but I bet if it was their kid..." He placed his hand on Phillip's back and led him to safety. Then, he talked a lot louder, so they could hear him. "If it was your kid, maybe you would have stopped it." I watched the reactions from the group of parents. Most of them appeared surprised, perhaps insulted by my dad's accusation.

The three of us walked away in silence. My heart was hammering and there was a knot stuck in the back of my throat. There was a part of me that felt like I was on the ground with him. I heard the two boys shout to my brother, "It ain't over! Loser!" Unfortunately, he and I knew that he never had a day off from being picked on. It would never be over.

When we were getting into the car, Phillip muttered, "I could have got 'em. I almost had 'em."

As I predicted, Dad gave Phillip the routine lecture about picking and choosing his battles. I think Dad felt sorry for my brother, but at the same time, he wanted him to let some things slide.

While Dad worked the stick shift, he calmly reminded him, "You don't have to fight everyone who makes fun of you. You can walk away. Believe me, I am not telling you to back down either, but you gotta' know when to fight, and when to walk away."

It was obvious to me that Dad's words meant nothing to my brother. I also knew that if he had the opportunity, he would do the same thing all over again. I tried putting myself in his place and wondered if I could just walk away.

The ride home was quiet. Too quiet. The silence was disturbing. I studied Phillip as he stared out his tiny window and tried to read his mind. I had so many thoughts going through my head; so many questions I asked myself. *What is he thinking? Maybe I should have done something. Why didn't those parents help? Are those boys going to beat him up again?* He never moved his body, or sighed a deep breath, or even blinked his eyes. I looked toward him and noticed small scratches on his face. At that moment, I felt a deep sadness that I could not explain and wondered what it must feel like to be him. I mean, it was okay for me to make jokes about him, but when I saw someone else hurt him, it bothered me. At that moment, I made a pact with myself that I would never make fun of his weight again.

I watched him stare out the window. I noticed a single tear roll down his red, puffy cheek. He chose to ignore it.

Without thinking, I reached over and wiped the tear away. Phillip never acknowledged my attempt to ease his pain. He sat motionless; numb. He was probably replaying the fight over in his head. Maybe he was preparing himself for his next battle.

Back on the hockey field, I couldn't help thinking about that particular fight between my brother and his teammates. I also felt a strange sense of loyalty to my brother, so ever since that day, every football player was my sworn enemy. After the brawny football team ran past me, I felt just like that little girl sitting in the back seat with my brother all over again. Maybe, deep down, somewhere hidden inside me, there was a trace of guilt. I was no better than those boys on his team. In fact, I was worse. When I heard the girls from the hockey team calling for me, I shook my head and tried to physically shake off that childhood memory. I swallowed hard and let out a deep breath. The two lines of royal blue and white faded. Their bobbing helmets were lost in the haze of the harsh sunshine.

I shook my head and told myself that all of that stuff was in the past. I tightly gripped my stick, tucked my mouth guard in my shin-guards, and sprinted as fast as I could toward my teammates. While running toward the huddle, I told myself to forget it- just wipe it all away. Shoulda. Woulda. Coulda.

t.m.i. (too much information)

Eighth grade was off to a great start. I attributed that to the fact that my brother was living in Florida. Or maybe it was my new attitude mixed with a hint of superiority. All I knew was that, for once in my life, I felt special. The field hockey team was undefeated, my grades were decent, my skin was zit-free, and a cute freshman boy asked me out. Unfortunately, we broke up in two weeks. When he tried to kiss me in the hallway after school, I panicked and wrote him a three-line breakup letter. It went something like this:

> *Jimmy,*
> *I like you, but I just want to be friends with you.*
> *Don't be mad. Hopefully, we can still play basketball*
> *after school.*
> *Sorry,*
> *Shannon B.*

Lizzie and I hung out in Westville almost every weekend at Tiffany Ledger's house. On Friday nights, the girls from the hockey team got together and sang songs from Dirty Dancing. We did typical girly stuff, like painting our nails and skimming through old pictures and magazines. Most times, we spent the night talking about whoever was not in the room. When the scrubby Westville boys rode their bikes past Tiffany's house, they would call out to us and we would run to her window to exchange typical thirteen-year-old immature banter. The boys hollered obscenities, laughing as they did figure eights on their bikes. They would tease me by calling me 'Size Three Reebok' because of my miniature feet. It could have been a lot worse. My friend, Jenny, was nicknamed 'Baby Frank' because of her huge forehead. I would never say it to Jenny's face, but I thought it was hilarious.

In South Jersey, fall was all about color. The orange, brown, and gold leaves that fell effortlessly to the ground were something that everyone was quite used to. It seemed as though every season in the Northeast created its own brand of colors to claim its territory. Autumn's strong winds blew away the crunchy leaves; the crispy reminder that just a few short weeks ago they were lush and green. The thin branches resembled skeletons, patiently waiting for spring to dress them up again. The leaves were by far the most noticeable change of the season; everything else just snuck up on you. The chill in the air that made you search the bottom drawer for all your tucked away turtlenecks. The friendly, earthy aroma that escaped from my next-door neighbors' fireplace reminded me that hibernation mode was coming.

Fall brought the arrival of bright orange pumpkins that would eventually be carved into ornate jack-o-lanterns. October invited white ghosts to peek out of the windows. I watched Charlie Brown's Great Pumpkin cartoon special, sat on the bleachers at football games, and ate homemade vegetable soup. It all just happened. Everything. All those things happened without my consent. In fact, I looked forward to the change of seasons. It reminded me that everything was running as planned. Natural. Yet, somehow that year, everything seemed so *not natural.*

My mom, dad, and I observed autumn's metamorphosis without Phillip for the first time. I was secretly jealous that he could see fertile green palm trees any time he wanted. The warm weather would allow him to spend his days fishing on a pier. He could still enjoy riding his bike past five o'clock at night or keep his window open to feel a dewy breeze. Even though his move was supposed to be permanent, I knew his stay in Florida was just temporary. To me, his absence from our house never seemed completely real. In fact, I viewed his move as an extended rest and hoped that Florida would serve as a semi-vacation or semi-rehabilitation.

Phillip stopped calling me sometime in September. Everything was going by so fast. Once school began, the days flew by. He was thousands of miles away, but he was always lingering around me. Phillip never had to be in front of my face because he was everywhere. He was in every memory that I had. His shadow was all around my neighborhood, in my school, on my teacher's faces. Not only did he reveal himself in my everyday life, but he dominated my thoughts.

The mystery surrounding his departure puzzled me. Unfortunately, I spent too much time and too much energy wondering why he was the way he was. We lived in the same house, had similar experiences, went to the same school, and lived in the same neighborhood, yet we were so different. My only links to figuring him out were left behind in his old bedroom. His abandoned room left tiny clues that were hidden in his dressers, under his bed, on his walls, and in his closet. I needed to find a shred of evidence to prove that Phillip was normal, or could be one day.

On a chilly November morning, I visited his room that was located just ten feet away from mine. I slithered in slowly and stood next to the door for a couple of minutes. I did this so I could inspect his room from a distance before completely entering his realm. I never closed the door, never went in at night, and never stayed for too long. As I held my breath, I walked to the center of his barren room and stared at the white walls. His walls were sparsely decorated with hand ripped Garfield comics and a homemade X-Men poster. His walls were depressing: no medals, no glossy pictures of his friends, no favorite NFL player hung on his wall. Maybe it was hope that was missing.

I crossed my arms and shrugged my shoulders to take away the chill. After inspecting from a distance, I decided to investigate his dresser drawers. I rifled through a couple drawers and became weary after finding old boxer shorts, rubber bands, pens, and Life Saver wrappers. When I reached far back in his sock drawer, I heard something scrape the bottom of the wood, so I drug my right hand on the bottom of the hard splintering surface and felt something cold. I could easily remember why he was never normal. In my right hand, I held sharp medical scissors that had traces of dry blood on the edges. My brother used what I held in my hand to cut his skin.

I never knew the correct name for what he did, but I knew that he used scissors, razors, or anything sharp to slice into his flesh. I stared at the scissors, felt those butterflies in my stomach again, and remembered when I learned about his dark secret. I wondered how his life could have been different if I had said something. I found out about his secret when I was in the third grade. It rained that day, so during our recess period we stayed in the classroom. The options for entertainment during those wet, miserable days were math flashcards, old board games, or hangman on the blackboard. I made a picture for my mother. I drew a picture of Mr. T. for the front of the refrigerator. With a scowling face, eyebrows down, and a bubble above his head, Mr. T. declared, "I pity the fool who leaves the milk with only one sip left." Mom always complained that we put milk back with just a tiny bit left and, for some reason, it drove her crazy. Just as I rose to show Joanne Guilda my masterpiece, I noticed that my teacher, Mrs. Rollins, was walking into the hallway to greet Phillip's fourth grade teacher, Mrs. Shultz.

Immediately, my senses were sharp and my stomach became uneasy. Those ominous butterflies were back. I wearily sat down in my seat and prayed that my brother was not out there with her. I heard Mrs. Shultz's raspy, scotch-sipping voice in the hallway, muttering my brother's name when she greeted Mrs. Rollins. My entire third grade class gave their full attention to whatever was going on out there, leaving their games and flashcards behind. Instead, I put my head down and silently begged that it would stop, even though I had no idea what it was all about. Ten years of life had taught me to listen to my gut, and my gut was telling me to be alarmed.

There are moments in everyone's life: moments of clarity when time seems to move in slow motion. The day Mrs. Shultz shoved my brother into my classroom was one of those life-changing instances. Phillip tripped and almost fell on his face when he entered. I wasn't surprised to see him, but I was concerned about the look on his face. Over the years, with every one of his confessions, infractions, or disappointments, I never ever saw him look so terrified. What could he have possibly done to warrant such a worried face?

Mrs. Shultz followed my brother into the classroom, dismissing the fact that she shoved him and he nearly fell down. She was in charge and she made sure that everyone-especially my brother- was aware that she was running the show. She was enraged by whatever my brother had done. Mrs. Rollins followed behind her, allowing his personal catastrophe to unravel in front of everyone. Mrs. Shultz nudged Phillip. She persisted, "Go on! Get in there!" She rolled her eyes, sighed deeply, and shook her head from side to side, revealing her disgust for the pathetic boy in front of her.

That boy, the pitiful little child, was my brother who I loved dearly. Her detest for him, along with her anger, was indirectly affecting me. After Phillip staggered into my classroom, he strategically propped himself against the cold, yellow wall near the door. His face was blotchy and his chubby hands were tucked in his pockets.

Mrs. Shultz cried, "Can you even believe it, Mrs. Rollins? I mean, have you ever in your life seen such a thing? What kind of a person does something like that? "

Mrs. Shultz looked astonished as she shifted her glare from Phillip, to me, and then to Mrs. Rollins. I suppose she was making sure that she had all of our attention. She and Mrs. Rollins took turns interrogating my brother. Then, she rhetorically asked him if he was crazy or just stupid.

Every now and then, Phillip would look up to find me and he would catch my eye. I watched him cross his arms several times, only to nervously uncross them. Instinct told me that he was desperately trying to tell me something. I could see it in his eyes when he lifted his head and peeked at me, but I did not understand. I sighed, and wondered if it was going to be like last year when Phillip peed in the electrical socket in the boys' room. Upon hearing the news, my second grade teacher had informed my entire class that an idiotic, stupid third-grader urinated in an electrical socket. After blabbing that it was in fact my brother, she drilled me for several minutes, in front of everyone. That night, when I went to bed, I heard her overbearing voice ask me over and over, "What is wrong with your brother? What is wrong with him? Why would he do that? Does he do that at home? Shannon, what is wrong with him?" She even asked me if he was a retard. I learned at a very young age that if I just sat perfectly still, shut my mouth, and acted disinterested, most people would stop asking me questions. What could I possibly say to defend him? What did they want me to say?

Judging by my brother's timid disposition, I knew it was going to be much worse than peeing in an electrical socket. Phillip was constantly getting into trouble, so his uneasiness should have been my cue to expect the unexpected. Mrs. Shultz grabbed Phillip's shirt sleeve, physically pulling him away from the wall.

Phillip stood defenseless only ten feet away from me. Mrs. Shultz repeated, "Show 'em! Show 'em! Go ahead. Show 'em!" She glanced in my direction to make sure that I was watching. "Show 'em your arm, Phillip! Come on!"

Phillip was visibly upset. He tried to walk out of the room twice. Both times, Mrs. Shultz pulled him back. She was not going to allow him to get away without revealing his arm first. Mrs. Shultz demanded, "Go ahead, Phillip!"

Phillip stood alone. He crossed his arms tightly, almost hugging himself. I sat perfectly still in my chair. The entire class gasped when he reluctantly pulled his sleeve up to his elbow and showed his left arm. I gasped along with them and immediately felt nauseous and dizzy. His pale left arm had several thin red lines going up and down, side to side, and in every direction. His white flesh looked translucent, in total contrast to the crimson traces of blood. His blood stained the inside of his gray sweatshirt, absorbing the disturbing evidence. When I saw his arm, I felt the butterflies in my stomach plummet and nearly threw up at the sight.

Who did that to him? Why would someone do that to him? What was mom going to say? Mrs. Shultz held his shirt sleeve up to ensure his arm remained visible, so she could prolong his excruciating humiliation.

Phillip never looked up once his arm was revealed.

Mrs. Shultz demanded answers. She angrily asked, "Who did this? Who did it?"

Mrs. Rollins joined her colleague and began questioning him, too. Phillip stuttered and mumbled in a feeble attempt to avoid answering both of them. He stood helpless with his left arm behind his back and his head down.

She repeated, "Who did it?" Mrs. Shultz grabbed his right wrist and bent over to look him in the eyes. "Tell me!"

Phillip swayed nervously back and forth. He did his best to avoid everything, but the pressure was too high. He pulled his arm back, looked back at her, and defiantly whispered, "I did."

Mrs. Shultz threw her hands up in the air and hissed sarcastically, "I don't think we heard you, Phil." She leaned in close to him with her hand cupped to her ear. "What? What was that?"

It was so hard to watch. I just wanted it to end.

"Me," he muttered with his teeth clenched.

Mrs. Shultz glared at me as she shook her head from side to side. "You?"

My entire class seemed mesmerized by the odd situation. They watched his darkest, most wicked secret come to light. Then, Mrs. Shultz became eerily calm as she stood next to my brother with her bony hands clutching her tiny hips. Phillip rolled his sleeve down and then he narrowed his eyes with contempt, perhaps blaming her. His mood changed. He was no longer humiliated; he was furious.

Phillip never looked at me after his arm was revealed, and I was grateful for that small favor.

She snidely asked, "How? How did you manage to cut yourself?"

After slight hesitation, Phillip murmured, "Scissors."

He never lifted his head when he spoke, never shifted his weight, or sighed. His body language indicated total defeat.

"Whose scissors?" she asked. I was aware that Mrs. Shultz kept checking in on me, watching me, wondering if I had any awareness about the situation.

"The art room," he snapped.

It seemed like my brother amused Mrs. Shultz, almost as if she was getting some kind of sick enjoyment out of it. She rolled her eyes and mocked, "The art room, huh?" She threw her hands in the air and cynically remarked, "What are you, an idiot? You're supposed to cut paper… not your arm."

My class laughed at her comment. I slithered down in my chair, desperately wanting everything to end.

"Shannon!" she called out.

My name sounded foreign coming out of my brother's fourth grade teacher. She pointed her long, red fingernail at me and asked, "What is wrong with him? Does he do this stuff at home?"

I shifted my eyes back and forth from her to my drawing of Mr. T. I tried to avoid her question and became angry with my brother for putting me in this position. Again.

Mrs. Rollins felt that it was necessary to question me, as well. She barked, "Seriously, Shannon, did you know about this?"

I figured if I just sat still, twiddled my thumbs, and appeared ignorant, maybe they would leave me alone. I shrugged my shoulders and said nothing. It worked. They stopped asking me questions.

After Phillip left the room, the class went about their business, back to their flashcards and board games. But I sat silently in my seat, put my head down, covered my face, and tried to pretend that it never happened.

I felt weird- like I was supposed to do something... but what?

On the way home from school, Phillip and I walked in silence until the crowd of children dispersed and we were finally alone and able to talk. Phillip begged me not to say anything to Mom or Dad. He pleaded, "Shannon, please don't tell Mom!" He pulled on my book bag to get my full attention.

I pulled back, irritated by his crazy behavior and for, once again, putting me in the middle. I asked, "Why? Why did you cut yourself? Are you some kind of crazy freak?"

He stopped in the middle of sidewalk, scratched his head, and exhaled. He was surprisingly composed when he whispered, "Maybe. Maybe I am a freak." Then, he clicked his teeth and began to explain, "Shannon, it doesn't matter. You just can't say anything. You need to just forget about it. Just don't tell Mom or Dad, please?" Then, he placed his trembling hands over his face, trying to hide the unavoidable tears. "Please don't tell!" Phillip could barely talk when he softly repeated, "Please."

I shook my head and asked again, "Why? I don't understand. Why did you do that?" When I asked him about it the second time, my voice was much calmer.

He wiped his watery eyes. "First, you have to promise me that you won't tell." His eyes darted toward mine and I could understand the desperation in his voice. "You can't tell her. Please! I will *never* forgive you. I am asking you really nice... don't tell her or *anyone!*" He continued to vie for my confidentiality. "Not even when you get mad at me, Shannon. You can't tell anyone. I will hate you forever. 'Til the day I die if you tell anyone."

I never saw him like that before. He looked sincere and I wanted to protect him. I also wanted to know why he would cut himself, so I made a promise to him and to myself that I would keep his secret until the day I died.

I swore, "I won't. Okay? I won't tell. I promise." I recited, "Cross my heart and hope to die- stick a needle in my eye." Then, I placed my hand over my heart to prove my commitment.

I needed an explanation. "So? Why? Why did you do that? How could you do that? I mean, didn't it really hurt?"

We started walking slowly on the broken sidewalk. Children ran past us, giggling as they made their way home. Phillip sighed as he searched for the right words.

He explained, "I don't know. I wish that I knew why I did it." He made a tight fist with his right hand and pursed his mouth. Then, he confessed, "I just get *so* mad sometimes. I just get so mad that I want to hurt someone. I don't know. I guess I want to make everyone feel what I feel, but I just... I don't know... hurt myself, instead." He exhaled a puff of air and then whispered, "You'll never understand."

"Understand what?" I asked.

"What it feels like to be me. Nobody does."

"So, you're really mad and..."

He interrupted. "No! I mean, yeah. I'm pissed. Wouldn't you be? Do you know how it feels to be called a fat-lard by a total stranger or made fun of just because of your…" He paused to catch his breath: "It's just- it's hard."

"Are you mad at me?" I questioned.

"Whatever, you know what I mean." Phillip stopped walking again. He tried to explain it so I could understand, "It's just that, I get so mad, or maybe, like, sad. I can't explain it right. Maybe, a little bit angry. If I cut myself, then it takes my mind off everything."

"Uh-huh." The look in my eyes indicated that I did not understand at all. I pressed him for more details, "Well, I don't get it. Wouldn't cutting your arm hurt you more?"

He looked up to the gray sky as if the answers were up there. He commented, "I guess it's like being really, really mad, you know? And, all of a sudden, you stub your toe." He shrugged his shoulders and added, "You just forget about being mad and think about your toe."

I nodded as if I understood. "Oh. Yeah. I get it." I kind of understood, but not really.

Feeling as if I had some sort of control over him, I made him promise me that he would never do it again. I gave him an ultimatum: "If I don't tell anyone, then you have to promise to never do it again, okay?"

He placed his hands over his heart, just as I had done earlier, and vowed, "I promise. It's the last time."

Looking back to that cloudy day, I wished that I was smarter and understood how serious his cutting was or how bad it would get. I believed his promise that day, or maybe I wanted to believe he would stop. Either way, his cutting continued throughout the years. I never told my parents about his arm mutilation in third grade and I always regretted it. While standing over his dresser, I caught my reflection in his mirror and whispered the words, "You should have said something." It was so hard to admit that my silence and sworn promises may have led to him moving away. He should be in New Jersey, drawing Garfield comics in his room.

When I found the bloody scissors and relived that day, I became very angry. Furious. For the first time, I was not angry with Phillip, but with myself because I did not do anything to defend him or help him. I knew my brother did weird things. I knew he did things that could not be explained, and I knew he couldn't help it. So, why didn't I help him? With the tiny scissors in my hand, I closed my eyes and wished that I could go back in time. I would grab my brother and pull him out of that room. Then, I would tell both Mrs. Rollins and Mrs. Shultz to go shove the scissors up their insensitive asses.

My visits to Phillip's room, especially after that day, were infrequent. Searching his room only conjured up painful memories that often made me feel weird inside or maybe- guilty. I closed his door, walked to my room, flopped down on my unmade bed, listened to INXS, and swore that I would never go back to his bedroom.

smell ya later

When fall transformed into early winter, basketball season began. Unfortunately, hockey was over, along with all the team pizza parties, football games, and fall dances. I hated basketball. I hated wearing those squishy high tops that made my legs look short and stumpy. I hated the smell of my hands after touching a dirty basketball for what seemed like five hours. Basketball was the reminder, the blatant reminder, that I would be indoors for the next five months. The crisp fall days playfully echoed in the breeze, but the sun's departure at four in the afternoon diminished any hope of sunlight. I developed a love/hate relationship with winter.

No doubt, summer was my favorite season for obvious reasons, but there was something undeniably sweet, maybe nostalgic, about fresh, white, powdery snow. Sometimes, rarely, I helped Dad shovel the sidewalk in the early morning after the snow fell at night. The peaceful silence that we honored while shoveling snow humbled me temporarily, teaching me that sometimes the most insignificant moments in one's life often become the most cherished. Dad and I never said much to each other while piling snow by the sidewalk. It was an assumed agreement between the two of us that we both appreciated.

The snow reminded me of Phillip. While shoveling the heavy, wet snow, I thought about the anticipation we both shared after a night of snowfall. We opened our windows at seven o'clock in the morning and anxiously waited for the fire siren to grant us our freedom from the school day. Phillip and I would jump up and down with joy once we heard the wailing fire alarm. Instead of going back to bed, we put on our mix-matched winter clothes, skipped breakfast, and quickly joined the kids in our neighborhood. Sometimes, we would grab our sleds and walk to Dead Man's Hill over on Chestnut Street. Of course, I didn't have enough courage to actually go down, but I never missed the opportunity to watch my brother- the daring one. I bit my fingernails and shivered while giving him last second advice before his deadly launch. When I thought about those times, the good times, I wanted to recapture that innocence. Could he change? Could I? Would things be different when he came home from Florida?

On November 17, 1988, it snowed for the first time since Phillip left. That morning, I opened my bedroom window and waited for the siren, but it never went off. I wasn't sure if I was disappointed that it didn't go off, or if it was the reality that Phillip wasn't there. The sight of flurries brought about those familiar memories along with an unexpected, yet much appreciated letter from our skinny mailman. I recognized Phillip's distinct, chicken-scratch writing on the flimsy envelope. After it was in my hands, I ran to my room and ripped the envelope open. I held the white sheet of paper in front of me while biting my nails and visualized him writing the letter in his new room.

Shannon,
How are you doing? Well, I'm doing fine and everything's great. Thanks for all your letters. Is

*mom making you write them? I like the looks of the
new dog, Sandy. Do you like her? Well, I'm all tan
with my shaved head. I hang out with skaters. They
dress like fags, they look like fags but they're alright.
Rob is the only cool dude. There's a couple of babes
where I live but there's some dogs too. (Wuff-Wuff!)
We go to the beach and body surf. Well, L.L. sucks
and all the pop-tart-farts. Metallica is kicking. No, I
don't have MTV. Well, that's it little sister.*
   Love,
   Phil

*P.S. "Parents Just Don't Understand" is a cool cut.
This is your Ravingly Rad, Totally Tuff, Massively
Muscular, Chilled Out-Dude.*

I read his letter twice and snickered occasionally,
cupping my hands over my mouth when I imagined him
body surfing. After reading it, I looked out my window at
the thin tree branches and began to daydream about the two
of us becoming closer again, possibly even friends.
Phillip's life was so new and exciting. He had a brand new
father, new skater friends, and a new school. There was
hope; hope that whenever he came back to New Jersey, he
would be brand new, as well.

For the majority of last year, Phillip's presence in our
home was nearly invisible. I referred to him as "the
stranger who slept ten feet away." We shared the same
kitchen, we used the same bathroom, and came home to the
same address, but we became absolute strangers. His
isolation began sometime in late January last year. He hung
out in his room all the time, playing his obnoxious music,
lying around, sleeping, or reading his comic books. If he
did make an appearance out of his bedroom, it was only so

he could play his Nintendo. He never joined the family at night to watch TV, or ate at the dinner table, or woke up early in the morning to greet us in the kitchen. Mostly, he just slept the days away like a hibernating bear in his cave. I never saw my brother in school either. Mrs. DeStephano stopped asking me where he was because my answer was typically an uncaring shrug. Instead of viewing his isolation as weird, I enjoyed the solace of walking through the halls without the fear of my brother teasing me.

My brother, who was once my idol, became the weirdo who stayed in his room all day and all night. The only evidence to his existence was the tiny crack of light that peeked from the bottom of his bedroom door. Phillip wore the same clothes everyday, never showered, and had little interest in his appearance. My brother, who was once the life of the party, the class clown, and the center of attention, became a prisoner of his own room. It was as if we were living with a ghost. I knew he was there. He was just ten feet away from me most of the time, but it felt like he was a million miles away.

Phillip's isolation came as a blessing in the beginning. My parents figured that if he was quiet in his room, then he was not causing any problems; therefore, they overlooked the significance of his new quarantined lifestyle. Throughout Phillip's life, my mom tried to understand him. Both she and my dad tried various methods of discipline to reform my brother, none of which ever worked. After all the threats, deals, pleading, and punishments, Phillip was always the same. He was never the type to conform or be tamed, shaped, or molded. Mom and dad never told me why Phillip was on the verge of permanent expulsion from school and I never asked. The less I knew about my hermit-crab brother, the better. To me, Phillip's decision to remain in his room seemed like a good idea. As long as I could walk through the halls of school and know for sure that he wasn't going to embarrass me by urinating in a socket or cutting up his arms, then I was satisfied.

After stuffing his handwritten letter underneath my mattress, I turned on my radio and looked up at my pictures that were tacked on my corkboard. While gazing at the glossy picture of our family smiling near a small waterfall at Shenandoah Mountain, it occurred me to that life went on with or without my brother around. Our family went about our everyday routines. We visited Niagara Falls and rented a house in Ocean City over the past summer. I thought that vacations would be more fun, calmer, or more enjoyable. Instead, I found road trips and vacations surprisingly boring. He was the one who stirred up a commotion, and, since he left, I quietly looked out the window for Volkswagen Bugs with one head light and smirked when I thought about how much fun it would be to punch Phillip in the arm.

I thought about him a lot in school when I was forced to remain stationary in my designated seat. Instead of taking notes about Nova Scotia, or memorizing the Periodic Table, or figuring out the Dewey Decimal System, I daydreamed about my brother. I replayed the past and imagined a better future for him while ignoring my own. With my hand resting on my cheek to prop up my head during class, I tried to look somewhat interested, but my thoughts were often drifting off to salty waters. The visual of my chubby brother wiping out several times on his body board made me laugh inside. While thinking about it, I could hear the opening drum solo to "Wipeout."

The view out of the window in my social studies classroom allowed me to gaze at the frozen hockey field that only a few weeks ago was green and full of energy.

After living in New Jersey for most of my life, I had become accustomed to the weather and the inadvertent way it altered my moods. That day, my mood matched the thin gray sky and whipping winds that shook the windows. As I traveled to white, sandy beaches, inhaled coconut oil, and sipped homemade lemonade, I sighed when I looked at the bare trees outside. They reminded me that it would be several months before spring supplied them with buds of life. In my Social Studies daydreams, I imagined Phillip getting up late on weekends, calling his friends, and then pedaling his bike to the beach. He would grab a ham and cheese sandwich (with a crunchy dill pickle) and a Dr. Pepper for lunch. His new skater friends would joke around with him, and say things like, "Man, this is the life. Forget Jersey. It's a total armpit!" Phillip would lie to them about why he left. He would never mention the real reasons. He would smile and reply, "Yeah, this *is* the life."

I sat in my hard chair at school and wondered if he was really happy or really sad.

Occasionally, I had fake conversations with him in my head. During our pretend conversations, I was always clever and wise and magically had all the right answers to any of his unresolved questions. He would tell me about how great he was doing in school, his new girlfriend, and how much he had changed. I would tell him about the field hockey team, our new yellow Labrador, and about how much I had changed. I would tell him that I would be nicer to him if he was nicer to me. We never discussed drugs, cutting, depression, or hospitals.

My contrived conversations with Phillip inevitably led to questions that lingered in the back of my mind. As Mr. Jenner lectured our class about South America, I tried to appear interested in the history of Ecuador: *Does it really matter that they were the leading exporter of bananas?*

Who cares? I get my bananas from ACME. Behind my phony facial expressions of being interested, my thoughts were stuck in the past. During Mr. Jenner's insightful knowledge of tintos, I was revisiting a brisk April day eight months ago. The day my brother left our home and ventured out into the unknown to his new life in Florida. Mom let me stay home for half the day, and I spent the entire time watching Phillip play Super Mario Brothers. With his departure looming, we never spoke to one another. We simply distracted ourselves with Duck Hunt and Kung Fu.

That morning, Mom and Dad were busy making sure Phillip had his plane ticket, his luggage, and any legal documentation that he might need for his new school/life. Being thirteen allowed me to believe that life was simple, so I minimized his move and told myself he would be back by Christmas. When Dad announced that it was time to leave, I stood next to Phillip and waited for a powerful or memorable moment. Instead, I was met with a cold, unemotional farewell. Phillip never took the effort to get out of the recliner. He simply extended his right arm out and smugly blurted out, "Smell ya later!"

With slight apprehension, I shook his clammy hand and quickly responded, "No... I'll smell *you* later." Phillip never responded. He just turned back to his game. Obviously, my reply did not interest him, nor did my existence.

That was it. I got a handshake and a "smell ya later." My false expectations of sharing something profound was completely shattered when I heard the echoing sound of Mario changing from a little pipsqueak to a large, dominating figure. I felt foolish walking out my front door, still believing we could rekindle our relationship with a tender goodbye. As I looked out the car window on my way to school, I realized that there was just too much stuff between us to make amends with a simple hug. After all of my snide remarks and harsh comments wishing he was gone, his departure was secretly more bitter than sweet.

I told myself to focus on the history of South America, instead of the history between my depressed brother and me. I suppose being his sister meant that my role in his life was minimal. I had to re-establish myself as the one born fifteen months after him, reinvent our relationship out of daydreams, and remember that I had no right to know all the answers. I sunk in my seat and wondered if he would miss me... *just a little.*

My parents had no idea how much I used to think about my brother. Most of the time, I tried to ignore my feelings about him. His issues were always so secretive. I heard a saying when I was ten years old about a 500-pound gorilla that is just sitting in the room and no one ever talks about it. He was like that gorilla. He was there, his problems were immense, but for the most part, I didn't know how to talk about him. There was no denying that his isolation was a result of his spiraling depression, although I had no idea what depression even meant. Depression, to me, seemed like a state of mind. My thirteen year-old mind believed that depression was a contrived official label to call someone sad. On some level, I always knew that my brother was sad, but my anger toward him justified my lack of concern. For some reason, I thought time would make him happy. But, I was wrong. According to his doctors, time turned his acute sadness into a full-blown clinical depression.

The day I told Lizzie that my brother was in the hospital, she assumed (like everyone else) that he had a physical ailment. Hospitals were for the sick, the old, for people with broken bones, heart attacks, or cancer. Phillip did not belong in a hospital... did he? It was a Saturday morning when I told her about my sick brother. We sat in her bright living room, ate Elio's Pizza, and watched *Yo! MTV Raps.* Telling someone (even if it was Lizzie) that Phillip was a lunatic that required psychotropic medications and, at times, physical restraint, felt like I was admitting that our family was just as crazy.

After I confessed that he was in the hospital, she licked her salty fingers, sipped her Pepsi, and then asked, "What happened?" Lizzie was the type who asked several questions and never waited for an answer before she asked another question. She predictably rattled off several more follow up questions before she allowed me to answer the first one. "Did he break something? Are you gonna visit him? Is he at Underwood?" She bit into her rectangular block of pizza and added, "That's where my sister went when her appendix burst. Is it his appendix?" She put her pizza on the flimsy paper plate and finally allowed me to respond.

Even though I was talking to my best friend, I found it very difficult to talk about Phillip without stuttering or blushing. "No. No. No," I coolly responded. Although I appeared calm, inside my heart was racing. It felt so nice to just talk about him; so nice to release all the secret information. Why was it so hard to say mental hospital? At that moment, I wished that his appendix had burst. I scratched my head. "It's not, like, that type of hospital. It's not Underwood, either," I said. "It's called Lawrence."

She looked up into the air and narrowed her brown eyes as she tried to recall a hospital by the name of Lawrence. Confused, she asked, "Where the hell is Lawrence Hospital? Washington Township?"

The truth was that I really didn't know where Lawrence Hospital was located and it didn't really matter, but it served as a buffer for our impending conversation. I guessed on the location. "I think it is in... I don't know. It's, like, north of here. It's forty-five minutes away. It's, like, up the Turnpike. My mom and dad are there right now." I could hear the words come out of my mouth, but it seemed as if someone else was talking. "I don't know. It's a mental hospital. It's just for kids," I added while keeping my eyes on Lizzie the entire time. I tried to study her facial expression, so I could read her response without her even saying a word.

She looked me over with eyes of disbelief. Her eyes were clearly saying... *are you kidding me?*

"Shut- up! Wait! Hold it! Uhh, did you say mental hospital?" Lizzie snapped. She used her fingers to highlight the word mental. "What do you mean mental hospital... for kids? Like, a nut house? Do they wear straitjackets and get electric shocks? I didn't know they had places like that for kids. And why is he there anyway? He's not crazy. Is he crazy? No, he's not. Is he?" She persisted with her questions without taking a single breath.

I tried to appear calm about the situation when I began to explain everything, but my heart was pounding so quickly that the façade of acting casual was a constant struggle. Why was it so hard to talk about this? Shrugging my shoulders and avoiding her glare, I glanced to the TV and saw Rob Base dancing, singing about joy and pain. "He went yesterday when I was in school. My mom said that a task force came and got him," I confessed. Immediately, I put my hands in the air again because I knew she would ask about the task force. I quickly added, "Don't ask. I have no idea what they are. Mom said that trained people had to come in and take him away."

But I really did know what a task force was. I wasn't supposed to know what happened, but I overheard mom talking on the phone to a social worker from the hospital. Mom could barely complete a sentence when she told the person on the other end about how Phillip left the house. Apparently, mom caught him in his room cutting up his arms and stomach. According to mom, Phillip forced her out of his room by shoving her out the door. Mom told the person on the phone that she pounded her fist on the door and screamed for him to let her in, but he held his weight on the door to shut her out. Eventually, mom had no choice but to call 911. So a team of counselors came in and took him by force.

Mom started crying when she explained how Phillip cursed at her. "I didn't know what to do! I just, I was so scared. I didn't know what he was doing in there." She cried. Mom blew her nose before continuing, "So, yeah. He was so mad at me. I mean, he called me the worst names, you know? He, he…" She began sobbing, "He told me that he would never forgive me."

I listened to the conversation and knew that I would be replaying that scene over and over in my head. Apparently, it was just bad- really bad. Phillip had to be sedated with a needle. After mom talked about the needle, I immediately saw Phillip screaming, kicking, and yelling while the people stuck a needle in his arm. The image of him lying there unresponsive gave me chills, making me wish I never listened to Mom's phone conversation.

Lizzie was trying to absorb- or believe- my story. Her eyes were getting softer, but they still betrayed a hint of disbelief. I could tell she needed confirmation. "In his room?" She cynically remarked. "Like, he's just hanging out and, all of a sudden, people come in and just, like, take him away." She scoffs, "Like a freakin' swat team… they just grab him and take him away."

"Yup." I nodded.

Rob Base was still singing about sunshine and rain when she confirmed, "So, right now, as we speak, your brother is at the mental hospital and your parents are there? Right now? This minute he is, like, in a strait jacket?" Lizzie pointed to the clock, so she could point out the severity of the situation. "Right now?"

I delicately answered her pressing question. "Yes." Then, I sarcastically barked, "Right now. He is…" Lizzie interrupted me by putting her hands in front of her body to stop me from going any further.

She asked, "Okay. So what did he do? What happened? Did he do something crazy? Or, I don't know… is he crazy? Seriously, why would he go there? I don't get it."

I tried to pretend that I knew nothing regarding the exact reason why he was there. I knew he was a cutter, I knew he was depressed, I knew that he needed help, and I knew that I wasn't supposed to tell Lizzie.

I blankly replied, "I don't know." I sipped my Pepsi and then nervously breathed in and out.

After soaking up the gravity of the situation, we both looked at one another with blank faces. Lizzie tried to come up with some possible reasons why he might be there, maybe to help in some way. "Shan, maybe he just needed to get away for awhile. You know? Maybe your Mom and Dad just want to know how to, like, handle him better." I shrugged my shoulders at her suggestion. I breathed in deep again and totally understood that it was way beyond simple discipline.

I began telling Lizzie more and the more I spoke about him, it seemed like Lizzie wasn't even there. It was as if I was talking to myself and I liked it. "My mom said that he was all depressed and she was, like, all worried. And you know what? Maybe he is kind of depressed. I mean, Phillip never comes out of his room or talks to anyone. I mean, I don't even know what depression is, but he's always in a bad mood." I tried to give her some examples. "He's kind of gross because he never takes a shower. He used to go out with his friends, but not anymore. He never, like, eats with us at dinner. Wait. Come to think of it- he never really eats. Phillip used to be funny and make jokes, but he never does anymore." I continued to ramble. "I remember my mom calling so many places. She was on the phone all the time, trying to get help. It was like doctors, therapists, and just all these places. The phone book was out all the time. It seemed like she was always on the phone talking about him. I just assumed she was talking to the school because of all the trouble he was in." I stopped talking and finally looked toward Lizzie. "That big, yellow phone book was always on the kitchen table and, now, I know why."

Lizzie asked me, "Do you think he wanted to go? I mean..." She sighed and went on to say, "Maybe, like, deep down, he wanted to go, but could never say so."

I scoffed at her suggestion and casually replied, "No." Then, I had a second thought. "Well, maybe." The more I thought about her suggestion, the more it made sense. I looked at Lizzie with a new perspective. "That's a good question. I guess I never thought about that."

When I walked home from Lizzie's house, I took my time soaking in spring and the new buds on the Dogwood trees. I looked like I was curiously observing the flowery canvas, drenched in the sweet smell of spring, but, truthfully, my head was spinning with confusing thoughts of Phillip. If I could just figure him out, then maybe I could help him.

I gave serious thought to why my brother was in a mental hospital and surmised that, throughout our lives together, the clues were always there. When we were kids, Phillip confided in me. He trusted me with his deepest secrets. After hearing them, I was never sure what to do with all the information, so I stored them in my head and inventoried them like tiny snapshots. As his head rested against a hospital pillow and while he was safe with his doctors and nurses, the need for my parents to have a clinical diagnosis from a therapist was crucial. I, however, didn't need a therapist to tell me that his way of thinking has always been skewed. My parents wanted someone with experience, someone with a degree or a professional license to tell them exactly why he cut, or why he slept so much, or why a task force had to come get him. On my way home, I picked up rocks and threw them over the power lines, and felt strangely guilty. *Why should I feel guilty?*

As I sniffed a couple of rhododendrons, I remembered that sunny morning when I was nine years old: the morning Phillip and I sat on a sappy stump of wood. It was the day I heard his most chilling confession. It all started the day before when Phillip, Jimmy (our next door neighbor), and I were playing in our front yard on the last day of our summer break. We rode our bikes up and down the sidewalk, marking our territory, and pretending to be The Three Musketeers. The three of us chanted in unison with our homemade stick-swords held high: "We're all for one and one for all. Together we stand and divided we fall."

The undesired arrival of the two girls who lived four houses down compelled us to protect our territory. Though they were unaware that they were trespassing on our land, we began an attack on the foreign intruders. We threw rocks, called them names, waved our stick-swords, and sent them home in tears. We celebrated as the girls retreated; however, our victory was short-lived. We hid in our tree fort while we nervously peeked through wooden planks as their father stormed up to our front door.

After a few minutes, Dad was waving me and my brother to come inside, so we could receive our inevitable punishment. We ran up to our bedrooms with tears rolling down our faces along with warm, sore butts. Dad told each of us, "This is gonna hurt me more than it's gonna hurt you." I took my punishment, cried, and swore that I would never throw rocks at those ugly, stupid girls ever again.

The sun was bright that afternoon. I sat on my bed, totally pissed because I had wasted my last day of freedom. I peeked out my window several times with envy as I watched those two little brats ride their bikes on our sidewalk. They smugly rang their annoying bike bells and I knew they talked louder to remind us that they had won the war. The next morning,

I could barely remember the entire incident because of the excitement surrounding my first day of second grade. After I strapped on my white shoes, gobbled down some Cheerios, and filled my new Barbie backpack with fresh notebooks and pencils, I began searching for Phillip. His room was empty, his stuff was gone, and Mom informed me that he had already left for school. Darn! I hated going to school by myself.

With frustration and a little anger toward him for leaving without me, I sprinted out of the house and made my way toward the corner. Then, I heard my brother's voice calling for me in the backyard. When I found him, he was sitting down on a broken log near our pine tree. While sprinting over to him, I could read his face. Instinctively, I knew something was terribly wrong.

Gasping for air, bending down with my hands perched on my knees, I looked over at him. "What are you doing?"

He lowered his head, avoiding my probing stare as he mindlessly chucked pinecones at the garage. I watched him throw four pinecones at the stucco. Finally, he murmured,

"Just hanging out. Hiding. Waiting for you." He picked up a sappy branch, wiped off his sticky hands, and sadly remarked, "All by myself."

The warmth from the sun was a sorry reminder that it was technically still summertime. The morning birds praised God for another day. I listened to the squawking, peeping, and tweeting as I blocked the sun with my small hand to see his face. I didn't know why he was sad or why he was waiting for me. Furthermore, I wasn't even sure that I wanted to know. I advised, "Well, come on. Get up. We have to walk to school now. You ready?"

I strategically placed my body sideways, indicating the direction we needed to walk. Phillip never moved, not even a single flinch. He remained on the stump, throwing dirty pinecones. He looked up at me and scoffed, "I don't wanna go." He sifted the dirt by his feet in his hands. "I wanna sit here for a while," he barked.

I began fidgeting, hoping that my uneasiness would remind him that we needed to go to school. I bumped his shoulder and whispered, "Come on, Phillip. It's time to go to school. You ready?"

He pressed his small fingers in the dirt while I sat next to him. Phillip clicked his tongue, shook his head, and slowly said, "I wish…"

"Huh?"

"I kinda wish…"

I cocked my head to the side and cautiously asked, "Who? What are you talking about?"

"Yesterday. I wished that he would have killed me," he blurted and casually continued to play with the dirt on the ground.

"Oh!" I smiled. I knew it was about yesterday and knew that it was Phillip's way of telling me that he was angry, which translated to sad. I was used to him saying odd things, but when he added death into the mix, I became alarmed. After all, death was final and unknown.

I asked, "You mean when Dad spanked us?" I hugged my knees as I sat next to him. "Did it hurt?"

Phillip never looked at me when he spoke, but I stared at him the entire time. He narrowed his eyes, pursed his lips, and searched for the right words to explain his declaration. "No! It didn't hurt."

He was lying. Simply by having this conversation, it was obvious that he was lying. He lowered his voice to a whisper, turned toward me, cupped his hand to my ear, and confessed, "I wanted him to kill me."

I gasped. "Phillip! What!" I pulled away from him to look him in the eye. "No, you don't mean that! Do you?"

He defended his wishes. "No! I do mean that! I'm sorry. No, I'm not sorry. That is the way I feel. Last night, I dreamed about what it would be like if I was gone."

At that moment, while he was confessing his desire to die, I sat on the stump with my face blushing, butterflies swirling, and heart racing. Part of me thought that he was just being overdramatic, but the other part, the intuitive part of me, was terrified.

It seemed as if he was in some sort of trance throughout the conversation. He gazed off into the distance. I was just his witness. He went on, "Sometimes, I think everyone would be better off." He shrugged his shoulders and swiftly wiped a small tear that dribbled down his face with his sleeve.

"Phillip!" I exclaimed. "You shouldn't say stuff like that! Anyway, you're just mad."

He sat still for a couple moments, perhaps considering my statement. After hurling another pinecone, he coolly replied, "No, I'm not mad. Just sometimes, I wish I wasn't here."

There were no words to say because nothing could prepare me for his morbid confession. I wanted to say something profound and meaningful, something that would instill an immediate zest for life, but I couldn't think of anything. Nothing. Nada.

I played with the Velcro straps on my new shoes as a distraction, placing the straps down and then pulling them back off again. After his statement, I assured him, "You don't mean that. Really. You are just mad right now. You don't really want to die. I mean, that is just a horrible thought. I don't want you to die. And, and Mom and Dad don't want you to die. And Jimmy, he doesn't want you to die. Your friends don't want you to die either. Nobody does." I hurled a pinecone at the stucco and confidently confirmed, "You'll be fine. You'll forget about it by the end of the day." I, awkwardly, patted his back and then went back to playing with my shoes.

I blushed as I said the words to him. I felt stupid for saying those words. It should have come out better, smarter, or just better.

Phillip was thankful for the words; I could just tell. However, his theory, his belief about dying, remained unchanged. He muttered, "Yeah, well, I still wish I could leave this place."

Trying to get some clarification about his use of the word "place," I asked, "What place? Like, home or…" He interrupted me, clearly irritated that I did not understand.

"This place, Shannon!" He barked. "Sometimes, it just… I don't know. Whatever. Just, just forget it." He put his head down between his knees and began to cry.

I hated when he cried. It was so hard to see him break down, but somehow hearing the sniffles seemed much worse. *What should I do? What should I say? I can't tell Mom because then he will never tell me anything. Should I hug him? Should I tell him that everything would be okay?* I didn't know what to do, so I just sat next to him. I just sat by him shoulder to shoulder, played with my strap, and said nothing.

Phillip wiped away his tears and then quickly rose to his feet. He brushed himself off and motioned to me that it was time to go. I really wanted to help him. I wanted to let him know that he was scaring me. I wanted to tell him that it would all be better someday. Instead, I followed his lead down Elm Avenue. The only words spoken between us were Phillip's request for secrecy and my allegiance. Once again, I promised my brother that I would never tell anyone.

"Cross my heart and hope to die… stick a needle in my eye."

After I told Lizzie about my brother, I felt a little bit relieved that she knew and it wasn't my secret anymore. I was so tired of keeping everything to myself about Phillip. When I came home, I ran up to my room and listened to INXS. I flopped on my bed with my sneakers still on and listened to Michael Hutchinson's savvy voice. Life was so much easier when I listened to music. It was my escape. Everything about life could be summed up with just a few exciting lines and a catchy chorus. As Michael sang about tiny daggers, I drifted in and out of reality. Michael's words fit the moment and, as I listened, I felt sorry for Phillip.

While listening to the song, I recalled the time I watched Phillip light his hand on fire over our gas stove just because he saw it on: *"That's Incredible!"* Afterward, he went to school with a homemade bandage, only to be sent to the emergency room with third degree burns. Then, there was the time when were walking to school and he threw a can of Hawaiian Punch at a car just because someone dared him. The man who was driving stopped his car and chased my brother all the way home. I ran along, cheering for Phillip, hoping he would make it safely home. Or the time he pretended to be dead in the white ocean waves down the shore, so the lifeguards would have to go in the water to retrieve him. I winced remembering the time he was busted at ACME for guzzling down Nyquil to get high. Possibly the oddest stunt he ever pulled was the time he strategically placed a knife in his pants with ketchup oozing out... just to see my reaction.

While listening to Michael Hutchinson's voice echo his sentiments in *Never Tear Us Apart,* I recounted all the fights around town, the fat jokes, and his failures. I felt an overwhelming sense of sadness and guilt. I felt like a helpless observer in his chaotic life. There were so many situations when I could have said something or done something to defend him. Instead, I did nothing but watch.

Phillip and I did not communicate very much before or after his hospitalization. He did not confide in me the way he used to because he saw me as the enemy, rather than a confidant. He and I were both aware that we were labeled the 'good one' and the 'bad one' and we chose to play our parts. If he were to sum me up in one sentence, it would read like this: she is a superficial, preppie, little bitch who acts just like all her stuck-up, snobby friends. I hate to admit that part of me was somewhat proud that he viewed me that way.

The only thing I heard from him directly about his brief stay in the hospital was that everyone there was certifiably insane- except for him. He never (or at least it seemed that way to me) took his hospitalization seriously. He would often joke about 'those crazy people' and told my dad that the longer people stayed at that place, the crazier they became. Whenever he talked about it, which was rare, his description often reminded me of the movie *One Flew Over the Cuckoo's Nest.* My knowledge of any place like that was only from what I saw on TV, which led me to believe that people who were in mental institutions slobbered profusely, ate checkers, and yelled into open spaces. Phillip was always clever and he knew that by calling everyone else crazy, he would appear normal. My brother only stayed in the hospital for twenty three days, perhaps a lifetime to some. Every time Mom and Dad would visit him, he begged and pleaded for them to take him home. He made sincere promises of changing; claiming he would go to school every single day, assuring them that he would stay out of trouble. He would willingly agree to any new rules or regulations. He just wanted out of that place. He had a written aftercare plan, some medications, and three new diagnoses. He was officially clinically depressed, had some weird sleep disorder, and had an oppositional defiant disorder. Two weeks after he came home, he had a one-way plane ticket to Lake Fort Worth, Florida.

Christmas of 1988 was my first holiday without my brother and I tried to act like it didn't bother me, but it did. I put my head down on my pillow at midnight on Christmas Eve, and prayed for the first time in a long time:

Dear God, please bless everyone in my family. This year, I want to be better. I want to be better and do my homework and be nicer to Mom. Do you think you can help me? I know that I am not very religious, but I do believe in you, and since you are there... can you help me to be nicer and smarter? God, can you really make everything all right? I mean with my brother and all? I heard that you love everyone- no matter what, so can you, like, help him? Can you somehow let my brother know that I do love him and I am sorry for being so mean to him this year? God, I promise that when he comes home, I will be a good sister. Bless Mom, Dad, Phillip, Lizzie, my dogs, and all my friends. Okay. Bye. Thanks. Happy Birthday Jesus. Amen. Shannon Bennet.

in the still of the night

I slept over Lizzie's house on New Year's Eve night. We ordered cheese steaks from Pizza City and flipped back and forth from *Dick Clark's Rockin' New Year's Eve Show* to MTV. That night, as I drifted off next to Lizzie, I thought about making a perfect New Year's resolution. It seemed like everyone I knew wanted to lose five pounds. I never understood the significance behind looking like everyone else until I entered junior high. I soon learned that every girl competed against each other in nearly almost every category: their looks, their clothes, their ability to flirt and attract boys, and they did all of this covertly- on the down low. Even though I tried to ignore it, I tossed and turned all night thinking about my brother and all the reasons he never quite 'fit in.' He was the fat kid, the dirt-bag kid, and, later, became the weird kid. I flipped over on my side in Lizzie's bed and tried to remember that he was *just a kid.*

When I began taking out all the stored snapshots of my brother, I replayed a morning several years ago; a morning that reminded me that my brother was just a vulnerable, little boy. I could almost feel the speckled bright rays of sun flickering and dancing around my eyes. It was early springtime. The smell from our prized dogwood sweetened the air and, as I gazed at the white branches, I swore the flowers sprouted over night. Morning brought so many options. I could ride my bike or pick the new flowers for Mom or play Barbies outside or jump hopscotch on the sidewalk. With all those plans in mind, my day never officially started until I confirmed my brother's plans first.

On my tippy toes, I crept into Phillip's bedroom with intentions of scaring him. I cracked his door open, jumped out, and shouted, "Raaaahhh!" When I realized he wasn't startled, I teased, "Hey! Fart-face! Wake up!"

I was disappointed. He didn't move or even flinch in his bed. When his eyes met mine, he only slightly acknowledged my presence. Half concerned and half disappointed, I sat Indian style next to the foot of his bed. I asked, "Why are just laying there? Didn't I scare you?"

He rose from his horizontal position slowly, pulling his Star Wars covers over him like a swathe, and placed his body sideways while resting his head on his elbow. I could tell that he had been awake for some time because his eyes were clear and wide open. He traced his pointer finger along his blue Star Wars sheets and sighed. Then, he rolled onto his back.

With a touch of sarcasm, I asked, "What is wrong with you?"

Phillip put his pointer finger to his lips signaling for me to be quiet. I asked why. He hissed and then he scolded me and told me to shut up again. So, naturally, I shut up. Phillip rose and sat on the edge of his bed with his sheets hovering around him like a protective shield. Perhaps he was heavily debating on whether or not to let me in on one of his untold secrets. I knew that eventually he would tell me; he always did. He exhaled deeply and with a sharp gust of hot air escaping from his mouth, he pulled his sheet tighter and began inspecting me- studying me. I sat completely still by the side of the bed, waiting for him to ask for my confidentiality.

He began, "Shannon, I want to tell you something. But, you can't tell anyone or I'll never ever talk to you again. I mean it!"

Phillip was about to let me in on another one of his confessions, and all I had to do was verbally commit to secrecy.

I pleaded, "I won't! Duh? Do I ever?"

Phillip and I pinkie-swore that from that day forward that anything that was said within his four walls would forever remain within his four walls.

He began, "Okay. I know you're gonna freak out, but it's alright. Okay, well, last night, I sort of made a big decision." He paused and began picking at his toes, which I watched with total disgust but decided to overlook.

I curiously asked, "And what decision did you make?"

"Well, more like a deal," he admitted.

Judging by his vague response, I knew he wanted me to figure it out on my own. Phillip and I used to play that game all the time. I would take guesses and he would coax me on, letting me know if I was remotely close. I looked at his ceiling, held my fingers to my chin, and tried to figure it out. "Hmm... last night, you made a deal. What kind of a deal?" I was talking to myself while he intensely watched. "A deal? Last night... hmm?" I guessed. "Did you make a deal with Mom?"

He replied, "Nope."

"With one of your friends?"

"Nope." He shook his head and with his eyes, he told me to go on guessing.

I traced my chin with my pointer finger, just like I saw in the movies. "Hmm. I don't know." Stumped and bored, I asked, "What kind of a deal?"

He hesitated before he began to speak, almost as if he was giving me a moment of silence to prepare for his news. He began, "Well, as you know- I can't lose weight." His look to me was an indication that he wasn't waiting for me to disagree. He went on: "I just can't lose it. I try and I try, but I can't." Phillip clicked his tongue and rattled off a bunch of reasons why he was fat. "I try to eat better or eat less or not eat at all, but whatever- I end up gaining more. I don't know why I am this way. I mean, I don't think I eat that much." When his eyes caught mine again, we both silently agreed that he needed to lose some weight. He leaned in close to me and whispered, "If I could just lose a couple pounds, then maybe people would be nicer to me. They wouldn't have any reason not to like me. For once, I would be kind of normal. You know?"

I knew just by observation alone how incredibly horrible people could be to my brother. I made a feeble attempt to make him feel better by mentioning, "You're not *that* fat. I mean, you play soccer and you ride your bike and stuff. You could be a lot worse."

He unexpectedly grabbed his stomach and began rubbing it just like a pregnant woman caressing her unborn baby, and muttered, "Nothing is worse than being fat. Nothing." He looked at his round stomach and sighed. "I hate it."

I gulped after he said those words, slightly embarrassed by watching him grab his portly stomach.

He put both hands over his eyes to hide the tears that trickled down as his large shoulders shook.

I tried to make him feel better by saying, "Awww, man- don't cry."

Upon hearing my request, he toughened up and instantly wiped his tears away. He admitted, "I'm tired." He wiped his nose with his sheets that rested on his arms and went on, "I'm so tired. Tired of being the fat kid…tired of… looking this way. I've been up all night tossing and turning. I decided that I don't like being fat, so I made a deal."

"A deal? I don't get it."

"I made a deal with the devil." Phillip peeked timidly at me, so he could read my reaction. "Last night, I sold my soul to the devil…"

Gasping with fear, I shouted, "What! What do you mean! You can't do that! You can't make deals with him!" I inched closer to his bed. "Tell me you're lying. You are lying, right? Tell me!" I demanded.

He defended himself by stating, "Does it really matter? I mean, who cares? God isn't helping me, so maybe if I sell my soul to the devil, maybe he will." His voice became soft and trailed off as he muttered, "I don't care anymore, Shannon. I don't really care."

Once again, I got more than I bargained for by swearing to secrecy. This was huge. This was out of my control or his control or anyone's control. This involved Phillip's sacred afterlife.

Infuriated, I began ranting: "What do you mean? You don't care? You cannot make deals with the devil. There are other ways to lose weight! You did it before and you can do it again." I reminded him, "Remember, when mom brought you to Weight Watchers and you lost weight? You can do that again."

"Yeah, but I gained it all back. Anyway, that was, like, so embarrassing." He gave me a sideways look and bitterly scoffed. "All you do is clap for each other and tell stupid stories."

Phillip laughed when he mentioned that he was the only boy and the only one under the age of twenty. "I just don't want to go to Penny's and have to buy Husky jeans anymore. People call me husky when I wear those ugly jeans. Uhh, those jeans! They even have like a stupid wolf on the pocket to, like, remind people that I am fat. I feel like a retard. You don't get it because you've never been called a fat-ass or a lard or tons of fun."

He did have a point. I never had anyone make fun of my size, let alone call me a fat-ass.

After we talked some more, Phillip described to me how he was laying when he made the request. He showed me how he placed his hands over his chest and crossed one over the other just like a dead person in a casket. He repeatedly told me that he was not sorry and that he would do it all over again. I felt compelled to convince him to change his mind. I said, "There are other ways. Trust me. What if you go to hell?"

"Who cares, Shan? I don't care what happens when I die. All I know is, right now, I don't want to be fat anymore."

"Can you take it back? Can you change your mind?" I asked.

As if he had extensive knowledge about selling one's soul, he confidently replied, "No. Once you sell your soul-you belong to the devil."

I was not sure what the statute of limitations were or the laws regarding deals with the devil, but I tried to advise him about his options. I retorted, "No. No. I don't think so. You can definitely change your mind." I was making it all up. "You can definitely change your mind. My friend, Tara, told me so. She said that God is the most powerful thing in the universe and can overrule that kind of thing. So, you can ask God to help you. Maybe if we pray to God really hard, He will undo it." I advised. I rose up next to his bed in a kneeling position, hoping that he would join me in prayer.

Phillip murmured, "It won't do any good. I asked God so many times to help me lose it and it never worked. God just doesn't listen to me."

I tried again while emphatically pleading, "Yes. Yes, he does. Tara said that God hears everyone. He can help you." I was still in my kneeling position and still making it all up. I reminded him about the time we went to Vacation Bible School together, and the teachers said that God could hear any request and that He could do miracles. "Remember?" I pleaded. "You were there. Remember?"

Phillip shook his head and held up his hands to stop my talking. "It's done and I had to let you know. But, now you can't tell anyone or you'll go to hell, too." His warning put a knot in my stomach and I suddenly felt nauseous. I wasn't sure if I was angry or scared that his secret involved my salvation in the afterlife.

The idea that we would not be in heaven together made me sad. As my last resort, I brought Mom into the situation. "What is mom gonna think when you're not in heaven with her?"

He whispered as he began to make his bed, "She won't care- nobody will."

I was about to walk out of his door, but something made me turn around. I said, "Well, just so you know- I will and mom will, too."

After that day, we never talked about it again. For two weeks, before I went to bed, I prayed for God to help my brother. I was happy when Phillip never lost any weight. In fact, he steadily gained more.

The morning I prepared for the first day of school in 1989, I decided to spruce up my looks considering it was a new year and I had a boyfriend (it all went down at the winter dance.) I used a flatiron to get the kinky waves out of my hair and applied bright, glossy, pink lipstick, which would probably be off my lips before I walked out the front door. I coordinated my clothes the night before (even my shoes and socks) and dabbed Love's Baby Soft Perfume on my neck and wrists. There was a new air surrounding me as I listened to The Beatles sing *Ob-la-di, Ob-la-da.* I, playfully, winked in the mirror and blew myself air-kisses as I belted out the catchy tune that made no sense. I laughed along with the song and winked in the mirror again, and then danced while singing, *"Life goes on."*

Thirty-six days later. I could never prepare myself for February 8, 1989. That day was the beginning of the end. The blistery air, the smell of looming snowfall, the whipping winds served as a warning (maybe it was my own personal slap in the face.) It was a Wednesday; a typical February night, a night that required you to hide your head in your jacket and sprint indoors in order to escape the fierce winds that stung your cheeks like tiny bee stings. On February 8[th,] my junior high basketball team beat Woodbury to a pulp. Of course, I had nothing to do with it. I watched the girls hustle up and down the court with their ponytails slapping their faces and asked myself why I even played... I hated it. I hated being inside, I hated high top sneakers, and, mostly, I hated the smell of contained sweat mixed with body odor that swirled in the gym. I swore that season would be my last.

I twirled my hair while sitting on the bench, totally bored. I studied the referee who resembled Burt Reynolds. (I think it was the mustache.) As I gnawed on the skin around my fingernails, I thought about *Cannon Ball Run,* and laughed inside a couple times thinking about Dom DeLuise's raspy laughter. I told myself that, when I went home, I would try to imitate it. I cheered, high-fived, and narrowed my eyes when our coach would look my way- as if I was concentrating on picks, plays, or rolls. However, I was fantasizing about Dom DeLuise, salt and vinegar chips, Thomas, Bobby Brown, my two papers that were due tomorrow, and making inside jokes with the girls on my bench. With a cushy twenty point lead, I was in the game for my three minutes of mandatory playtime. My only contribution was stealing the ball only to miss an easy lay-up.

On the ride home, dad and I joked about my mediocre playtime. We complained about the cold weather as if the weather was a big surprise. Dad and I talked about a winter storm that was forecasted on the radio or, shall I say, "blown-up" by overzealous weathermen. I think weathermen became giddy with the slightest possibility of a storm arising in the north. The tumultuous Nor'easter of the century would most likely end with a couple of inches on the ground; not even enough for a decent snowball. When dad and I pulled into our icy driveway, we noticed that every light was on downstairs. The illumination seemed odd in my usually dark house. Mom's friend, Sherry, was over. Her car was parked unevenly on our street, as if she jumped out of her car while it was still moving. At first, I was eager to tell Sherry about my lay-up, but my excitement fizzled when she practically hit me in the face with the front door. Sherry never looked at either of us. She simply muttered, "Sorry." Then, she quickly dashed away and slipped on the wet grass to her car.

She sped away, nearly leaving skid marks on the street. I suppose the visual was somewhat funny; kind of like a cartoon character bolting to the car, jumping in the window, and then speeding away without even turning on the ignition. However, her departure wasn't funny at all- it was an ominous warning of what was waiting inside for us.

Dad shrugged it off, but I knew (because of that fluttering feeling in the pit of my stomach) that whatever was going on inside was not going to be remotely funny.

I walked into the kitchen first, but when I caught sight of my mother, I wished that, just for a moment, I could somehow be invisible, so I could watch everything from a distance. My frail mother sat by herself at our kitchen table. The ashtray was full of butts, the morning paper scattered on both ends of the table, and the cordless phone was in her left hand. The low vibrations from our old refrigerator served as a buffer; a welcomed distraction. She said nothing. She just stared at the phone as her bony hands shook. I felt like everything was in slow motion. I hated that I had to ask her what was wrong, but I knew I had to.

"What's wrong?" I asked.

Mom just clutched that phone, possibly waiting for dad to make his entrance.

Watching her was kind of like watching a doctor perform surgery. I wanted to look, but afterwards, I wished that I turned away from all the guts and gore. She rapidly alternated her gaze from me to the phone and then, eventually, my dad. It reminded me of a lizard moving its head from side to side viewing everything in such an awkward motion. I stood in the kitchen, wearing my winter jacket, sniffling from the cold, patiently waiting. Before she could get the words out, I already knew what she was going to say. I just prayed that I was wrong.

With the arrival of my father, mom finally gave herself permission to holler like a ferocious animal in the wild. The noises she made sounded like barking or snarling or whimpering (perhaps all three.) Dad and I stood a mere five feet away from her while we observed her mad display; both fearing the words that might come out of her mouth. Mom gasped for air, placed her hands over her forehead, then she cupped her mouth with her fingers. She was physically trying to stop the words from coming out. Mom screamed. She lost her breath. Then, she screamed again.

When she ran out of breath, her body went limp, her eyes rolled back, and she nearly fainted from exhaustion. Mom startled me when she slammed the phone on the kitchen table, nearly cracking it into pieces. "He's gone!" Breathing sharply in and out, trying to catch her breath, mom looked in our eyes to finally acknowledge our presence. I remember one of the girls on my hockey team became so faint and exhausted from the heat that she needed a paper bag to breath. As my mother sat in her seat, unable to breath, I could only think about that girl on my team. Mom crossed her arms over her chest and rocked back and forth in the small, wooden chair. With her face red and blotchy, she finally shouted, "He shot himself! He shot himself!" She uncrossed her arms looking to us for a response. Even though she was screaming, I could not hear her anymore. Her lips were moving, but I couldn't hear her. I blanked out after the words "shot himself" because I knew who she was talking about. Anything said after "shot himself" didn't matter. No matter what she said or how she said it, the truth was my brother was dead.

Dad put his hands out in front of him, trying to calm her down. He wearily asked, "Who? Who is gone?" By the tone of his voice, I could tell that he already knew, too.

She never looked directly at dad when she began to explain. Her eyes were blankly fixated on the phone that rested on the table. She appeared sedated, but her piercing cries revealed an untapped energy that scared me. "He is dead! Goddamn it! Don't you hear me! He killed himself... with a gun!"

I knew it was Phillip. I could never quite explain what exactly went through my mind when I heard that he shot himself. My senses were up: I could hear things clearly, see with 20/20 vision, and I could feel things that were inches away. Unfortunately, that was a time in my life when I wanted to remain numb or unaware.

I actually thought that I could run out of the room, go outside, come back into my house, and make it all disappear. I even contemplated the idea of picking up the phone and calling Phillip to prove that she was wrong. I had to find a way to make it disappear. How can I make it disappear? After hypothesizing several alternative ways to prove that Phillip was alive, I snapped out of my delusions when I heard dad's voice next to me.

Dad remained to my left and, with the refrigerator humming, he calmly asked, "Maddie? Who is gone?" He looked toward me. I ignored any interaction between us and continued to stare at my mom while thinking about that girl on my hockey team. I visualized her flushed, sweaty face breathing heavily in and out of an old, brown paper bag. As I thought more about that girl, I became aware that it was becoming increasingly difficult for me to breathe and, if I looked at my dad, I feared he would sense it.

Mom was practically scratching her skin off as she muttered to herself. Mom looked like a crack-head going through detox, suffering from the physical reactions of withdrawal. Her long fingernails traced her face, leaving several tiny scratches on her forehead. She remained slumped in her chair, rocking back and forth and holding herself. Mom continued muttering to herself, ignoring the two of us who watched her meltdown unfold. Part of me hated her for telling me like this, but I knew mom had little to no control over her emotions, even on a good day. While dad and I stood in front of her, my thoughts became selfish. This should be different, I thought. Mom should sit me down and tell me calmly. I am not supposed to see her like this. Instead of focusing on the death of my brother, I became annoyed that mom didn't have the fortitude to ease the blow. In the movies, they sat the girl down on the bed, caressed her hair, and softly whispered the unfortunate news. In the movies, the girl cries and then grabs her teddy bear, even if she is thirteen. In the movies, the girl on the bed with the teddy bear is comforted with hugs and forehead kisses. In the movies, the girl hears token metaphors and clichés to try to make death seem natural. However, it was not Hollywood and his death was far from natural. Everything was wrong. His death was wrong, the timing was wrong, and the delivery was wrong.

"Maddie. I'm sorry. We can't hear you. Who is gone? What happened?" Dad curiously inquired. Mom continued rocking back and forth, furiously shaking her head, and whispering to herself.

Dad pushed a little harder. "Maddie?"

She hesitated and then looked at my dad as if he was crazy. She asked, "What do you mean, who? Phillip! He shot himself in the head with a shotgun." After her announcement, she dropped her head on the table and sobbed while her frail shoulders bounced up and down.

She repeated, "He's gone. He's gone. He's gone." Mom stopped, then nestled her head in her elbows on the table. Instinctively, I thought about anything but what she was saying. I thought about how she looked like she was playing *Thumbs-Up-7-Up* or the girl huffing and puffing in the brown bag or the humming of the refrigerator. Dad and I stood helpless while she hid her face on the table. I was thankful for having an old refrigerator that hummed; otherwise, we would have heard that proverbial pin drop. The room was so quiet, too quiet. The silence echoed realities in my head. He's dead.

Dad tried to get the details, hoping to find some flaw or missing link that would disprove the morbid news. "When?" he asked.

She mumbled as she held her forehead in her hands, resting her elbows on the table, "A week ago. They found him in the woods." When she mustered enough strength to look at us, I noticed the tiny scratches on her forehead and speckled, red blotches on her neck. She wiped her soggy cheeks with her long, decorated New Jersey nails, only to have fresh tears roll down her moist face. I focused on her coral nail polish, embellished with painted roses on every single finger. I loved to make fun of her Jersey nails, but at that moment, I was grateful to her for being so cheesy. I found it much easier to study her fingernails, instead of looking directly at her face. While I watched her hands shake, I was in a trance, hypnotized by the flashing spots of coral.

She sobbed, "He must have been just rotting away… just rotting away." She tried to catch her breath in between each sentence. "Why didn't his father call sooner? He was missing for a Goddamn week and nobody called me!" Mom pointed to herself with her pointer finger that flashed a single red rose and repeated the word, "Me!" Thank God for those long, tacky Jersey nails.

Mom began talking to herself in between the uncontrollable sobbing and primal snorting. "Rotting! My son was rotting in the woods… I can't…my little boy?" She phrased her last statement as a question, obviously a rhetorical question. "I can't even…I cannot even, I mean, in Florida, the heat and all. My son in the woods! Uhh!" Then, she suddenly stopped. Her sparkling blue eyes, now blood shot, looked peculiarly toward my dad. "Can you imagine how he must have looked?" After blowing her nose, her eyes met mine for the first time.

As I stood there absorbing mom's words, I had gruesome visions of his body decomposing in the blistering Florida sun and I was sure that my face showed it. Then, there was more silence. We shared a moment of much needed stillness. My dad took the patriarchal role by gathering us together for a much needed group hug. While embracing, I could feel mom's warm body and could equally feel dad's strong arms surround us both. We stood in a small triangle, holding hands with our heads down. As I peeked down at the floor, I wondered if Phillip could see us and see what he had done to us.

When we looked to one another after holding hands, I noticed that both mom and dad were crying, but I was not. Not one tear rolled down my face, not one. It was wrong. Everything was wrong.

"Shannon…" Mom began. "You need to go upstairs. I have to talk to your father for a while," Mom requested after she blew her snotty nose.

"Are you sure it's him? I mean, maybe they got the wrong person," I valiantly suggested.

She quickly responded, "Yes. It's him. It's him. I know for sure that it's him." Mom sharply exhaled, and then added, "I will be upstairs soon. I need to talk to your dad right now, okay? Just, please, go upstairs. Please." After she said the word, "please," mom began crying hysterically. She plopped down on the wooden seat and gradually settled back into her *Thumbs-Up-7-Up* position.

I ignored her request and looked to my dad who was already smoking one of his Marlboro Reds and cracking open a cold Heineken. His lips quivered after he blew out a plume of smoke from his mouth. When he turned his head to concur with mom, his movements were lethargic and mechanical. He looked like he was wearing an invisible neck brace. The sight of my dad broken down at the kitchen table broke my heart, but watching mom's shoulders shake with every sob hurt even worse. The brave leader of our family and the silly woman who playfully danced to Rod Stewart were gone and Phillip was to blame. Dad puffed his cigarette, sipped his beer, and watched mom cry in silence.

Turning my back to my parents was exceptionally difficult and I considered sitting on the bottom step, so I could listen to their private conversation. I will always regret the fact that I did turn around, only to see my dad cover his face with his large hands to hide his weeping. I have never seen my dad cry like that. He was not aware that I was watching as he pounded his fist on the table, and repeated, "Oh God. Oh my God." His voice cracked and then became stronger when he added, "God! No! No! No!" The sight of him weeping petrified me, so I ran as fast as I could up to my room wishing I could erase everything that happened in the past thirteen minutes.

I entered my room, shut my door, stood perfectly still in the center and blankly stared at the walls. Then, on an impulse, I ran to my mirror to see if I looked any different. I checked out my eyes- they looked the same. I checked out my hair- same. I checked out my mouth- same. My reflection was the same, yet somehow, when I looked harder, everything seemed different. I stared at myself in the mirror and knew that my life would never be the same.

I wanted to believe he was still alive, so I convinced myself that it was all a mistake. In the mirror, I shook my head up and down in agreement with all the thoughts in my head, while reassuring myself that it would be okay in the morning. I actually believed there was some sort of mix-up or a terrible case of mistaken identity. Funny how the mind does whatever tricks necessary to ease the shock or, in my case, avoid it. I mean, he had some issues, but he would never kill himself, would he? It was easier to believe that he would never do such a horrendous thing, but I knew it was exactly something he would do. The warning signs were always there, right in front of me, sometimes confessed to me. I continued to stare in the mirror, having an ongoing conversation in my head, feeling as if I had helped him pull the trigger. If I just told my parents all of his secrets then he would probably be alive.

Alone in my room, I became oddly uncomfortable with my thoughts, so I scurried to my bed and hid underneath the blankets, still wearing my sneakers and basketball uniform. What do I do now? I asked myself. What does one do when they learn that their brother just shot himself? Should I listen to music? Sleep? Stare? Call someone? Cry? Scream? Read? I chose to remain underneath my covers and hope that it was a mistake. If I stayed perfectly still, pleaded ignorance, and waited... it would all go away.

100 feet west of fernley drive

I crawled into my bed and wished that I could just have one more conversation with Phillip. In the nine months since he left, I never once felt the urgent need to talk to him the way I did on that night. As I hid under my covers, my thoughts raced with noble last ditch attempts of talking him out of it. I even indulged in fantasies of coming to his rescue in the nick of time, and for some reason, he would change his mind simply because I asked him to. While lying in bed, I wrestled with how I was *supposed* to feel and how I was really feeling. Why am I not crying? Why? I am supposed to cry... so, why do I have this urge to save him, instead? I mean, he's gone. I can't save him anymore. Why am I not sad? I should be sad. Under the covers, sweating from the dry contained heat, I talked in circles in my head. Why did he do it (really)? Was he mad at me? Was he trying to tell me? Who found him? What did he look like? How many times did he try before he actually did it? Did he ever wonder how this would make me feel? Then, I covered my head with my hands in frustration. I should have done something... said something... told someone.

I shut my eyes as tight as I could and, with one deep breath, considered the tragic reality that I was going to be walking around this earth for the rest of my life without him. I would graduate high school, get my driver's license, drink my first beer, go away to college without my brother around to watch me.

I rose from my bed and checked the mirror again. Still the same. I carefully cracked open my bedroom door, hoping to catch the conversation between my parents talking downstairs. Creeping down the steps, I was aware that my sense of sound had amplified with extreme intensity and I could easily make out every sound from the kitchen. I could hear everything, even the sound of them inhaling their cigarettes. When mom spoke, her voice echoed harsh vibrations, yet within the next breath, it was supple and weak. She was repeating the details of the dreaded phone call from Phillip's dad. Both dad and I would hear it for the first time.

At first, she sounded exhausted, borderline comatose, when she reported the information to dad. She mechanically recited, "I was home. I was making dinner. The phone rang. I picked it up. I heard a voice that sounded familiar... and... I..." She cleared her throat. "And, I... was uh, was making dinner." Then, she could not put one sentence or one word together. "He said, uh, that he had some bad..." Mom lit up another cigarette. "...some, uh, bad news and..." She took a drag from her smoke. "And, he said, um, that... that he had some awful news. So, I... I just thought he was, like, maybe, hospitalized again. I don't know." Mom began crying hysterically as dad tried to assure her that it is okay to continue. "I don't know. I just... there were so many things going through my head. You know?" Mom smashed her butt in the tray and deeply sighed. "I guess I thought he was cutting his arms again, but, uh, I never, ever thought that he..." She didn't have the strength to finish the sentence. She didn't have to. Dad already knew what she was going to say.

Dad responded quickly and compassionately. "I know. I never thought he would either." Neither of my parents could say "kill himself" in the open air. They couldn't fathom, let alone declare, that the boy they raised took his own life.

While listening to their conversation from the top of the stairs, I wondered if they were looking at each other or hiding their faces or holding hands. My curiosity was put on hold when I heard the squeal of my dad's chronic cough. After the coughing was over, he sympathetically, and with the utmost sincerity, whispered, "I'm sorry. I am sorry that you were alone. Maddie, I am so sorry. This is an awful situation... just awful. There is nothing I can say right now or do to make this better."

Silence. What are they doing? Are they staring at each other? Are they embracing? What is going on?

"I am so sorry, Maddie. So sorry that you were here all alone," he remarked.

Then, they each started to smoke another cigarette.

Mom never responded. Maybe they were hugging each other. I replayed visions of them powerfully embracing while dad caressed her hair and lovingly whispered to her that it was okay to cry. However, those tender moments were only in the theater or read about in Shakespearian tragedies. In the real world, my world, they were probably smoking their cigarettes, staring numbly at the table, and waiting for each other to say something meaningful. I sat on the third step down, biting my fingernails, nervously hanging on for a shred of confidential information.

Then, finally, mom cleared her throat and mentioned, "Phillip did it with another kid. Another boy." Mom sniffled, and then added, "Some friend of his..." She scoffed, "Hmm, some friend, huh?"

My legs were bouncing up and down on the stairs as I listened to mom. My fingers were raw from biting my skin around my fingernails. Go on. I kept repeating in my head. Go on. Tell me more.

"He, uh, was Phillip's age. His name was Daniel, I think."

"What?" Dad quickly interrupted her. "Together? What do you mean- together?"

Mom sarcastically remarked, "Together! I don't friggin' know... as in... *together*. All I know is what Phil told me. You'll have to forgive me if I blanked out after the words *shot himself*." Her voice trailed off and became softer. "The story got a little fuzzy. All I know is they found Phillip in the woods with another boy his age, and they both committed suicide."

Uhh! I cupped my hands over my mouth with the shock of my brother lying dead in the woods with another boy.

Dad commented, "Sounds suspicious... are you *sure* it was a suicide? I mean, was there a note or anything?" Dad's question made me wonder about that possibility, too.

"Yes. His father found the letter... it was a suicide, Tom. Phillip killed..." Mom began to cry and I knew why her tears fell at that moment. She just couldn't say it. She couldn't continue. She finally mustered up enough strength to admit what happened and whispered, "Phillip killed himself."

I was just about to go up to my room when I heard the phone ring. The echoing noise shook me up a bit and I crossed my fingers that it was Phillip's dad reporting more news. I ran upstairs to pick up the cordless phone before mom, so I could eavesdrop. When I picked up the receiver and put my hand on the bottom to block my breathing, I was secretly pleased when I heard a man's voice ask for mom. It was the first time I ever heard his voice; a voice that gave me life, the voice of mystery, and the voice that would confirm my brother's death.

He began talking business right away. He said, "Maddie? It's me... Phil. Yeah, uh, I'm at the police station and I need some information." He cleared his throat. His voice was soft and slow, perhaps because of the circumstances or maybe it was his natural prolonged southern draw. He added, "And the officer who was at the scene needs to talk to you."

"Okay," Mom responded eagerly as if she had waited years for his phone call.

The officer hesitated. He identified himself, gave his heartfelt condolences, and seemed a little uncomfortable (although I was sure he had the same conversation with other parents) asking mom routine questions. I knew something bad was coming, so I prepped myself by sitting on the edge of the bed and covering my forehead with my left hand. First, the officer asked mom if she was alone. Mom told him that her husband was sitting next to her. Then, he asked her if she knew of his whereabouts before the death, and if Phillip tried to contact her. Mom gave the officer all the information. Then, he paused briefly and mentioned, "Uh, well, let's see, first, I just want to let you know that this might be really difficult to process at this moment, but we really need all the information you can give us."

Might? That was an understatement.

He sighed. "I need you to be strong and try to focus on this investigation. Due to the fact that there were two minor youths involved, we are investigating thoroughly. "Um, okay... the uh, the coroner just took their bodies in and... um, well, they need his... dental records. I..." He paused for a moment, and I could vaguely make out talking in the background. It sounded like he was getting instructions or directions from another police officer who was also at the crime scene. The officer blurted, "Yes. That is correct. It was 100 feet west of Fernley Drive."

I clung to my phone with my left hand and repeated to myself- *Fernley Drive?* Where the heck is Fernley Drive?

"Why?" she snapped. "Why do you need his dental records?" When mom asked the question, her voice trailed off at the end when she realized the answer on her own. The police officer was repeating an address while calmly giving more instructions to the investigator. I heard mom sniffling and blowing her nose while she waited for more instructions or any information.

Phil was back on the phone, I could tell by the long voice. He sighed deeply and reassured her that the investigation was being handled with the greatest of detail; no stone was being left untouched. He said, "They need to be absolutely certain that it is him." Then, his voice became lower, as if he was about to give secret information. He softly warned, "He shot himself, Maddie. I know the officers here have to do their job and do all this stuff, but I know he did it. It's bad. I'm not gonna lie… it's bad. But, I know it's him, Maddie. They just need the records to close the case… I don't know… routine stuff. I guess. So, I need you to…"

"So… the dental records are because, uh, he shot himself in the face? Do you mean that he… I mean you weren't able… Oh my God! I can't do this! I just can't do this!" She lost what little composure she had and began sobbing.

Immediately, I hung up the phone and threw it on the bed, wishing that I did not listen in on the conversation after all. The visual was ingrained in my head forever and it almost made me throw up. I sat on the edge of the unmade bed paralyzed as if some uncontrollable force had taken over my body and left me unable to move any limbs. My head was spinning, my fingers were shaking, and the butterflies intensified to sharp stomach pains. I told myself not to think about it, but the more I focused on not thinking about it, the more I visualized him lying in the woods, rotting away. I was too shocked to cry, so I stood up in the middle of the room and stood perfectly still, torturing myself with that nightmarish image.

The sound of thumping feet up the stairs broke my inability to move. I ran out of the room and jumped into my bed, turned off my light, put my head underneath my pillow and tried to pretend that I could disappear into the night. I heard the door creak when mom opened it to check up on me. I felt invaded. Go away. The last thing I wanted to hear was mom crying next to me. Go away.

From the edge of my bed, she softly whispered, "Shan? You awake?" The smell of cigarettes filled my room, suffocating me. I ignored her.

She gently pleaded, "Shannon... wake up... I have to talk to you."

My muffled response should have given her a clue. "Mom? I'm sleepin'." I tried to play it up by softening my voice and rubbing my eyes, but, of course, she sat next to me anyway.

I prayed that she would just rattle off a couple one-liners and then leave me alone. The tears, the sniffling, and the noises that went along with them were too much for me to handle. She cried next to me and I did nothing to soothe her.

She asked, "Shannon, you ok?"

I understood what she was really asking. I began laughing in my head by the hypocrisy of the question. Of course, I was not even close to being "ok."

I lied, "Yeah." My voice cracked. I wanted her to believe that I was only half-awake, so I only had to half participate.

Unfortunately, mom could not take a hint. She continued, "It's just that... I... I want you to know that..." She struggled to find the right words. Once again, she began weeping in the darkness next to me, and I did nothing to console her. Just leave me alone, I kept repeating in my head. Go away.

She barely got the words out. "I want you to know that I love you very much and I... I don't know what is going to happen now." She started to pull herself together as her words became stronger. "I just don't know what to do... I just cannot believe this is happening to me. Why did he do this to me?" I knew it. I knew that somehow she was going to ask me questions that I could not answer.

The tears, the sobbing, the questions... I hated it. Just go away!

After moments of silence, she left. She left me in my room. When the door shut, when the light from the hall was gone, that was when I wanted her to come back. I just needed someone to sit near me. Of course, I could do without the crying and the sniffling and the questions. I just wanted company.

Sleep- impossible. Visions- unbearable. Reality- unbelievable. Every time I began drifting off, my mind immediately replayed graphic images of my brother lying in the woods. At 2:36 a.m., I rose slowly from my protective cocoon with my uniform still on, serving as a reminder of the simplicity of the early evening. I slithered my way out my door and tiptoed to the bathroom. I heard muffled whimpers coming from mom's bedroom and did my best to ignore them. After I closed the bathroom door, I looked in the medicine cabinet and hoped there was something in there that could make me drowsy or knock me out. It wasn't fair. I was sure mom had some pills to help her sleep and dad had beer to help him sleep, but I had nothing.

I looked around the medicine cabinet and thought-maybe, some cough syrup. I read the label with chills going down my left arm when I remembered that Phillip used to guzzle down the syrupy liquid. After reading, I gently placed it back in the medicine cabinet and, as my face caught the mirror, I stared at my reflection. I focused on my tired blue gray eyes and tried to force out tears, but... nothing.

I tiptoed back to my room, ignoring the noises from mom's room, still holding onto desperate hope that it was all just a terrible misunderstanding. My digital clock displayed 3:03 a.m. in large, red numbers. Time seemed insignificant. Actually, everything but the recent news seemed insignificant. I curled up in a fetal position, held my arms in tightly to my body, and covered myself with my comforter. With my safety blanket engulfing my body, I reminded myself that if I just stay still enough, plead ignorance, and wait... then, everything would be just fine. My basic need for air seemed less important than hiding away from the dark night, from the darkness that surrounds me, from the truth. I began to pray:

Dear God, it's me, Shannon. Shannon Bennet. God, please make this all go away... please, just make it not be true. God, I know it might be true. I do. I am not stupid. But, anyway, can you just make it a mistake? Please, make everything okay. God, I know

*I am not the best person in the world and I know I
should be nicer, but please... help me... or... help us.
You can make it all better. I know you can. Amen,
Shannon.*

That night, I awoke every forty-five minutes to pull my
covers securely over my head for protection. I was not sure
what I needed protection from, but I needed to feel
protected. I never opened my eyes to look at the clock or
look around my room; I kept them closed tightly (which
was extremely hard to do) the entire night. I was afraid that
if I opened them, I would see Phillip standing there at the
foot of my bed. I was not even sure why I feared my
brother perhaps I couldn't handle what he might think
about me or what he might look like... with his head
missing or whatever.

The squawking of black crows woke me around six in
the morning. Funny, I never heard those birds before. As I
stretched out my legs to expand from my safe fetal
position, I allowed myself to open my eyes. There was a
brief moment of wonderful denial. A brief moment when I
actually believed that all I had to do was put on my shoes
and socks, and go to school. That thought was fleeting,
concocted in my subconscious mind to ease the shock.
Unfortunately, the sobbing from mom's room reminded me
that everything was real and that putting on my shoes and
socks would not make it go away.

When I heard mom cough, I covered my head with my
pillow to avoid her or anything that reminded me of his
death. Suddenly, the thought of telling Lizzie served as a
distraction. I panicked. How do I tell her? How do I tell
everyone? I imagined everyone staring at me, pointing their
fingers, and cautiously whispering into each other's ear.
They would say, "Yeah, that's her. That's the girl. Her

brother killed himself... Oh my God! You remember? That weird kid, uhh, Phillip... yeah, that was his name. Eww, he was so weird. Oh my God. What a sin!" I hated thinking about what people might think; perhaps, even worse, I hated myself because I cared about what they thought. I dozed off again with my head smothered underneath my pillow agonizing over the thought. Then, I felt an immediate rush of shame for posing such thoughts when they should have been on my brother, and the blatant fact that he was dead.

"Your dad wants you downstairs," mom shouted after she knocked on my door. She never waited for a response. She just walked away. (Thank God.)

I stomped down the steps... left, right, left, right... I repeated it military style in my head. Stomping was my obnoxious way of alerting dad that I was going to be in the kitchen soon. Just in case he was crying, my loud thuds would give him ample time to stop. When our eyes met in the kitchen, our stare made it perfectly clear that our conversation was going to be nothing more than details.

"What should I say?" I asked dad as I picked up the phone.

He didn't hesitate with an answer. "The truth." He looked at me with both softness and sincerity. I responded with harsh eye rolling and sarcastic scoffs that served as my thirteen-year-old way of wishing there was another version of the truth. The truth was unbearable. Why couldn't it have been a car accident or some incurable terminal illness? "Just tell her the truth and get it over with," dad muttered just before he sipped his coffee. Under his breath, I heard him say, "Oh boy."

I confirmed, "So, just tell her? Just, like, tell her what happened? What if she tells everyone else?" I needed permission to tell the absolute truth. Dad nodded to reassure me that it was okay.

"It's going to come out eventually. It should come directly from you, right?" He nodded his head again and granted his consent. "Go ahead, Shannon. I am right here if you need me." He got up to fix another cup of coffee.

I held the phone in my hand and began dialing her phone number. 8-4-8, I don't need his help. 4-5-4, I can do this on my own. However, as I was on the verge of dialing the last number, I watched dad carefully, following him around the kitchen with my eyes, just in case.

Lizzie picked up the phone too fast. I wasn't prepared. "Hello?" she said.

Trying to sound normal, I replied, "Yo. It's me... uh, I won't be going to school today," I claimed. I nervously bit the skin around my nails.

"Why? You sick?" Lizzie asked.

I scoffed, "Uhh, yeah... I wish."

"Huh?"

"Well, umm, there has been a death in the family."

"Who?" She demanded. Lizzie's question was so simple, but it reminded me that this was going to be harder than I thought.

I struggled for the nicest way to say it, but quickly concluded that any way it came out was going to be awful. "Um, well, it's my brother, Phillip. My mom told me after we came home last night, after the basketball game." It was impossible to say anything beyond the facts.

Her voice became low. "What! What do you mean?"

I added, "Phillip died."

Her voice was nothing but a raspy whisper. "Oh. My. God. Are you serious? I mean, I know you're serious... oh my God! Shan, oh my God! What happened?" I could hear her breathing intensify and it scared me. Everything was so real.

"Well, how do I say this? He, like, um... I don't know." I began holding my head while trying to find an easy way to say it. "He kind of, well, shot himself... in the..." I decided not to finish that sentence. "He committed suicide," I blurted out, slightly proud of myself for saying it.

I glanced to dad. I needed his reassurance that what I just said was acceptable. He was just staring at the kitchen walls, sipping coffee, and half listening to my phone conversation. Lizzie went silent. The line between us went mute. There were no words, no sighing, no heavy breathing, or throats cleared. Nothing.

I thought that she hung up the phone. "Lizzie? Liz? Did you hear me?" Still no words, but she did give a heavy sigh. I never took into consideration how the information might affect the person who was receiving the message. The phone call to Lizzie was the first of many conversations to come and judging by our conversation it was going to be a long road.

Finally, she softly whispered, "Oh." Then, another pause, "I mean..." She sighed again, "I can't believe it. I, uhh, I guess you won't be at school for a couple days, then... huh?" I didn't know how to tell her and she didn't know how to respond.

Finally, she commented, "So, yeah, I'm, like, sorry." I knew that was all she was going to say about it and that was totally fine.

"Well, I have to go... I don't know... I'll talk to you later. Okay?" I said. I ran my hand through my tangled hair and continued nervously bite the skin around my nails.

She automatically recited, "Okay... well... bye."

"Bye." I quickly hung up the phone.

whatever, I'll be fine.

A fter the dreaded phone call to Lizzie ended, I slowly walked up the stairs to my room, flopped on my bed, and curled in my contorted, little ball. The light from the sun comforted me because I no longer feared the darkness; the unknown. Within seconds, my body went completely limp and, with the daylight shining in on my weary face, I drifted off. I drifted to a place where time was a simple illusion. My body was no longer aware of my five senses when I was in that distant place; it allowed me to forget, allowed me to rest, and allowed me to believe everything would be fine.

Sometime that afternoon, dad woke me from my peaceful dream state. After knocking lightly, he requested my permission to enter- which I greatly appreciated. I was certain that he was going to give me the predictable fatherly advice about death, although, I could not remember dad ever talking about death or even knowing anyone close to him that died. I sat up against my headboard with my back to my pillows and wondered what his beliefs were about death. I knew dad would be the one to console me. Mom could hardly put a sentence together, let alone dispel any words of wisdom. I didn't expect her to even try to ease any of my pain and, quite honestly, I didn't expect her to make me feel better. Then again, mom could never hide her feelings and, at that time, I really needed her to. Dad was different. He was the calm one who could find a way to put things into perspective. However, as I sat with my knees to my chest, waiting for dad to speak, I highly doubted that he could put it all into perspective. While waiting for his noble words, I gulped the dry air and bit my fingernails. Dad would know. Dad would know what to say. I watched him slump his back and rest his hands on his legs and waited.

Dad peeked up at my poster-covered walls, possibly for the first time, trying to absorb my hidden adolescent world. Dad patted his leg with his wrinkled hands as his cue to begin. "Shannon," he began. "Shannon, we are leaving tomorrow. Early. Very early."

Dad never looked directly at me and part of me was relieved. When the conversation started, he just blankly stared out my window. "We are flying to Fort Lauderdale and then driving to… uh." He scratched his elbow, trying to buy more time. "Uh, Lake Fort Worth." I sat perfectly still, waiting for direction, hoping he would tell me something important. He finally looked toward me and said, "You need to get dressed because we have to go pick up your homework assignments at school. You will be out for a while and I don't want you falling behind." He glanced over to me to make sure I was listening. Not quite the direction I was hoping for.

No fatherly advice. Maybe it was for the best. I slipped into my jeans, pulled over my field hockey sweatshirt, then pulled my hair up tight. I looked like shit. While fumbling around to find my sneakers in my pig-sty room, I cursed the entire time, using the f-word to follow everything I said under my breath. It was difficult to find anything in my room, let alone sneakers. I skipped putting on socks (two matching socks… I don't think so!) and caught a glimpse of my freshly painted garnet toenails. I thought about Phillip's chubby feet that I made fun of throughout the years. Then, even though I told myself not to, I thought about what his toes must have looked like upon his discovery. I put on my already laced sneakers and sighed. Damn! Was this going to continue? Was I going to always visualize him like that? Distorted? Unrecognizable? Decomposed? Would I just remember him as a rotting corpse?

I became angry with myself for allowing the visual to seep into my thoughts. I had to get ready. I told myself not to think about it. I sprayed some hairspray and checked my face in the mirror one last time. I intensely studied my eyes and whispered, "Just don't think about it. Just don't think about it." I nodded at the girl in the mirror, convincing the reflection that it was possible to temporarily forget- that it was imperative, a matter of survival. I grabbed my jacket, ran out of my room, and softly repeated, "Just... don't think about it."

When dad and I entered the main office at school, he took control and ordered me to sit and wait. I tried to pretend that I was invisible as I quietly observed everyone scurrying in the crowded office. As familiar faces passed by me, I worried that they already knew what happened. Then, I saw my two friends pass by in the hallway. They ecstatically waved to me with bright, cheery smiles. They yelled, "Yo! Bennet! What's up, kid." They didn't know. I could still pretend to be invisible. Thank God.

I studied everyone in the room, trying to figure out who they were just by watching. I followed a young student teacher while she retrieved her mail and created her entire life story within a matter of seconds. She was single. She graduated from a college in California. She colored her hair herself because the salon was a rip-off. She wore braces because her family was too poor to afford them when she was little. She liked horses, Chinese food, and Madonna. I watched the unknowing woman until she exited the office, telling myself she was going to the gym to do a step class.

Dad gave me permission to go to my locker. "Everything is arranged. Your teachers are waiting for you," he said.

The dismissal bell sounded. The ringing bell was my cue that it was safe to walk in the halls.

My locker held up glossy pictures with gooey chewed up gum. It was a painful reminder of the simplicity of yesterday. What a difference a day makes. I glanced at my prized baseball card of Darren Daulton, remembering my social studies daydreams of Phillip and me going to Veterans Stadium to eat big Philly pretzels and eat ice cream out of a small plastic helmet, maybe, even wave on Fanovision. The notion that every single aspect of my life would somehow remind me of his absence was really depressing. His absence was permanent, and permanent meant forever. No pretzels, no ice cream, no waving. Nothing.

Thomas (my new boyfriend from the dance) spotted me at my locker. He sniffed me out like a cadaver dog sniffs the scent of death. Death was all around me. As weird as I was about the situation, the even weirder thing was how people reacted to me. His steps were slow as if he was asking for my permission to approach. I hated that. I hated the weirdness. I half smiled at him to ease the awkwardness.

Thomas knew Phillip, or rather he knew of Phillip. I do not believe they ever shared one conversation. Thomas knew him as the kid who was in a mental institution, but he also knew him as my brother. When Thomas approached me, he placed his hand on my shoulder and asked me how I was holding up. I lied to him when I shrugged my shoulders and muttered, "I'm alright."

Funny, after my rehearsed response, our conversation turned to the most trivial things, considering the situation. He told me that they played waffle ball in gym, that there was a storm coming, and that Denny Bilchecki got caught cheating in math class. I listened to Thomas with relief; relief that he was not asking about Phillip.

"I am leaving tomorrow," I announced as I stuffed my books in my backpack. Thomas asked me how long I would be gone. I replied, "Well, I don't know how long, I think, like, three days, maybe. I don't know. They don't tell me anything." I bit my skin around my nails, sighed, and then admitted, "I don't know." I began twirling my ponytail when I nervously added, "We have the funeral, and, uhh, the umm, the whole, the whole..." I rolled my eyes. "The whole *thing*."

Thomas looked down at his black Adidas Sambas and then his eyes darted directly toward mine, immediately making me feel really uncomfortable. Then, it hit me. He was sad. I could see sorrow in his eyes. I wasn't sure if he was sad for me, my family, or just the fact that he indirectly knew someone who committed suicide. It was something that I never considered until that moment.

He placed a letter in my hand and covered his sweaty hand over mine. As he delicately held my hand, he warned me that things might not sound right. He said, "I wasn't really, umm..." He squeezed my hand. "I wasn't sure what to write. So, I'm sorry if it sounds all messed up." Thomas stuttered a little and spoke with a low voice when he said, "I'm sorry. I am real sorry." I was blushing. He was the first person to say sorry to my face.

After much needed silence, I mentioned, "I have to go. My dad's waiting for me and my teachers need to give me my work. I will try to call you. Anyway, thanks. Thanks for the letter." I walked away and stuffed his note in my left jean pocket.

After many heartfelt apologies and clichéd references about God, I retrieved all my assignments and wearily walked into the main office where dad was sitting alone in the same chair that I sat in earlier. He appeared so lost, so vulnerable, almost childlike. I lightly tapped him on the back, indicating that I was ready. On our way out the door, we stopped when we heard an urgent voice call for us. We turned around in unison and saw Mr. Brown nearly out of breath while waving for us to come in his office. Mr. Brown's gesture was not just an invitation, rather a strong request.

Mr. Brown, Gateway's principle, was certainly not a stranger to either of my parents or to me. Phillip's one and a half year stint at Gateway, however brief, proved to be a roller coaster of complexity for everyone. My parents had an extensive history with Mr. Brown, as well as the school faculty and the school administration. Certainly, Phillip deserved his punishments, but even I could not deny that he became a target. When something bad happened, anything bad, Phillip was the first to receive blame. Part of me believed that he lived out everyone's negative perception of him. He once mentioned, "Well, if everyone says I am bad... I must be bad."

In the past, Mr. Brown's interactions with me were often overly kind and overly compassionate. My only guess as to why he saturated me with canvas smiles and well wishes was out of pity or perhaps obligatory compensation to make up for the distraught relationship between him and my parents. When passing in the hallway between classes, he was excessively friendly and once remarked about my Temple University sweatshirt, claiming it was his alma mater. (Alma... what?) I politely smiled with agreement, but I had no idea what that even meant. That was *one* of the confusing things about being Phillip's sister. I would constantly second guess people's motives, wondering if they were genuinely nice or just reaching out to me in sympathy. Overall, I liked Mr. Brown, mostly because his efforts to be friendly toward me mixed in friendly conversation about soccer. His daughter played soccer against me on Sundays, so soccer was our neutral topic.

Unlike my brother, I have never seen the inner workings of the principal's office... ever. As I absorbed the sanctity of a principal's office, I noticed his walls decorated with degrees, official awards, Gateway banners, and several plaques with positive quotations. On his desk, he displayed a small plaque that read, *"All our dreams can come true, if we have the courage to pursue them."* -Walt Disney. There was a red and white pennant over the door with Temple University in capital letters. Mr. Brown wasted no time in telling us how very sorry he was for Phillip's death. I sat with my legs crossed on the seat, clutching my royal blue softball jacket in my pale hands. I sensed my dad was not up for this conversation, not at that moment. Dad was uneasy in his chair, shifting every couple of seconds to adjust his position. I also noticed that my father was becoming irritated, or defensive, or whatever. It was obvious that he wasn't comfortable with the words that were coming out of Mr. Brown's mouth. In my chair, I sat perfectly still. My face revealed nothing but mild interest. My mouth was dry. My eyes were stinging. Those old familiar butterflies began to attack my stomach, yet I remained perfectly still.

Mr. Brown seemed concerned, apologetic, and borderline responsible when he admitted that he was hoping that everything 'worked out' for Phillip. He remarked, "To hear this news is simply devastating."

Dad never acknowledged his benevolent attempts to console us. As the conversation became stagnant and, with no response from my dad, Mr. Brown turned toward me and smiled. Then, he looked back toward my father with his eyebrows down and his lips pursed together, looking like he was trying to figure out a calculus problem he commented, "You have a great kid. I..."

Mr. Brown never had a chance to finish. Dad placed his hand on my left arm, looked Mr. Brown deep in the eyes for the first time, and snapped, "I know she's a good kid... you don't need to remind me." The words came a little too quick off his lips and it reassured me that my gut feelings were right.

It was not dad's intention to remain in the chair and listen to someone ramble on about his kids. The tension between them led me to believe that there was something in their past that was resurfacing, obviously about my brother-always about my brother. Dad began zipping up his brown, leather jacket, quickly rose from his chair, and motioned to me that it was time to leave. Mr. Brown earnestly requested that he remain seated, while thanking him for taking the time to talk during "this very difficult time." I got the impression that dad sat back down simply for my benefit.

Mr. Brown folded his hands on his desk and leaned toward my dad. "Mr. Bennet." His voice was low. "I think it might be a good idea for Shannon to see one of our counselors at school."

I sat with my eyes low to hide my sudden interest in the conversation. I knew dad's opinion about *counseling*. Dad had a strong belief that most shrinks were only there to twist the truth, take your money, and, ultimately, screw you up more. I also knew that he would deny any type of counseling or psychological assistance. Mr. Brown, with good intentions, pressed on and raved about the grief counseling available at the school.

"I don't think so," dad barked sarcastically. "My daughter will not need any... *counselors.*" He raised his hands and used his fingers to quote the word 'counselor.' Mr. Brown leaned back on his black desk chair as he crossed his arms to take a moment to soak up what dad said. I was sure they never taught him how to handle that at Temple University. I almost laughed in my chair thinking about it.

Mr. Brown's demeanor changed. He stated, "Mr. Bennet, I am truly sorry if I offended you. It's just that..."

Dad interrupted, "Yeah, I know. I know...you're just trying to help, right? No, thank you, but no. She'll be fine." As I sat still in my chair, I could not help but think that I was not supposed to be there, but I was there and I was taking it all in.

Mr. Brown tried to be diplomatic about the touchy situation: "Well, maybe Shannon would like someone to talk to about all of this." He shrugged his shoulders and added, "Maybe not now. Maybe... later. But, just the same, I wanted to extend our services and let you know that we are available." Mr. Brown settled into his chair and gave his final remark. "Mr. Bennet, it is a service we offer all of our youngsters."

Youngsters? Did he really just say youngsters? Ewww! Who uses that word? I was laughing inside- perhaps it was my way of dealing with this heavy situation.

Dad repeated, "No. No. Thank you. I understand. She'll be fine."

Mr. Brown wearily smiled and then added, "Well, if you change your mind, let me know." He rose from his chair while fixing his red shiny tie and shook dad's hand.

I grabbed my jacket and headed for the door, but before I left his office, I looked back to my principal and waved goodbye. As our gaze connected, I knew I would never forget the conversation. It defined my life. I walked outside and was greeted by small, white flurries tickling my face. I knew. I knew from that single conversation, from those three words how I was supposed to act, live, and deal with my brother's suicide. Dad didn't need to have that fatherly conversation or expel words of advice.

I understood those words: "She'll be fine."

the trip down south

After packing my suitcase with my belongings and my outfit for his funeral, I slithered in my bed and prepared for another sleepless night. My comforter served, once again, as my protective shield. Early the next morning, I crammed into the backseat of our tiny Volkswagen Rabbit. Viewing Philadelphia at 4:30 in the morning was an intriguing sight. From the Walt Whitman Bridge, I could see the blinking lights from the airport. I took in the United States Navy Yard with all the retired war ships that shared tired tales of the sea. Then, I saw my beloved Veterans Stadium. I followed the puffy, white, billowing smoke circling the sky from the forgotten factories that sat along the Delaware River. I watched in awe as the smoke traveled aimlessly at the mercy of the gusty winter air. I closed my eyes when we came to the tollbooth and hoped that when I opened them again, I would magically be in Florida.

Dad struggled with every twist, turn, sign, or direction that he encountered on the way. I wasn't sure if that was due to the current situation or his lack of knowledge regarding the airport. At any rate, I sat in the backseat and ignored my parents trying to interpret the arrows to the parking garage lot. I rolled my eyes and half listened to dad mutter under his breath due to his inability to find the correct departure gate. He asked attendants the same questions many times. The leader of our pack was out of his element and I sensed the panic in his voice. Ironically, mom remained silent, and, for once, she was non-argumentative. I followed behind both of them like a stray puppy, listening to my walkman, so I could block out everything. I made up my mind that I would remain a mere observer on this trip, so my disinterest in the airport fiasco was deliberate.

I plopped down in my designated seat on the plane next to my father and continued listening to my Walkman until the snotty flight attendant asked me to, "Please put away my belongings." What was I going to do now? The light sobs that I heard from mom annoyed me, so I threw a tiny pillow over my head while the captain gave us the flight announcements. Why would anyone care that we are taking a flight path right by Chicago? How the hell could we possibly know where we were up there? I laughed under my pillow wondering if anyone on the plane was wondering the same thing. I slouched in my seat, covered my head, and repeated the chorus to *Toy Soldiers* in my head until I could put my headphones back on. While in flight, I tried to sleep, but the turbulence along with all my disturbing thoughts of my brother's dead body decaying in the woods, not to mention meeting my biological father, kept me awake. I listened to my new mixed tape and pressed fast forward over all the sappy lovey-dovey slow songs. Ton Locs' *Wild Thing* played four times before the stewardess offered me a drink. After declining a soda, I finally dozed off listening to Jimmy Buffett. Hearing a grown man sing about cheeseburgers and getting drunk kept my mind off what was to come in just a matter of hours.

I motioned to the stewardess so I could take her up on the soda and reread my note from Thomas.

> *Dear Shan,*
>   *Hey. I just heard the news from Liz. I can't even believe it. I really don't know what to write except that I am soooooo sorry. I wish that I could write something that would make you feel better, but I don't think that is possible. I am here for you, and your friends are here for you... we love you. I feel terrible. I wish I knew how to make you feel better. Sorry. I can't wait to see you again.*
> *Love,*
> *Thomas*

After sleeping for what seemed like five minutes, dad gently shook my arm, waking me from my visions of a pencil thin mustache. As I prepared to exit the plane, I reminded myself to "just be strong." No matter what happened, no matter how terrible, I had to stay strong. I shuffled my way through the small aisle while repeating in my head, "Just be tough. Just tough it out. Don't be a total Sally. Be strong. You can do this."

The three of us staggered around the airport like lost tourists, pointing and second-guessing as we chaotically navigated our way to baggage claim. We rolled our belongings behind us and wearily ventured outside to retrieve our rental car. The wide, tinted, automatic glass doors glided open revealing the blinding sunlight, smothering us with our first gust of humid air since early September. We were not prepared for it. We were not prepared at all. Mom and dad were going back and forth about the location of the car while I followed behind. They walked, talked, and lit up their cigarettes, turning around occasionally to find me. When we found our rental car, we stood by the trunk and everything became eerily quiet. Standing in the hot sunlight, feeling the warm breeze in my hair, and looking at the puffy clouds cluster above proved that the trip was very real. We stood in the Florida sun facing reality and it totally sucked.

The three of us soaked in the weather as we stowed our belongings in the back. It was a gorgeous day with palm trees dancing in the blue sky and colorful tropical birds hovering above us. The birds in flight were so much prettier than the Canadian Geese that did nothing but waddle around and poop all over our softball fields. Looking down, I spotted a miniature lizard slinking in and out of the bushes and rocks. Although I was pretty sure we were all thinking about it, dad was the one who said it out loud. He shook his head, peeked at the swollen clouds in the sky, and dared to ask, "How?" He lit another cigarette, deeply inhaled the orange and white stick, and then looked down at his brown shoes. He asked, "How could he do it? It's so beautiful here. How could someone..." Dad stopped after he saw mom's face. She knew his death had nothing to do with the weather. After that, none of us spoke to one another until it was necessary.

My aunt, who overestimated our budget, made our hotel arrangements. The hotel itself was gorgeous. Everything about it was ideal for a family ready to enjoy a pleasurable Florida vacation. It offered prime location; an oceanfront view overlooking the glistening emerald and turquoise waves. I opened the sliding glass door to view the beach, again surprised by the humid air that hit me when I stepped out. Then, I pressed my weight against the wrought iron fence that enclosed the balcony, closed my eyes, and took in the intoxicating scents that filtered through the air. After

I wiped the sweat from my brow, I watched families fly kites and old men search the sand for lost treasures.

Mom and dad were busy inside making phone calls. I liked the solitude and occupied my time by watching the hypnotic waves from the open balcony. The salty air reminded me of Ocean City, New Jersey. I thought about Phillip. The sun will rise, the waves will break, the sand will retreat, but I will never see him again. I will never see him again. I repeated those strange words in my head while watching the effortless waves crash. I always liked being alone by the sea. The ocean never gave me permission to feel completely alone. The sea was eternal and would remain long after I left this earth. The sea held secrets under its deep waters. Like the ocean, I, too, held secrets of my own: secrets that should have been told, secrets that might have saved my brother.

I let out a deep sigh that was stored up since crossing The Walt Whitman and crept over to the cabana chair. I wasn't sure how long I was sleeping; I could only remember drifting off to the sound of seagulls squawking above, and, of course, that dream. My dream was about a robin flying frantically against the wind. The robin looked distressed, but, as I looked on, I wasn't too concerned. It flapped its wings chaotically. The robin would climb against the wind only to be knocked back down, over and over again. The bird began descending slowly down to the ground and, with every few feet it dropped, its feathers began falling off one by one. The robin, helpless and barely alive, was on its way to an inevitable death. I watched with no concern. As it plunged to the ground, nearing the green grass, I placed my hands over my eyes. I woke up before its expectant crash due to the smell of cigarette smoke. I peeked with one eye and watched my mom smoke a newly lit cigarette. Her hair was wild, her chapped lips quivered, and her eyes were concealed by her black sunglasses.

She never looked away from the ocean when she asked, "You up?"

"I guess," I muttered. I was exhausted. I could barely pick myself up to rest my elbows on the chair. "Yup... just dozed off... I guess."

I asked, "Mom, do you think that later we can go to the beach and take a walk?" Once again, she stood frozen against the balcony rail, still gazing blankly at the ocean.

"We'll see," she muttered, and then flicked her cigarette out in the open air. I knew what her answer meant; it was the grown up version of no. "We'll see" was what my parents always said when they meant no, but did not want to expel energy to explain. She held onto the rail of the balcony, shifting her weight back and forth, almost as if she was in a trance. What started out as tiny sniffles became wet sobs, eventually turning into full-blown hysterics. I sat on the cabana chair, peeking toward her only to quickly look away. I thought of one hundred things to say, but every word, every thought seemed so corny and rehearsed. I was relieved when mom dashed to the sliding glass doors and went inside the hotel.

After she left, I told myself that I just needed to be strong and be tough. Then, I rose from the chair after hearing children laughing below. I watched with envy and closed my eyes while I wished that I could trade places with them just for a little while.

Just as Luke Skywalker had to eventually face the inevitable, I, too, had to face my personal Darth Vader. I hoped that my limbs would remain intact after our meeting. I was pretty sure that I would be okay. As I traveled with my parents in our sparkly rental car, the anticipation of meeting the last person who saw or talked to my brother seemed intriguing. I felt nauseous over the fact that I was meeting the man who abandoned me thirteen years ago. After all the years of distance, the only reason we were meeting was due to the death of my brother. My unexpected and forced reunion with him was merely one aspect of my uneasiness, but was, admittedly, a big one. Within a matter of minutes, I would be standing in the same place my brother lived, the place where he decided that he would kill himself, the place of pain. My job was to simply observe; observe the mood, observe the clues, observe everything- then I could figure it all out... later.

When we took that final right off the highway into the entrance of his trailer park, I assumed that we would be traveling down a dirt road. My stereotypical mind concocted a stereotypical red-neck scenario: rustic trailers would be propped on cinderblocks, small children in bare feet and frayed cut-off jean shorts would be running down the road, carrying sticks and throwing rocks. Rebel flags would proudly sway in the backs of pick-up trucks along with a mounted shot-gun. Those thoughts quickly diminished after I saw the bright, nearly brand new trailers. The driveways had perfectly new black gravel (the smell from the topcoat was still in the air) without any rowdy riff-raff in sight. Leafy, green palm trees waved and welcoming me after I passed each one. The giraffe neck trees lined the manicured road as if they were strategically placed. American flags proudly flew over doorways and mailboxes. Everything was new. The trailers were bright and shiny, almost as if they were driven off the lot that morning. There was even a pristine lake or some kind of waterway serving as a centerpiece in the middle of the trailer park. In the middle of the lake, a large fountain sprayed water ten feet high, almost tickling me as we drove by.

I became fidgety the moment we arrived at his seashell driveway. My fingers were already in my mouth and my leg bounced in the back seat as we drove closer and closer. Mom could barely keep her hands off the car handle and I seriously believed she contemplated jumping out before the car came to a full stop. She knew the last shred of evidence to the life of her son was in that trailer. I walked behind my parents, prepping myself for my meeting with my own 'Darth Vader.'

Before we could knock on the door, Phil greeted us at the walkway and I could not have been more shocked if he had boobs and a blond Dolly Parton wig. The sight of the man standing in front of me took several moments to absorb. Trying to connect any resemblance between the two of us was difficult, if not impossible. He stood a mere five foot seven inches with shaggy, blond hair, dark circles under his beady eyes, and severely sun-damaged skin. His appearance probably had more to do with his years of smoking and boozing than the trauma surrounding my brother. He was an unfortunate sight that took a lifetime to create. He greeted us in front of his trailer steps that seemed more like a ladder. He wore a tan, buttoned-up, short sleeve shirt and dark brown polyester pants that were about two inches too short. As I climbed the three tiny steps to enter, I noticed that his big toe on his left foot was completely black.

Once inside, I told myself to focus on anything but the polyester pants and black grotesque toenail, but, of course, that was all I could think about. During our understandably awkward greeting, I scanned the trailer trying to examine any evidence that would give me any information about my brother. Like boys and girls at a sixth grade dance, we looked at each other with curiosity, dreading the first move. The four of us stood motionless in the kitchen and waited. I wasn't completely sure if it was a kitchen. It did have a tiny sink, a tiny range stove top, and a tiny elevated refrigerator to match. In the center of the kitchen, there was a three-foot high raised island, littered with old newspapers and crumpled cigarette boxes. Empty Styrofoam coffee cups were scattered all over the counters; some still had black coffee with cigarette butts floating on the top. Gross!

Mom and dad did their best to initiate any sort of conversation by asking the safe and routine questions about the weather. I could tell that there was going to be a whole bunch of trivial, meaningless talk followed by several cigarettes and a lot of coffee. As I predicted, Phil offered the first cup and, naturally, mom and dad graciously accepted. The coffee percolated, their cigarettes were lit, and the anxiously awaited conversation was about to begin. As they took their first sips, mom and dad politely asked me to go to the living room. Fortunately, the living room was only three feet away, so I could hear everything anyway. I thought it was hilarious that they actually thought sending me two steps away was going to give them privacy. Those fools!

I delicately sat on the edge of the putrid, orangey-brown floral print couch and pretended to watch TV while I covertly listened in on their 'private' conversation. I noticed the fake wood paneled walls were completely bare and small portions were several shades lighter from the sunlight. The television was beyond outdated with worn fabric lining the bottom and hand sewn buttons to match. There weren't any sneakers, hockey sticks, book bags, or comic books in sight. The only proof that Phillip resided there for nine months was an earth science textbook that sat on the coffee table, untouched. After years of taking my brother's belongings for granted, the sight of his science book was a treat. I opened the cover to look at his signature on the inside flap and smiled as I read, "Boys rule- girls drool."

The three fumbling adults stood in a crowded miniature kitchen while I sat alone in a living room four times the size. Mom began the string of questions that reminded me of grade school. She started every sentence with: what, who, when, why, where, or how. Phil did his best to answer her questions in the most dignified way possible. Of course, since I was thirteen and a professional gossip, I knew he was withholding information. I wasn't sure if that was for my benefit or for hers.

While trying to figure out the layout of the trailer, I heard my mom ask, "Where's the note? Did he say anything in the note? Do you have it? Can I read it?" Phil reached to the refrigerator to grab the note held up by a magnet from Circle K.

I made my entrance in the kitchen, figuring I was privy to the intimate information, secretly hoping that my name was on that piece of white, lined paper. Mom held it close to her face and ignored everything around her. Her lips moved as she read to herself. Then, with disappointment in her voice, she asked, "That's it?" Her reaction stunned everyone. "I don't understand this part." She pointed at the sheet of paper and flashed it toward Phillip's father.

He shrugged, nervously chuckled in defeat, and shook his head. "I don't either." His pale blood shot eyes squinted as he read the part on the bottom of the page. Phil muttered, "What is *the truth?*" I thought maybe you guys would know. Seriously, I've wracked my brains out trying to figure that out and... yeah... um... I have no idea." He examined it once again. His perplexed facial expression confirmed his uncertainty.

I was the last of them to read the letter. When I finally had the sliver of paper in my sweaty hands, there was a moment of uneasiness. These were his last words. As I read it, my hands began to shake and I kept skipping words just to find my name somewhere, anywhere. He never mentioned me in the letter. I suppose I was in the same category as "family." His letter seemed rather generic. There was nothing to indicate a specific reason or flaw or trigger to explain why he was going to kill himself. Phillip did try to pass on that it wasn't any of our faults and begged for our forgiveness. After he signed his name, he wrote a P.S. on the bottom of the sheet that read, "Find out the truth." After reading his obscure last request, I was sure that I would spend my entire life trying to figure it out. I stared at his chicken scratch penmanship and felt like that last line was written just for me.

After reading the letter, I returned to the ugly couch and pretended to watch TV again. They talked endlessly about conspiracy theories, possible reasons, and the signs they should have seen earlier. Phillip's father brought a large manila folder out of a drawer and plopped it in front of my parents. It was the official police report along with newspaper clippings and some phone numbers of people who possibly knew any information. He gave mom and dad permission to make copies but demanded the original copies.

Simply by eavesdropping, I learned that Phillip and his friend Daniel were both found dead in the woods from self-inflicted gunshots. Apparently, Daniel shot himself first and Phillip covered him up with a blanket. The police report indicated that the gunshots were no more than minutes apart and there was a cassette radio with Led Zeppelin inside. Both of them personally made their own tombstones out of Styrofoam and inscribed their tombstones with the letters- R.I.P. After learning about the Led Zeppelin tape, I knew he played "Stairway to Heaven" as his farewell message and I knew he questioned whether he would actually go to heaven.

Phil explained that during the past several weeks, Phillip had been increasingly distant. Apparently, Phillip was giving his things away to his friends. Phillip's dad also mentioned that during the past couple weeks they rarely talked to each other. As the conversation turned to the other boy, Daniel, Phil became visibly upset. He raised his voice and angrily ranted about Daniel. He felt Daniel was a bad influence on Phillip. The last time they saw each other they had a terrible fight about a robbery in the trailer park. Phil talked in detail about how he accused my brother and his delinquent friends of robbing a house down the road to get money for drugs. According to Phil, Phillip denied everything and an awful fight ensued. Mom pressed for more information about the fight, but Phil refused to give more details, claiming, "It's so stupid now... you know... it was a bad fight." Mom dropped it.

Mom walked into the living room to examine everything, just as I did. She waved to me, motioning me to follow her. Mom led me to my brother's bedroom that was only a few steps from the living room. Even with the bright Florida sun, the room was dark, very dark; dark and creepy in a very literal and metaphorical way. We searched the room for a light switch or a lamp, but found nothing. Mom finally opened the single pane window that allowed just enough light to see half of his room. We stood in silence, observing the sorry excuse for a bedroom. I could literally feel the negative energy exuding from his tragic room. I didn't like being in there. Dirty clothes, candy wrappers, old homework assignments, and half-empty Coke cans were scattered around the floor. There were no pictures on the wall, no photographs of home, no typical fifteen-year-old posters- nothing. It was simply depressing.

While searching every nook and cranny of his room, we tried to find something that would give us more information. My mission was to find some evidence that *I* existed in his world. Did he at least have a picture of me or a letter... anything? My search ended in disappointment when I realized that there was nothing in his room to remind him of me. It felt like I was forgotten; completely absent from his life and that hurt the most.

Mom focused most of her attention on the closet, grabbing things and throwing them in a small pile on the floor. Within minutes, the closet was almost empty. Uneven wired hangers swung back and forth after mom's investigation. I sat on the edge of the twin mattress watching her sift through all his stuff, irritated by her need to smell every single item she pulled out of the closet. I knew that if Phillip were watching her, he would either laugh or be totally disgusted.

Mom quickly rose from her kneeling position and shouted, "This smells just like him! This one! It's his smell... oh my God! Come here... Shan... smell it." Her request made me cringe. There was no way in hell I was going to smell a shirt that she found lying on his dirty floor. Mom held his shirt to her chest, turned around, and remarked, "Look, Shan. We got him this one for Christmas last year... remember?"

Of course I could remember!

It was a t-shirt that had California raisins dancing and glittery letters that read: *"I Heard it through the Grapevine."* It was the dumbest shirt ever, but mom loved it. Phillip, however, hated it, and I was surprised to see it in his closet even if it was on the dirty floor. Mom still did not get the concept that boys didn't wear stupid crap like that, and she was so disappointed when Phillip refused to wear it.

"Gross mom- it was on the floor. How can you, like, smell it like that? Ugh… gross," I complained.

"It's not gross. I don't know. I just, I guess…" She stopped to smell it again. "It's all I have left of him." Then, she held the shirt up to her chest as if she were pretending to wear it. "Just think, maybe he wore this. Maybe. I mean, it smells like him."

"Seriously, Mom? He would never wear that… it just smells like him because it was with all his other crap. Trust me." I put my hand in the air. "He would not wear that."

We picked around some more, occasionally laughing and reminiscing over certain articles of clothing that reminded us of events or fun moments. It seemed like everything that we talked about revolved around fun memories. It was the most comfortable I felt since arriving in Florida. I found his green army jacket and gave it to my mom knowing she would want to keep it. His clothes, his material possessions, and his stuff were all we had left that was tangible.

I got up from the floor, dissatisfied with my search. As I made my way to the door, mom gasped. She hollered for me to come back to the closet. She held something with her two fingers far away from her body.

Mom cupped her left hand over her mouth and cried, "Oh my God! I cannot believe it! He promised!" She held something that looked like a shirt far away from her body. "He promised."

I walked back to examine the shirt. Holding it only with two fingers, she transferred the shirt to the small window so she could reveal the dried bloodstains on the sleeves.

Mom never looked directly at me as she softly whispered, "See?"

I looked over the shirt and said nothing. Mom clutched the shirt as if she was holding onto a long lost treasure, delicately caressing the bloodstains. Slowly, she sat down on the edge of his mattress, rocking back and forth. She started to weep. Then, she began repeating, "My baby... my poor, poor baby." She sniffled and then angrily hissed, "He promised!"

I could not handle it. The sight of my mother holding a bloodstained shirt while rocking and calling my brother a poor baby was just too much. I crept out of his room and never said a word.

After leaving mom in Phillip's room, I sat on the ugly couch and watched the local afternoon news. Instead of listening to the news anchor talk about the recent mystery behind demolished mailboxes, I heard Mrs. Rollins and Mrs. Shultz ask in unison, "What is wrong with him! What is wrong with him? What is wrong with your brother?" It was my fault. Even though Phillip physically cut his own body, I should have told my parents many years ago. I gazed blankly at the TV and blamed myself.

I shook my head back and forth as I tried to shake it off until I heard an unfamiliar voice. "You want something to eat? Are you thirsty?" My biological father stood next to me with his chubby hands resting on his hips.

I politely smiled and responded swiftly, "Oh, no thanks. I'm okay."

He sat next to me on the recliner, rocking back and forth with his tiny, black-toed foot exposed. Ugh... seriously... can't he just wear socks? His beer gut hung over his belly revealing a tiny sliver of white flesh that peeked out from underneath his shirt. I could not get over the brown, ugly, polyester pants that fit him like a body suit. Sitting next to him (alone) was complete and absolute torture. I could tell he was trying very hard to drum up some idle conversation. The TV served as a great distraction while I contemplated how on earth mom could ever hook up with a guy who wore skin tight polyester brown pants, not to mention the fungus infested black toe.

"Oh yeah! I have something for you," he exclaimed. He struggled to get out of the recliner, which was probably the funniest sight I have ever seen. I nearly lost it when I watched him get out of the chair like a pregnant woman in her third trimester.

My mind raced with all the possibilities. Please be a letter. I crossed my fingers and hoped that I had my own letter. Phillip would tell me everything, just like he used to when we were little. The anticipation was driving me crazy. I thought of everything he wrote before even reading it. He would tell me that he was sorry and that he would miss me the most. He would tell me it wasn't my fault or that he just couldn't live in this world anymore. He would tell me not to worry and that he loved me. I heard a muffled noise coming from a room in the back and knew he was searching for my long lost goodbye letter. Instead, he walked in the room holding a shiny, leather, royal blue and white soccer ball.

He smiled proudly and handed me the blue and white soccer ball. I took it from his chubby hands and asked, "What is this?" That was a stupid thing to ask... duh, Shannon. "I mean, did he play here?" I inspected the ball and searched for his signature.

He shook his head and then replied, "No. No. He never played soccer here, but..." His eyebrows rose up. "There is a story behind that ball." He plopped back down again.

I smiled with slight interest. "Really?" I was intrigued but kept my eyes steady on the soccer ball. "What's the story?" I inquired. For the first time in thirteen years, I made eye contact with him. For the slightest, smallest moment in time, I saw his soul coming through those small, blue, beady eyes. I knew, simply by looking into his eyes, that he was a sad, unhealthy, depressed man.

"Well..." He began, pausing to readjust his shirt that crept up his bulbous beer belly. He leaned in closer. I eased myself back as he came forward. "When your brother moved here, he was a little homesick." He rocked in his recliner as he told me the story behind the soccer ball. "So, after a couple weeks time, I asked him what I could get him to make him feel better. And you know what he wanted?" Hmm... let me think. Could it possibly be the soccer ball? What a reject.

Phil continued, "He asked for a soccer ball and do you know why?" Here we go again- just tell me.

I guessed: "Um, maybe 'cause he played soccer when he was younger?" With a proud smile, he replied, "No, Shannon..." Eww, gross, he said my name out loud. "Phillip said that soccer reminded him of you. He wanted to remember you." His voice was soft and sentimental for the first time. I smiled, and then watched him sit back in his chair as he folded his chubby fingers across his bloated belly.

I held the soccer ball in my hands, tossing it up and down a few times, thinking about the possibility of my brother actually missing me. The blue and white ball seemed like my only connection with him and I would cherish it forever (or until I needed a soccer ball.)

My mom finally came out of the bedroom with impeccable timing. She held a small collection of clothing, along with random belongings like woodcarvings, pillowcases, and pencils. It was weird. When mom noticed the soccer ball, she smiled and asked if it was Phillip's ball. I explained the story behind the ball and, before I came to completion, she nearly lost it. Her eyes became watery as she began to cry and barely whispered, "That is so nice.

Wow... he really loved you." She brushed the ball with her free hand and then traveled to the kitchen to show dad her new treasures.

I did not believe her. I could not and did not believe that he loved me. I just couldn't figure out how he could do what he did if he really loved me. I remembered the day he left and how all we exchanged was a simple handshake. If anything, I believed he hated me.

Time had come for us to leave (thank God.) We all stood in the sorry excuse for a kitchen, theorizing one last time about possible 'reasons.' Phil grabbed a sheet of paper from the refrigerator and showed it to my mother. It was a bunch of numbers written down that looked like whoever wrote it was trying to divide large numbers. Phil thought that Phillip was in "big trouble" with drug dealers and the numbers indicated money he owed. The other theory centered on an ex-girlfriend. Over the past couple weeks, Phillip and his girlfriend broke up and, evidently, he was heartbroken and that may have set all of this into motion. Mom and dad listened closely to the possibilities and asked several questions. I stood holding my soccer ball, trying to figure it all out along with them. They just didn't understand. I mean, it just seemed so silly to assume he would kill himself over a girl. He wasn't like that. The soccer ball rested on my hip while I watched the grown-ups debate, and thought to myself... doesn't anyone remember he was in a mental hospital a year ago?

Mom informed me that she was staying to "do some things" which meant she needed more time to talk and go over the paperwork. Dad and I pulled away from Phillip's last residence and I wondered if anyone who lived around the park knew about his death. I watched a little red-headed boy ride his bike down the road. He was laughing and doing wheelies. Life went on. Anyone who heard about his premature death would probably just say, "Man, that's a shame." Then, they would do another wheelie.

it's official

Dad and I didn't speak much on the way out of the park until I got enough courage to ask him why mom was staying. I shielded my eyes with my hands and looked out the window. Eventually, I rolled it down to expose the salty air and bravely asked, "Dad? Why is mom staying there?"

He hesitated before giving me an answer. I normally had to leave a five second grace period before he ever answered anything. He finally mentioned, "Shan, your mom has to do some things."

"Like what?" I inquired curiously, while waving my right arm like a snake outside the window.

His response was matter of fact: "Well, for one thing, she has to help make all the funeral arrangements for tomorrow. You know? And, uh, let's see, she has a lot of stuff to go over with the police... sign some papers- that sort of thing." He paused, then mentioned, "And I suppose she is going to meet the mother of the other boy."

"Really?" I was shocked. "She is going to meet her?" Just the thought of meeting her was fascinating and, at the same time, kind of creepy.

Dad added, "Your mom is going to be really busy and, I am sure, exhausted. Shannon, look, I know I have said this before, but this time it is different and I really want you to listen to me. Do you hear me?" His head kept turning quickly from the road and then back to me, trying to engage me in his one-person conversation.

I already knew what he was going to say. He began his well-intended lecture by stating, "You need to be very patient with her right now. This is just not going to blow over and be okay in a couple weeks. I want you to be on your best behavior and just get along. Just do what she asks of you and don't give her a hard time. Okay?" After his request, his head swiveled from the road and then back to me in quick flashes.

As he waited for my response, I imitated him in my head, mocking the classic requests, "Be nice... don't talk back... just do as she says." I've heard them all thousands of times. I clicked my teeth, slowly sighed, and muttered, "Yeah, I know. I know." As I rested my chin on my elbows and looked out the window, I really wanted to say was- *whatever, dude.*

We stopped at the first fast-food place, which, luckily, was McDonald's. When we entered, the smell of French fries made me salivate and I could already taste those salty fries in my mouth. We sat in an empty, frigid area and ate in complete silence. I dipped my French fries in my pool of ketchup three at a time. I thought of several conversation starters involving my brother, but every opening seemed contrived. It probably would have been a good time to talk about my brother, but we chose Quarter Pounders instead.

I waddled to the car, bloated from too much Dr. Pepper and casually burped the entire alphabet. (Personally, I was impressed- Dad was not.) Dad informed me that we were going to take a walk on a pier. I felt guilty for getting a little excited and then reminded myself that my alternative was to hang out in the hotel, watch *Golden Girls* re-runs, and grieve (whatever that meant.)

On the way to the pier, Dad and I rode in the car in silence, which served as a perfect time to think about Phillip. At first, my memories were foggy, but then they became very clear- almost as if I was watching it all on TV. My brother and I spent most of our childhood near the water. The framed pictures hanging on the walls at home were cherished snapshots of us beaming with pride as we held our freshly caught fish from the Atlantic in our tiny hands. Dad would lay the slimy fish on wooden boards to clean them. We would poke them with sticks or chase each other with the slippery fish in our hands. Passing neighborhood children would throw their bikes down so they could get a peek at the ocean's untouched treasures. The kids cautiously ran up to our yard to watch my dad run his razor sharp blade into the stiff fish with pinpoint precision. The brave boys became a bunch of sissies as they squealed like little girls and covered their eyes when the fish guts came out. It never bothered us because we were used to dad filleting the fish; sometimes, he let us help. Being near the water again and watching people fish off the docks would forever remind me of those long afternoons with my brother. There was an odd feeling within the pit of my stomach during our visit. Butterflies. I could tell those familiar butterflies beginning to rise. *What is coming? Why do I feel this way?*

Dad and I walked slowly along the long, wooden pier that was lined with several fishermen of all shapes and sizes. The only thing you needed in order to be on that pier was a pole, some bait, and a little bit of patience. I liked looking in the small buckets that held live bait. Most fishermen used minnows, crabs, squid, or leftover fish from a previous catch. I watched closely when they baited their hooks and cast their lines in the water. I could always tell an experienced fisherman just by the way they cast their line.

Dad pointed out various things to me, like the circling of sea birds above the ocean. He told me that if you saw birds clustered in one spot, then there was probably a school of fish underneath them. "Always look for the birds," he advised. Dad pointed out the choppy water about two hundred feet away and told me that was where the bay met the ocean. "When the waves get sharp and curl over, you are in very shallow water and most likely caught in a sandbar." We watched with anticipation while people attended their curling rods to reel in their prizes. Most times, we were disappointed when they pulled up seaweed or tangled their lines with the guy next to them. When someone caught an actual fish, I would run over to them to find out what type of fish inhabited the crystal blue water. It didn't seem to matter what they were called or if they were edible. I was simply fascinated by their features. They were a lot prettier and more colorful than any fish we ever pulled out of the north Atlantic. After tossing the turquoise and silver fish back into the ocean, I looked as far as the ocean would let me and came to the conclusion that everything was prettier down there- not just the fish.

After checking out the pier, we went for a walk on the powdery beach. We rolled up our pants, carried our shoes and socks, and walked quietly along the water's edge. Again, Dad did his best to give me some insight surrounding the wonders of the ocean by educating me about the tides. He passionately talked about the coordination of low tides, high tides, and the delicate role the moon played in regulating it all. I half-listened to him talk and found it quite interesting, but within a two second span, I forgot everything. Our conversation reminded me of school. I could sit through an entire lecture or take notes or read a paragraph three times and still have absolutely no idea what it was all about. However, for some strange reason, I could remember useless, trivial, unimportant, pointless things. I mean stupid things. Dumb things.

I could remember what kind of cake I had at my third birthday party or what I wore on my first day of school. I could recall smells, feelings, and passing words from years ago. I could easily remember who I sat next to on my first day of Kindergarten, the first time I ever saw a woman's breast exposed on TV, a vivid dream, or music that played in passing cars. Most people (usually my friends) were completely fascinated by my skills. Friends would often confirm their forgotten memories by asking me to recount any small detail- and I could. I could recall facts about a random person I met one time, but I could not remember what my dad just told me three minutes ago.

I watched the waves filter in and out of the sand. It was mesmerizing- hypnotic. The ocean never rested. I wondered if Phillip was ever on the same beach, looking at the same foamy water. I wondered if he ever thought about me while he walked along the beach or if he ever considered how I would feel about his suicide. While searching the sand for a perfect shell, I suddenly felt sad. *Why did he do that? Was he mad at me?* Then, I picked up a white seashell, brushed it off, held it to my ear to listen to the ocean, and then reminded myself to ask those questions later. At that moment, during the entire trip, I had to stay strong and distanced from the situation.

Just as I was telling myself to forget the situation, Dad asked, "Are you okay?"

After the question was posed, I looked down at the seashell and wondered if he heard my thoughts. *How did he know I was thinking about him?*

The butterflies were back. The subject was too deep. Distraction was a must to keep my sanity. I just wasn't ready to talk about him. I knew the situation, my thoughts, the shock, had not set in yet. Even if I wasn't okay with everything, it seemed like telling dad that I was fine could buy me some time; time to sort it all out.

"Yeah," I replied.

Dad walked by my left side with his hands in his pockets. "Shan?"

I stopped to look at him and noticed he was standing still, studying me. "What?" I asked.

His pale, white feet gingerly traced the sand. He seemed nervous. When his eyes met mine, I had a sense that he wanted to avoid the subject, as well. "Listen. I wanted to just talk to you about all this."

"Okay." We slowly walked next to each other as our first real conversation about the death of Phillip was about to get started.

Dad began, "I've been thinking. I've been thinking a lot about everything that has happened in the last four days." I knew dad was trying to read me. I suppose he needed to know that I was going to be okay for tomorrow. "Shan, I've been thinking a lot about you. You know? This, to me, anyway, has been a total nightmare. I mean, every single aspect of it. A nightmare that I just want to wake up from-only, I know that when I get up in the morning, I have to face this all over again. It just... I don't know, it rips my heart out. I mean, there is so much pain. I've never felt like this before."

I listened to him talk about his experience and it seemed as though I was listening to a story. It was like a story that I was connected to, but, at the same time, completely distanced from. It was a weird feeling.

"Shannon?" Dad stopped walking and his pause meant he wanted me to stop, too. "Do you want to tell me anything? Do you have any questions? Look, I don't care if you think they sound stupid- just ask me."

I immediately shook my head, indicating that I was fine. "No." I looked down at the seashell and mentioned, "Dad, I'm good. I'll be alright." After my response, dad smiled sideways and cocked his head.

"You sure?"

"Mmm-hmmm."

"Okay. Well, my door is always open."

I nodded my head and told him that I was fine again. At that moment, when I was talking to dad, it seemed like I was acting in some sort of off-Broadway play. My response was more recited than real. I didn't want to get into it with him. It hurt to hear his turmoil, so telling him mine seemed abusive. Ever since we heard the news, I watched my parents closely. They were so traumatized, so deep in a black hole; how could they possibly help me? It was just easier to tell them that I was fine. It was obvious that there was nothing that they could say or do to make me feel better about the situation. So, why bother them with more crap?

On the way back to the car, I showed dad my seashell. But before we left for the hotel, I turned around one last time to watch the fishermen on the pier and caught a glimpse of the most magnificent bird fly above. It delicately danced in the blue sky, lacking any sense of direction. It just floated along with the wind, as it effortlessly flapped its enormous wings. Careless. Free. Beautiful. I watched the bird and thought about Phillip's desire to become a bird and fly far, far away. Immediately, I was sad again. I watched the bird circle above and whispered into my tiny seashell, "I'll think about that later. Not today."

We moved to a different hotel- a cheesy hotel to match our mood. The night before Phillip's funeral, I tossed and turned for what seemed like hours in my lumpy twin bed. Mom had her prescription sleeping pills, yet she managed to get up every half an hour to smoke her cigarettes outside. Dad had his beer to ease him into slumber. I, of course, was present with nothing artificial to numb my body or numb my mind. Every time I began to find that comfortable state of sleep, visions of my brother walking into the woods instantly woke me. I recited sappy love songs in my head. I had to keep them sweet; Lionel Richie or Stevie Wonder or Babyface- anyone would do. After all the love, all I could hear was Jimmy Page's sultry voice singing *Stairway to Heaven*. He was the one voice that told the truth. The mellow flute whispered in my ear, drawing me in for some unwanted advice. I heard Jimmy's enchanting voice tenderly serenade me with his prophetic words when he told the story about a sad, lonely, superficial woman. It was *his* song: Phillip's song. It was his way of saying good-bye. I just knew it.

From time to time, I would glance at the alarm clock and roll around the bed to get comfortable, only to hear lyrics from *Stairway to Heaven* in my head. The gentle introduction served as my own form of medication that soothed me into deep sleep. It literally felt like I was sleeping for three minutes when the front door opened and struck my face with the cruel morning sunlight. I pulled my blankets over my head to shield myself like a vampire about to be evaporated. Dad came through the door while balancing two cups of coffee, an orange juice, and a Boston cream doughnut.

I hid under my covers, irritated by the bright beams of light and the whirling noise from my mother's blow dryer. I took a sip of the pulpy orange juice, rolled my eyes, and told my mom to turn that friggin' blow dryer off. (In my head- of course.) Everything annoyed me in the morning- everything. It took tremendous effort, but I managed to get out of bed to turn on the TV and prayed that our shit-hole hotel had MTV. After flipping through every station four times, I clicked and scoffed with my left hand resting on my hip until dad politely asked me to keep on the local news. Then, I rolled my eyes and plopped back on the bed, took a bite of the round confection, and blankly stared at the TV.

Mom's appearance startled me. My eyes were drawn to her like a magnet. For a fraction of time, I mean a miniscule moment, I could sense a little of what she was feeling simply by watching her. I was completely fascinated by her soft humming rendition of Amazing Grace. *How come I didn't notice her yesterday? Did she lose five pounds over night?* Ironically, mom's efforts to lose a measly five pounds often ended with failure after several attempts. With this tragedy, ten pounds almost evaporated from her within four days. She reminded me of Skeletor. Her cheeks were shrinking into her face, revealing her petite cheekbones. Her long-sleeve, black shirt and black ankle-length pencil skirt accentuated her dissolving body.

Mom stopped humming and sighed at the sight of me lying in bed. Her attempt at sounding composed came out demanding when she barked, "Shannon, get dressed. Come on, get going. Make sure your clothes are not wrinkled and do your hair nice- okay?" She took a careful sip of her coffee and continued humming, *"Amazing Grace, how sweet the sound, that saved a wretch like me. I once was lost but now am found. Was blind but now I see.*"

Mom never waited for my response as she proceeded to light up her cigarette and head outside with her steaming coffee. She never tried to console me or hug me or give words of wisdom, and I was quite aware that she would not be available to do any of that for a very long time. It might sound weird or even unemotional to distance myself from my mother during a time when we should have been close, but I needed the space. I didn't expect her to save me or help me. I was in survival mode. Being in survival mode meant staying isolated, being strong, and getting through it.

I wiped the sugary, white powder off my lips and thought about how silly it was to look good for my brother. He didn't care what I looked like. Shoot, I didn't even care what I looked like. He was not going to care who was there or what we were wearing... he's dead. Funerals were not for the dead; they were for the living.

I sat quietly in the backseat of the rental car on the way to Phillip's funeral and listened to Mom talk about Daniel's funeral that she attended the previous day. According to mom, Daniel's mom was a very sweet lady and Daniel was her second son who died. Her younger son drowned in a pool when he was only five years old- about five years ago. Mom told dad that Daniel's father sat in the back pew without any expression on his face and never muttered a single word. Mom said Daniel's dad wore his military uniform and left the ceremony half way through and never returned.

"He never came back?" I asked.

"Nope," mom casually replied.

"That's weird. I mean, that is kinda strange, right?"

Dad chimed in, "I suppose everyone is different. Maybe it was all too much."

I thought about Daniel's father some more- probably too much. I wondered what it was like for him, for his family, and for all his friends. It was all so complicated- there were so many people involved. I winced and felt mildly ashamed for my thoughts at that moment. *It was all their faults.* My face became red with the realization that I was conflicted with the way I was supposed to feel and the way I really felt. *Phillip (and Daniel) did this- all of this- and now, we have to suffer.*

Instinctively, I knew I was supposed to observe. Mom was supposed to be the outward griever. Dad's role was masculine protector. We all had our roles. We all played our roles very well. I suppose it was the only way to make it through the trauma. I only questioned whether we had to keep those roles. Furthermore, I wondered how long we would have to remain in character. As I rode in the backseat pondering those questions, I visualized my dad sitting in the principal's office while advising, "She'll be fine."

We took a left into the empty parking lot. There were only three other cars there and I assumed that two of them were probably staff members. I peeked at the rearview mirror and looked at my face for a final inspection. I looked the part. Hair: sprayed and teased. Make-up: perfectly applied. Clothes: wrinkle free. It all looked very neat and polished in the reflection. I played my part very well.

Mom led our trio and didn't bother to wait for us when she opened the double glass doors. I always figured that my first funeral would be for someone old, someone who died from a stroke, or someone who lived their life; not a fifteen year old and certainly not my brother. It was against the laws of nature to bury someone who was born only fifteen months before you. Death? What happened when you died? I figured that everyone thought about death from time to time. I mean, people had to at some point. The unknown of death fascinated me. The part that bothered me was that, once you died, there was no real evidence to conclude that you actually went to heaven or hell. As a child, I was told that when people died, they went to heaven, but I was also told that there was a Santa Claus and a Tooth Fairy. I had to know if there was a heaven, and if there was an afterlife-would Phillip even be there?

The funeral home was predictably peaceful and serene. The design intentionally gave the perception of tranquility. Even if it was an illusion, I liked believing for a little while that heaven was all harps, angels, and everlasting, unconditional love. The strategically placed plants, the crucifixes, the biblical passages, and the sincere organ music were inviting, yet, at the same time, deceptive. The lighting, just like our hotel, gave me the impression that I was somewhere else in time. I could not tell if it was day or night. The radiant, stained glass windows, adorned with Jesus along with his faithful disciples, seemed churchlike. The ambience tricked me into believing that Phillip was exactly where he should be.

The first person I saw was my biological father sitting with his head down in the last pew. He was staring to the front where Phillip's picture stood on a large, white column. His nod directed at us indicated that he was in no shape to engage in conversation. For the first time, I felt a deep sadness for him. He found him. That thought alone made me shiver. I studied my biological dad for a moment; dissected him. What does it feel like to be him? Did his parents love him? Did he get bullied (like his son?) What did he want to be when he was five: fireman, fisherman, or teacher? No, he was none of them. He was the depressed, middle-aged man sitting in the last pew, crying over his dead son.

After my thoughts of Phil faded, I noticed the spectacular flower arrangements that surrounded Phillip's seventh grade picture. The sight of his 11x14 glossy school picture above all the arrangements of yellow carnations, extravagant calla lily flowers, and white roses with generic banners with generic messages made me nauseous. Phillip's ashes rested in a large urn about the size of a candy jar. Mom traced her tiny, quivering fingers over the urn, caressing it as if he could somehow feel her. Watching her embrace his ashes secretly repulsed me. I mean, the thought of how he became ashes was just gross. I hated to be within ten feet of the urn. She pointed out the large flower arrangement the field hockey team sent for the funeral. I read every signature on the card which confirmed that they all knew- a realization that made me feel strange inside.

"It's so permanent," Mom whispered as she held her son's ashes.

"Yup. It is. It's kind of weird, huh?" I muttered.

"Weird, how? Like, weird that he is really dead?"

I nodded my head, but that was not what I meant. I explained, "Weird, like, I don't know. It's just so freaky to be holding that thing."

Mom turned to me with bloodshot eyes and declared, "It's all I have left of him."

I didn't agree with mom, but I chose to drop it. She was wrong. I was only thirteen and I knew she was wrong.

The funeral director tapped mom on the shoulder, whispered in her ear, and then gently shook his head. Mom looked at me and quickly mumbled, "I gotta go. I have to go to the front to greet everyone." She patted me on the back and left me alone with Phillip's ashes and his 11x14 photograph. Before she left, she looked in my eyes and softly said, "I'm sorry. Shannon, I'm sorry."

"For what?"

"For everything. I don't know. I am just really sorry. That is all I can say." After her statement, she turned and walked away.

After mom left, I scurried to my pew and thought about what her apology really meant. Then, it dawned on me. I suddenly knew what her sorry implied. She wasn't able to help me. She couldn't. I understood. After watching unfamiliar people walk in the front door, I flipped through the Bible and hoped that there was a passage to prove that everyone went to heaven- even if they committed suicide. *Was suicide a sin? Would Phillip be sent to hell because he self-murdered?* With those deep questions, my head began to pulse, the butterflies swirled, and I felt like a helpless, lost girl in the second pew.

"Shannon?" Moments later, I felt a light tap on my back. Mom half-smiled with hidden pride when she introduced me to a plump woman. "This is Olivia." She nodded toward the lady. "It's Daniel's mom." I knew what mom's smile implied. I was the normal one; the evidence that our family was not crazy. It was time to play my role of normal and put together, so I stood up to greet the mother of the boy who committed suicide with Phillip. That thought alone made me feel nauseous again.

I got the vibe that Olivia was the type of woman who baked homemade apple pies for church bake sales. By looks alone, I speculated that she called little girls "honey," never forgot to send a birthday card, and owned several scrapbooks of her beloved family members. Her wide arms reached around my small body and squeezed me tight. Olivia reminded me of a boa constrictor as her massive arms wrapped around my small body, nearly suffocating me. While we were in full embrace, she began to weep.

She slowly inched away and grabbed a strategically placed tissue from her D cup bra. With wet tears rolling down her soggy cheeks, she said, "I am so sorry, dear." I knew it. I was right. She called me *dear*. She whispered, "Ugh, I am so sorry. I just, I just don't know what to say." She blew her nose and then maneuvered my mother so we were all facing each other in a three-way circle. "This is just, I don't know. It's horrible."

Olivia monopolized the entire conversation, repeating the same sentiments that I heard several times since Phillip died. Mom and I allowed her to ramble. I guess it was easier listening to someone else expel their own raw emotions than actually feeling anything for myself. She dabbed her forehead with the same tissue that she used for her nose, and then confessed, "It's my fault."

Mom reassured her that it wasn't her fault. Her comforting words sounded rehearsed, and I knew it was because mom heard those exact words from everyone else. I knew mom blamed herself. Dad blamed himself. I blamed myself. Guilt. We all felt guilt. Death was supposed to be sadness or longing; anything but guilt. It wasn't fair to put that emotion on top of sadness. It just wasn't fair.

Olivia kept her head down while soaking in mom's encouraging words. She clutched my right shoulder with her powerful Kung-Fu grip, and advised, "We have got to be strong. We have *got* to be strong." She looked up to find me and remarked, "With God's strength, we will all move on. Just have faith. Oh. Lord Jesus. Please. Please, be our guide." She blew her nose with the same snotty tissue, and then advised me, "Shannon, you need to be strong for your mom- she needs you." Olivia gasped and held onto mom when she said, "God knows, she needs everyone."

Before she left, Olivia had these parting words: "We just have to keep praying. I have to believe that there is a reason for this; that God has a plan for them. I don't understand, but I am sure He does." She slowly nodded her head, so she could believe her own words.

I liked Olivia. I really did, but she was just like everyone else. She talked freely about God's will, afterlife, and having faith without proof that any of those things existed. Furthermore, why did I have to be strong like Olivia suggested? Why can't I just fall apart? Why can't we all just fall apart for awhile? What was so wrong with that? Maybe it was in times like these when we are supposed to question whether or not God actually exists. Olivia only confirmed what I already knew. I was supposed to be there for mom. I was supposed to look like I had my act together. I was supposed to continue the charade of the cool and controlled daughter.

When the ceremony started, I sat behind mom and dad. Actually, I was quite content sitting behind them, so they couldn't see me. I was on my own and totally fine with that. I tried not to look at his picture, but my eyes were drawn to that glossy portrait; it portrayed a young boy who was unaware that his life would be over shortly. The picture became blurry, the words coming out of the funeral director's mouth sounded muffled, and the people in the room didn't seem to exist. I stared into my brother's eyes and visualized him walking in dark, lush woods while carrying a shotgun on his shoulder.

I began daydreaming of that night- the night he walked into the woods. I imagined myself nervously waiting for my brother by the trees and bushes, somehow knowing the location, knowing his plans, and knowing the future. At first, Phillip seemed surprised, but at the same time, happy to see me. Then he became curious about my presence. "Why did you come here?" he asked me. I began telling him that I knew what he was going to do. I calmly, but intensely, warned, "I know. I know what you are going to do." Phillip seemed relieved. He seemed thankful that someone came to rescue him.

I begged him not to do it. "Please! Please! Wait!" I grabbed his arm, forced him in my arms, and held him tight. I told him, "I'll be nicer. We'll get help. We'll help you. I promise." I saw tears come down my eyes when I admitted that I was wrong. I told him that his death would crush us and that it would devastate our lives. I looked him in the eyes with my hands pressed firmly on his shoulders and begged him to stay out of the woods. "We love you," I cried.

The sound of mom crying took me out of the woods. Why didn't I say those things before? Why did he have to die for me to say those things? I would never be able to tell him that I was sorry. I would never be able to help him. In my daydreams, I could cry, but in real life, I never shed a tear since I heard. Even when I tried to cry… I couldn't.

The funeral director conducting the ceremony never met my brother, yet he delved deep into Phillip's personal life. I wasn't sure how everyone felt sitting in the pews, but I was sure that we all needed guidance. His death left all of us with questions, with guilt, and without direction. What could that simple man say to ease our pain? How could he know what happened to my brother? I was the skeptic sitting in the second row, who doubted a human man could reassure me that Phillip was happier, more peaceful, and most importantly, going home to heaven.

He began, "Phillip was a young man who was lost on his path of life. We can all rest assured that he is at home now and he is safe and comforted by the Angels of the Lord. Phillip left this earth too soon and we will never understand why he chose to leave this earth but..." He intentionally hesitated so he could raise his pointer finger to the sky. He softly continued, "We can find solace and seek shelter in God's love and know that God is a good God, who has his arms wrapped around him as we speak. We will miss him and will think and pray for him everyday and, perhaps, learn from his short life here on earth." He tried to comfort the flock of people who were desperate to hear something reassuring. I wanted to be part of them, believe with them, but it was too hard.

Next, the funeral director, with his hands clasped together, claimed that death was natural. "We were born to die," he said. He reminded us that life on earth was temporary and only our souls were eternal- limitless. My outward expression showed intense belief, but inside I was laughing to myself and thought about how I used to believe that Santa Claus lived at the North Pole with tiny elves, who intuitively knew if I was naughty or nice. The funeral director declared, "We shall remember Phillip's life and those he touched. We shall remember only the good times and the love that he shared with his family and friends. Phillip is a child of God, and no child of God is alone at home." He looked directly at my weeping mother and nodded his head. I suppose his words were mostly for her benefit.

When the funeral ended, I was relieved. What seemed like an eternity was really only 45 minutes. The smell of fragrant flowers, the sound of sobs and noses blowing, and the organist's rendition of Amazing Grace were supposed to aid with my official goodbye. However, it only strengthened the distance between me and my brother. The funeral was my opportunity to forget him, my chance to deny that he ever existed. That was the only way I could live my life. I had to abandon him. Again, it was a matter of survival. "Don't think about it. Think... later," I reminded myself.

Mom collected every single tiny card from the flowers and cradled his ashes in her arms. I waited patiently in my pew and then followed behind mom and dad. Dad wrapped his arms around mom, protecting her from harm until he had to let go. She occasionally looked back to his glossy picture and wiped the flow of tears away with a damp tissue. Her eyes were distant, her movements were slow, and her thoughts were probably miles away from me. I tried not to take it personally. While walking out of the funeral home, I realized that life with mom would never be the same.

The unrelenting sunlight struck my face after I opened the tinted glass doors. I heard his friends behind me. There were about seven or eight kids following behind us, laughing, shoving each other, proving that my brother would just be a story they would tell in the college dorm. Mom and dad were completely oblivious, but I wasn't. Like the constant observer, I watched them- their movements, their lips, their laughter. They engaged in normal conversation disregarding the fact that my brother just shot himself and unaware that I was staring directly at them. At that moment, I hated them. I hated the fact that their lives would go on and Phillip would be just a horribly tragic 'thing' that happened. His old friends might mention Phillip's name once or twice over the years. As I watched them pile into their tiny, red car, my hateful thought swirled in my head and revealed its wrath through my piercing eyes. Oh, how I hated them. I hated them because they would never be able to take any accountability for their inaction. After all, I had to blame someone.

When we drove away, I immediately reached for my headphones and listened to *Martika*. I let out a deep sigh and zoned out for a while. "I'll figure it out later," I said to myself.

I slept the entire way back to Philly. It was effortless, dark, and uninterrupted. From The Walt Whitman Bridge, the bird's eye view of Camden made it hard to believe that someone so prophetic and magnificent as Walt Whitman ever visited, let alone, resided anywhere near that dirty, washed-up place. However, while passing the once fabulously thriving metropolis, I felt a strong connection with the lost, desolate city. Camden was the city of heartache, the city of failure, and the city that longed for revival. The city's hovering air, gray and thin, was merely pollution filtering the once clean sky. Camden was one of the most depressing places in America and I shared a common bond with the forgotten city. We were both very, very lost.

Lizzie and I talked briefly about the trip, but whenever the conversation became too deep, the subject was conveniently changed. I laughed when I mentioned my biological father's skin-tight, brown, polyester pants and hideous, black toe. Thomas did his part to ease the transition back to school. He wrote me funny letters in between our classes, played basketball after school, and hung out long after his last class was over. I never cried about my brother to my friends or even to myself. I never showed any anger about the situation. Most of the time, I convinced myself that his death was black and white- he was dead and I had to forget him.

I had perfect attendance in school; never late, never missed a basketball practice, and never missed one pitching class. All of that had nothing to do with my capability of dealing with the situation, but everything to do with staying away from home. My new life since Phillip's death was all about distraction. Being home, near my mother, and only ten small feet away from Phillip's old room sucked. My house was an infestation of continuous grief and sadness. I could sense the inevitable misery before I opened the front door.

Due to mom's inability to function, dad did most, if not all, of the daily upkeep. He did the grocery shopping, he cleaned the dishes, he did the cooking, he took out the trash, and he worked full time. The first several weeks following Phillip's death, mom's presence in the house was limited. Physically, she was present, but emotionally she was somewhere else. Mom was the mood barometer in the house. Both dad and I adapted by allowing her to slip in and out of her new reality. Mom was the fragile one, so we catered to her and gave her permission to do whatever she wanted. Unfortunately, that meant dad and I walked around the house on eggshells. We never knew which woman was going to show up in the morning.

Judging by mom's erratic moods and sly remarks under her breath, I knew she felt alone. Mom never came out and said it, but I knew she was secretly angry with dad and me. She couldn't understand how we could function; how we laughed at TV shows or how we became excited over anything. What mom didn't know was that we were simply diverting our pain in order to cater to her needs. The three of us struggled to define normal. Normal? What was normal anymore? I suppose normal was coming home to a trashed kitchen. It was accepted and completely normal for mom to stay in bed all day. Normal was expecting the worst when I walked through the front door. Normal was redefined after Phillip killed himself and, as much as I wanted to grieve my dead brother, I secretly resented him. After all, he was the reason my life, our lives, were turned upside down.

A couple months after Phillip died, I began having horrible nightmares about him. During the waking hours, I put on my best act to show that everything in my life was ordinary, which left me exhausted. Sleep, my only escape, was interrupted by visions of my brother walking into the woods. My dreams began to change. Instead of begging him to leave the woods, I watched him from a distance. Most of the time, I would follow behind him as he slowly walked deep into the thick woods. Even if I wanted to say something to stop him, the words never came out. Phillip never turned around to acknowledge me, and I allowed him to do the inevitable. It scared me. I began sleeping with my lamp on and covered my entire body with my thick comforter. It served as my protective force field. Before I closed my eyes at night, I prayed to God:

Dear God, it's me Shannon. Shannon Bennet. God, please let me sleep tonight. I don't wanna have those bad dreams. I know I am not perfect, not in some starving country, not homeless, but I do need your help. Maybe my dreams are trying to tell me something- but can you please just take 'em away. God? Is he there? Do you know if he's there? I hope so. I wasn't a good sister and I don't wanna feel like I am mad at him, but sometimes... I am. I wish so bad that he didn't do that. Why did he do that? Was he mad at us? Was he mad at me? Is Mom gonna get better? God, can you just help me sleep tonight? Please, can you just take all of that ugly stuff in my head away? Anyway, thanks. I love you. Amen, Shannon Bennet.

The frozen branches that were motionless during the winter months began to thaw. Spring finally came... finally. The dates changed. The Easter bunny made his appearance. St. Patrick and The Mummers did their annual parade in Philly. Time pressed on, but everything was the same at our house. Things got worse. Mom basically lost her mind or, perhaps, her soul. She was in the house or sleeping in her bed or on the couch, but she *really* wasn't there. I wasn't sure what she did during the day when I was in school. Most days, I struggled to concentrate on a math word problem because I was thinking about Mom. Was she okay? Was she going to get out of bed? Will she ever be Mom again? Regarding Phillip's death, dad and I casually ignored any conversation about our feelings and concentrated on taking care of mom. By definition of taking care of mom, I meant, we tried to let her depression run its course.

It was during that time that I felt strange for being angry all the time, instead of sad. I was *supposed* to be sad, but I really wasn't. Confused? Yes. Sad? No. Nobody gave me a book on how to behave, how to react, or what to feel. My true feelings surrounding Phillip were a mix of anger, guilt, and remorse. I was angry with him for making my life suck. I was guilty because I should feel sympathetic. I felt a deep sense of remorse for not being able to stop him or help him.

Dad and I shared a common bond that allowed us to focus on winning. Winning felt good; losing felt bad. He taught me to be a champion. Dad educated me on the ways of working hard, getting ahead, and striving to be number one. The bond that solidified our relationship was sports. When we practiced outside or went to games or talked about athletic strategy, we didn't need to think about Phillip. Dad told me I was strong. He always encouraged me to be a winner. Dad believed that I was something special and because of those reasons, I could not show any weakness. If I faltered in his presence, then I felt like a failure. If I showed emotion, then I was vulnerable. If I cried, it was like admitting defeat. Dad was the only one who pumped me up during that time, and, as a token of gratitude, I acted like I was fine.

"You are a champion," he would say. He would raise his fist in the air to emphasize the point. Every time he raised his fist, I winced inside and felt like a complete fraud. To him I was normal, and that was all that mattered.

the popcorn man

Inever told anyone about the way I really felt and so, with each passing day, I became more detached from my own feelings. I was so embarrassed and ashamed of my relationship with my mom. I resented her. I suppose, I hated her for focusing on him and ignoring me. That thought was selfish and totally mean; it killed me to feel that way. My days were intentionally busy with school, softball practices, games, and hanging out with Lizzie or Thomas. It was easier to function when I filled my days with clutter and noise. Unfortunately, the distraction was temporary. I guess I could compare it to holding my breath under water or placing a band-aid over my severed leg. It never lasted long.

During the spring, mom became even more isolated from dad and me. She occasionally and slyly mentioned that she was the only one suffering. I would never know what it was really like for her at that time, but I knew for sure that I was suffering, too. Mom failed to realize that I kept my stuff quiet in order to protect her, and, I suppose, I knew on some level that she could not help me. During that time, there were a few moments of peace between us. Sometimes, mom and I could have a normal conversation about the weather, a movie that was coming out, or something random that didn't eventually involve Phillip; regrettably, those times never lasted long enough.

As the weather allowed me to wear short-sleeves and shorts, Mom was often outside riding her bike or taking the dogs for a walk. It was also during that time that I began to have a gut feeling that something was not right. It was so weird. I just knew the way she was acting was just an act. My suspicions regarding mom's real feelings about her life were confirmed on a late May night.

It was not that unusual for me to hear faint sobbing or crying coming from mom's room. Actually, it was rather common, but on that particular night, she sounded different. Along with her sobs, I heard muffled words that were loud enough to attract my attention. I was in the midst of writing a paper for English class; a paper that I should have started a week ago. I rose from my floor and carefully cracked my door to listen in on her private phone conversation. Mom's door was open enough to allow me to hear every word, every sigh, and every single sniffle.

Mom was noticeably choked up. With desperation in her voice, she cried, "I don't know. I just don't want to be here anymore. I really don't..." She stopped talking to give her full attention to whoever was on the other end of the phone. She went on, and it seemed to me that she was trying to defend her statement. "It's not that," she replied. Then, she proclaimed. "No! I am sure! I'm positive!" She continued to vent after blowing her nose. "I just can't do this anymore. I don't wanna pretend. It's like my life is one big lie- you know? I wake up everyday thinking that things will get better, but... and now, it is spring, and I foolishly thought that things would get better. You know? I'm just stupid. Stupid for thinking the weather would change things. And you know what? Now, it just hurts even more." She paused so she could listen to the other person respond.

"I'll go! I will. I want to leave this place. Just…" She let out a huge sigh, and then stated, "I don't care about this stupid house or money or anything like that! I just want to get the hell out of here!"

The way she said those things led me to believe that she put in some serious thought about it. My interpretation became personal. She wanted to leave me behind. Just like my biological dad; just like my brother.

I was on my knees, listening in on her private conversation, trying to figure out who was on the other line. *Who did she want to run away to? Where did she want to escape?*

Then, Mom's voice became low and attentive. "What? Yeah. I mean, it's just- it's hopeless. There's no point. I miss him so much. I just want him back. I got cheated! Nobody understands. Nobody cares." Mom's voice went silent with only the occasional soft "uh-huh" and "ummhmm" that was muffled by her stuffy nose.

"I am serious!" she hollered.

I backed away from the door. My pulse became deep and fast at the same time. I wanted to hear the truth. I wanted to know how she really felt. Mom kept repeating the same things. She was desperately trying to convince the other person that she was serious.

She began yelling. I could not understand why she was yelling so loud. I mean, she had to know that I could hear her. She shouted, "I just don't care! Don't you hear me… you're just like them… you don't hear me! I don't care about them. I don't care! I need a break! I just want to go! I want to be alone- by myself." She said it. She finally said it. I calmly rose to my feet, grabbed my jacket, and searched for some quarters in my backpack. Just like my mom, I just wanted to be alone.

The idea of confronting her only occurred to me when I found myself outside in the middle of my road, staring up into her open window. As I gazed up to her window, I could still hear her faint voice. I felt slightly victorious, perhaps even brave, to make such an unexpected decision. She was completely unaware that I was on the outside looking in, and that thought alone made me feel great. I had the power to do whatever I wanted. I was on my own. I was free, and nobody knew where I was or what I was doing.

That May night was created for better times. The sweet air was perfect for a first real kiss or playing jailbreak or just sitting around, watching lightning bugs. The moon was full and bright, so I took a minute to soak it in. As I walked further from my house, I playfully counted stars. I began to trace them carefully with my pointer finger- just like when I was little. For a brief moment, I thought about how small and insignificant I was on the planet. I was so small. Tiny. It was a fact; a fact that somehow made me feel better about my current situation. The grandness of the large, white, glowing object promised to me that things would get better- one day. They had to get better. Mom's words hurt, but as I walked underneath the mammoth circle in the sky, they began to fade with each step.

The brightly lit neon sign that proudly displayed, "Open 24-7," was a welcomed sight. The clerk had a patch over her left eye, but managed to carefully watch me as I entered the store with just one eye. She nodded to me, which was my cue that I had permission to come in so late. My money was limited, so I took my time skimming through the magazines from the familiar rack. *Tiger Beat* was getting old, *Teen* magazine was boring, so I tried a new issue of *Sassy*. On the glossy cover, a pretty, blond girl was smiling flirtatiously while she playfully touched each of her fishtail-braids. The caption underneath her read: "How to know if he is *really* interested." She was so pretty; painfully cute in almost every way. *How did she get those perfect teeth? Does she look that way when she gets out of bed in the morning?* Inside the magazine, little snip-its and serious articles with bright pink headlines tried to decode the secret lives of teenage girls. The magazine featured 'Every Girl's Guide' to proper make-up technique, boyfriend dilemmas, and how to handle life's most embarrassing moments. What I could not find in that magazine was all the good stuff; the relevant stuff. *Sassy* failed to write about my life. Perhaps, *Sassy* could write an article called: "How to look cool when your life totally sucks." I scoffed a little louder with every flip of a new page. If making eyelashes look seven times bigger, or being embarrassed by a wad of gum that became stuck on the bottom of my shoe were the most pressing issues in a teenage girl's life, *Sassy* would be a Fortune 500 company. I grabbed cheddar cheese popcorn off the chip rack and paid the pirate-clerk the money. When I got my change from her, I half expected to hear a parrot squawk. I giggled a little at the possibility.

My walk home was intentionally slow. I was in a better mood. The superficial magazines, my new friend- Pirate Clerk, the cheesy popcorn, all served as a wonderful distraction. I took my time inspecting details that ordinarily would have passed me by. I picked flowers, kicked rocks, and peeked in a few mailboxes. I threw popcorn up in the air and tried to catch it in my mouth, which left a trail of popcorn behind me. My English paper, or the fact that it was getting close to midnight, did not seem to matter. In fact, I wasn't worried about anything at all. I gobbled my popcorn. I hummed to myself as I leisurely walked under the full moon. I was free. Mom had no idea where I was and she probably didn't know that I heard her confidential conversation. It was an exhilarating feeling that quickly disappeared when I saw the light from her window.

I was supposed to have my paper completed. I was supposed to be resting in my warm bed. Instead, I was lingering outside my house, stuffing my face with cheddar cheese popcorn. My steps became even slower as I approached my house. I heard the slightest sound behind me. After inspection, I guessed that it was a couple behind me with their arms wrapped around each other. The light from the street hid their faces, but the silhouette appeared to resemble two people walking arm in arm.

The idea that other people were out so late at night did not alarm me until I realized that at my slow pace, they should have passed me. I was about one hundred feet away from my house when I decided that it was time to speed up. I began feeling strange. Those familiar butterflies came on quick and my senses were instinctively up. I needed to get home. My back stiffened and my strides became longer and quicker, but my decision to speed up came too late.

At first, I thought it was some kind of joke when I felt two large arms wrap around me. By sheer size, I knew there was a man holding me captive. My breathing was swift as I exhaled and, for once in my life, I struggled to inhale. I could see mom's light from the window, but I could not manage to yell; nothing would come out of my mouth. I froze. I could not believe someone was attacking me. My body seemed stronger than I remembered it- swifter. I could smell his manly scent that reminded me of vinegar or something oddly sweet. In the first few seconds, I believed that I was going to turn around to see one of my guy friends messing with me. Maybe that theory was what I was hoping for.

He said nothing. He just held me tight with both arms and began to carry me backwards. Then, with one quick maneuver, he threw me down on the road. We were facing each other, but I could not see his face. He was about ten feet away when I realized that, yes, it was a man, and, yes, it was a strange man. I scraped my butt and both of my hands when I wiggled my way back on the hard, gravel road. As I slithered back, my eyes focused on the man in front of me. I still could not see his face. He was smaller than I had anticipated. Even though it was May, he wore a puffy, winter jacket that was lined with fur around the hood. His large hood rested over his head- intentionally low. It strategically hid his face and his eyes. As I crept back, it occurred to me that he must have planned it. Maybe he saw me leave my house earlier, or maybe he was planning the attack for weeks. The streetlight near my house worked against me. Instead of revealing his reflection, it only allowed me to see his small, shadowy frame.

My mind began racing with so many thoughts. *What are his intentions? Do I know him? Does he know me? What does this man want? Why is he throwing me down?* I somehow found my voice and began shrieking like a primitive animal. As the man drew closer, I inched back. When he moved a little closer, I scraped my butt moving back. He was trying to get close to me. *Why did he want to get so close?* Every time I moved back, he crept closer. Suddenly, his arms extended toward me, and I knew he was going to try to grab me. I kicked my feet and scraped my hands some more on the road. I screamed, "Help! Help! Anyone! Help!" Nobody responded to my cries, so I directed my screams toward him. "Go away! Go away! Leave me alone! What do you want! What do you want!"

Nobody came to my aid. The houses on my street were dark; not one light went on. After all my yelling, the dogs on my street kept quiet. Even though mom's window was open, my voice fell on her deaf ears. The man staggered closer. He never spoke or revealed his face as he extended his arms my way. I was still on the road trying to back away, and then something very odd happened. He ran away. I could hear his sneakers press against the gravel as he sped away. I turned my head quickly, sprung up, and sprinted as fast as I could to my house. As I approached my driveway, I glanced back and hoped he was not watching me go in my house. Nothing. It appeared that he was long gone. It was like he vanished into the moonlit night.

I slammed the front door and frantically ran up to mom's room. I was red in the face, out of breath, and hysterically screaming.

"Mom! Call the cops now!" I demanded.

Mom hung up the phone without saying goodbye. Her eyes crinkled and her eyebrows went down. She curiously asked, "What the hell is going on?"

With no time for explanations, I barked, "Just call 911 now!"

Mom dialed the number without any further questions.

As I peeked out the window and tried to catch my breath, I demanded, "Tell them… tell them!" I gasped for air. "I've been attacked!" I could sense mom's unwillingness to believe me given that I was supposed to be in my room. I shook her up a little bit when I shouted, "Just do it!"

After talking to the dispatcher, mom slammed the phone down and demanded an explanation.

"What the hell happened?" She asked.

"Nothing. I was just attacked."

"What do you mean? Where the hell were you?"

In my mind, I did not feel that I owed her any type of explanation.

I was vague when I muttered, "I went out. 7-11 and…"

"You what? What do you mean? Out? It's almost midnight. Are you out of your mind?" Mom began questioning me, lecturing me, and totally bothering me. I ignored her. After all, she wanted to leave anyway, so she didn't deserve to know any details.

I turned off the lights, so I could peek out the window again. Mom's words meant nothing to me. I could only think about that man who was waiting for me. I never looked at my mother when I shouted. "I don't have to tell you anything! What the hell do you care? Just go away!"

We both ignored my last comment when we heard the police car pull into our driveway. The police officer took down some notes, asked the same questions three times, and found it odd that I was out so late. The police officer seemed baffled that I never saw his face, even though we were facing each other. I got the impression that he didn't believe me.

"You know, the curfew for anyone under the age of eighteen is 10 p.m., don't you?" He never looked up at me after he asked the question. He kept scribbling in his tiny, yellow notepad.

Okay, so, somehow this was going to be my fault! I admitted, "No, I didn't know that."

He asked why I was out so late, so I told him that I wanted some popcorn. He finally looked up from his notepad and repeated, "Popcorn?"

He asked my mother why she was not aware that I was out of the house. Mom appeared confused, maybe a little angry when she told the police officer that she had no idea that I was out. She told him four times that she thought I was in my bedroom doing my homework. As she spoke to the police officer, I kept thinking about her phone conversation. Inside, I was fuming. I blamed her for my attack.

Ultimately, I looked like the idiot who went out after curfew for cheddar cheese popcorn. The police officer told me that I was lucky to be unharmed. Unfortunately, he gave me an unwanted lecture about respecting my mother or whatever. All I heard was: "Bla-bla-bla. Your mother is worried. Bla-bla-bla. You should be smarter. Bla-bla-bla. Don't do it again."

"I'm goin' to bed!" I ran upstairs and slammed my door as hard as I could.

Mom knocked on my door five minutes later. "Shan? Shan- are you okay?"

"Go away!" I shouted. "I'm tired."

Mom never responded. She just went away. I cried myself to sleep that night. Everyone wanted to leave me; it was so obvious. In my tear-stained pillow, I began to pray:

Dear God, it's me, Shannon. Shannon Bennet. Is he going to come back for me? Please, please, please God. Please, make him never come around here- ever. Okay? God, why does she hate me? I am not the one who killed myself, so why does she want to leave me? I know that I am supposed to love her- but I don't! I hate her! I'm sorry. I shouldn't hate her because it said so in the Ten Commandments, right? But, sometimes, I wish that I had another family- except for my dad. Oh, I'm sorry about that. That was mean. Wait! No, I really do want another family. I deserve to be happy, right? I don't know. God, why am I here? Sorry, but I really hate my life right now. Do you think you can help me or do something? Whatever. I'm going to bed. Love you. Amen, Shannon Bennet.

When dad came home from work the next morning, I wanted to be the one to tell him what happened. Mom would only manipulate the facts and make me look irresponsible. He was upset, maybe he was confused. He kept asking me why I went out so late. I never told him why I left. I just blamed it on my need for cheddar cheese popcorn.

When I met Lizzie at the corner in the morning, I showed her the popcorn that was scattered all over the street. At first, she laughed and thought I was joking, but after replaying the story, she eventually believed me. Lizzie aptly named him, "The Popcorn Man." When she mentioned his name, she let out a shriek of frightful laughter that one might hear in a Halloween song. When she joked about the situation, I could laugh about it. However, when that man grabbed me, I was horrified and, for once, I felt completely vulnerable. I was no longer the indestructible girl I thought I was. The memory of that night would forever remind me of cheddar cheese popcorn, my mom's phone conversation, and my mistrust of the moonlit night.

The aftermath of my attack brought on jokes, cynical questions, and raised eyebrows. Nobody bought my story. People had a hard time believing that anyone could be assaulted within the safe haven of Woodbury Heights. I kept Mom's secret. I held it inside. I never told her, or anyone, the real reason I left that night.

There was a new sense of alarm that I had never felt in my entire life. The darkness was not my friend, either on the inside or the outside of my house. I made Lizzie drop me off in front of my house instead of down the street when the sun went down. I feared the man was still waiting for me. I no longer lingered around the streets or took late night walks to the 7-11. Lizzie was the only person who knew about my paranoia.

On my last day of eighth grade, I got out of bed, looked in my bathroom mirror, and cynically laughed. My wishes all came true; he was gone. I looked in the mirror, again, and softly whispered to my reflection- *I can't believe it.* The truth seemed too cruel, so I ignored the subject any further. I simply brushed my teeth, put on my make-up, and walked to school.

The last week of school was always a chaotic mixture of anxious kids and equally anxious teachers just hanging around until summer vacation. Usually teachers (the cool ones) allowed us to do whatever we wanted as long as we sat quietly in our seats. On my last day of eighth grade, Lizzie and I had to clean out our locker. We took little effort sorting out trash from treasure. We simply threw everything into a big, black garbage bag. I found old socks, crumbled letters from Thomas, a bag of sour cream and onion chips, and several missing homework assignments. On the very bottom of my locker, I found an old picture of Phillip.

When I picked it up and looked into his blue eyes, my head became light and my breathing was out of sync. Without hesitation, I quickly threw it with my pile of pictures that hung in my locker. I told myself that I would look at it later. Lizzie and I continued to dig through our locker and laughed when we found long, lost drawn pictures, scathing poems, and all our immature mementos from our eighth grade year.

The final bell went off. The piercing sound was a delightful echo that gave us permission to leave; permission to enjoy our ten weeks of freedom. Lizzie and I walked home that day and filled ourselves with all the possibilities of summer. Summer was a fantasy concocted in the minds of young people. It was a time of imagination and creativity; a world of our own. We talked passively about September. Within a matter of weeks, we would officially be freshmen. After saying goodbye to Lizzie at the corner, I saw mom sitting all alone on the front steps. She watched me walk up the street and took long sips of her Coke. She placed all her attention on me as I walked up the driveway. She never waited for me after school, so the sight of her on that step made me nervous.

She held up her Coke and smiled. "Hey kid! What's all that stuff?"

I took advantage of her chipper mood and decided to indulge her with more information than necessary. "Uh, it's all my stupid locker stuff. I got some Phillies pictures, dirty, old socks, a messed up Cat Stevens tape. I found an old coffee mug- which is kinda weird considering that I don't even drink coffee. Who cares? I'll probably just throw it all out." I stood on the sidewalk with the small bag in my arms as beads of sweat surfaced on my forehead. I never mentioned the picture of Phillip. In fact, it had been several weeks since I said his name out loud.

Mom rose from her pretzel position, stretching out her legs as if she had been sitting for a long time. She opened the front door for me and politely requested that I drop off my things. "Come on- let's go for a walk."

She called up to me as I threw my stuff on the floor, "I got you a Coke!"

As I was walked toward her, I muttered, "Mom, how long is this gonna be? Because I'm going over to Lizzie's in, like, a half an hour."

Mom placed both hands on her hips. She lowered her chin and retorted, "Lizzie can wait. Anyway, it won't be that long. Geez!" She scoffed, "You can't make time for your own mother?"

I had to seriously think about her last question.

Mom handed me the Coke. I popped it open, guzzled it down, and then burped like a man who just chugged a six-pack. Mom was not impressed.

At first, she was talking small talk. She inquired about school and my plans for the summer. (Bla-bla-bla.) My one-word nonchalant answers were typical communication between mom and me. Most times, my responses were simple phrases like: "Yeah. Uh-huh. Nope. Um-hmm." Then, Mom became noticeably agitated, even nervous. She pursed her lips, bit her nails, and avoided looking in my direction. She seemed fidgety. Intuitively, I knew she was about to deliver big news.

Mom announced, "Shannon, I am going away for a little while. Actually, a long while."

Bingo. I was right.

I immediately asked, "Where?"

She answered just as quickly, "Florida."

"Florida?" I repeated. "Why?"

She shrugged her shoulders, smashed her mouth sideways, and sighed. "It's just that I need some time. A break. You know? Some time... by myself. I am not sure if you can understand, but it's just something that I need to do. I have to figure some things out on my own." She paused and took a sip of the Coke, indicating that she was waiting for my response.

As I watched her drink the soda, I thought about how great it must be to be an adult. You can just get up and go-whenever or wherever you want. She needed a break? It sounded like she was breaking up with me. I half expected her to start the next sentence with, "It's not you... it's me." Maybe she was going to tell me that she, "Just wants to be friends."

The only question I asked her was, "When you leavin'?"

She cracked her knuckles and cleared her throat.

While looking up to the blue sky, she flatly responded, "In three days. I guess I'll be gone for the summer or until late August." Her face looked puzzled as if she was calculating time in her head.

"The whole summer!" I shouted. "The entire, like, summer?"

She went on, "Probably August. It's a one-way ticket, so whenever I want, I guess. I haven't really decided yet."

After the initial shock wore off, my emotional state was a cross between total shock and resentment. I mean, how could she just leave? Then, after further consideration, I changed my mind. I smiled. I suppose one could compare me to Thomas- the cat from *Tom and Jerry*. My face must have looked just like his whenever he was scheming up another plan to catch that mouse. A wonderful new thought occurred to me. For the entire summer, I could do anything I wanted.

I calmly said, "Well, whatever you need to do."

My statement was intentionally snide and crass. I tried to relay that if she did not want me, then I did not want her either. However, mom was pleased with my response. She half-smiled and nodded her head with agreement. She totally missed the point that I was trying to make.

After our walk, I ran up to my room to put on my bathing suit, and then quickly dashed out the front door. As I ran down the street in my flip-flops, I heard mom's voice calling to me from her bedroom window, reminding me to be home by five. I cheerfully waved back to her. When I turned back around to go to Lizzie's house, I smirked with a devious thought- *in one week, I can do whatever I want! You can't boss me around! Ha-ha!*

Mom's flight was on a Friday. Dad and I drove her to the airport and waved goodbye as the plane left the Philadelphia runway. Instead of focusing on the gravity of the situation, my only concern was biting into a *Jim's* cheese steak. *Jim's* was on South Street, and I easily convinced Dad to detour our trip home, so we could indulge in my favorite treat. As Mom boarded the plane, I began to salivate with thoughts of gooey, provolone cheese that was always perfectly melted on top of the salty, tender steaks.

Keeping Bennet family tradition alive, we ate our steaks and never talked about the fact that Mom left for the summer. I never asked Dad why she left, and he never bothered to explain it to me. So, we ate our cheese steaks with tangy ketchup, fried onions, and salty French fries with a side of sweet denial. (Yum-yum.)

Dad believed that kids should have the summer off. He always told me that his father used to say, "Tom, you will have your whole life to work, so just enjoy being a kid." Oh, how I loved that statement. Dad had rules and I followed them, but most of his rules were basic. He didn't care what time I woke up or went to bed. He just needed to know where I was going and who I was going with, but Mom needed every single detail regarding my private/social life. Mom made my life difficult. Dad made my life easy. I took advantage of my '*Summer of Freedom*' by doing exactly what mom hated: staying up late, eating junk-food, hanging out with whoever I wanted to, and simply living without so many rules. In one word- it was awesome!

The sound of the alarm clock pounding my head at seven in the morning was a distant memory. Occasionally, the annoying buzzing from a neighbor's lawn mower would motivate me to get out of bed, but I usually got up whenever I desired. Next, I would putter around the house and make myself a bite to eat. Then, I would prep myself for a lazy day of lounging by the pool. I took mom's magazines that came in the mail, poured some homemade iced-tea with a slice of lemon, turned on the radio to Q102.1, and floated carelessly in a tiny raft for hours. Life was good.

My summer vacation plans also included several sports camps. I understood why dad signed me up for so many camps. My time was intentionally busy and meticulously planned. Dad created a genius way to keep me distracted during the summer. It became obvious to me that he and mom knew long before I did about her decision to leave for the summer. Nevertheless, I welcomed summer camp, especially since they were sports-related and most of my friends would be there. Not only did I attend day camps, but my nights revolved around sports, as well. I had at least two softball games during the week. I was on a summer field hockey league that met every Wednesday night at Gloucester High School. Every other Thursday, I played on a summer basketball league, and weekends were booked solid with softball tournaments.

I felt like mom only called when she knew that I wouldn't be home. I only talked to her when she called specifically for dad. I didn't miss her and that made me sad. She was staying with her family in Edgewater, Florida. Edgewater was a surf town near New Smyrna Beach. She bounced around from house to house. One week, she stayed with my aunt and the next week, she was living with her dad, or my uncle- I could not keep track. Every time she talked to me, it seemed she was staying with someone new. On the rare occasion that we did speak, she made certain to fill me in on her beach days, fishing trips, and the late night shrimping adventures. I tried to pass along my excitement regarding her happiness, but really, I was kind of pissed off. *Why was she happy there and not here?* Again, I personalized it: she didn't need me.

Late nights and early mornings were my most cherished times of the day. During the hours of stillness, I became creative- alive. There were endless humid nights that I spent in my room doing absolutely nothing and everything all at the same time. I was often busy making a collage, painting my toe-nails, writing crappy poems, looking at the yearbook, or skimming through magazines. Most times, I drifted off into sleep when the birds were squawking to greet the new day. My radio never went off at night. I often listened to mom's old tapes. I liked Jimmy Buffett, The Steve Miller Band, and Cat Stevens. By far, my favorite late night song was a tribute to my brother. It allowed me, in my own special way, to reminisce about Phillip. I listened to *The Long and Winding Road* hundreds of times that summer. I even wrote down the words on a white piece of paper in my best penmanship and hung it up on my wall.

I remembered hearing that song many years before. It always seemed so sad to me. Mom told me that it was about a personal connection with God. She also mentioned that it was an actual road that The Beatles used to walk on. I wasn't sure about either. That song, to me, was the only way I could feel connected to or sympathetic toward Phillip. I felt like listening to it gave me permission to look for answers, or to think about the situation that I purposely stored away for the past six months. Hearing Paul McCartney admit that he, too, felt alone and abandoned reassured me that I was not crazy to assume that my feelings were isolated. As I listened carefully to that painfully slow song, I gave my mind the freedom to wander into deep, dark places that I rarely permitted myself to go.

It was my opportunity to be still and all alone with my thoughts of Phillip. I was present. All the "think about that later" thoughts danced around my head, but it seemed okay because I was in the moment.

Paul's lyrics made me feel like I was reciting the words to my brother. If Phillip could lead me to his door, or if I could understand why he did it, then maybe, just maybe, things would get better. Perhaps the song was a connection to God or maybe heaven. *What happens when we die?* The Bible claimed that there was an afterlife, so I crossed my fingers, closed my eyes, and hummed to the melancholy message. I sat Indian-style on my floor and prayed to God that we would reunite under much different circumstances.

Mom was in Florida for forty-seven days. She called me twelve times. I received two generic postcards in the mail. The kind of postcards that have beautiful, oily people tanning themselves on the beach until their skin looks like leather. Nothing deep was written; nothing profound was mentioned in her writings. I hoped that, with the passing of time, mom would come home completely changed. I created a fantasy in my mind about our future when she returned. The picture I created was so different from the hell on earth we endured in our house. I predicted that she would make me white-chocolate macadamia nut cookies every day. (Okay, that was just a fantasy.) She would attend my field hockey games; perhaps she would even bring me a snack. (Just like the other moms.) I visualized us going shopping for my first homecoming dress, exchanging motherly/daughterly trivial banter in the kitchen, or sitting in a huge pedicure chair with our hair wrapped up like swamis. It was all so picture-perfect, just like a *Hallmark* movie. My optimism grew when I got in the car to go pick her up. Mom's respite was over. She could be my mother again.

Dad and I picked her up on a Wednesday night. Upon seeing my mother for the first time in forty seven days, my pulse rose when I looked at her blue eyes. I didn't know how to react, but I did know that I missed her. My reaction was different than I had anticipated. When I saw her, I kind of felt like I was five years old again, and she was picking me up at kindergarten. She was my mom and I missed her. It was just that simple.

She wore a floral dress that accentuated her tiny frame. Dad must have noticed her beautiful transformation, as well. She looked different. Mom's appearance was simply glowing; time alone had done her good. Dad kissed her, hugged her tight, and held her hand through the airport. In all my years, I could not remember seeing that kind of public display of affection between them. Even though it was totally gross to watch, it was kind of sweet and endearing.

On the car ride home, we exchanged our summer stories. We talked about uplifting things; good things. We simply enjoyed our time together. All my anger about her leaving me seemed to dissolve. Even though it was late, mom searched through her suitcase to find the gifts she bought for me. She held up Florida Gator boxer shorts, along with several other University of Florida trinkets, leading me to believe she purchased all the items at the airport gift shop.

When mom returned home, I studied her. (The new her.) My investigation began twelve hours after she arrived home. My first clue that life on Linden Avenue was going to remain a war zone was when mom complained about the lack of food in the house. Next, she whined about the condition of the house. She called it a pigsty and accused us of living like "pigs." After a few short days of New Jersey, mom's gripes became personally directed toward me. She blamed me for not keeping the house clean. She reprimanded me for getting up too late. She made me feel like I was useless within a matter of hours. She sipped her morning coffee, smoked her morning Reds, and spewed her morning complaints.

It took four days for me to start avoiding her again. I had to acknowledge that my hopes of change were simply that- hopes. Mom began pointing out all the flaws in the house. "When is the last time you dusted?" she scoffed. "How hard is it to vacuum a floor?" she vented. Then, she let it all out. "You guys live like pigs, and I am not cleaning up your mess!" she shouted. I heard her mutter under her breath a few times that she should have stayed in Florida. She gave me several chores to finish. My summer of freedom, of waking up at noon, of lying by the pool was (gasp) over.

It was a total slap in the face. I mean, she comes home from her sunshiny vacation and returns as 'Super Bitch.' I vacuumed the floor with indifference, putting in about an ounce of effort. Mom noticed. She whisked into the room and grabbed the vacuum cleaner. She shouted, "This! This is how you vacuum…" She vigorously vacuumed the floor. "But you wouldn't know that, would you?" She bumped into the coffee table with the vacuum cleaner with little effort to be careful. "You! You do nothing. It's so like you- isn't it? All you wanna do is play softball and have fun with your friends." As she was venting, I was thinking- *yeah…what's so wrong with that?* Mom shook her head, and rolled her eyes, leading me to believe that we were both much happier when we had thousands of miles between us.

She looked at me as she turned the vacuum cleaner off. "I should have stayed there!" she barked. Then, she told me to leave.

I left her in the room and under my breath I whispered, "bitch." Then, I shouted, "Then go back!"

Four days. Four days was all it took to pick up exactly where we left off. She was happier without me. Maybe Florida reminded her of Phillip. Maybe New Jersey reminded her of the loss she suffered. I didn't know. I just knew that nothing changed... just the date.

The week before school started, mom and I did our best to avoid each other and tried to appear pleasant whenever dad was around. I was thankful that I had the summer alone and I was sure mom was glad, as well. Mom was still depressed. She began isolating herself from us again. My relationship with her seemed impossible. She forgot all about me and memorialized him. Phillip was all she could think about. I could not understand why she lived in an imaginary world with him when I was right in front of her.

our Father, who art in heaven…

Ninth grade was going to be different. It had to be better than the past school year. The night before my freshman year started, I thought about how last year I was so happy that Phillip moved away. That thought really stung; it hurt so badly. Just before I drifted off to sleep, I told myself that I would think about him later. High school was an entirely different world that I was anxious to explore, and those unsettling thoughts regarding my brother would have to wait. Phillip was too complicated. I just couldn't understand it, and, during that time, I really did not have anyone who could explain it.

I observed everything during those critical first few days of school. For the first time in my life, I would share a lunch period with older boys. No, scratch the word 'boys;' guys. The halls were swimming with junior and senior guys; eighteen-year-old guys who emanated total manliness along with a license and facial hair. It was so different from last year. I mean, the food was the same, the location was the same, but the scenery was completely different. The girls were more refined. Some of them were going to college next year. They walked with confidence, had perfect make-up, and knew exactly how to act around hot guys. I hung out with my freshman circle of safety and wondered what it would be like to be a senior or, better yet, in college.

On a Friday, I found myself staring into the distance in the cafeteria as my ice-cream sandwich melted down my arm. The jovial laughter from the football team caught my attention. They were probably laughing at a perverted joke or a perverted thought. (Perverts!) Everything guys laughed about was sexual. I began daydreaming while I watched the perky cheerleaders giggle and act like 'stupid girls.' The cheerleaders hiked their skirts to their butt cheeks, listened to the same Top 40 music, used the same dull lingo, and all blushed with hormonal delight when they flirted with a varsity football player. My thoughts transitioned to my brother. I imagined Phillip with them. I could literally see him laughing at those stupid jokes (probably telling them) or flirting with the pretty girls or receiving praises from teachers for representing the Gator football team. The memory of my brother had long left those boys. Phillip was never even so much as a thought to them. I licked my ice cream and wondered if any of them even remembered that chubby kid who played on their team for one season. I must have been staring for a while because Tom Ridley looked over to me and smiled. Tom cocked his head, waved slowly, and grinned as he elbowed Carl Kindsay.

I quickly turned away from Tom. The only thing I could possibly do to help the situation was to act like I was looking at something behind him. It was no use- my red face was a dead giveaway. Tiffany elbowed me and sarcastically commented, "Your face is, like, beet red."

I touched my cheeks and began to panic, "Shit! Oh my God! No, it isn't. Really? Is it?

"Yeah, uhh, like a tomato." She chuckled.

"Don't look now..." I requested softly, "But, is Tom Ridley looking over here- or am I just crazy?"

Tiffany, being a clever girl, dropped her pencil to appear as if she had a reason to look over. "No, he's lookin' the other way. He's talking to buck-toothed Bridget. Uhh, I hate her! Everything about her is, like, so fake. Ewww! I bet she has fake contacts in to make her eyes look that blue." Tiffany grew silent, and then announced, "Oh wait, he is looking over here…" She turned to me with disbelief. She announced, "I think he's smiling at you. Yup, he's definitely looking at you."

I cupped my head with embarrassment and then mumbled, "Eww, gross. Why is he looking over here?"

When the dismissal bell rang, I immediately clutched my backpack and hauled my butt down the hall with Tiffany by my side.

"Hey! #55?" I heard a voice calling to me at the end of the hallway. I turned around and saw Tom Ridley approaching. He playfully asked, "Yo! Why you wearin' #55?"

Tom marched toward me while stretching out his hands, gesturing that he wanted a response.

"What? Who is #55?" I scoffed.

Tom gave me a sarcastic grin. "Yeah, okay…duh? Turn around, Sherlock." He pointed to the numbers on my field hockey jersey, and read them out loud: "Five and five. That equals fifty-five. Right?" He laughed as I slowly bobbed my head in agreement.

I turned around to face him and in my best smartass voice, I replied, "Yeah, well, that's not really my number. If you look close…" I pointed to my back. "…You will see the strategically placed plus sign, so that means, five plus five is…?" I waited for him to finish.

Tom put his hand to his mouth, pretending to be deep in thought. He joked, "Oh? It means you love Lenny Simms. You know- 'cuz he's #55."

I pulled on Tiffany's arm as an indication that it was time to go to class. Before we entered Spanish class, I coyly turned to Tom and said, "Lenny Simms has no neck and he has a full blown Grizzly Adams beard. I would hardly use the word love." After my comment, Tiffany and I giggled as we swaggered into Spanish class. I never waited for his rebuttal, but I was pretty confident that he was somewhat amused.

I learned shortly after our conversation that most senior guys were interested in freshmen girls. We were in some new world with an abundance of eighteen-year-old guys at our disposal. Only their interest in naïve, freshmen girls usually centered on our vulnerabilities. In one month, rumors circulated every Monday about some freshman girl who instantaneously became a slut at a weekend party. We never needed proof that anything actually happened. In the high school world, being easy or slutty was the worst reputation a girl could get.

After our brief conversation on a Friday afternoon, Tom Ridley and I became friends. We talked about everything. He mostly talked about football, and I mostly asked personal questions about senior girls. Most of the time, we just joked about random pointless things or the gross lunch we just inhaled. Thomas hated when I talked to Tom. It was all very innocent. I saw Tom as my inside connection to upperclassmen information. He was my personal informant who divulged secret details about who was hooking up and who was breaking up. He talked a lot about all the colleges he visited, and I loved hearing those stories. Our relationship was simple and I knew what I wanted out of Tom and, besides, what idiot would hook up with a senior guy who would be leaving for college? Duh?

The first few weeks of school held a refreshing newness that temporarily alleviated the drudgery of getting out of my bed in the morning. There were the annual pep rallies, the new field hockey season, and the new hook-ups. With all the distractions around me, fall only made me think about him. Phillip. It was my first autumn since his death. In fact, the fall, for some strange reason, made me think about him more than ever.

It was when the dark nights came early that I really started to grasp that he was gone. Inside, I was reasonably proud of myself for holding everything together and making my life look so ordinary. However, most of the time when I was with my friends, my thoughts were off in some distant place. I was always foggy. Pretending that I was fine was exhausting. Trying to act as if his death was something in the past began taking its toll, and it usually revealed itself in odd ways or at the most inopportune times.

My decision to ignore everything that bothered me was necessary to keep me sane. I suppose another reason why I chose to keep him out of my head was because I didn't want to feel guilty, angry, or horrible all at once. The tragic reality of Phillip's death, my volatile relationship with mom, my insatiable need to impress my dad, and my overall fakeness crept up on me in my dreams. My dreams replayed the same theme nearly every night. I was lost. I was lost in the woods, in school, or in my own house. I was always lost. I was always trying to find my way.

Sometime in the fall, mom attempted to save Phillip's soul by joining the local church. Her need to find religion or God or faith became her obsession six months after Phillip died. For the first time in my life, Mom forced me to get up on Sunday morning to attend a church service. Every Sunday at 9 a.m., she knocked on my door and, every Sunday at 9 a.m., I would ignore her. She shouted, yelled, and cajoled until I gave in and lazily crawled out of bed.

Mom resorted to bribery, promising to take me out to breakfast afterwards. Church was foreign to me. I attended briefly with some friends down the street when I was little, but my parents never formally directed me to any religion or belief. We had a Bible in our house that was somewhere between the dictionary and a *Stephen King* book.

My dad did not join us. It seemed mom's only ally was me, and I only went because I was forced. Church, to me, was another institution telling me what to believe. They told me when to pray, how to pray, when to sing, and what to sing. My philosophical beliefs regarding religion were simple: there was *something* out there, but I could not commit to believing in something that seemed so *made up*. Phillip and I attended a couple different churches with friends, and we attended vacation bible school every summer. In fact, one summer we both accepted Jesus into our hearts. The young missionary lady told us, "Jesus can knock on the door, but only you can let him in." Phillip and I both blankly stared at the woman while we looked at a poster board of Jesus Christ who waited patiently near a door without a door handle. That was our only form of education regarding Christianity. To be honest, I wasn't even sure if I was Christian. I mean, I told people that I was a Christian because if you said that you didn't believe in Him, then you were some kind of atheist freak. Going to church was a reminder of my ignorance regarding the sensitive subject. It also forced me to think about Phillip... in the afterlife. Would he be there? Could he be there?

I walked behind mom as we entered the Presbyterian Church on Elm Avenue. There was an overwhelming sensation of wonder and of disparagement all at the same time. My assumption was that anyone who entered the church was high and mighty, was saved, and guaranteed a spot in heaven for just showing up. The white-haired ladies walked down the aisles waving and smiling with their painted red lipstick and old lady perfume lingering long after they walked by. I watched them closely and judged them before they could judge me. What would they think about Phillip's death? Would they say it was selfish? Would they say that suicide was a sin against God? Probably.

With each passing Sunday, I assimilated to my new environment. I smiled. I waved. I sung my psalms when requested and I even prayed with my eyes closed (not even a peek.) I tried very hard to understand the scriptures when the preacher told stories about the Apostles and Jesus, but it was too confusing. I mean, if God loved us unconditionally, then why did I feel like I was never doing the right thing? I wasn't praying passionately enough; I wasn't sure if I believed in Jesus or Moses or the parting of the Red Sea. If I didn't really believe that Mary got pregnant by Immaculate Conception, could God love me? There were so many rules and regulations to follow; rules that determined if I was a good Christian. Was I a good Christian? Wait... again, would I even be considered a Christian?

I tried to absorb the wisdom that my preacher spewed every Sunday. When he spoke about forgiveness, my shoulders pressed against the wooden pew with interest. He said that God was a forgiving God, and that He loved all his children unconditionally. So, I smiled as I sat anxiously in the pew and figured God would not mind if I daydreamed about plate-sized pancakes. The preacher spoke in the front of the congregation with his long, purple robe along with a yellow sash across his chest. He slowly raised his arms to the sky, nodded when he spoke, and occasionally twitched his caterpillar mustache. The biblical stories of the Old Testament reminded me of Greek

Mythology. I winced with confusion trying to relate any of those ancient stories with my lifetime. Unfortunately, I needed some kind of interpreter. Instead of getting the gist, I bit my nails and, once again, dreamed about buttery pancakes.

Everything the preacher talked about went right over my head. Mom sat next to me, muttering soft uh-huhs and hmm-hmms with agreement. Was she really getting it? Maybe I was just stupid. I didn't get it. I felt like my job in life was to get closer to God. My interpretation of religion was simple- I was supposed to live my life to gain God's favor... but why? I felt like I was trying to impress someone who already loved me. Where did God go? How could we be separate? What about Phillip? Was God mad at him? Nobody was telling me what I needed to hear.

The only person who ever comforted me regarding Phillip's whereabouts in the afterlife was my friend, Sharon. She told me that all souls go to heaven, but sometimes when people die, they get confused. Sharon explained that when humans die violently, too soon, or whatever- sometimes they get lost in between two worlds. They don't know that they are supposed to go to the light, and so they stay in a place called limbo. Sharon told me that everyone goes to heaven, even bad people. Everyone, she repeated. Her words calmed my fears. Everything else I heard regarding his death just seemed like static. People never told me what I really wanted to know. Was my brother in heaven? I needed reassurance that everyone, regardless of who they were or what they did, could go to heaven. I wasn't sure if Sharon was accurate, but I wanted to believe her so badly that I chose to.

On Sundays when I sat in church, I contemplated my own sins. According to the Bible, simply by being born, I was part of the original sin; therefore, I was separate from

God. My preacher reminded me that my only salvation was Jesus Christ. Then, I thought about Jewish people... are they just always separate from God? The fact remained that I was a sinner. I cursed. I lied. I cheated on my math test and, to top it all off, I wasn't even sure if I believed that Jesus was the Son of God. So, how could I enter *The Kingdom of Heaven?* I hated thinking about those questions; hated questioning what I was supposed to believe. I was the skeptic sitting in the fourth pew every Sunday morning. I was the hypocrite who sung the songs, read the verses, and went to church because I had to and not because I wanted to. Regardless of whether or not I believed, I sat on the hard wood next to mom every Sunday and prayed for Phillip. I prayed that we would meet again in the afterlife.

I kept every church hymnal that I received upon entering the front door. It outlined the psalms that we were going to sing and the scriptures we were going to study. At night when I was alone in my room, I would study the flimsy piece of paper and re-read the scriptures. I reread them so many times trying to dissect the meaning, but the words were too complicated. I read; "But he that shall blaspheme against the Holy Ghost hath never forgiveness but is in danger of eternal damnation." Luke 3:29. Upon reading the passage, I closed my flyer and prayed. I prayed with my eyes shut tight:

Dear God, I don't get it. I guess that is alright... right? God, I know Phillip killed himself, but he didn't know what he was doing. I think he was confused. I think he was sad. God, please help my brother. God, please allow him into heaven. Can you let him in? I promise I will try harder, you know? I will try to pay attention in church and be nicer to mom and I'll be good. Phillip is a nice person, or was. I don't know. He just, just... I don't know. Am I supposed to know? Please let him in. Maybe one day we can meet up again. Maybe we can be like we were when we were little. Okay, that's all. I love you. Amen, Shannon Bennet.

In the confines of my room, I played *Autumn Leaves* repeatedly and, when I was totally bored in school, I hummed it under my breath. Nat King Cole had the voice of an angel. It was so soft, but equally confident when he sung about autumn in a gloomy, yet realistic way. I understood his words. I understood his loneliness.

I wrote the song on the inside flap of my English book and looked at the words while drifting to far away places. In science, I sat in my designated seat and listened to my poorly dressed teacher talk about rock sediment or rock formation (whatever.) Most of the time, my chin rested on my palms as I tried to hold my head up and I daydreamed. I even laughed cynically in my head when I thought about how silly I was for assuming that last year during that time, Phillip was body surfing and eating vinegar fries at the beach, when he was really contemplating and plotting his own death.

I found myself getting more and more annoyed by the most miniscule things. Thomas suddenly got on my nerves and my friends became irritating. In my mind, everyone I knew had some kind of hidden agenda against me. I walked around the halls like a zombie. I was half-present and half-gone, never really sure which half I was in. I hated my planned days along with the monotony of school that seemed to serve no purpose in my life. What does it matter? Who cares about fractions? Dewey Decimal System?

Periodic Table? Who cares? Phillip was gone and I will never see him again.

Sometimes, I sat in class staring at random people and suddenly felt an uncontrollable urge to just yell at them or hit them. Nancy Deiner, who was an annoying know-it-all, raised her hand to answer every single question and waited until the bell was about to ring to ask some dumb question that nobody cared about. She sat next to me in English class and, after another one of her irritating know-it-all answers, I totally lost it. I shouted, "Shut up, Nancy! You're such a freakin dork!" She looked me over with a face of stone and, after my outburst, she never talked to me again. I didn't blame her and I really didn't care. After my explosion, the class fell silent, probably wondering if I was insane. However, *I* knew I wasn't insane. I was just angry. After yelling at Nancy, my body felt like it had released something, like a huge weight was lifted off my shoulders. Nancy wasn't the only one I attacked. I was on the attack almost twenty-four hours a day. I blew up at everyone. I hated when people walked too slow, talked too slow, chewed their gum like a cow, asked me a stupid question, or didn't ask me a question. I hated watching girls giggle, boys taunt, or teachers lecture. I hated when my coaches ordered me around, when mom bossed me, or when *anyone* looked at me the wrong way. I hated going home. I hated being at school. I hated, well, just about everything. Most of all, I hated hating my life.

After another boring day at school and a long basketball practice, I came home in a bad mood. The smell of spaghetti sauce drew me into the kitchen, but I had no appetite. Mom was stirring the saucepot while humming a Rod Stewart tune. Just the sound of her humming annoyed me.

When she noticed me in the kitchen, she quickly snapped, "Oh, Shannon. I need you to set the table. Dinner in ten minutes." She hummed some more as she added salt and pepper.

In the most defiantly bitchy way possible, I announced, "I'm not eating- going upstairs." Then, I lugged my backpack and darted up the steps.

I knew mom would react to my tone, but I didn't care. Just as I thought I was going to make an escape, mom called up to me from the bottom of the steps. "Uh, where do you think you're going? I told you to set the table and... you *will* set the table."

I turned around, trying to make it seem like she was bothering me, and flatly stated, "I am not hungry. I am not eating, so why do I have to set the table? You've been here all day, so you do it!"

I knew she would get pissed. Maybe making her feel bad was my motivation. I didn't know why, but it seemed like pushing everyone's buttons was amusing. Mom pointed her wooden spoon at me and demanded that I immediately come downstairs. She shouted, "It's not an option, and what the hell does that mean? I've been home all day. You need to start doing things around here. It's your house, too." She caught my eye and then emphatically ordered, "Get your ass down here and set the table. Now!"

I scoffed, "No thanks. I'll pass."

Surprisingly, her voice was calm when she pleaded, "Shannon, I am asking you nicely. Please, set the table." With her hand pressed on her hips and the wooden spoon pointing in my direction, she held her breath and waited for my submission.

I cocked my head and sarcastically barked, "No, correction." I began waving my hands to emphasize my point. "You didn't ask me. You told me. You never ask-you just tell. I can't remember the last time you asked me anything. You just tell me. All the freakin' time!"

She retorted, "Are you seriously talking back to me right now? I mean, seriously. I asked you to do one simple thing like set the table and you have the nerve to turn this on me. You know what? It doesn't matter if I asked you or told you- you are supposed to do what I tell you anyway because I am the mother and you are the child. And that is the name of that tune." With her eyes glaring, she dared me to go further.

I gave in.

Defeated, exhausted, and livid, I threw my bag down, stomped down the steps and began haphazardly pulling plates out of the cabinet. I muttered under my breath loud enough for mom to hear all my gripes and moans. I threw silverware down, chucked napkins close to the plates, and flung the salt and pepper shakers.

"There, I'm done! Happy now? I'm goin' upstairs," I declared.

Mom inspected my appalling table setting, then she coyly mentioned, "Uh, I only see two plates. You need another one. You *are* eating with us."

I flat out refused. I barked, "No. I'm not. I'm not hungry."

"I don't care. You will sit and stare at the wall for all I care, but you are eating dinner with us at this table. Got it?" She began humming Maggie May, coolly ignoring me.

I screamed, "No! I don't want to stare at your ugly face! You can't make me!" I rushed out of the kitchen, running up the steps to the comfortable confines of my bedroom.

She shouted, "Excuse me!" She raced behind me, yelling up the steps, "You don't talk to me like that!"

I lost it. I just lost all control (if I had any to begin with.) I screamed like a crazy lunatic. "You can't tell me what to do! You! You!" I pointed directly at her. "You don't own me!" My veins were probably protruding from my forehead and my words were incomprehensible. I spewed out awful words and several accusations along with spit and unreleased tears. During the battle, I had no remembrance of what I actually said.

Somehow, I managed to yell, "I'm not hungry! You eat my gross spaghetti!"

I slammed my door behind me, two times for the dramatic effect.

She never followed me. She left me in my room. Afterward, I felt terrible. Why did I do that? I should have just eaten that stupid spaghetti. With my door closed, I could hear faint music from downstairs and, with every second that passed, I wished I could take back everything. It was so stupid. Then, I looked around my room, hating myself, hating my situation, and just hating the fact that I was so mean. Why was I so mad at everyone? I walked slowly to my mirror to look at the stranger who inhabited my trembling body. Then, with one swipe of my arm, I sent every item on my desk onto the floor. The rage building within took over. I ran to my wooden closet doors and began to punch the hard surface as hard as I could. Thump! Thump! Thump! My hand was completely and comfortably numb. Surprisingly, it felt great to hit something. I repeatedly smashed the wooden closet door, never noticing the trickles of blood scattered on my hands and my lavender walls.

After pounding my fist and making an impressionable gash on the closet, I began tearing down all the pictures from my wall, shredding them as I cursed wild profanities under my breath. It felt good to rip things apart, too. I found pleasure in destroying my room. Completely out of breath and, on an impulse, I picked up a mug that read,

"Virginia is for lovers" and hurled it at my mirror. The alarming sound of the mug shattering into small pieces allowed me to stop and catch my breath to view my destruction. I stood in the center of my room, wondering how I was going to hide the mess from mom and wishing I had just set the table for three.

Mom never came to check out the noise. I lifted my right hand and watched the tiny speckles of blood ooze out of my knuckles and, for the first time in a long time, I felt something. Relief. The uncontrollable rush of anger that came over me was gone. Instead of cleaning my hands, I inspected the tiny, red lines, faint scratches, and torn skin. I chose to blast INXS, hoping Michael Hutchinson could clarify my feelings. I went under my thick covers, curled in a ball, felt the warm pulsating sensation in my hands, and hummed along with *Devil Inside.*

The next day, I wore my Gateway field hockey sweatshirt, using the extra long sleeves to hide my raw fingers. I covered my closet doors with posters from my wall, pinning Michael Jordan's long arm span over my closet doors to cover up the holes. It could take years for mom to discover the holes, so I figured that I could plead ignorance with no recollection.

School carried on as usual: still lame- still boring. After my explosion, I couldn't help but wonder if other kids had crazy tantrums like me. Maybe I was the only one. For that reason alone, I contemplated if I was "normal." What was normal? As usual, school kept my mind in a state of monotonous routine, allowing my mind to wander. The only thrill that day was catching the end of Christina Kennedy and Jennifer Ammirati cat fighting in the hallway. Then, there was the unexpected/expected fire drill. When the teachers actually told us that we were going to have a fire drill, it kind of ruined the entire point. When the piercing noise and white flashing lights went off, my class methodically rose to our designated spot in line and waited for further instructions. After I marched outside, the tingle from the bitter November wind made me shiver and hug myself with my extra large, gray sweatshirt.

Kimmy Walton walked beside me. She confirmed that the wind was wicked. We talked about the possibility of missing the entire class, our basketball practice, and finalized our plans for the upcoming weekend. Kimmy was my friend, or rather, she was like me. We dressed the same, liked the same music, hung out with the same people, and probably were interested in the same boys during our years at Gateway. We were classified within the same species, the same social rank, or to a casual observer in the high school world, we were lumped close to each other in the cafeteria. Knowing that we shared the same beliefs made her next remarks nearly unbearable. Kimmy and I huddled near each other for warmth, bending our shoulders as we shivered and watched kids push each other playfully.

"Eww!" Kimmy hissed as she tapped me on the shoulder. Her humid breath warmed my ear when she whispered, "What a total scumbag? Do you see him... he's, like, totally gross. Why do they dress like total freaks?"

Kimmy did not have to wait for me to concur as she pointed her finger to a boy standing alone. She knew that I would agree simply because we were in the same high school clique. I was already nodding with agreement before I laid eyes on her target. Kimmy whispered in my ear, "Ewww- imagine bringing that thing home to meet your mother!" Then, she rolled her eyes at the sight of Todd McManus. Before I could respond to Kimmy, I took my time looking Todd over for the first time in years.

He did look the dirt bag part with his ripped, acid wash jeans, black Pantera t-shirt, and his wispy mullet haircut.

Todd, oblivious to Kimmy's accusations, stood alone with both hands in his pockets while he exhaled tiny trails of puffy air that escaped his mouth every time he let out a breath. Todd never looked at me, but I was staring at him for quite some time, wondering what happened in his life during our three-year hiatus. Sixth grade seemed like forever ago. Todd seemed to represent all the loathing and love hidden deep inside me. It suddenly bothered me that Todd was considered one of the dirt bags, but it bothered me more that I was the one who was judging him. I liked him. So, why would I shake my head and agree that he was one of them? I considered the question for the first time in my life.

Kimmy never waited for a response, but I knew she assumed that I felt the same way. What she did not know was the effect her statement would have on me long after the fire drill was over. Back in English class, I though about how Todd and I had something in common- his father's death and my brother's death. I wondered if he ever punched walls, threw things, or was confused, or hated everyone like I did. Kimmy probably would have judged Phillip the same way and I would be one of those shallow girls who joined her. Who cares what his hair looked like? Who cares about his clothes? I knew Todd, and I knew that Todd was a good person, so why did it matter? Sadly, I knew my thoughts of Todd were mere reflections of my brother. While daydreaming in class, I envisioned kids in Florida laughing at Phillip and calling him obscene names while I watched.

I sat in English wondering how *I* became so superficial. I *was* one of those girls and I fed into the belief that your exterior defined you. I shook my head with shame, knowing what my brother went through for several years. Phillip's suicide was complicated, and I didn't think that I could ever pinpoint one single reason why he did it, but I did know that constantly being ridiculed and being made fun of had something to do with it. I was no better than Kimmy. I was worse.

After my stroke of insight, I got a pass to go to the bathroom and took a long, hard look in the mirror. Who was I to judge? I asked myself as I fixed my ponytail and reapplied lip-gloss. I took my time looking at myself until I heard the sound of the bathroom door creaking. I pretended that I was busy washing my hands. Then, I caught a glimpse of Keri Metz. She was a sophomore and she terrified me. Her eyes were lined with black eyeliner around both the top and bottom lids. She outlined her tiny lips with red lip liner. Keri defined the stereotypical Jersey girl in nearly every way which included her faded jean jacket with the signature Guns-n-Roses patch. Last year, in gym class, she blasted the hand dryer nozzle up while spraying Aqua Net hairspray to enhance her already huge bangs. I used to secretly watch her, totally amazed by the height of her bangs.

When Keri's eyes met mine, we both ignored each other with mutual disgust. She clicked her teeth as an acknowledgement of my presence and then briskly strolled into the stall and slammed it hard. After she closed the stall door, I shook my head and laughed to myself in the mirror with the irony.

I walked out of the bathroom and took my time before going back to English. We were reading Romeo and Juliet, so maybe if I took long enough, I wouldn't have to participate. My English teacher rambled on about Shakespeare with a passion that no fourteen year old could even comprehend. Shakespeare, to me, was as confusing as the Bible passages I tried to understand. I yawned in my seat, checked the clock eight times, and waited for the "B" lunch crowd to pass by.

Funny, as I tried to comprehend the words of Shakespeare, my thoughts were consumed with him. Phillip. I wanted a do-over. I thought about having just one chance for a do-over. I would do it all over so differently… just like Romeo and Juliet.

Christmas time for many people was a time to rejoice, to celebrate, and just be happy. I have lived under the impression for the past fourteen years that Christmas would magically and, without any effort, instill joy. There was an almost unspoken pressure to be happy during Christmas and if, for some strange reason, you were down- you were "weird." How could one ignore the vibrant colors in the store windows or the catchy holiday jingles? What would we do without the festive commercials filtering our airwaves, sending us subliminal messages of Christmas bliss? Then, of course, the rich foods, the freshly baked cookies with red sprinkles inviting us to taste- afterward leaving their everlasting pleasure on our hips. The fragrant pine tree that twinkled, the Charlie Brown cartoon special, the hopes of a picture-perfect landscape donned with fresh snowflakes. If you could fog a mirror, you were supposed to love Christmas. After all, what loser dreaded Christmas?

I was the loser. Even with all the sparkling red, green, and white lights that hung high on the roofs in Woodbury Heights, I was lost in a place that was so dark that no amount of sparkling lights could make it bright. Not even the birth of Jesus Christ, who promised eternal salvation, could make my spirits rise. Christmas was no longer a celebration, but rather, a pinnacle marker that Phillip was no longer on this earth to celebrate, nor would he ever return. It seemed the nostalgic memories of my childhood

Christmases would be replaced by sour visions of what would never be.

I would never have the chance to give him another present. I would never watch the fake burning fire on PBS with him by my side. We would never swap our traditional Christmas chocolates. We would never have a future of coming home from college to greet each other. He would never be an uncle to see my children tear open their presents. He was gone. Christmas only magnified the intensity of the pain.

Mom made feeble, yet noted, attempts to lighten the mood by hanging up a couple decorations. She bought some Christmas eggnog and placed the red and white wrapped presents under the tree. As Christmas drew closer, it was evident that each of us in our family was heading in different directions. We dealt with Phillip's death in our own way. Every emotion was just fluttering around, festering, perhaps waiting for a particular moment to reveal itself. My means of survival was to simply remain silent. I avoided talking, mentioning, or even whispering my brother's name, hoping that somehow avoiding the situation would make it all go away.

Mom and I attended midnight mass on Christmas Eve. Although mom mandated that I attend, I really wanted to go to church on Christmas because attending the celebration made me feel like less of a religious hypocrite. Over the years, I soaked up the Christmas presents, ate the sugary confections, and sung about Jesus, but I never once officially celebrated his birth. When I walked into the candlelit church, the warmth of the candles immediately comforted me. It was a welcome contrast from the bitter cold just ten small steps outside. The old, gossipy, white haired women were fast asleep. In their place were college kids returning home for winter break and youthful smitten couples.

When I sat in my usual Sunday spot, I wondered if everyone attending really, wholly, and undoubtedly believed in the birth of Jesus. Was I the only one questioning his existence? After I glanced over my hymnal, I prayed:

> *Dear God, I am sorry. Oh, it's me Shannon. God, I want to believe. I do. I want to believe that someone could love me so much that they wouldn't care if I was good or bad. Or if I cursed or talked bad about people. How can it be true? Can you help me? Maybe something tonight... I don't know... will, like, change my mind. Okay. Well, it's about to start. Bye. Love, Shannon.*

The sermon began after a passionate rendition of "Joy to the World" by the organist. It sounded kind of creepy. Then again, everything sounded creepy when played on an organ. The preacher began his sermon by praising the Virgin Mary and then the birth of Jesus. Virgin Mary? I chuckled inside when I envisioned Mary confessing to Joseph that she was preggers and, oh by the way, you are not the father. When I really tried to understand the story, literally, it just sounded like some sort of myth. I sat on the hard seat and thought about all the fairy tales that I believed as a child, and then, it hit me. The story of Jesus was the grown-up version of a fairy tale. Literally, the story was next to unbelievable, but when I listened to the message with only my emotions, I melted inside. Jesus was an amazing man. The pastor praised Jesus. He worshipped Jesus. He loved Jesus. "Jesus came to wipe away all of our sins, to save us, to teach us. Jesus is the way and the life," he said.

I bowed my head down during the singing of "Silent Night" and wondered if I was worth saving. Then I wondered if Phillip was worth saving. Was Phillip in Heaven? I bowed my head and prayed:

Dear God, it's me again. Shannon. Well, I just really want to know something. If Jesus came to save us from all of our sins... could Phillip be forgiven for killing himself? It must be true, right? God- is he forgiven? Can you let me know, please? Amen. Shannon Theresa Bennet.

After the congregation finished their long drawn out "Ahhhhhmeeennnn," the pastor closed his eyes, raised his hands to the high heavens, and passionately spoke: "And through the love of God and the birth of His only son... we are *all* loved and forgiven." He kept his arms lifted to the sky, smiled, and urged, "Now, go in peace."

My eyes became wide, my heart felt a little tinge of something, and I felt the presence of God. Maybe he did hear me? A peculiar, loving sensation circulated throughout my body that filled me with hope. I bowed my head again, smiled back, and said, "Thank you, God."

happy freakin' new year, you lush!

The week before Christmas vacation, the gossip circulating rapidly throughout freshmen classrooms was all about Tiffany's party. The anticipation of her New Year's Eve party was practically mandatory conversation of every freshman- maybe, even sophomores, too. Tiffany, Lizzie, and I spent our study hall periods planning the party, enjoying the power of playing gatekeepers to those who could come and those who absolutely could not. Parties were great. New Year's Eve parties were grand. A party that promised no parental supervision was beyond our wildest dreams. Without an adult eye to watch and discipline our every move, we had permission to be on our worst behavior. Of course, there was always the possibility of upperclassmen crashing our party; guys- not girls.

A couple weeks before the party, I began to visualize New Year's night and all the possible scenarios. I bought a new outfit from Contempo, meticulously plucked and arched my eyebrows, and perfected my flat ironing skills. When the dark sky settled over the sunlit sky that late afternoon, I began the ritual of getting ready by blasting my music. I played my new Beastie Boys tape and danced to

She's Crafty. After just a couple beats, I thought I heard mom calling for me downstairs.

I cracked my door hoping that the music would indicate that I was in no mood to talk to her. I sung.

I heard her call for me again. I sat Indian-style in front of my mirror while swiping pink blush across my pale cheeks. She called for me, yet again, forcing me to get up from my sitting position.

"Mom? Mom!" I clicked my teeth with the realization that I would have to go downstairs. I stood at the top of the steps and shouted, "Did you call me?"

I held my breath as I walked downstairs. "Mom? What?" I hoped that whatever she was going to say would only take up fifteen seconds of my precious time.

Mom's tiny body hunched over and rocked slowly with a Santa Claus throw blanket covering everything except for her head. Soft music echoed on her stereo while she methodically rocked. She sung along with the miserable country music. I think it was the Oak Ridge Boys... anything country totally depressed me.

When I saw streaks of gray smoke escape out of the blanket, I knew that my plans for the night were going to change. I sighed deeply before cautiously walking to the end of the couch. The sight of her in such a vulnerable position made me both nervous and sad. I wearily approached her and tried to think about The Beastie Boys, but all I could think about was how everything was my brother's fault.

"Mom?" I timidly asked, "You okay?" I kept my body distant and crossed my fingers that she would simply nod.

Only her lips and cigarette were visible when she exhaled a puff of smoke. Her hands trembled, reminding me of the night she held the phone in her hands when she told me Phillip killed himself. She covered her eyes to hide the tears. "I can't do this. I just... I don't know." Part of me wondered if she even knew that I was there. After she mashed her cigarette butt in the ashtray she looked up to me with tears welling in her eyes and warned, "Don't leave me alone tonight." Afterward, she covered her eyes with her shaky hands.

I kept my cool and thought that I could somehow churn out some reassuring words that would serve as a band-aid, so I could get back to my plans. Part of me felt incredible guilty for casually dismissing her obvious sorrow; however, there was a larger part of me that felt justified for wanting to leave. It wasn't fair. I wasn't sure how to cope with his death- let alone help my mom. Torn, I gave a half-hearted attempt to ease her pain by calmly assuring, "Mom, you'll be okay." I crossed my fingers hoping that a little pep talk would make her recant her request. I suggested, "Why don't you go out with Gina? Or, I don't know- maybe watch Dick Clark. You know?" Using Dick Clark to relieve the grief of her dead son was a long shot, but I was really desperate. There was no way I was staying home. There was no way I could watch her deteriorate. I couldn't. I simply wouldn't.

"Dick Clark?" she sarcastically repeated. "Dick f-ing Clark? Do you think Dick Clark is gonna make me feel better or bring him back? Do ya?!" Her blank expression was a small reminder of the absurdness behind the suggestion.
I began breathing a little faster. I knew that it wouldn't matter what I said or didn't say to make her feel better; she wanted me to stay home. Yet, I tried to remain diplomatic.

"No," I responded with sympathy. "But, I don't think I'll be able to bring him back either." I played with the magazines on the coffee table as I wracked my brains trying to figure out what I needed to say to get out of this situation.

"Well, I'm, I'm gonna go back upstairs to get ready." I began slowly walking backwards, praying that she would turn on Dick Clark.

Mom began shaking her head back and forth in disgust. She reached for another Marlboro Red. Mom's face contorted as she repeatedly tried to get her lighter to cooperate. I hated the sight of her eyes squinting, lips curling, and nostrils flaring when she struggled to ignite her lighter. After a long drag, she looked into the distance and muttered, "You are so selfish. You know that?" She exhaled and repeated, "So selfish."

"Why? Why am I *so* selfish?" I asked as I used my fingers to highlight the word "selfish."

We were both silent for about twenty seconds. She took another drag while I mentally prepared to defend myself. Mom held the orange stick between her two tiny fingers and asked, "Do I really have to explain it? I mean, you see me crying, you know I'm totally upset, so I simply ask you to stay home one night- one night! And you can't even give me that..." Mom crossed her arms, rolled her eyes, and softly hissed, "God! I can't believe how mean you are to me."

There were about one hundred things racing through my mind. Every single thought centered on how mean she was to me, however, I was aware that if I brought up one false or misconstrued accusation, then it would just would escalate into a full-blown fight.

I tried to defuse the situation. "Mom, you're just upset. You know? I mean, it's tough and I wish there was something I could do to..."

She interrupted me by requesting, "You could stay home tonight."

Her puppy dog expression indicated that it was more than just a request.

I stewed inside, secretly furious by her unrealistic request. Within the same moment, I began to feel twinges of guilt when I caught sight of her delicate body hunched over on the couch. The mix of emotions was killing me inside. If I left, then I would be a horrible daughter, but if I stayed, I would be totally bitter.

After brief contemplation, I told her the truth: "I don't want to. I want to go out with my friends."

She sighed. Then, she stared at the twinkling Christmas lights and coolly replied, "Well, tough shit... you're staying home."

"What!" I yelled. "But, I don't want to stay home! I wanna go out and you know that! Talk about being selfish!"

Mom ignored me. She slowly rose from the couch, unveiling her body from the blanket, and handed me the phone, "Call Lizzie and tell her that you are not going." She nudged the phone toward me. "Do it now!" she warned.

I pushed the phone away in defiance. I yelled, "No! I am going out! You can't make me stay home. Not tonight!" Then, I grabbed the phone from her fingers and threw it as hard as I could on the couch.

Mom and I began yelling back and forth. Sometimes we used incredibly hateful words that had little, if nothing, to do with the current situation. We argued about taking out the trash, cleaning my room, and curfews. Somehow, we began to debate about who left the hair in the bathroom tub. It was an endless cycle of old stuff that never got resolved. As we became louder, our words became meaner, our intentions were more hateful, and we began bringing up grievances that were more serious.

"Shannon," Mom began, "Don't you even care? I mean, how can you go out and hang out with your friends? Don't you even care? I mean, are you ever upset? How can you just leave me like this? Don't you even care that your brother died? How? Tell me 'cause I just don't understand how you can be so unfeeling."

Unfeeling? I took a moment to digest the accusation.

I retorted, "Unfeeling?" I stood in the middle of the room pointing to my chest and sarcastically laughed. "Seriously, you're kidding me, right? Is that supposed to be funny?" I asked while cocking my head. I mocked her by raising my voice and clapping my hands. I pretended to laugh as I remarked, "Ha-ha. Oh, no- that is hilarious! It's a friggin' riot, right?" I shook my head, grabbed my stomach, and slapped my knee as if it was all a big joke.

Mom wasn't sure how to react to my blatant disrespect. I addressed her accusation about not caring by asking, "How would you even know how I felt? Seriously?"

She seemed amused by the question as if she was waiting for me to ask the entire time.

She quickly replied. "Nobody cares. Nobody. Not like I do." Mom shook her head up and down. I was sure she was proud she finally said it aloud. She added, "I mean, isn't it obvious? You go out with your friends all the time. Even tonight- it's more important to have a good time than help me. Yeah, I truly believe that I am the only one who cares."

I threw my hands in the air and sternly asked, "Why, 'cause you cry? Or because you drink? Or because you go to a therapist? Do I have to behave a certain way to prove that I care? Who are *you* to tell me how *I* feel?" I turned away from her, ran up the stairs, and then snidely remarked, "If you had it your way... you'd rather leave! So, who is the one who really cares? Huh?"

I felt proud of myself for finally getting that out in the open. Mom, however, darted after me. "What the hell is that supposed to mean? You know, you come up with the meanest things to say to me. You really do!"

I stopped before entering my room. This was just the chance I needed to finally confront her. "I heard you. I heard you on the phone that night." Mom's face revealed both confusion and curiosity. I wasn't sure if she was trying to remember or trying to forget.

After cautious hesitation, she asked, "Shannon, what are you talking about?"

I exhaled a deep breath. "That night... the night I was attacked. I heard you on the phone talking to someone about how much you hated it here and how you wished you were gone and that you didn't care about leaving... and that is why I left. I ran away from you!" I looked down to the floor. It was too difficult to look directly at her. I muttered, "You are the one who doesn't care."

She seemed stunned, yet interested at the same time, but I knew she would deny it. "Shannon?" She shook her head, laughing under her breath at my insidious allegation. "Where do you come up with this stuff?"

I screamed, "Don't deny it! Just for once- fess up! You said it and you meant it!" My voice cracked as my words became softer. "You said it. And you meant it."

I ran in my room. I slammed my door only to have it immediately fly open with mom standing with her hands on her hips in the hallway.

She began waving her right hand at me. "How dare you!" she shouted. "How dare you treat me like this! Why do you make up such wild things? I am your mother! You need to respect me."

At that point, it didn't matter. It didn't matter to her if she said it or not because ultimately she was going to deny it. I stood firmly in the center of my room. I barked, "Well, then, act like it! You want to be my mom- then act like it!" Her face became rigid as she listened from the hall. I began, "Moms don't leave. They don't even think about leaving." Then, I shrugged my shoulders and whispered, "You know? You are here. You're in the house and, like, physically here, but you're not *really* here. Are you?"

Mom went into defensive mode by stating, "Can you blame me?" She pointed to her chest and repeated, "Can you blame me?" She added, "I am sorry that I'm a little, uh, I don't know, out of it. Excuuuuuussssee me!"

She kind of sounded like Steve Martin; I almost cracked a smile.

I looked down to the floor at my make-up bag and flat-iron, wondering how my fun plans could go so wrong within minutes. I sighed. "Mom, you just don't get it. You just don't even understand." I gave up. Otherwise, we would be standing in the same spot for hours defending our own points of view. All the confusion surrounding my brother's death would remain safe inside me because I knew mom could not help me. I also knew that, deep down, her inability to ease my pain was not her fault. She just wasn't there. She left a long time ago.

"Shannon, you are not going out tonight. You will stay home and think about the mean things you said to me." She shook her head and headed for her room.

I calmly stated, "No, I *am* going out tonight and *you* can't stop me."

Mom was not impressed with my strong rebellion. Personally, I was quite impressed by my defiance. She turned around and smugly recited, "No, you are not and that is the name of that tune."

She slammed my door after making her final statement. I stood alone. I was angry. I was hurt. I was going to that damn party. I quickly and quietly prepped myself to go out. As I applied my mascara, I visualized myself running away and never returning home. The thought alone thrilled and excited me. I imagined mom crying hysterically just like she did for Phillip. I slipped in my old jeans, a white t-shirt, and my Bass moccasins. I grabbed my hair and pulled it in a tight ponytail (so much for the flat-iron and new outfit.) Getting out of the house unnoticed would not be easy, but after some minor consideration, I decided jumping off the roof was my only option.

My house had a sunroof that rested just below my window and was only a fifteen foot jump. The only way to ensure my escape was to exit through the bathroom. I dashed to the bathroom. My heart was beating out of my chest, but at that moment, I was not worried about any repercussions. I wanted to run away and I was willing to do it any way possible, even if it required me to jump off my roof.

The plan was simple: jump off the roof, run as fast as possible from the house, and then go to Carl Kindsay's house. Tom mentioned he was stopping by Carl's to play Nintendo before they left for a party in Westville, which was conveniently just down the street from Tiffany. While looking at myself in the mirror, I laughed thinking how ironic it was that Tom called me that afternoon. I convinced myself that it was a universal synchronistic sign telling me to go to the party. Before opening the window to shimmy through, I wrote a message on the mirror to mom in capital letters with my red Clinique lipstick:

MOM,
I HAVE TO GO. I CAN'T STAY HERE!
YOU WILL NEVER SEE ME AGAIN!
SHANNON.

After I wrote the last line, I smiled and hoped that she might believe it. I stepped on the toilet, wiggled out the window, and landed feet first on the icy roof. I crawled to the edge of the roof and scanned the ground for the best spot to jump. I needed a place where the snow would be high enough to cushion my fall, but with all the adrenaline pumping through me it probably would not have mattered where I landed. I jumped and landed on both knees. I heard my jeans rip and after a quick inspection, I saw two dirty holes that exposed my bloodied knees. At that moment, I couldn't feel a thing. I ran as fast as I could to the gate and darted to the streets behind me with the triumph of victory keeping up my pace. I ran past Carl's house and headed down Beech Avenue. Then, somehow, I found myself in front of St. Margaret's Church.

The cold air pierced my lungs which created sharp chest pain with every breath I took. When I made it to the church parking lot, I bent over with my hands resting on my stinging knees to catch my breath. There were several cars in the church parking lot and I could hear faint singing with organ music coming from the congregation. The statue of The Virgin Mary was just steps ahead of me, so I drug my feet, placed my hands in my jean pockets, and moved toward her. She looked so peaceful and untouched, the complete and total opposite of me. I looked deep into her white, marble eyes and whispered, "Why? Why am I here?" I stared in her eyes, praying that a profound miracle would occur and she would answer me. Surely, she, of all people, must understand pain. Maybe she could understand my pain. Then, as I bent over again, I could hear the choir singing, "Ahhhh, ahhhh, ahhhhmen."

I took a step closer to her, merely inches away from her serene face. I touched her cheek with my frozen fingers and began to cry.

When the tears began to streak down my face, I landed hard on my knees and began sobbing with my shaking hands covering my face. I had no control over the tears rolling down, and, for once, I did not try to stop them from falling. I allowed them to trickle down my face, down my chin, and onto the hard asphalt. There were no words coming out of my mouth, just muffled cries. As the warm tears rolled down my cheeks, I was surprised to realize that I actually liked the sensation.

I remained on my aching knees that scraped the icy gravel, cupping my face in my hands. My tears were a mixture of sadness, anger, and an overdo confession. I confessed my deepest fears to the marble statue, glad that I had a chance to say horrible words, even if it was to an inanimate thing. I spoke about my doubts about Jesus and about God. I cried because I could not help my brother. I was angry with Phillip, yet, I felt a tremendous amount of sorrow at the same time. I wondered if I was a good person or just an evil bitch.

My mom would leave me if she could, my brother hated his life so much that he shot himself in the head, and I just jumped out my bathroom window to run away. I was supposed to be a winner. I was supposed to be strong. I was supposed to be the golden child: the one who made my parents proud, the one who listened to teachers and coaches, the one who smiled happily while playfully chewing bubble gum in the hallway. So… why? Why did I feel like my entire life was a lie? I felt like I was living the life of someone else. Who am I? I wiped the snot away from my nose with my sleeve, tightened up every muscle in my body, picked up a large rock, and threw it in the distance.

I looked up to The Virgin Mary and asked, "Why am I so angry?" I toyed with the idea that she would somehow answer me. "Why am I angry?" I bent my head down and muttered, "I should be sad, but I'm mad!" Then, I raised my head to Mary and softly asked, "Does God even love me?" After wiping away some old tears, I wished, just as my brother wished two years ago, that I was a bird, so I could fly far away.

I rose from the kneeling position realizing that I had to run to Carl's house, so I could catch a ride with Tom before he left. After wiping my cold tears, I looked up to The Virgin Mary one last time. Her stillness momentarily soothed me. I cupped my hands over my face and told myself to think about mom later, to think about Phillip later, and think about me… later. During that moment, I understood that getting a ride was more important than self-pity. I slowly jogged toward Carl's house while devising a phony reason for asking Tom for a ride.

When I slowed down to catch my breath, I looked to my left to a house with a large bay window and stared. I watched as a family gathered around a table, eating, drinking, smiling, and enjoying the New Year festivities. The bay window revealed what I had been longing for and, after watching the family inside, my chin gave out and I began sobbing again. *Why couldn't we be like that? Why was it so hard to be normal?* My body stiffened, I bit my upper lip, sighed, and forced myself to move on. After every other step, I would turn back to gaze at the bay window. Everything that I had hoped for, everything that I was not, we were not, was shining in that bay window. I could almost touch it, yet, it was so far away.

The bitter Jersey winter night was unrelenting and I did my best to stay warm with just a sweatshirt. As I approached Carl's house, the reality of going in after Tom suddenly terrified me. My legs turned to jelly and my eyelashes were frozen from the watery tears that met the bitter air. His house illuminated the dark night with tiny, sparkling, fake candles framing each window. His lawn reminded me of an amusement park. There was a large, plastic Santa Claus along with plastic, glowing reindeer, and a cheerful snowman standing next to ten oversized candles glowing in a row that paved the way to his door. Although it appeared inviting, I reminded myself that Carl was no friend of mine or Phillip's. I shook my head, laughing at the situation.

Every step closer to his door became more difficult until I found myself robotically knocking at his front door. The outside light seemed like the wake up call that I needed to put on my best act. A friendly, almost cherubic-looking, older woman answered the door.

I knew her. She worked at the Heights police department. With her half apron and oversized glasses, she warmly said, "Well... hello." It sounded more like a question than a welcome.

I managed to warmly reply, "Hi."

With her eyes scanning mine, I could tell she knew that I had been crying and it bothered me. She smiled, extended her hands to open the door, and asked if I wanted to see Carl.

I quickly responded, "No." Without letting her catch her breath, I asked, "Is Tom here?"

As if she just remembered, she put up one finger and cheerfully mentioned, "Oh, yes. Tom is here."

I stepped back, indicating that I had no intention of going inside the house, but she insisted that I get in from the cold.

I reluctantly stepped inside. When I entered, I felt safe. The fireplace was glowing and I could smell the delicious aroma of freshly baked chocolate chip cookies. Everything I smelled, everything my eyes were drawn to were all painful reminders of what I did not have and it made me want to cry all over again. I didn't even know Carl and I already envied his life.

Carl's mom called out from the hallway, "Tom? Tom. You have a pretty, young lady here to see you." She smiled while admiring me and probably thought that I was Tom's girlfriend.

Funny, I didn't feel "pretty," but I liked hearing it. Girls like me do not feel pretty even if we were. We just feel crazy most of the time. Pretty girls do not jump out of windows, cry in front of churches, or fight with their mothers, and they certainly do not knock on a stranger's door for a ride.

With an intense game of Sega on the line, Carl yelled for me to come back there. Carl's mom led me down the hallway and left me standing in his doorway, which I refused to enter. She placed her hand on my shoulder and asked, "Hon, do you want some cookies? Just made 'em." I smiled politely and wasn't quite sure to laugh or cry. Just moments ago, I was asking The Virgin Mary if there was a God.

"No thanks. I just ate," I lied. She half smiled, knowing my reason for refusing her cookies had nothing to do with my appetite.

Tom pressed pause on his Sega game, looked toward me and seemed pleased when he saw me standing there. He asked, "Shan! What are you doing here?"

I avoided any eye contact with Carl but managed to look at Tom for only a second. Sensing that something was wrong, Tom looked at me like a wounded puppy and sympathetically asked, "Shan, you okay? You wanna go?"

I nodded my head, never looking up because I could feel my chin quivering *again*.

"Hey…" Tom began, "What's the matter, Shan?" He dipped his head trying to make eye contact. I could feel four eyes on me, as if I was some kind of lost soul just waiting for salvation. Tom should have known that I wanted to leave, so I darted a look back to him revealing my impatience.

"Oh!" Tom chuckled, "It's gonna be like that, huh? Okay. Alright. Don't tell me. I understand." He was obviously trying to make the situation lighter, but I refused to give in. I shook my head again, flashed another dirty look, and continued to act like a bratty four year old.

Carl felt it necessary to make small talk. "Aren't you a freshman?" he inquired.

I placed my hands on my hip, shot him a cocky look, and blurted out, "Yeah." I was the epitome of fourteen-year-old immaturity and I liked it. Carl didn't even deserve a nod from me, let alone a verbal response. I stood silently in his doorway picking at the skin around my fingernails.

Tom finally realized that it was hopeless. He grinned and then asked, "Shan, you wanna go to Tiffany's, don't ya?"

"Yup," I muttered as I stared at my new Bass shoes that were totally soaked.

Tom quietly got up and told Carl that he would see him at the party. As he grabbed his jacket, I bolted from the entrance of the room and headed to his car. While shivering in the cold, I balanced my back on Tom's car as I looked up at the sky. The stars were bright and the moon hung over me, reminding me of that night with the *popcorn man*. I scoffed at the thought that the moon lit night must be God's way of mocking me. I heard Carl's voice along with Tom's, and rolled my eyes with the thought that Carl just wanted to see the freshmen freak show.

I stood by the passenger's seat as I blew hot air into my hands and waited for Tom to open my door.

Tom playfully laughed and said, "Come on, little girl, let's get you out of here." Then he shook Carl's hand and headed toward the driver's seat. Carl stood on his front stoop waiting for us to drive away. Carl waved to me as I went by him. I looked down and tried to act like I never saw him.

For the second time since I crawled out of my window, I felt safe.

"Do you want to talk about it?"

I snapped back, "About what?"

"Duh? You show up all upset at Carl's house. Obviously, something happened." He sarcastically replied as he turned up the heat. He continued, "I think you would feel better if you just, I don't know, talked about it."

I reached for the radio and ignored his offer. I smugly replied, "No. There's nothing to talk about."

Tom shrugged his shoulders and allowed me the chance to talk on my own terms. Instead, I listened to the radio. Roxette began singing *Listen to Your Heart* and I found myself watching the moon, completely lost in the silky words.

What was my heart telling me? If only my life was that simple. If only life could be explained in a song. I sneered at the ignorance of stupid love songs. Love songs made life seem magical and wonderful and hopeful. I wanted to hear a song about a stupid blonde girl who escaped out the window, cried to herself in the bitter night, confessed her sins to a statue, and begged for a ride at a stranger's house. How would that ballad play out? It seemed all songs had long forgotten the angst of being fourteen.

When we arrived at Tiffany's house, Tom turned off the ignition but allowed his radio to play. I could feel his eyes.

During that still moment, I wanted to blurt out everything. I wanted to scream. However, I was aware that there was nothing he could say to make me feel better, so, why bother?

He finally asked, "You okay? Tell me, Shan."

"It's okay. I am fine. I am fine now. I just… needed to get away. So, yeah, I am cool. I guess, like, I just needed to get away."

"From what?" he asked.

I shook my head. What did I want to get away from? Everything that bothered me was in my head, so I how could I get away from me? I tried to ease out of the conversation by saying, "I just needed to get away. I don't know how to explain it. Just out."

"Okay. Okay. It's just that I know, you, uhh… I mean…" He hesitated.

"What?" I insisted.

"Well," he raised his voice a bit, trying to convince me that he was just helping. "I am guessing that it's been kind of, like, hard for you." I looked over to him and saw his sympathetic grin.

My stomach felt weird after he said that. Why did he say that? I tried so hard to hold onto the lie that my life was fine. Tom was exposing me. I didn't like it.

"Look, Shan. If you *ever* want to talk about it…"

I interrupted. "About what?" I asked sharply.

"Your brother. I am sorry. I can't remember his name." I was completely vulnerable and, once again, my damn chin began to quiver. I hadn't said his name in so long.

"Phillip?" I replied. It was shocking how uncomfortable I was with saying his name. "I can't. I don't even know where to start." I managed to look at Tom with sincerity and softly admitted, "I can't. It's too complicated."

He pressed, "Shannon, it's okay. You can talk to me. I'm a good listener." He put his right hand up to the sky as if he was swearing to both God and me that he was a good listener. He promised. "I will not tell a soul and I will not give you any unwanted advice. I promise." He smiled. His smile was genuine and I did appreciate it.

I was grateful and perhaps, under different circumstances, I would have taken up his offer.

I shrugged my shoulders and wished that our conversation was different. "Thanks. That's really cool of you- for real. Maybe some other time." I grabbed the door handle and said goodbye. Tom called to me from his window and reminded me that he was only one block away if I needed him. I waved and knew that in less than two hours he would be totally shit-faced.

That night, for the first time in my life, *I* got totally shit-faced. I entered Tiffany's house with a mission. For one night of my life, I wanted to forget who I was. I knew if I drank a lot of liquor, I could accomplish my goal. Tiffany cheerfully answered the door and hugged me with delight. I playfully asked, "Where's the hard stuff?" Her face lit up as she offered me her parents' finest alcohol.

Of course, being a novice drinker, I sampled everything and nearly gagged while sniffing the pungent smells. Everyone seemed to encourage my drinking. Their interest in alcohol was quite different from mine. My goal was to forget and I was on my way to total amnesia. Tiffany showed me the dark bottles with silver labels and took out each one to sample. I chugged Peach Schnapps, whisky, bourbon, and gin straight from the bottle. It was quite possibly the most repulsive liquid I had ever consumed, but the result would outweigh the awful taste.

The effects of sampling several types of liquor did not take long to set in. My mouth was tingly with a hint of what tasted like cold medicine, and my head began to get dizzy. Everyone I looked at was blurry and seemed to be talking without words coming out. Within an hour of drinking, my head was spinning and I became someone else. I became overly friendly, hugging and squeezing anyone who would allow it. Everyone laughed at my stupid jokes. I had an incredible feeling that I was totally loved and was totally invincible. I *was* someone else. Mission accomplished.

While in my drunken stupor, I forgot all about the night. It was as if my life before gin never existed. My friends flocked to me, daring me to say stupid things, to sing or dance or whatever. I voluntarily pleased everyone, including myself. While rapping along with Biz Markie in *Just a Friend*, I could see Tiffany run toward me in the living room. She looked panicked and I began cracking up when I saw her worried face. I hysterically laughed when she warned me that it was my mother on the line. With the phone in my hand, I began cracking up.

Tiffany tried to hide the phone, so she could shield my blatant laughter from my mother. Tiffany cried, "Shannon! Shannon!" She tapped me on the shoulder and sarcastically barked, "Hey dip-shit! It's your mom!" Tiffany led me upstairs as I happily continued to yell lyrics.

I held the phone tightly and swayed from side to side, using the wall to help me stand. Tiffany grabbed me and threw me on her bed. She sat next to me, propping the phone in my ear to coach me along. My head was pounding and all I could do was respond with one-word answers.

I gulped and slowly closed my eyes. All I could manage to say was hello.

"Shannon?" mom's voice cracked. "Is that you? Shannon? What the hell? How could you do that?"

"Yeah," I was responding to her calling my name. Tiffany's head was close to mine as she tried to feed me the right words.

My eyes were shut and my head was thumping. "Shannon, how could you do that?"

Holding my breath and trying not to laugh, my words came out slow and lethargic. I replied, "Mom. Whatever. I just…"

She interrupted, "Don't whatever me. Don't. You have no idea how worried I was."

"Oh, oooooooooopppppppsss!" I giggled.

Tiffany nudged my side and silently worded, "Say you are sorry."

"Huh?" I heard mom whisper.

I closed my eyes, twirled my ponytail, and then repeated anything Tiffany whispered in my ear. "Mom, you're sorry."

Tiffany nudged my side. "I mean, I'm sorry." I had to place my hand over my mouth to stop laughing.

Mom exhaled and cynically asked, "You are, are ya?"

"No. Not really." I began cracking up. Tiffany nudged me again.

Mom asked, "What the hell is wrong with you?"

I fell back on the bed and scoffed. I muttered, "God! I am just kidding, relax. Oh my God! I said I was sorry." Tiffany put her hand over my mouth to shut me up.

Mom imitated my last remark. "No, not really, huh?"

"No," I said with an exaggerated sigh.

Mom was rambling on and on about being irresponsible, selfish, or stupid while I held the phone up in the air and mocked her by using my other hand to mimic her talking.

Mom yelled, "Shannon? Shannon? Hello? Are you even there?"

Tiffany quickly placed the phone next to my ear. I retorted, "I'm fine!" I looked to Tiffany and imitated a man making muscles while nodding my head rapidly.

Mom wanted answers. I wanted to get off the phone. "Why did you do that?" she asked.

"Why?" I repeated. "Oh my God, Mom! Seriously, I can't do this right now!" The room was spinning and what mom did not know was that- I *really* could not answer her questions.

She muttered, "Fine!"

"Alright!" I shot back.

"Okay," Mom whispered. She said goodbye, but I hung up the phone before saying a word.

Afterward, I flung the phone on the bed and belted out, *"You. You got what I need. Oh baby you!"*

Tiffany shook her head, laughed, and then called me an idiot.

The next morning after throwing up macaroni and cheese four times, I experienced my first hangover. I told Lizzie and Tiffany that it was like riding The Gravitron fourteen times in a row after eating chili hot dogs and milk. They made gagging noises with the thought. The room didn't just spin in one direction; it spun sideways, backwards, and forward. My body was extraordinarily weak and I struggled with the littlest movements that left me exhausted. I was thirsty, weak, tired, and I looked like shit. Mission accomplished; I never wanted to feel like that again.

auld lang syne

Pain. The pulsating, rhythmic beating that pounded the inside of my skull was in one word- *intense*. The constant drumming made it impossible to concentrate or focus. I woke up with the harsh rays of the sun striking my pupils and Tiffany's hair dryer on full blast. The contrast between day and night in New Jersey was incomprehensible.

With my right arm covering my face, I whined, "Tiff! Turn it off!" I lethargically reached for a pillow to drown out the sound, or better yet, last night.

Physically getting myself out of bed was more work than I had anticipated. It took effort just to sit up and watch my surroundings. After checking myself out in the mirror, I remarked, "I know that I didn't look like this last night." Both Tiffany and Lizzie belted out thunderous chuckles when they agreed that I looked even worse. I checked my reflection again. I shook my head with disgust. Inside, I thought about what a loser I was. How could I become that stupid, drunk girl?

During the ride home, I gazed out the backseat window, sinking lower with every mile closer to my house. The tiny south Jersey houses that crowded Route 45 appeared inviting with their Christmas decorations still lit from the festivities of the night before. Soon, they would all be gone. The missing decorations would ultimately lead to the doom and gloom of February.

I caught glimpses of Lizzie and her mom talking about the food from the party Lizzie's mom and dad had attended. All I could remember hearing was lobster and tuna "tar-tar." Tuna tartare sounded like a name that I might be reprimanded for saying out loud. They could enjoy a trivial conversation like that, while I dreaded my complicated conversation with mom. The repercussions for last night were waiting for me when I walked in my front door. Oh, how I wished that we could just discuss lobster. I questioned my sanity: was last night real or just some dream? Did I really jump off the roof? Was it really me in front of The Virgin Mary? I shook my head and wondered how on earth I ended up in Carl Kindsay's bedroom. Most of all, I questioned the purpose of life. What am I doing here? Why is it all so hard? I sighed just before we turned down Linden Avenue, and then I began to pray:

Dear God, my pastor said that you have a plan for all of us… that you never leave us… is that true? I have to tell you that I don't really like this plan; actually, it kind of sucks. Sorry. I know I am not supposed to say bad things to you, but I hate this life, right now. Can you make it different? Please? Pretty please? Love, Shannon Bennet.

When I opened the front door, both dogs barked which made my headache intensify. The house was empty. There was no sign that either mom or dad were home. With my lips sticking together and my insatiable need to hydrate, I drank three full glasses of water. Tiffany advised me to take Tylenol for the headache, but I didn't know how to swallow pills. Funny, I could do shots of Jagermeister, but I couldn't swallow a tiny pill. My room looked the same, the bathroom mirror was clean, and the window was back to its original state. I put on my sweatpants and slunk deep in my bed with the lights out and shades drawn.

The silence combined with the darkness of my room made it simple to fall asleep. I had a dream that started with my mom coming home to a brand new house. She purchased a very large and expensive Victorian style home that was meticulously furnished with modern furniture and sleek design. She was so excited about her new home, taking pride in her selection and showing me all the modern amenities. She made a point of showing me all the decorations that hung from the walls and an old, oversized, wooden rocking chair that took up a large portion of the living room. I asked her if she had an inspection before she bought it. She admitted that the man who sold her the house guaranteed her that the house was in impeccable condition and there was no need to worry. With disbelief and shock from her foolishness, I began to scold her and repeatedly warned her about the dangers of not getting a home inspected. Mom's demeanor quickly changed. She became defensive and quite hurt that I did not trust her judgment. She abruptly asked me to leave. Then, dad entered the new house and shared my sentiment as he began pressing her for the details surrounding the inspection. She blushed, admitting again that there was no inspection. Both dad and I began to chastise and belittle her. Mom became frustrated and started yelling at us. Then, I noticed a crack in the floor. I lifted up an area rug, pointed to the crack, and continued to demean my mother. Mom inspected the crack and began weeping as she followed the crack line through the house. Disappointed, she fled the house in tears. Dad and I stood in the room, wondering what to do. We never ran after her.

I woke up at that moment and tried to go back to sleep to find out if we ever ran after her. I woke up feeling terrible for not being more sensitive. Uggghhh, just what I needed- more guilt. I told myself that I should have been nicer, should have been more sympathetic, and I should have run after her. Going back to the dream was impossible. My head was feeling better, but the dehydration from lack of water made me nauseous. Dragging myself out of bed, I went downstairs for three more glasses of water.

While chugging my cold water, I noticed that it was dark outside. The day was nearly over as the clock read 6:30 p.m. It was only twenty-four hours ago that I made my escape and probably just as long since I last ate. Starving, I reheated leftover wonton soup, drinking the broth and nibbling the wontons. I flipped through the channels and settled on *America's Funniest Home Videos*. I belted out a couple of laughs but became quiet when I heard the sound of mom's car door.

Mom arrived with several shopping bags and her "know-it-all" friend, Gina. Seeing Gina walk through the front door was worse than seeing my mother. I braced myself for her unwanted advice. I despised her attempts at making me a better daughter, or listening to her and mom gossip about my latest disappointments. I vowed that when I had kids, I would never complain about them to my friends, especially when they could obviously hear it. I was shocked when they both greeted me warmly, even asking me what I was watching.

After they settled in the kitchen and fixed a pot of coffee, mom called into the living room. "Shan? You want pizza? We're going to Pizza City. You want some?"

Huh? I wasn't expecting her to ask me that or even be civil. Pizza sounded fantastic. "Yeah, pepperoni." I tried to sound normal, but I was thrown off by her calmness regarding last night.

After sipping coffee and complaining about some lady in Caldor, they left together to pick up the pizza. Feeling kind of tired, I went upstairs to take another nap. Before settling back in my warm bed, I washed my face in the bathroom. My reflection revealed hollowed cheeks, white pasty skin, and pale blue eyes. I looked different, somehow. My face showed a girl who looked frail and weak. This was not the reflection that I was used to. I didn't like it. The confident winner was replaced with a worthless loser.

The smell of pizza swirled around my room, inviting me downstairs to taste the gooey cheese and salty pepperoni. Gina teased me about sleeping all day commenting, "Must be nice to go to parties all night and sleep all day." I ignored her statement, inside telling her to, "Suck it!" All I needed was another person reminding me that I was a rotten, stupid girl.

The Color Purple was on channel two. I perked up as Nettie and Celie clapped hands and happily sung. I hated to admit it because most of my friends would laugh at me, but *The Color Purple* was my all time favorite movie. It was the only movie that made me cry, and I was somewhat embarrassed over that fact. I happily ate my pizza, watching Nettie and Celie clap hands.

After Nettie and Celie reunited, I got an insatiable desire to write down my dream in my notebook. I took out my notebook, began writing down the dream, and then started to write random things down. I wrote: *New Years 1989, window, run, field hockey, fall, leaves, orange, ugly hair, ponytail, girl, Celie, sister, dead brother.* I decided to try it again. I wrote: *Pizza, Ocean City, body surf, dead brother.* I gave it another try. I wrote: *Lizzie, best friend, kindergarten, Pledge of Allegiance, America, New Jersey, Garden State, tomato, red, blood, dead brother.*

I gave up in defeat and decided that it was a good time to look at his old pictures.

Phillips' pictures were stored in my desk, like ancient archives, only to be taken out during special occasions. With my word association doodles and last night's break-down, I decided that the occasion was special enough. I made up my own unique ritual by placing all his pictures face down on the carpet. I picked one picture randomly, looked it over, and then placed it facing down again. A full year had passed since I stashed them away and viewing them gave me the feeling that I was looking at a ghost.

The pictures reflected proud smiles as Phillip held up freshly caught fish. He hugged me from behind as we sat in front of our Christmas tree on Christmas morning. He held a wooden bat and wore a green baseball uniform, smiling with his left front tooth missing. I only allowed myself to look at one picture at a time, so I could absorb everything. My favorite picture was of the two of us standing in the living room with our arms around each other. He wore a striped blue and red shirt, and I wore a red shirt with a jean jumper. We both had platinum blonde hair that flashed little curls with streaks of natural highlights. We smiled and gave the peace sign with our tiny fingers. The picture mesmerized me. Instead of feeling sad or sorrowful, I was happy. I was happy because I knew, in that moment, we both were happy together.

On the radio, I heard *Look Away* by *Chicago* and placed the picture down. It took a lot out of me to look at his pictures because they usually reminded about his death, instead of his life. His death was so violent, so calculated. I couldn't understand how a person could take a gun and shoot themself, to actually put it to their head and pull the trigger. Realistically, I knew that Phillip was responsible for his own death and no matter what we did... he would have found a way to end his life. However, there was a huge part of me that blamed everyone and everything except Phillip. He was the victim, right? I wasn't sure. Most of the time, I felt like the victim of his death, of his decision. With the pictures scattered in front of me, I thought about the kids who bullied him because of his weight. I replayed all the bizarre conversations we had, including him selling his soul and the time he admitted to me that he wished he were dead. I replayed the memory of third grade when he cut his arms. I thought about the isolation, the drugs, and the mental hospital. It just seemed like the signs were there. I blamed myself for not being smarter or telling anyone about his odd behavior. I blamed the teachers for misunderstanding him. I blamed everyone, especially myself, but I knew that he pulled the trigger. I also he knew that there was nothing I could have done to stop him. Intellectually, I understood the situation. Emotionally, I was drowning in a dark cloud of confusion.

While reviewing all his pictures, I toyed with the notion that his life was meaningless. I didn't understand why he was on this earth. It bothered me that most people simply forgot him. His friends no longer asked about him or mentioned past experiences, and his death was only a year ago. By the time I graduated, nobody would remember him, including me. Behind all the anger and resentment, I still had an overwhelming sense of loyalty. My loyalty to him was hidden deep inside. Phillip's death raised too many questions, stirred up emotions, and left me wanting answers. So, in many ways, he *was* still alive.

School began one day after my first hangover. Walking with Lizzie through the back doors to enter high school was like reliving New Year's night all over again, except, I had to pretend that it was somehow funny. We shielded our eyes from the bitter morning winds that persistently reminded us that it was January. When our red, blotchy faces met the dry indoor heat, both of our cheeks glowed and pulsated from the fifteen-minute walk outside. I was quite sure the news spread about Thomas and I breaking up and, of course, my crazy, drunken night at Tiffany's house. I wasn't proud of myself. I hated that I was that girl who got totally trashed and ended up hugging the porcelain god. Nobody wanted the label of being that stupid freshman weekend chick that gets piss drunk at parties. I didn't want to be that girl, but as I took my first steps into school, I had the distinct honor of holding that worthless title.

Tom approached me from behind while Tiffany and I waited like zombies in the lunch line. He placed his big bear paw hands over my eyes and asked, "Can I cut in?"

I knew it was Tom. I also knew that I had to act cool. I had to act like New Year's night never existed. He cut the line without my consent.

"Soooooo," Tom said in a drawn out, overdramatic voice. "I heard someone had a little too much fun. I mean, a little too much al-kee-hawl the other night. Hmmm? Who could that be?" He laughed and leaned over to whisper in my ear, "Did you have a good time?"

I rolled my eyes, and then stated, "'Good' is not the word I would use."

"Next time," he warned, "just talk about it. Don't try to drink it away." Tom winked at me, grinned, and waited for my clever response.

I playfully agreed, "Talking- good. Drinking- bad. Got it." I pointed to him and sternly lectured, "And that is one to grow on."

"You'll learn, Bennet. Stick with me. I am older and wiser than your freshmen buddies." Tiffany punched him on the shoulder, showing her discontent for his last remark.

Tiffany and I sat down with our French fries and frozen yogurt on a large, red, plastic tray. She dipped her fries in our communal pool of ketchup and asked, "So, how much trouble did ya get in? How long are you on house arrest?"

"No punishment," I admitted.

Tiffany challenged my last statement. "What? Are you bull-shitting me? You are such a liar!"

"Well, there is a catch, but I was supposed to do it anyway." I licked a spoon full of frozen yogurt, gulped, and leaned in close to her body. "You have to promise not to tell anyone. I only told Lizzie. You cannot tell anyone. If you tell anyone about this, then I will look like a total freak. Got it? Not a single soul. Okay?" Tiffany nodded with full confidentiality.

I took a deep breath and confessed: "I have to go to therapy with my mom this week."

She pulled away from me. I wasn't sure if she was shocked or amused. She replied, "That's it?" She gobbled down three more fries. Tiffany continued, "Just go in and talk to some old dude for like an hour. Man, you got off easy." She smirked, shook her head, and sarcastically repeated, "Man, you so got off so easy." Then she began to imitate a therapist by using a dignified, manly voice. She mumbled, "So, tell me about your childhood? Oh, by the looks of it, um, you are a child. Okay, well ummm, how do you feel about that?" Tiffany imitated the therapist by pressing fake glasses against her nose, "Further, how do you feel about the way you feel?"

Tiffany and I laughed at our new inside joke. We talked to one another as if we were both therapists having some deep theological, yet, useless debate. However, the fun came to an abrupt end when Sammy Torres rudely interrupted us. Sammy sat down at our lunch table (uninvited.)

Sammy wanted all the details about the New Year bash. Mostly, Sammy wanted to know about Carl Kindsay. She pressed me for any pertinent information regarding him, his room, his pictures on the wall, or anything. She annoyed me. I figured it might be the perfect time to totally humiliate her. I leaned over to whisper in her ear and acted as if I was going to share some dirty gossip. Instead, I shouted so everyone within an earshot could hear me. I yelled, "What! What! You're in love with Carl Kindsay?" Then, I looked over at Tiffany and loudly stated, "Hey! Hey! Tiff, Sammy wants to make out with Carl Kindsay!"

The kids sitting next to our lunch table stopped talking to each other and stared at us. I smiled coyly trying to act like I was just making a mere observation. Sammy was not amused.

First, the girls at my lunch table gasped. Then, they asked, "How could you do that?" After watching Sammy stomp away from our table, my friends and I began cracking up hysterically.

Tiffany slapped me five and then she added, "Ugghh, she is such a bitch. She totally deserved that."

The truth was simple. She did deserve it. She deserved it because she was so giddy about a stupid boy who used girls like trash and dumped them after just forty-eight hours. She deserved it because she cheapened herself by liking someone with no morals.

As I got up from my seat, I looked over to the football table and saw Carl flirting with Carolyn Romito. Carolyn had big boobs that swayed from side to side when she walked in the hallway. She often wore low cut shirts to flaunt her butt crack cleavage. She was also notorious for going out with guys who were over 22 years old. (Eww!) She was definitely a stupid girl, although I never once had a conversation with her, it was implied. I could sense her "stupidness" as she gushed at Carl's attention, finding any excuse to touch him. I shook my head, looked down at my flat chest, and vowed that I would never act like Carolyn Romito.

The snow covering the ground that once looked so pristine disappeared into black slush lining the streets. Weeks passed since I last saw the grass, and almost two months had gone by since I last saw green grass. The dry air from constantly running the heaters made me long for the humid days of summer. At night, I opened my window and sat on my dresser to escape the stuffy air, and face my hidden secrets that only the light of the moon could reveal. The moon served as my dearest confidant, my cherished friend, the universal reminder that, at one time, Phillip saw that same light.

The full moon always captivated me. Often, when we were small, Phillip and I would stare at the round orb and ponder who or what was up there. He told me the moon was really just one big chunk of cheese, and I believed him. I always believed him. The luminous glow revealed the dark night in a way that no amount of manmade light could. The earth appeared different, sounds were magnified, dreams were achievable, memories fonder, and my thoughts were clearer. Although, scientifically, I knew little about the moon, I felt its power from hundreds of miles away. The infinite space immersed with tiny blips of light almost gave me unwritten permission to tell my secrets. The sky and all its wonders reminded me that I was never alone.

As I sat on my dresser, window opened, and legs crossed, I listened to The Beatles sing *Across the Universe*. I could feel the presence of my brother.

I replayed snapshots of Phillip and me running wild in the rain. It was late August. We were soaked. We were laughing. We were jumping rope.

I could almost hear Phillip laughing. I remembered him dancing on stage when he was in second grade. He was Smokey the Bear. He happily pranced around the stage as the entire school laughed with amusement. I was proud. That was *my* brother on stage. I remembered that for a very brief time on this small earth, we did love one another.

Unfortunately, my fond memories and love for him often transitioned to that night. The night he decided to end his life. Why did his death overshadow his life? Why was it so hard to accept that he was gone? Death scared me. I suppose it scared me because of the morbid way people react to death. I mean, I was not a smart girl, but I understood that death was inevitable. His death, however, was intentional. I suppose, part of me worried that I would never see him again, not here or in the afterlife. Perhaps that thought alone was much scarier than actually dying.

my beautiful distraction

I turned fifteen three days before St. Patrick's Day. To celebrate my birthday and St. Patrick's Day, mom, dad, and I piled in the car for a trip to Maryland for green crabs. (Artificially dyed- technically blue claw crabs.) Mom and dad sat in the front seat, occasionally talking, pointing at signs, but for the most part, they sat in a peaceful silence. I immediately placed my headphones on my ears and drowned myself in my new music.

Mom never made me come with her to therapy. I suppose she needed all the "alone" time possible. When she told me that I didn't have to go, I pretended to act relieved, but secretly, I was disappointed. On the way to Maryland, I sat by myself in the backseat; the backseat my brother and I shared for many years. Fourteen months have passed and it seemed like I have been sitting back here alone forever. I grabbed my headphones and listened to Kate Bush sing *This Woman's Work.* Lizzie told me that all the music I listened to was depressing. After reviewing all my new music, I suppose she was right. Somehow, depressing music made me feel better. There was someone out there, somewhere, singing sad lyrics just for me. I listened to Janet Jackson sing *Lonely* until the highway signs on Interstate 295 became foreign. The last time I went to my favorite Chesapeake Bay spot, things were different. We arrived by boat. It was summertime. I was twelve and my brother was alive.

March, known for "coming in like a lion and going out like a lamb" looked more like a spring monsoon. The sight of my favorite summer place looked cold and uninviting. The northern Atlantic atmosphere differed so greatly from season to season. It seemed my moods and fond memories shifted along with the changing weather. In August, I could smell boiling shrimp, seasoned perfectly with Old Bay and lemons, before we even docked the boat. In March, all I could smell was damp grass and wet clothing. My memories of the great Chesapeake Bay included sunny days, drinking Cokes, and the salt water splashing my face on our boat rides. My brother and I ate crabs off the bow of the boat as we dipped our feet in the cool water and chugged root beer. I wanted desperately to recapture the times we shared at the Pub, but everything looked so unfamiliar. I couldn't find Phillip anywhere.

The suspension bridge that stood close to the pub looked different, too. The cars that once looked synchronized were passing each other chaotically, rushing and jockeying for road space, speeding to their destination. I watched the winter-worn cars whistle by and thought about how irrelevant time was at that particular moment. In the summer, the disappearing sun competed with the moon for just a little more time; time to shine brightly on my face. It was brilliant. I used to sway back and forth with the waves on dad's boat while soaking in the sky. While taking in the scenery, I would sing loudly, never caring what I sounded like because nobody could hear me through the hum of the motor and the waves crashing. I told myself to remember that sky forever. After turning away from the bridge and to the distant choppy water, I knew why that landscape was etched in my memory.

Because it was St. Patrick's Day, I expected to enter a pub filled with loud mouth frat boys chugging green beer, giddy with a reason to celebrate their red-haired heritage. Surprisingly, there were only a few people in the place, most of which were older couples casually sipping their wine glasses filled with White Zinfandel. We sat at a small, round table that overlooked the bay and my once beloved suspension bridge. We ordered boiled crabs with Old Bay, three cokes, French fries, corn on the cobb, and several wet napkins. The waitress placed black and white newspaper on the table, threw the crabs on top, and then walked away with a smile.

The three of us devoured our crabs, picking them over with tiny instruments; we congratulated each other when large pieces of sweet crabmeat were extracted. The three of us sipped our Cokes and dipped our crabmeat in melted butter. We sat at the table for quite some time, dissecting our dinner, laughing and enjoying each other. It was nice. It gave us hope. Maybe we could make happy memories without him. The atmosphere was a little different, the company was a little smaller, but I had hope that things were looking up.

In the northeast, softball season began with cold, cloudy skies and ended with humid afternoons that made you sweat simply by standing in the sun. The weather changed everyone. The arrival of short skirts and tank tops brought on the hormonal hollers of awestruck boys. Teachers gave less homework, my friends and I stayed out later, and windows that were shut for nearly seven months were finally open with the arrival of spring. It was all so natural. As the flowers bloomed, and the trees sprouted- I had hope.

I attributed my new zeal for life with the changing atmosphere.

Instead of hearing thunderous salt trucks pass by, I could hear crickets singing their praises of the night. Gusting winds and skinny branches hitting our roof were replaced with gentle breezes of spring caressing the emerald leaves. The fragrant spring night signified my freedom from winter's hibernation. Everything was going to be better. I had hope.

In the early morning, the sweet smell of pink azaleas lingering by my window made the pain of getting out of bed a little bit easier. (A little bit.) I didn't mind the passing rain showers that appeared out of nowhere during April. In fact, I quite enjoyed the furious storms that flashed cracks of lightning along with roaring claps of thunder. I felt alive. It was like breathing new air; sweet air that promised change, hope, and possibility. Instead of negative thoughts drowning my soul, I began hearing a soft voice, a gentle voice relaying the joys of life. I began a constant dialogue in my head, a running conversation that was kind instead of cruel. I smiled more, laughed more, and felt joy for the first time in a long time. Most days, I liked the girl I saw looking back in the mirror and, occasionally, I loved her.

Although the honeymoon phase of my springtime euphoria was still present, I began to feel it drifting away when spring became more familiar. That friendly reflection in the mirror was nearly gone, my nightmarish dreams of Phillip abruptly returned, and that self-defeating negative voice made its return. Perhaps I was more comfortable being miserable, or maybe I felt guilty for being happy at all.

My phony smiles, fake laughs, and cliché, cheeky expressions gave everyone the impression that I was happy. It was a lie. In fact, the façade that my existence was something like a Norman Rockwell painting was so exhausting. Trying to juggle school, sports, my social life, and doing it all with a smile gave me a small sense of satisfaction. Some people even referred to me as a role model. Every morning, I layered my make-up on my face and with every different shade I brushed on my skin, I hid the truth of how I was really feeling. The weight of trying to appear happy literally drained all my energy. I nearly collapsed after a long day of school, of practice, of running away from what I was feeling inside.

The truth always catches up... eventually. Teachers complimented me. Friends joked around with me. Boys noticed me. Mom and dad were proud of me. People I met seemed to like me, but they didn't really know me- not the real me. Occasionally, I experienced twinges of pride. However, when I was alone watching the moon with no one to deceive, I felt very lonely. I was still that girl kneeling on a cold winter's night in front of The Virgin Mary. Why did I sit by my window at night feeling an overwhelming sense of sadness? The timing was so off. I should have felt this way a year ago.

Like a non-stop roller coaster, my moods shifted from low valleys to high peeks, eventually shooting me downward. One year after his death, my emotions were uncontrollable, and I felt like I was riding without anyone turning the switches. As I looked outside my window and gazed up toward the glowing moon, I wasn't even sure what I was sad about. I didn't really think about Phillip or his death like I used to. I understood that he was dead. It was obvious that death was inevitable. I was also well aware that death was permanent. I could not understand why that was so hard to grasp or why my mind just would not let it go.

There was a ritual involved whenever I looked out my window for solace. I liked to surround myself with music and get completely lost in the moment. I listened to Pink Floyd religiously and hoped *The Dark Side of the Moon* could offer some secret insight. *Breathe in the Air* was my favorite for so many reasons. The shrilling call of insanity set the tone for that song. I loved the melodic guitar that allowed me to contemplate my life for a minute and a half. The lethargic riff of the guitar took my emotions in any direction I desired. Entranced by the sultry words, I bounced my head softly with agreement as I compared the words to my twisted life and really believed that someone understood me.

After absorbing the words, I allowed every thought, every secret thought, to reveal itself. I never answered any questions or skewed my thinking. Pink Floyd served as my own personal shaman. As if I was in some sort of meditative state, I soaked in the suspicious night sounds, smelled the spring air drifting in my screen window, and was somewhere between fantasy and reality, almost dreamlike. Caught in the odd contrast between the light of the moon and darkness of the sky, I was authentic and pure.

My thoughts transitioned from stupid arguments with mom to lunch table banter to future aspirations. Eventually, my thoughts always came around to Phillip. I visualized that night; the night he killed himself and I hated to admit that my thoughts were often self-centered. I wanted to create that night for myself, even if it was traumatic, even if I saw something that I would regret. Sometimes I envisioned his chubby cheeks with little lines of tears trickling down. Other times, I watched him pace back and forth with a gun in his hands, his feet making footprints in the dirt while he paced nervously, contemplating his decision. I felt his pain, instead of my own when I saw him in the woods. Selfishly, I needed to know that at that moment, the seconds before he ended his life, that he loved me.

The last week of May, Shelly and I attended the varsity banquet together. Shelly and I practically clung to one another for mutual support. We were the scrawny freshmen surrounded in an upperclassmen world. Shelly and I had a circle of friends from the softball team, but beyond the familiar faces from the field, we hardly knew anyone. Instead of looking like lost girls in a strange land, we inhaled buttered rolls and told each other inside jokes. We casually whispered vicious things about the cheerleaders who, for some reason, thought that they were athletic. Luckily, we were entertained by the baseball players sitting at the table to the right of us.

The only guy I considered a friend from the baseball team was James Hafferty. James, a junior and self-proclaimed National Park dirt bag, and I became fast friends two summers ago. James' interest in me had everything to do with Shelly. She was the love of his life; every guy's life. James was cool. The reason I dubbed him "cool" was because he had friends within every social group. He was one of the few who could have a meaningful conversation with the punks, druggies, and preps. I don't think James fit any social category and, for that reason alone, I liked him. Once, James told me that I should have been a "dude," and I took that as a compliment.

James was displaying his affections for Shelly by throwing packets of butter at her. Shelly giggled flirtatiously, fueling his desires as she playfully repeated, "Stop it!" It did not take a genius to see through her words; I knew she loved the attention. James began tossing packets on my dinner plate, so I took the opportunity to use one of my worthless skills. I placed the packet on the table and flicked it with my finger, just like the boys did with their triangular footballs in class. To my surprise, and everyone else at the table, I nailed him right between his eyes. The baseball team howled in laughter, demanding that I do it again. I had the distinct honor of helping create his new nickname- Mr. Butterworth.

James took advantage of his close vicinity to his true love by staring and giggling, and I mean girl giggling. If that was not bad enough, Carl Kindsay began taunting and teasing Shelly, too. What a loser! When Carl looked over to our table, Shelly's interest increased. My thoughts began centering on that night; the night I knocked on his door. Shit! Why does everything revolve around Phillip? I peeked over to Carl and wondered if he thought that I was some sort of freak. Whatever. It doesn't matter.

The more James and Carl teased Shelly; the more I thought about that winter night. I could not help wondering if Carl remembered. As the banquet progressed, everyone began yawning and made half-hearted attempts to appear mildly interested. James and Carl intermittently took turns whispering in each other's ear and pointing at Shelly. They reminded me of gossipy middle school girls, but they were high school guys, so they looked like total rejects. Eventually, Shelly placed a napkin by her face, blocking their view and playfully cried, "Stop staring at me!" James and Carl took that as a sign that she wanted more. I did not. The whole scene was just beyond pathetic.

I peeked over Shelly's shoulder and snapped, "What the hell are you guys staring at?!" I pressed my shoulders forward and added, "Take a freakin' picture- it'll last longer." James immediately grabbed his stomach and began hysterically laughing. Then, he put his hands up and waved his white napkin in defeat. Carl also found my outburst humorous. He raised his eyebrow and backed up in his seat, pretending that he was scared. James barely got out the words, "Alright, tough guy. Okay... take it easy."

When the banquet was finally over, I sat by myself at the table waiting for Shelly to finish taking pictures with the varsity field hockey team. I watched people take group pictures, shake hands, and give congratulatory hugs. I didn't mind waiting for her; in fact, I liked watching everyone. I watched and tried to interpret conversations that I could not hear. I was in the midst of making up a story about a guy who played tennis. He was with his dad... probably. He was smart... most likely. He was skinny... naturally. I wondered if he ever hit on a girl or kissed a girl or even had sex with a girl. Ugh... yuck... I don't want to think about that. After that thought passed, I was startled when James sat down next to me.

I teased, "Dork... you scared me. What are you doing, anyway?" I began to smirk and then added, "Shelly is going out with a senior. Sorry."

He chuckled. "Ha-ha, thanks for the update." He paused. "Really? A senior? Who?"

I shook my head and then admitted, "Just kidding! I bet you're ready for triple by-pass, huh?"

He tapped the saltshaker and casually mentioned, "Well, well, Bennet. Actually, it looks like a senior has eyes for you."

I gasped, "Oh God! Not that nose bleeder, Michael Heller! Eeew, he like, wrote me a letter and asked me to check a box... yes or no. How fifth grade!"

James laughed because he knew Michael was a nose bleeder. He said, "Uh, no, not Michael." James looked at me like I was missing something. "Duh? Shug."

"Shug?" I sarcastically repeated.

James threw his hands in the air, "Oh my God... you are so dumb. He was staring at you the whole night. Well?"

He shrugged his shoulders and added, "Umm, yeah, he was staring at you until you told him to take a picture."

I was confused. "Carl?"

He nodded his head with agreement.

James asked, "Can he call you?"

Why me? Why not Shelly? I mean, Shelly was clearly more his type. She was pretty, said the right things, and had plenty of boyfriend experience. I just walked around in jeans, t-shirts, and wore my hair up. The only boyfriend experience I had was with Thomas, and he was more or less a puppy.

I cynically replied, "No!" I scoffed and then rolled my eyes with contempt.

Stunned, James chuckled, and then repeated, "No? Why?" he asked.

I could think of hundreds of reasons why I didn't trust Carl. In my mind, I recalled all the lunch table talk about how he broke up with a girl because she laughed too loud. Tiffany told me that he asked a girl out and then broke up with her twenty-four hours later. My opinion of Carl would forever be tainted by the night I came to his house for a ride. Mostly, I associated him with those horrible memories of Phillip's football team. Furthermore, I wasn't going to sell myself out because I was some little freshmen who got all gushy when a boy asked to call.

I cocked my head and snapped, "Why? Why should I let him call me? So, he can break up with me in a week? I don't think so. Anyway, how come he didn't ask me himself- instead of sending you?"

"Bennet," James cocked his head back. "What do you want me to tell him?"

"Tell him..." I wanted to say something clever. "Tell him... I'm not an idiot."

"Yeah, but, can he call you?" he persisted.

As I got up from the table, I turned back to James and ordered, "He can do whatever he wants- it's a free country." I walked outside, secretly curious to see where that last comment would lead.

When I walked into my house, I glanced at mom, who was lying on the couch, intensely watching Melrose Place. She put her finger over her lips to hush me up when I made noise coming in the house. I never told her about the night or my awards... her reaction would just be disappointing.

The phone rang ten minutes after I walked in the front door. After one ring, I promised that I would not cave and pick it up. After two rings, I reminded myself that Carl probably picked on Phillip. After three rings, I wondered what he wanted. On the fourth ring, I picked up the phone, anxious to find out why he was calling my house.

I picked up the phone, held it in front of me, and quickly exhaled. "Hello?"

"Is Shannon there?" A very unfamiliar voice greeted me on the other end and I knew exactly who it was.

I tried to answer him in a matter of fact voice, "This is Shannon. Who is this?"

"Well, the last time I checked it's a free country, so I thought I'd give you a call. Don't hang up!" He laughed while making an effort to plead his case.

Trying to seem clever, I asked, "Give me one reason why I should stay on the line." I really didn't want him to hang up and I probably would have settled for any dumb reason.

"Let's see... hmm. I know!" His voice became low as he sarcastically asked, "I want to know why you didn't want me to call. Am I that bad? I'm not that bad... am I?" Carl laughed.

Trying to appear calm and uncharacteristically serious, I replied, "Well, let me think here... hmm? Why would I not want you to call me?" I tried to say it as if he should have already known the answer. "How many girlfriends have you had in the past year? Past month? Week? Hmmm? I wonder?" I tried to make my point by laying on the cynicism. Thick.

Without hesitation, he snapped, "Girlfriends… none."

"Liar!" I challenged, just as quickly.

"You said girlfriends, right? And that number is zero," he protested. "Or none. Nada. Take your pick."

I countered, "Oh my God!" I laughed so hard I could hardly breathe. Does he think I am that stupid? I could barely get the words out as I continued to laugh. "You are such a liar. Every week you ask out a new girl." I chuckled again. "I bet they all buy into it, too." I whispered, "Oh, those stupid girls… gotta love 'em. Dude, you are so typical."

Carl tried to state his case, but the visual in my head was bursting and I had to share. "I bet you have a yearbook by your bed and late at night, you cross off every girl that you've called." I was so amused with my own story that I continued to laugh at my own description. "Or, or maybe, you have, like, little markers on your wall, like a prisoner getting out of jail, you know? Oh my God… you are at the freshmen… aren't you? You are starting with the Bs, right?" I settled down, then advised, "Well, Shug or Shag or whatever, keep movin' along… just go right to the Cs." I was still trying to calm down from entertaining myself when I noticed Carl was not responding.

Perhaps the silence signaled his need to absorb all my feeble theories. I waited nervously for his response. Carl's voice indicated that he was amused. I giggled when he began taking his shots at me. "You're no angel either." He remarked, "Oh, hold up. Wait just a second and let me just enlighten you on what I've heard." He took his time to clear his throat then proceeded to make his case. "I may ask girls out, but that doesn't make it T.L.F., does it? You specifically asked about *girlfriends* and that would imply that we were, I guess, together and a simple phone call doesn't cut it."

"I see... hmmm." I could not think of one clever comment. Damn!

Carl said, "Shannon, you're not too shabby in the guy department." His voice was antagonistic as he threw out a bunch of accusations. "I heard that John Boggs asked you to prom and you wrote the word 'no' on a blank piece of paper. I mean, come on... that's pretty pathetic."

When Carl playfully teased, I felt like I was talking to one of my friends. His humor was in line with mine. Surprisingly, there were no awkward silences or need to make up trivial conversation... our words flowed. He added, "And I heard that David Ringwald sent you flowers and, like, a day later, you sent them back! Tell me, who's the mean one? Come on. God, I had to pump myself up by looking in the mirror and quoting Stewart Smalley just to get up enough nerve to call you!"

I chuckled with the thought of him gazing at his reflection and saying, "I am good enough. I am smart enough. And, gosh darn-it, people like me."

I pulled the phone away from my ear, staring at the receiver, wondering how he even knew about David. Carl was right. I did send the flowers back, but only because David was totally stalking me. I went to the movies with him one time and I totally regretted it.

I retorted, "Okay, we're gonna get technical?" I giggled. "First of all, John is my friend and, by friend, I mean, I say hi to him in the hallway. So, there is no way in hell that I'm going to the prom with him. Second of all, who told you about the flowers?"

I tried anything to defend myself. I wasn't the bad guy. "Whatever," I muttered. I tried clearing up the misunderstanding about the flowers. I explained, "David used to drive by my house really slow and totally stalk me. He called me, like, eighty times a day and, if I didn't answer, he would hang up on my mom and dad. *And* he told everyone on the softball team that he was my boyfriend, so he totally deserved it. Anyway, who told you that?"

Carl was practically in tears from laughing so hard. "Shannon, everyone knows about that! *Everyone.* We rag on him all the time."

"Well, he deserves it. He was, like, all Fatal Attraction."

"Fatal Attraction?" He scoffed. "That's a bit much- don't ya think?"

"No, I was afraid there would be a dead rabbit in my yard." I tried to sound convincing.

Carl and I talked for a while until my mom told me to get off the phone. I suppose we could have talked all night long. I wasn't sure if I was happy or sad about that. Throughout our conversation, during the most inopportune times, I was wondering if my brother would be mad at me for talking to Carl. *Was Carl mean to him? Was I supposed to be mean to Carl? What the hell was wrong with me? Why was everything so complicated?* I panicked. "Carl... I, uhh, have to go. Listen, um, it's been unexpectedly kind of cool talking to ya, but, well, you know." I hesitated. I wasn't sure what to say. I blurted out, "Well, I guess I'll see ya around."

"Whoa! Hold up. Just a second. I mean, I don't wanna get all Fatal Attraction or anything, but when can I talk to you again?"

I was torn. I wanted to talk to him again, but I didn't want him to *think* I wanted to talk to him again. I smugly mentioned, "Well, Carl, you're a smart guy with almost a high school education, so you figure it out." Then, I quickly hung up the phone. I held the phone in my right hand and snickered as I covered my mouth with my left hand. That night, I hardly slept as I thought about our conversation, taking it into hundreds of directions, dissecting every word, sigh, and laugh. As I twisted and turned that night, I wondered if he was nice to Phillip. How could a guy who was so cool be so mean?

The next morning, I woke up terribly late. I saw the alarm clock and then went into total panic mode. Without hesitation, I flew out of bed and was immediately wide awake. I picked up some clothes off the floor, washed my face, brushed my teeth, and pulled my hair up. Looking out the window, I could see Lizzie waiting for me. I called out to her, and begged her to wait for me. While flying out the house, I forgot my lunch, money, and all my homework assignments.

That morning, I found a tiny note stuck in a tiny crevice of my locker. I pressed myself against my locker and read the letter.

> *Dear #10,*
> *Not bad for an almost high school diploma, huh? Don't get too crazy- Tom told me where your locker was. I'm not gonna get all "Fatal Attraction" on you, but I do know where you live (just kidding.) I am still shocked you took my phone call. I have been practicing my Stewart Smalley affirmations trying to get brave enough to ask you for a date. (Yipes!) What do you think? I'm not such a bad guy... movies...*

Saturday? If you say no ... I might have to put a dead rabbit in your yard!
  Fatally yours, #33

He's funny. The last line about the rabbit was actually kind of funny. I held the tiny, white piece of paper in my hands, blushing like a stupid girl. I was glad that nobody was around to see how dumb I looked- especially Carl. I stuffed the letter in my pocket and walked to my next class, trying to pretend that I didn't care. However, it was pretty obvious that I did.

Four days after our first phone call, Carl and I went to the movies for our first official date. It wasn't like he had to twist my arm too hard; I knew what I was getting into and I figured that I could handle it. I rationalized my feelings, convincing myself that I could get to know him without any emotional attachment. We watched Pretty Woman and, afterwards, we drove around Woodbury Heights because we didn't know what else to do. It didn't seem to matter what we did, just as long as we had a chance to be together.

Eventually, we parked the car at his house and walked around the neighborhood. Carl and I strolled slowly down Beech Avenue; the same street I ran down on New Year's night. We talked about trivial things and we found any excuse to touch each other; a playful shove accompanied by a flirtatious smile. We laughed about Julia Roberts in Pretty Woman when she said, "Slippery little suckers!" I professed my love for The Phillies, the Jersey shore, my best friend Lizzie, The Beatles, and my obsessive infatuation with Darren Daulton. Carl tried to convince me that The Mets were the best team in major league baseball and were going to win the World Series. I scoffed.

There was never a moment of silence between us. I almost felt like I was talking to one of my study hall buddies. Then, Carl's curiosity about New Year's night entered our conversation. "So..." He hesitated, slowing down his pace, stopping in almost the same spot that I broke down crying. I blushed a little bit as I looked to my right and saw the large bay window. "You know, I never understood why you came over that night. Tom wouldn't tell me, and I guess I always wondered what made you knock on my door. I mean, besides that fact that Tom was there and all." Carl tried to make it sound like a joke by adding, "I thought, *maybe* you came over to see me. *Maybe.*"

We were literally walking down the same street where I wept on my knees in the cold snow. It all looked so different. The ice was replaced with lush green grass and the sharp air that pierced my lungs filled me with sweet dogwood aromas. It was almost impossible to believe that I was the girl who jumped out the window and questioned God's existence, eventually ending up piss drunk on Tiffany's floor. There was one thing I knew for sure: I was not going to tell Carl about that night, not now or ever. I wasn't even sure *how* to explain that night. The last thing I wanted was for Carl to think I was some kind of psycho chick.

I played it down. "I needed a ride."

Carl wasn't letting it slide. He pressed, "Well..." Carl's voice trailed. "It kind of seemed like more, you know, like something was really wrong." He sighed. "I hate to admit this. Okay. Here goes- I hate to admit this, but it kind of bothered me. I don't know why. I don't know." Carl shrugged his shoulders while standing in the middle of the large asphalt road.

My face was becoming red. I could not turn around to face him because I feared he would be able to read my emotions. A strange sensation warmed my entire body and my guarded exterior melted away. Why did he care so much?

I turned around and faced him. I asked, "Why?"

Carl's response was uncomfortably serious, "I felt sorry for you, I guess. You looked sad." He smiled and then added, "*And* it was New Year's Eve... and you just, you just didn't seem like a sad person." Carl chuckled nervously after his confession. He continued, "I guess, for some weird reason, I wanted you to be happy- especially on New Year's Eve."

His confession caught me off guard. I couldn't believe that Carl had those tender thoughts. Instead of responding to his admission with sincerity, I chose sarcasm. I mocked, "Awww, poor, poor Shannon." I made an overdramatized sad face and pouted as I whispered, "Poor baby... you wooked so sad. So, I looked sad, huh? Hmmm. Awwwhh!"

I tried to make that night seem like no big deal, but, inside, I felt like a complete failure. The most important job in my life was to make people believe that I was happy and, after hearing Carl's concern for me that night, I felt like a complete disappointment.

I shrugged my shoulders and reassured, "Well, I just needed a ride- that's all."

Carl dropped it, sensing my disinterest in that night and my unwillingness to give details. We walked to St. Margaret's Church and sat on the marble steps. I cringed when I looked over and saw The Virgin Mary. We joked and reminisced about growing up in Woodbury Heights. We learned we had most of the same teachers in elementary school, played jailbreak together at some point in our lives, both loved The May Fair, and always went to the carnival every summer at the church. We had so much in common that we spent most of the night comparing stories about school, friends, and people we both knew. It was so easy to talk to him. I was very amused by his sense of humor and couldn't help but giggle at every other little comment, which I swore I would not do.

I didn't want the night to end, but I knew that it would. Carl insisted that we go back to get his car, so my dad wouldn't think he was a total loser. Before getting in his car, Carl and I stood in front of his house to say our goodbyes. That awkward moment was coming: the first kiss. I braced myself as I stood helpless on his curb. I could feel Carl's breath on my lips as he leaned in close to me. I froze. I pushed him back. I couldn't do it. I couldn't kiss him without knowing. I ordered, "Wait! Wait- just wait a minute."

Thoroughly confused, Carl cocked his head, and asked, "What is it? What's wrong?"

I was quite sure that other girls took full advantage of a moment such as this, but I suppose I was either an idiot or I was totally screwed up.

I rolled my eyes with disappointment in myself, wishing I just kissed him instead of making a scene. I wimped out and blurted, "Nothing. Nothing. I just, umm..." I felt about two inches tall and kept my hands in my pockets the entire time. Instead of looking directly at him, I shifted my gaze from side to side. That was not like me, I thought. Why couldn't I just ask him?

Carl gently brushed my cheeks, forcing me to look toward his blue eyes. My face turned a bright shade of red, and I could feel the blood rushing to my face. Carl curiously asked, "What's wrong? You can tell me," he persisted. He lightened the moment by making a joke. He reassured, "I told you- I am not such a bad guy. But, if you keep me hanging, I will totally cross off your picture in my yearbook."

"Ha-ha," I managed to say.

Instead of asking about his involvement with my brother, I brought up something else. It was easier to make up something else than to ask him about Phillip. I wasn't even sure if I could say his name out loud. I made up something, so he wouldn't think I was a total weirdo. I said, "Look, Carl. You are a nice guy and I kind of like you…"

"But…" he led me on.

I shook my head, stepped off the curb, and nervously walked away. I turned around to face him and confidently remarked, "Well, come on. You're leaving at the end of the summer and your track record with girls really isn't that great. And, seriously, I don't want to be, like, one of *them*."

He asked, *"Them?"*

I retorted, "I am not one of those girls who is gonna wait by the phone on a Friday night, cry herself to sleep, or drive myself totally insane wondering when things will be over." I began walking home, waved my hand in the air, and barked, "I just, I can't. I won't."

Carl yelled to me as I was walking away. "You still think that about me?"

I turned to face him and replied, "I don't know. Yeah." It was partly true, but it was not the only thing holding me back from liking him.

Judging by his face, I was sure the night turned out a lot different than we both anticipated. Carl calmly walked over to me. His voice was warm and the seriousness in his tone made me nervous. He began, "Shannon, I…"

I didn't allow him the opportunity to explain when I suddenly blurted out, "Were you mean to him?" My first official date with Carl, the date that was going so well, turned into wild accusations. It wasn't fair to ask such questions. I wasn't even sure if he could remember, but I could not go on pretending that it didn't bother me.

I rationalized my question by reminding myself that I needed to be Phillip's sister during that moment. I couldn't be with someone who potentially harmed him.

Carl's face gave me a clear indication that he knew exactly what I was talking about. He stepped closer to me, and, when I looked into his eyes, I knew in that moment that something big was about to happen- bigger than a first kiss. If he was the good guy, if he was nice to him, then, and only then, would I allow myself to like him.

He asked, "You mean… your brother?"

Looking down at my black shoes, I could barely nod my head. My body was numb and my hands became sweaty as I waited to hear the fate of our future. All I could do was stand on the curb and wait. Carl may be cute and he may be funny, but if he was mean to my brother, then there was no point in continuing. I had to be a loyal sister, perhaps to make up for the past.

I could tell his eyes were on me. I could feel the intensity. He said, "Shannon, I…"

Before he could begin, I began rambling away, "I know. I know you were on his football team. I saw the team picture. I was at the games. I was there. You were all mean to him."

Carl rolled his eyes.

I confessed, "I hated all of you. Every single one of you. You guys were just so mean." I stepped off the curb and looked back. "You know, I wanted to like you. I really did. I just, I just can't."

I exhaled as I walked away and wished that I never even went on the stupid date. Carl grabbed my shoulders lightly and gently pulled me back. I had adrenaline running through my body, aiding my strength as I confronted Carl. "I just want to know. I need to know." With a nervous deep breath, I asked him again: "Were you mean to him? Tell me the truth. If you tell me the truth, then I'll never ask you again." I picked at my nails and urgently pleaded, "Just tell me the truth."

Carl placed me back on the curb, so he could look at me in the eye. He tenderly took both of my hands in his. "I will. I will tell you the God's truth. I have nothing to hide," he promised, and then immediately looked down to his Nike sneakers. After looking at me, he said, "Your brother was... he was... I guess you could say- bullied. He was, well, not treated very nicely, to put it mildly, but..." His head went down and then quickly back up to make his bold statement or confession. "I was never mean to him. I used to tell the guys to lay off of him. You know? I remember him being so much younger than the rest of us."

As Carl continued to speak, I noticed he began talking slower and softer, which I took as endearing. He continued, "When I heard about your brother- I just felt so bad. You know?" I think Carl was blushing. He added, "I kind of felt like I should have done more, or maybe I could have been nicer. I mean, I wasn't one of the kids who made fun of him, but maybe if I said something to defend him, then..." I almost felt sorry for *him* as he continued to stutter. I never realized how difficult it must have been on him. He looked up and then deeply sighed, "I just, I just felt so- guilty."

Guilty? He felt guilty?

Carl held my hands tighter and made his stance clear. He swore, "But, as I stand here in front of you and in front of God, I was never mean to him. I promise."

His reference to God made me a little uncomfortable, knowing that once God was in the conversation, everything became very serious. I stood on the curb with relief. I admitted, "It's just so hard." I put both hands up to my forehead, feeling like a complete moron for exposing my fragile state (especially on our first date.) I muttered, "I just hated guys like you."

"Thanks!" Carl smiled which indicated that he understood my last statement.

After taking my hands away from my head, I cringed when I revealed my worried eyes. "I mean, not like you, exactly, just, you know, anyone who was mean to him. I mean, I know he was treated badly. Actually, I saw it myself. Isn't it weird that after all that time, I can still remember that?"

We both exhaled, took deep breaths, probably laughing inside about how the light conversation about jailbreak, turned into tragic memories about Phillip.

He never answered my rhetorical question; however, he said something that I needed to hear. "Look..." Once again, he caressed my cheeks with his big hands. "I can't stand here and convince you that I am a good person. As they say, 'talk is cheap.' But, if you hang around, then I will do everything to prove to you what kind of person I am." Carl laughed at himself, attesting, "I am really not that bad, er, at least, I don't think I am bad."

With Carl's promise, I finally allowed myself to like him. With my eyes shut, my heart open, and my brother's bad memories in the past, I allowed Carl to kiss me.

the stranger comes around

After that night, everything changed. Everything. The sun shined a little bit brighter, the stars in the sky seemed larger in the midnight sky, school was tolerable, and slow songs held new meaning. Instead of thinking about Phillip's death, I was distracted with mushy thoughts of Carl. Every moment, I questioned: *What is he doing? Is he thinking about me? When will we see each other again?* I listened to *Vision of Love* five hundred times on my Walkman. Ugghh! I was officially one of those stupid girls and I actually liked it.

The fact that Carl was leaving in two months seemed incredibly irrelevant because the only thing that mattered was the present. I didn't exactly care about what the future held. Keeping up appearances was most important to me. I never talked about Carl to my friends, parents, or anyone. Having someone in my life that brought out such emotions was both scary and awesome at the same time. Most times, Carl wasn't even aware of how I truly felt about him. If I acted like I didn't care, then it would be a whole lot easier to deal with when we broke up in August. I mean, obviously, we were going to break up when he went to college.

At night, when I opened my screen window and smelled the early morning air and listened closely to the owl curse the dark night in my neighbor's yard, I was, again, present. I allowed myself to feel happiness that, during the day, I thought I did not deserve. During the sunlit hours, I reminded myself that the happiness I felt was only temporary. In fact, I viewed everything of pleasure as strictly temporary, including my accomplishments with sports and school. No matter what wonderful things came my way, I still believed that I did not deserve it. I would always be the girl consumed with guilt, anger, confusion, sadness, and bitterness over the death of my brother. Everything else that came along in my life was just fleeting distractions to get my mind off reality. Happiness was never everlasting- it was just a distraction; just like Carl.

I never classified myself as crazy or insane, but I toyed with the idea that my thinking was tainted or, perhaps, skewed. Happiness to me was something I searched for but often denied with its first appearance. I never thought of it as depression, yet there was always a nagging or an aching that left me a little low. Like many people, I thought that having a bad day was not unusual. Actually, bad days were expected. The problem I had was my inability to be present. I was well aware that I was not completely there... I was stuck. I could never enjoy my life because I was constantly thinking about the past or worrying about the future. I often fantasized about changing my life; never really enjoying what was right in front of me.

Mom and I still ignored tough issues or, rather, we argued about anything, most times- everything. We battled back and fourth over stupid things, trivial things, but never the important things. Mom hung out with her friends again, enjoyed her afternoon walks, and occasionally went out just for fun. Mom and dad walked the dogs at the river and, sometimes, I tagged along. Even though the Delaware River was kind of bleak, it made us feel better. Mom's crying died down slightly. She moped around the house like a zombie, living somewhere between life and death.

We avoided discussing anything regarding Phillip; in fact, his name was rarely mentioned... if ever. Even though his death was a year and a half before, we could not talk about it. Dad never talked about it, so I assumed the worst. I never voluntarily brought up the subject. I was the constant observer, watching everyone while trying to figure it all out. Mom never tried to hide her emotions regarding Phillip. I knew how she felt, but dad was much harder to read. Lizzie and I never talked about Phillip either. I told myself that she just couldn't understand, but honestly, I knew she could grasp the gravity of the situation. Phillip was dead. It almost seemed as if he was never even alive.

Denial. Denial was my best friend. After a year and half of reflecting upon his death, or any death for that matter, I was no closer to figuring death out. There was no book or guide to assist me with my irrational thinking. I wasn't even sure if my thoughts were "irrational." If I could just stuff all that bad stuff away... just get rid of it, then I would be fine; however, it wasn't that easy. I was exhausted.

I, lovingly, referred to myself as "The Stranger." I suppose the stranger might have been my true self: the girl who looked out the window late at night, the girl who wore the satin mask during the day.

Running was always something that I loved to do, especially when I had something on my mind. I grabbed my sneakers, my Walkman, my digital watch, and hit the asphalt. My normal route took me to Oak Valley into Wenonah, and then I looped back around again to Woodbury Heights. On my journey, my breathing was the only thing that remained in sync as all my chaotic thoughts shifted randomly from one subject to another.

I tried to figure out how I could make everything better. I wanted to know when I would start feeling normal again. I wanted to know when I could think about Phillip in a different way... the way people said I would one day. I tried to hold onto the perception that I was fine. I made a deal with myself that I would try harder, be stronger, and just let it go. "Let it go," I told myself as the sweat poured off my brow. "Just let it go."

After stopping to stretch out my legs halfway through the run, relief spread through me, or maybe it was the runner's high that I always heard about. I truly believed I could do it. I could change the course of my life simply by being stronger and better. After all, being me wasn't that bad. I was pretty sure that other people had to deal with much harder crap than I did.

Before going home, I stopped by Carl's house. The fact that I was a stinky, smelly mess could not stop me from seeing Carl. Carl smiled when he saw me. His smile seemed to signal that everything was just right in my world. He was the distraction, the wonderful distraction that kept me going.

Carl slowly opened the door and mocked, "Well, well... look-see what we got here. If it isn't my long lost girlfriend- *Shannon Bennet?*"

"In the flesh," I replied. "Uh, scratch that. Sweaty flesh."

"Where have you been? I've been calling you, like, all day." He stepped outside sipping powdered iced-tea. (Yuck.)

Carl immediately began making fun of me. He made fun of my long gym shorts, my sweaty headband, and my big, yellow Walkman. He laughed, and I laughed along with him, as he imitated me jogging. I nearly fell to the ground when he pretended to be me. Carl mocked, "Oh, hi! My name is Shannon Bennet and I *don't* call my boyfriend because I am Shannon Bennet, and I am soooooo coooool! I like to wear headbands, run real fast, and did I mention, I am so cool! 'Cause, you know, I'm Shannon Bennet!" He imitated me running again (like a fem girl.)

There was no denying that Carl was funny. He made me laugh and it was the quality that I cherished most. Carl was truly my distraction from all the hidden problems that I tucked deep inside, and being with him was like a natural cure for my pain. We walked to my house, side by side, playfully teasing each other. Then, as we turned the corner to Linden Avenue, Carl stopped walking.

His voice trailed off when he began to speak. "Sooo?"

"So? What?" I responded with a smile on my face.

He paused and then announced, "I got my letter from Stockton. It was like some sort of orientation thingy. I am leaving August 18th." His statement clearly demanded some sort of sincere or serious response, which I was not capable of giving.

I nodded the entire time, wishing we could have just ended this day with silly impressions and inside jokes. Carl was completely unaware that I viewed our relationship as a summer fling. My skepticism never allowed me to believe that someone like Carl Kindsay would become a long-distance relationship. He was merely my future ex-boyfriend.

"Sounds good," I lied. "You got a roommate?"

Carl looked up to the sky, then back to me while slowly shaking his head in disbelief. He scoffed. "Good? What's so good about it? Don't you even care that I'll be gone? Jesus. What the hell? Do you have a calendar marking the days off?"

"No!" I protested with giddy laughter, glad we were back to making jokes. "No! I just, I don't know. I mean, duh, the fact is that you will be gone in, like, what?" I began counting on my fingers. "Six weeks? What am I supposed to do? Get all crazy and cry myself to sleep or crouch in a dark corner with the lights off?" I nervously fidgeted with my sweaty headband and sarcastically muttered, "Yeah, that'll happen."

"Well." He crossed his arms and stood in the middle of the street. "Maybe it would be nice for you to show *some* emotion. Any emotion! God! What is wrong with you, anyway? It's like you're just waiting for me to leave."

"No, I'm not!" I boldly denied his allegations with a hint of resentment in my tone, although his accusation had a ring of truth to it.

Carl lived in a fantasy world. I wasn't so naïve. I knew what happened at frat parties, and I also knew that college, long-distance relationships never worked... ever. Part of me wanted to share that belief along with him, but the risk was too dangerous. I was just glad to have someone to be with, laugh with, walk with, watch baseball with, eat Philly cheese steaks with, and, mostly, take my mind off my confusing life. Believing in dreams of living happily ever after would only generate more disappointment. Of course, the last thing I wanted was for him to leave me, but I wasn't going to kid myself because he *was* leaving. I was smart enough to realize that when he was out with his roommates playing quarters, I would still be in Woodbury Heights looking out my window- *alone.*

"Carl," I began, finding it very hard to be the slightest bit serious. "I know. I know you are going to college. I mean, I always knew that you would only be here for the summer, so, like, how do you expect me to act?"

"I don't know? Like you care. Is that so wrong?" He protested.

We stood in the street only three feet away from one another, facing our first serious talk. He needed to hear that I was sad about him leaving, or that things would be okay when he left. I needed to keep it all inside, so I could remain in control.

I tried to manipulate the situation. After years of choosing my words wisely to pacify my mother, I tried to minimize the situation. I said, "Look, let's not worry about it, right? I mean, what are we gonna do... we'll see what happens in August, okay?" Cringing, I recited the words that I dreaded. "If it's meant to be- it's meant to be."

It worked. Carl smiled after my cliché. He walked toward me, teasingly holding his nose and put his arms around my shoulders to walk me toward my door. He asked, "Is it meant to be?"

I escaped his embrace, looked him in the eye, and asked, "Is the Pope Catholic?"

It was the best I could do. I often questioned what was wrong with me. I had a good guy who liked me and wanted to be with me, yet I could not allow myself the freedom to enjoy it.

Mom and dad went fishing in Margate at least two times a week that summer. I liked being alone. With mom and dad gone, I could do anything I wanted. I chose to sacrifice my free day by organizing and rearranging my room. Sometimes I would get an irresistible urge to have some sort of order. Usually, after I finished cleaning my room, I promised myself that I would keep it organized, but I never did. After chugging a Dr. Pepper, inhaling two soft-Philly pretzels, and flipping through every TV station, I began to dissect my room. Bobby Brown blasted on my radio, escaping out my windows for all my neighbors to enjoy.

Under my bed, I found old socks, candy wrappers, a fork, a broken pair of Oakley sunglasses, and dozens of unfinished homework assignments. I changed my sheets, dusted my desk, threw out some old clothes, hung up and put away the piles of clothes on the floor. I even broke out the Windex and Pledge. I sung along with Bobby as he told me the "truth about Roni." I found a note from Thomas and read it four times. I got side tracked for twenty minutes when I found an old photo album. I picked out new pictures to place on my corkboard. I blushed a little bit when I hung Carl's graduation picture in the center of a homemade paper heart. I found the first and only letter Carl gave me. I reread it several times, trying to figure out what he was thinking when he wrote it.

When I cleared out everything from my desk, I found an old baseball card. (At least, I thought it was a baseball card.) It was stuck in between the drawers and the wood framing, practically waiting for me to find it. I thought it was one of my Darren Daulton cards. Instead of looking at one of my beloved Phillies, the tiny picture on the front exposed something I hated.

It seemed innocent, yet the intention of what I was holding in my hand was to hurt Phillip. It was a Garbage Pail Kid card. Time stood still for a minute and I couldn't hear Bobby singing in the background. My brother was an avid collector of Garbage Pail Cards, but the card did not belong to Phillip because it was mine. It was card number 83b... Sumo Sid. Sumo Sid was a morbidly obese Sumo wrestler, cracking the ground below due to his fat body. I suppose the reason I held onto the card initially was to tease my brother. I would often show him the card, so I could remind him of his weight, as if he needed me or anyone else to point out the obvious. I held the card in my right hand, caressing it with my fingers. Sumo Sid represented every cruel comment, every fat joke, and every reason why I was an awful sister. Card number 83b made me feel like complete shit.

Something as simple as a Garbage Pail Kid made my stomach queasy and my mouth dry. I started hearing all the nasty things I used to say in my head: "Fat-lard, fatty-Phil, and two-ton tubbalard." I asked myself: why was I so mean to him? What if I was nicer? Would he still be here? That was the problem... I knew in some way or the other that I contributed to his death.

I realized that it wasn't just the name calling or teasing. Many times, I ignored the awful things people said about him and, sometimes, I encouraged it. The truth was so hard to swallow. The truth sucked and there was no way to tell him that I was sorry. Grieving for him almost felt hypocritical. With a deep breath, I placed the card next to Phillip's old pictures and stared at my wall for about ten minutes.

I wanted to think about him some more, so I decided to visit his old room. I never went back after the scissor incident. Holding my breath and wishing that something in his room could prove that I wasn't terrible, I flicked the door open with one finger. I stood in the hallway while the door swung open. First, I poked my head into his deserted room, and, with my heart beating fast, I took my first step inside.

I took five baby steps to the center of his room where I could simply spin around to absorb the strangeness of his mysterious room. His free weights were neatly stacked in the walk-in closet, exposing the maximum weight his fifteen-year-old body could lift. Some of his winter clothes were hanging in the closet. I felt the fabric and tried to visualize what he might look like if he was wearing the clothes; I couldn't remember. I sniffed the collar trying to remember what he smelled like; I forgot. His memory that I intentionally suppressed made it impossible to remember.

The twin bed was still in the left corner of his room with white sheets and a single white pillow. After scanning his room, looking for something... anything, I felt so stupid for trying to recreate my brother by examining his old things. Sweat began dripping down my forehead from the stagnant heat accumulating in his unventilated room. I cautiously walked toward his wooden dresser, the same dresser where I found the scissors. I took a deep breath and opened his top drawer. There was a royal blue photo album just waiting for me to open it. Inside, there were dozens of Garfield comic strips, hand drawn army men in the midst of battle, a second grade class picture, and hand written scores from Super Mario Brothers. I could recognize his cursive penmanship anywhere. Then, I saw a picture of us.

We were hugging each other in the back of our blue Ford truck. The truck bed was loaded with leaves that we collected during the day. He was holding me from behind in a playful embrace. We were both laughing. I looked over the picture and smiled. I could smell the crisp leaves. I could feel his breath behind me. I remembered that feeling. Maybe that warm feeling was all that mattered. I felt as light as a feather during that moment and, just as I was about to leave, I felt a cool breeze tickle the back of my neck. Maybe, maybe that was him... laughing behind me.

that stupid girl in the mirror

Thursday, June 21, 1990 was like any other day that summer: predictable. I watched TV over at Carl's house that night and stuffed my face with not one, but two Klondike Bars. Carl walked me home. I remember that night was hot- ridiculously hot. I remember Carl teased me because I didn't have air conditioning in my house, so, therefore, I would sweat my butt off. I remember Carl said goodbye and was practically down my driveway when I called him back from my step. I was fidgeting my fingers, second-guessing if I should even ask him what I always wanted to know.

I blurted out, "I just need to know if you are happy?"

Carl's reaction was priceless. He crinkled his nose and stuck up his lip trying to think of something really clever to say. Instead, he shrugged his shoulders.

I looked into his eyes wishing that I never asked.

Carl smiled and said, "Yeah. Yup. I am happy. Why? Why wouldn't I be happy? I got a sarcastic, blond girlfriend. What more could a guy ask for?"

Perhaps I was secretly waiting for someone to ask me. I, blankly, responded, "Just wondering."

With his voice drawn, he pressed me for an answer. "Whyyyy?" Carl only knew me for roughly fifty days, but he seemed to have me all figured out. He knew that wasn't a typical question that I would ask.

The question was probably a statement in disguise. Deep down, I wanted someone to ask me the same exact question and I wanted to tell the truth so badly. I should have been joyous, I should have been taking pleasure in the summer, and I should have been head over heels, crazy in love. I should have told myself that I deserved happiness or that I was allowed to expect great things from my life, but I didn't. I wanted Carl to tell me things would be okay or explain why I was so sad. Unfortunately, he would never be able to do that as long as I pretended that I was fine.

I wanted to tell him that sometimes I blame everything on myself. I just wanted to blurt out all my thoughts. I was angry at my brother for leaving me with the mess, the guilt, and the inability to "just get over it." While Carl stood on my front step, I knew he would listen to anything that came out of my mouth, but I could not get the words out. He would think I was crazy or messed up or damaged goods. Carl told me he loved me, so I had to make him believe that I was that confident, strong, and fun girl he fell in love with.

After serious consideration, I decided to drop the subject, so I could remain normal in his eyes. I calmly replied, "Just wondering. Oh my God. I was just curious. Damn, can't a girl ask a simple question?"

He patted me on the back jokingly, almost congratulating me for asking. He asked, "Are you happy?"

He asked me. Someone finally asked me. I have to admit that it felt nice.

My response was quick. "Happy. I am the definition of happy," I lied. "Look up happy in the dictionary and you'll see my face." I posed for him, pretending that I was getting my picture taken and flashed a cheerful smile with my teeth deliberately protruding.

Carl laughed. Then, he came close to me and kissed me on the cheek. "Okay... I'll look it up when I get home." When I turned around to walk in my door, Carl mischievously slapped me on the butt and blurted, "Stay happy!" I swiftly turned around and watched him vanish into the humid, dark night.

Once inside, I went to the refrigerator like one of Pavlov's dogs, trained to inspect the contents of the fridge upon arriving home. Then, I opened the freezer and searched for something, not sure exactly what I wanted. The frigid air felt nice on my face. I stood there for quite some time, dreading the sweltering heat in my room. Before going to bed, I snuck into mom's room and saw her clutching her Bible with her right arm. The flickering lights from her TV revealed little sparks of light on her face, presenting a woman far, far away. I toyed with the notion that she was peacefully dreaming, but I knew she was diligently trying to find my brother in another world while I stood right in front of her. It didn't matter if she was asleep or awake; mom forgot about me and I was tired of trying to get her attention. I realized that she would always be my brother's mother. I was stuck with what he left behind. After I closed her door behind me, I pressed my forehead against her wooden door, and softly whispered, "Good night, mom."

I changed for bed. It was so freakin' hot, like, almost can't breathe hot. I found a pair of boxers and a tank top on my floor and figured, eh, clean enough. I flopped down on my warm sheets, became still, and relished the strange quietness. No static, no radio, no midnight breeze to distract my mind, and with that, I drifted off to The Greek Isles. I envisioned myself older, maybe late twenties, sitting on a lounge chair conveniently nestled under a palm tree. I could literally see myself watching distant ships in the crystal blue waters, surrounded by brilliant white buildings. I could smell the seawater and feel the ocean's ebb and flow from my chair. I was older, prettier, smarter, and free. The water, so clear, took my breath as my fingers traced the white, sandy beach. Skinny, tan, unfamiliar people walked by me and waved happily. They shouted to me in foreign words that I could not understand. I waved back to them, never knowing or caring what they were saying. It didn't matter anyway because they looked so happy. With the hooting of the owl in the woods next door, I woke from my impressive illusions, disappointed that I was still in New Jersey, in my ridiculously hot room, and sweating my butt off.

I tried to go back to The Greek Isles, but I couldn't picture them anymore. The stupid owl distracted me by hooting, perhaps his way of laughing at my thoughts. Stupid owl! My room was sweltering hot, sweat pouring down my back hot. I slowly got out of bed to fetch a rag, so I could run it under frigid water and place it on my head before I suffered through the night.

When I went to the bathroom, I felt an energy, almost a spark. I looked at the mirror, and then looked down to the sink with my shoulders shrugging to support my body. There I stood, all of five foot two, looking down, so I didn't have to face the mirror and that stupid girl in the mirror. I lifted my head to expose the stranger who reigned deep within my body. With my pointer finger, I played with my eyes, rubbing them, blinking them, only to reveal my bloodshot, blue-gray eyes that watched everything.

"I hate you," I whispered to my reflection.

At that moment, I knew that I was talking to myself, but I also knew that I was talking to my brother.

I crossed my arms and began to rant at my reflection. "I hate you for what you did. You are so dumb." I snickered, took a deep breath, and continued to confess my secret thoughts. I went on, "God! Look at you. Who do you think you are? You're nothing special. I mean, come on, just admit it. Just admit that you are an evil bitch." I nodded with silent agreement.

I was so ashamed. So, so ashamed. If only I said different things to him. If only I accepted him just as he was. If only I told someone about his cutting or all of his confessions. I didn't deserve to be happy.

"Why? Why didn't you do anything?"

My chin began to quiver. It was fascinating to watch it all play out in front of the mirror. I finally admitted, "You know what? You know it's your fault, right?" I nodded again, facing my fears, facing the mirror and that stupid girl in the mirror.

At first, one small tear trickled down my tan cheek, followed by a flood of tears stored up for over a year. I broke down and sobbed, watching my reflection the entire time. I wanted to see it. I needed to see it. I actually liked watching myself drown in my tears, but I could not understand why. I pressed my back to the door, slid to the floor, and sat Indian-style on the pink and white tiles. In a daze, I began counting the tiles, rocking back and forth, methodically counting the small tiles, and thought- I just don't want to feel like this anymore. I want out. I just wanted to be somewhere else or be someone else.

I lifted my body from the floor so I could search the medicine cabinet. I thought there had to be something, *anything* to numb me. I wasn't sure what I was looking for, but I just knew I needed something to take me away, so I could forget. I came across a new bottle of store brand cough syrup and, without hesitation, I put it to my lips and began chugging. Just like the alcohol on New Year's Eve, the result far outweighed the awful taste. All I wanted to do was slip away- just for a little while. I just wanted a break. I cried hysterically as I chugged, then sipped, then chugged again, and watched myself the entire time in the mirror. I never took my eyes off the mirror because I needed to know that the girl in the reflection was the real me, not the girl I always pretended to be. I finished the bottle of cough syrup and felt nothing. *Damn, this stuff doesn't even work,* I thought. I needed something else.

I searched for something else, but only found over the counter pain relievers. After reading Advil that promised to "temporarily relieve minor aches and pain," I took three at a time. Still, I felt nothing. At that moment, I needed instant relief.

I was obsessed with escaping. Just for the night, I wanted to break away. If I could just find a way to make it all disappear for just a short amount of time, then I would be satisfied. I began popping Advil, which surprisingly had a sweet, candy-like taste. After taking several swallows, I looked at myself in the mirror again, pissed because there was no numbing affects from the cough syrup or the Advil. I cried the entire time. I watched every single movement in the mirror. I sat back on the floor and counted the tiles again, feeling just a little bit heavy, and began humming *Come Monday* by Jimmy Buffett. Something inside me felt tingly. My toes, my fingers, even the hairs on my head felt weird. Oh, but it felt so good. I climbed back up to the sink, using both hands to support my body. There were so many things that I liked at that moment. The tingly sensation, the numbing all over my body, and my ability to watch it the entire time; it all made me feel powerful. While gazing at my reflection and touching my numb face, I began repeating, "I hate you. I hate you. I hate you." The words began to blend and it sounded like, "I need a tissue." The thought made me laugh.

I hated everyone. I hated myself the most. My entire way of life was a complete lie. I was a weak, idiotic girl who could not hold it all together. I looked at myself, my wet complexion an indication of my obvious vulnerabilities, and asked, "Why is it so hard to be strong... come on... Shannon. You can do better than this. Just suck it up!"

I began having a two-way conversation with myself, playing both defendant and plaintiff. As the tears rolled down my puffy face, I told myself, "It's okay. It's okay to have a meltdown. Just let it all out. Don't be afraid... just let it out!"

Then, I countered by mentioning, "Oh my God... Shan! You are such an idiot. Why are you being so freakin' stupid? Only crazy psychos act this way. You're better than that. Duh! You're a champion, remember?"

I cried harder when I heard the ongoing conversation in my head. Was I strong or was I weak? Was acting strong the same as being strong? Oh God- I felt so weak. I whispered to the mirror, "You are a stupid, weak girl. Get over it. He's the one who did it, so why should I feel bad?"

I shook my head while intensely watching my blue, watery eyes. My eyes proved to me, once and for all, that I was just pretending to be strong.

I whispered again, "I don't know." I shrugged my shoulders, feeling heavier than I remembered. I repeated, "I don't know."

I plopped down on the cool tiles once again. They felt so cool against my warm skin. My body dropped so fast that on the way down I scraped my right elbow. I began scratching my skin and, surprisingly, it felt wonderful.

My hot-pink nails made tiny marks in my strong, tanned arms. These arms, I thought to myself, have done a lot of work for me, but watching the new marks on my skin was beyond explanation. It felt nice and it looked hypnotizing. My nails dug in... harder... harder... yet, not hard enough.

I pulled my weight up to the sink. It was incredibly hard to stand perfectly still. I knew that I was going to do something drastic, and I knew that there was not one single person out there who would believe it. Sharp. I needed something sharp. The things in the medicine cabinet were getting blurry, coming in and out of focus. I found it. I found the shiny, silver strait razor. I held it in front of my face with so many thoughts running through my mind. What would mom say? What would dad think? Would Carl think I was a crazy psycho? I considered it odd that, at that moment, I could only think about my brother. In a bizarre way, I wanted him to see it. As I held the cold, shiny object in my tiny hands, I felt justified. I mean, it was all his fault anyway. I wished that he was there to witness what I was about to do. I wanted him to know what it felt like to watch someone deteriorate.

In my right fingertips, I held the sharp razor in front of my face. I smiled, chuckled a little, and hummed *Come Monday*. There were so many reasons why I wanted to cut my skin. I wanted to feel something physical, instead of emotional. I had the power in the palm of my hands to give myself temporary release. I wanted someone to walk through the bathroom door and tell me why I was acting this way. I wanted to get Phillip back for all the pain he caused me. Most of all, I just wanted something to take my pain away... quickly. Release me.

I sat down on the edge of the cold bathtub and bowed my head to pray:

Dear God, it's me Shannon. Shannon Bennet. God? Can you see me? Please, don't be mad at me. I'm not really a bad person. Or at least, I don't think I am so bad. Uhh, God? I don't know why I am here. Literally, I seriously do not know why I am here... this place can be so hard. I mean, I don't want to kill myself or anything... that would be stupid, but why can't you help me? I'm good, right? I am okay to my parents- most of the time. I have cool friends, I go to school on time, do my homework, and I have a nice guy, so why do I feel this way?

I took a deep breath. It was becoming increasingly hard to simply inhale and exhale without feeling tired. I continued to pray:

I hate my life. Yeah, I said it! Sometimes, I hate it. When will all this stupid crap be over? God, I believed in you or I kind of tried to. I went to church. How come you didn't help me? Okay, I'm sorry. No! Wait! I'm not sorry! I'm friggin' pissed! Where the hell are you? Sorry for using the word hell.

I laughed uncontrollably as I sat on the tub. Wondering if God cared that I used the word "hell." I pleaded with God; bargained with him:

God, I don't know why I am acting this way. Sometimes, I just hate myself. If you help me, then I promise I will do better. I promise. God? Are you there? I am sorry. I am sorry that I am such a failure. I want to be strong. I want to be good, but... I don't know how. Whatever...

I laughed cynically.

You're not there anyway. You're probably hanging out in a church somewhere, or healing the blind, or, or, I don't know- playing a freakin' harp!

The vision of God playing a harp filled with me rolling laughter.

I never said *Amen*. I felt an odd mixture of sadness and power when I held the tiny razor in my fingers. My tears were warm and salty against my skin. The more I wiped my salty tears off, the more they continued to fall. My heart began to thump in a fast rhythm. Alternating between wild laughter and deep sobs, I placed the razor back in the medicine cabinet, only to hold it in my hand again. Even with all the shame I felt at that moment, I desperately wanted someone to walk through the door, slap me on the face, and help me. In my darkest hour, I needed to believe someone would come rescue me.

My chin gave out and I began crying again. I affirmed, once again, in the mirror, and in front of God, that I was a total loser. My inner voice told me that I was no good and that I was a worthless idiot. I believed every single word. I found it difficult to hold my body up. I decided to take some more Advil, hoping that the pain reliever would do as promised. The razor quivered in my tiny, perfectly polished nails when I placed it close to my left arm. I flipped my left arm, exposing my veins, knowing I could never take it that far. I faked the motion of cutting the back of my arm several times, as tears fell on my tanned skin. I was starting to feel drowsy and tired, like I had been up for ten days in a row. The numbness was comforting. Then, I exhaled and cut a deep line down my arm from my elbow to my wrist.

Bright red trickles of blood steadily oozed out, covering my arm and dripping in the sink. For the first time, I didn't think. My mind was empty. Nothing. I watched with awe as my own blood traced my arm and exhaled, feeling an unexpected sense of relief. I made two more identical cuts to match my first line. I was meticulous with my incision and felt it was important to make three straight, uniform lines. As I watched the blood drip into the sink, I knew this would be my secret forever. Cutting my own skin, causing my own pain was a powerful experience and I, oddly enough, felt inexplicably at ease. My tears had vanished during my cutting. Nothing inside hurt; only the stinging of my arm bothered me. It felt like hundreds of bees took turns stinging me over and over.

I held my arm over the sink and washed my arm. My eyes followed the red liquid as it became pink while it mixed with cold water. I wrapped a cold, white washcloth around my arm and watched it become pink within seconds. I tried changing it several times, but there was too much blood. Eventually, I contained the bleeding and wrapped my left arm in toilet paper. I gently held my left arm with my right hand and glanced one last time in the mirror.

I whispered, "Happy now?"

My body, heavy and exhausted from cough syrup, Advil, and emotions, collapsed on the floor. My knee hit the hard tiles, but I didn't feel it. It was exhausting to lift my body off the floor, but I knew I had to make it back to my room before passing out. When I opened the door to my room, I lethargically grabbed my sweatshirt, barely able to slip it on. I fell on my bed wearing shorts and a heavy Gator softball sweatshirt. My head was pulsating against my soft pillow as my body succumbed to the rest it clearly needed. I only felt the tingling sensation of my freshly cut arm for mere seconds. I blacked out, no longer aware of my surroundings.

Friday, June 22nd, 1990 at 9:37 a.m., I woke up with my head throbbing and the low hum of the vacuum bumping my door; it was mom's way of waking me up. Before I could even open my eyes, I winced from the stinging pulsation on my left arm. I pulled the covers over my head, hoping to drown out the vacuum cleaner, or any noise for that matter. As I rolled over in my bed, I made the painful mistake of lying on my left side. I briefly flinched when the sharp pain alerted me to quickly roll back to my right side. Tracing my fingertips along my arm, I could feel my dried up, handmade toilet paper dressing, but I could not work up enough courage to actually look at the damage done. The heavy sweatshirt, along with my flowery pastel quilt, practically made me sweat off ten pounds. I laid in my bed with damp hair, the back of my knees sweating, and an overwhelming feeling of disbelief. The pain that I was feeling was intentional, and I was the stupid idiot who did it.

When the vacuum cleaner went silent, mom swung my door open with full force, hitting my wall and muttering under her breath. She looked so angry. It was only 9:30 in the morning, so why was she so pissed? Ughh... oh my God... maybe, she saw blood on the floor. Does she know? I traced my left arm to make sure my sweatshirt was hiding the evidence. I continued talking to myself wondering the entire time if she knew about last night. I bet she would get mad at me. I bet she would say, "How could you do that to me?" I bet she would think that somehow it was all her fault.

After muttering under her breath about how I slept too late, she asked, "Do you think you can make yourself useful today?" She wrapped the cord around the vacuum, never looking directly at me, which gave me relief. I was terrified that my face would give away what occurred in the bathroom last night. As I recalled bits and pieces of my late night saga, I became nervous wondering if there were any bloodstains on the bathroom floor.

The only thing I wanted to do at that moment was get out of bed to inspect the bathroom.

I quickly remarked, "Yeah." I was too nervous to be tired.

I sprung out of my bed, trying to hide the feeling of my Advil-induced heaviness. (My body felt like it had gained fifty pounds overnight.) Mom, clearly shocked by my peculiar actions, watched me closely. Her sudden interest in my odd behavior made me nervous.

I was afraid she was going to touch my sweatshirt or demand that I take it off. She stood in the middle of my room, grasping the vacuum cord. She cynically remarked, "It's like ninety degrees outside and you're wearing a sweatshirt?"

I couldn't look directly at her. I tried to convince her that there was a legitimate reason by returning her question with sarcasm. I replied, "Whatever- it was like totally freezing last night. Don't you remember?"

She hesitated for a moment and I knew that she bought it. "No," she said. "Huh? I was, I was hot last night." Her response sounded more like a question than a statement.

Good one, Shan.

After inspecting the bathroom and finding tiny specks of blood, I began cleaning the maroon dots with wet toilet paper, so I could easily discard the dirty tissue in the toilet. The bathroom was so bright with the sun shining steadily through the tiny cracks of the blinds. I couldn't help but think about how different everything looked last night. I exhaled and lifted my sweatshirt up to reveal the dried brown toilet wrapped around my left arm. Pressing down to test the amount of pressure I could take, I convinced myself that what happened last night was a fluke, a blip, a one time experimental thing that I would never do again. As I pressed down, I winced at the intense burning sensation. After revealing the sharp incisions, I began caressing my left arm and told myself that everything was going to be okay.

My body was still heavy and every movement took tremendous effort. While sitting at the kitchen table and munching on some toast, mom walked into the kitchen to pour another cup of coffee. She whistled a tune and drank her coffee while she gazed out the window. Mom would never know about last night and I wondered what she would do if she found out. Even though mom and I lived in the same house, I felt like we were two complete strangers. She knew nothing about me. I mean, she thought she did, but she really had no clue. I watched her take several sips from her morning caffeine fix and shook my head in disappointment. I was so ashamed about what happened last night and, at the same time, totally humiliated. What kind of freak cuts their arm?

After she left, I tried to envision the relationship she shared with her own mother. I was convinced that she never had love or guidance from her own mother. I never met my maternal grandmother before and I never heard anything about her either. I suppose the fact that she was in a mental institution in Florida for the past twenty years explained it all. Throughout the years, the only bit of information I knew for sure was that she was schizophrenic. To me, that meant she was a total whack job. What if I was a whack job, too? Maybe it runs in the family.

I ate my toast while contemplating the idea. *Nah... I'm not crazy- I'm just messed up.* The ringing of the phone diverted my thoughts. I picked up the phone, hoping it was Carl.

"Hey. So, you happy this morning?" Carl's chipper voice greeted me.

His voice sounded wonderful. He was the voice of sanity.

I faked a laugh, wondering how fast Carl would break up with me if he knew about last night.

I did my best to return his cheerful tone. I laughed again before saying, "I'm smilin' from ear to ear! What about you? Did you look me up last night in the dictionary? Was I cute?"

Carl snickered and said, "Yeah, you were the one with the bucktoothed smile."

As we chatted, I occasionally touched my self-inflicted wounds. Everything about that moment was weird. It was as if I was somewhere between reality and insanity at the same time. Carl and I made plans that night. How was I going to hide my arm?

After I hung up the phone, I wiped my brow and tried to forget about everything. It was over. I was fine. I was better than fine. Damn, I thought to myself, it is too hot to wear a friggin' sweatshirt.

summer of love

Carl and I played wiffle ball in his back yard almost every night. It was quite an impressive set up. He set up bases, a homerun fence, and even spray painted *Shea Stadium* on the concrete wall that was nearly covered with ivy. When I was in his company, I never thought about death or the future or anything heavy. Carl, to me, was all about baseball, playing wiffle ball, sappy Mariah Carey songs, inside jokes, and an occasional trip to Dippy's for ice cream.

The two weeks following my "temporary insanity," as I referred to it, were incredibly difficult. Hiding the trio of lines on my arm was difficult, but more difficult were going to be the permanent scars to follow. After wearing long sleeve shirts for ten days, I decided to come up with a made up story that my dog, Dewey, scratched me in the pool. Dewey had a habit of jumping in our pool, and it was basically impossible to get him out of the water, so I figured that would be a good story. I even showed people how it happened as I imitated Dewey's paw coming down on my arm with one hard swipe. Everyone bought it, including Carl.

I stopped trying to figure out why I did that to myself. In fact, I just stopped thinking about it in general.

Pretending that it never happened was a lot easier than trying to assess it or figure out what was wrong with me. My secret would remain in that humid bathroom on a hot summer night.

Like every summer before, the hot days went by incredibly fast. The end of August was looming, and I knew that the end of summer would destroy my wonderful distraction, Carl. I spent all my free time with Carl, thinking about Carl, or planning my doomed future around Carl. I rehearsed our breakup hundreds of times in my head, and with every scenario, I played it cool, trying to convince myself that it didn't matter. My predictions were simple: Carl leaves in August, we break up in early September, and then we never, ever talk again. I had the visual already set in my mind. I visualized his car riding past my street when he came home for the weekends. Or I would hear about one of his pretty, sophisticated college girlfriends from James. Or I would see him at the homecoming football game and we would conveniently ignore each other. I would watch him laugh with his friends and just remember him as that summer fling. I mentally prepared myself for the inevitable.

When Carl actually started packing his belongings into his huge locker, the harsh reality began to unfold. I watched helplessly as my wonderful distraction prepared to leave for good. Even after all my mental preparation and constant self-talk, it still hurt to watch him slip away. I told myself to be strong, and I *never* told Carl how I really felt. I began my nightly captain's field hockey practices, trying to get my mind off the obvious. The girls on the team asked me how I felt about him leaving, and I would respond, "Carl who?" They laughed, giving me a high five for my ability to let everything just roll off my back. I suppose it was a good show. Deep down, behind my bogus comments, there was tremendous sadness. Everyone eventually leaves me. Carl leaving for college was a loss that I could not even acknowledge.

He left on a surprisingly breezy Saturday morning just before eight o'clock. He walked over to my house to say goodbye. I was relieved that my grogginess from staying up the entire night kept me from feeling anything intense. As we sat on my front step, he held my hand and tried to soothe my fears that the summer was simply passing time.

I was not quite sure what came over me, but with a rare show of emotion, I wearily pointed out, "You're gonna forget all about me." I probably said it at the most inopportune time, but the statement was my truest and boldest declaration to date. I placed my head on his shoulders, sighing as I breathed in and out slowly.

The moment that was supposed to read like a movie script or a saccharine love song, but it was more like an awkward rite of passage. There was nothing sweet or simple about saying goodbye to someone. The words were just too hard to find with the future so up in the air.

Carl pushed me away. "Don't say that!" His face, rather serious, showed frustration with my last comment. Maybe I should have just kept my mouth shut. He added, "You are going to go back to the *same* school with all your *same* friends." He shook his head and helplessly admitted, "You'll start field hockey and go to football games, while I am, like, far away." He shrugged. "In the pines... at Stockton..." Carl laughed. "With the Jersey Devil."

That was type of stuff I would miss: the stupid jokes, the nothingness of sitting on the steps together, the silence that feels nice, the thirty second phone calls. It was all coming to an end.

Carl looked down at his new Nike sneakers, picking at the concrete that was falling apart on my steps, and softly whispered, "It's more like you'll forget about me. Everything is the same here and... I don't know... easy. Everything is routine and normal for you. Just don't say stuff like that... okay?" Carl's demands were not that hard. I could easily hold my tongue. Actually, I was a professional at not saying what I really wanted to say.

I smiled. "Okay. I promise." Then, I nodded my head in agreement. Trying to give some "girlfriendy" advice, I cheerfully said, "It's gonna be fine. I mean, it's your next step and you'll be fine. We can talk on the phone, write letters, and you can come home on the weekends, right?"

Carl kissed me on the cheek and handed me a red card. He asked me not to open it until later that night. As he turned to leave, I waved goodbye, watching him turn my corner. When I could no longer see him, I whispered, "Nice knowing you." Then, I headed inside to go back to sleep. I began mentally talking to myself in bed, trying to forget about him and reminding myself, once again, that it was only temporary. Perhaps he was right, life would be back to normal. As I flipped my body from side to side, I told myself that if I can deal with my brother's death and all that bullshit, then being alone would be a piece of cake.

Later that night, I read his Hallmark card by my open window with the late August moon.

Dear Shannon,
I may not be across the street anymore, but you are still in my every thought. Try to remember this summer and all the fun times when I am not around. I will be back soon to kick your ass in wiffle ball!
Missing you already.
Love, Carl
P.S. - Love you as long as Niagara Falls.

My identification had switched from being Phillip's younger sister to Carl Kindsay's girlfriend. It annoyed me that people were so interested in Carl's life. The girls at school asked, "How he is doing?" or "Does he like it at Stockton?" What did they care, anyway? Most of the time, I just gave basic one-line answers to keep them curious. I mean, they made it sound like he was my lifeline, as if I monitored his every move. I made it fifteen years without him, so I was quite sure I could make it to the weekend.

Lizzie and I hit the jackpot in school. We were in every single class together and sat next to each other in "B" lunch. We shared a locker, walked to school, ate lunch, and played field hockey together. The only class we did not sit next to each other was our third period biology class. Thomas sat right behind me, conveniently ignoring me while passing dirty letters to Keri, who sat right next to me. Keri let me read them, and we both gasped in disbelief at his disgustingly perverted jokes. He made cracks about her huge boobs, which went from tiny anthills to voluptuous mountains over summer vacation. I patiently waited for any reason to wear a bra; forget about sports bras... basically, in my sports bra, I looked like a ten-year-old boy.

I had to admit that one of my favorite times of year was September. To a student, it was truly a new year. Everything was the same, but, at the same time, everything was different. Summer was the opportunity to change and after a two-month hiatus, anyone could come back to school totally different. Even the smell of oily French-fries reminded me of the special time of year when everything was still mysterious and unexplored.

Lizzie and I walked to every class together, occasionally bumping into the cheerleading whores, who I was sure had Friday night bleach and peroxide parties. The poser skanks traveled in packs, bouncing their fake, white hair and big boobs all around, flirting with anyone who would give them any attention. I had good reason to hate them all: they all hated me. The fact that I was dating Carl irritated and confused them. I knew that they saw me as beneath them or somehow not good enough. I could just feel it. I received several prank phone calls over the summer with girls laughing in the background, harassing me about Carl. In the crowded halls, they walked past me, giggling while shouting his name loudly to get my attention. For the most part, I ignored them, but I welcomed any opportunity to make vulgar comments about them.

During field hockey practice, we ran a lot. I mean, five miles a day. Whenever I ran, my mind would wander. I shifted from one subject to the next, but most times, I asked myself, what it would be like if Phillip was still alive. What if he got some help and got better? What would he be like? Who would he hang out with? What would he look like? Who would he go out with? Would he like me? Maybe we would go to football games together. I had phony conversations with my brother on my long, five-mile runs. I told him that I was different and, if he were here, I wouldn't make fun of him or call him names. I told him that I was sorry. I told him that I should have come to his room and talked to him or just listened to him. In my head, I said the words "I am so sorry" hundreds of times and hoped that somehow he could hear me.

When I sat in class, I took the opportunity to observe, just as I did at home. I intently watched people and made up stories about them in my head. There were so many phonies and posers walking all around me, even those I called my friends. They were all wolves dressed in sheep's clothing. Girls in my class complained about the most trivial, unimportant things, usually stemming from their own insecurities. I rolled my eyes when the 105 lb. girl whined because she was "so fat." Give me a break. It was so clear that she just wanted to hear, "Oh, no. You are so skinny." Talk about insecurity. I listened to them, pretending that I even cared as they complained about their mothers, sisters, brothers, boyfriends, or whatever. To me, their issues were minor, and I laughed inside about their nonsense. Everyone walked around dazed and confused in the hallway, and I was able to observe, to study, and remain unattached until the day I saw Miles Donlon.

Miles Donlon and I have never talked to one another, made eye contact, or stood in line next to each other. He wasn't in any of my classes because he was in all level IV classes with the rest of the smart kids. Miles and I never once had a single word exchanged between us and probably never would. However, what Miles didn't know was that every time he walked by me, my heart sank and I felt incredibly overprotective toward him. Like my brother, Miles was the fat kid who was tortured by everyone, and I mean, everyone. When he walked down the halls, kids took liberties by pushing him around, calling him "million pound Miles." Silly girls giggled and hit their boyfriends as they smiled and giddily shouted, "Oh my God... stop... you're so mean." Unfortunately, those girls never did anything but try to *look* like they cared.

Miles had no idea that I compared him to my brother all the time. I actually looked forward to seeing him walk by me in the hallway, hoping I could replace my guilt with justice and maybe stick up for him one day. Miles had sad, brown, puppy eyes, and weaved his way in and out of the school crowd, as if he was in a big rush to get somewhere fast. His pants always drooped, exposing his butt crack, his shirt came up exposing his jiggly, white belly, and his hair always stuck straight in the air. Sometimes, I thought about what it was like for him at home. I wondered if his mom was nice to him, or if his dad took him out fishing. Did he have any brothers or sisters? Did his family make fun of him? I wondered if Miles had any dreams or aspirations. Miles was far more interesting than any chisel-faced football player. Miles reminded me of my past, and I anxiously awaited the opportunity to change it.

Exactly one week after Carl left for Stockton, he returned home to Woodbury Heights for his first visit. He called me three times during the week, mentioning repeatedly how much he hated it. Of course, I could not even fathom how someone could hate college life with all the freedom it had to offer.

I had practice early that Saturday morning. I just went through all the motions, pretending to listen intently to my coach, Ms. Phillips. Instead of focusing on corner plays, I was daydreaming about my boyfriend (soon to be ex-boyfriend.) I stared in the distance, making up several scenarios for our reunion with each one of them ending poorly. It was just my nature to expect the worst in any situation, my mind's way of preparing for a catastrophe. Whatever happened, I had to play it cool and never expose how I truly felt.

At six-thirty, the doorbell rang twice. I took my time answering the door, trying to appear preoccupied, so he would never suspect that I had been literally counting the minutes. I opened the door with an expected rush of bottled emotion released at the sight of his face. Embarrassed for feeling like a stupid girl, I tried to say something sarcastic to hide my true feelings. "Back so soon?" I asked. I followed my comment with a giggle and checked a fake watch on my wrist. I asked, "Didn't you just leave like five minutes ago?" Grinning, or possibly expecting that remark, he revealed a single red rose hidden behind his back.

"For me?" I asked. Then, I curtsied like a southern belle. "Why, Mr. Kindsay, for little ol' me? You shouldn't have."

Carl was pleased with my performance. He sarcastically warned, "Yeah, please don't send it back..." After grimacing with confusion over his comment, I started laughing as I remembered the story about John Boggs.

Talk about awkward? The first ten minutes of our reunion had several moments of uncomfortable silence that we filled with stupid comments and tedious lingo.

"Come on," Carl insisted. "Let's go for a walk."

I put on my sneakers and followed him down the street. I told him all about school. We talked about my classes, field hockey practice, and the nasty cafeteria food. I went on and on about how much I hated every single bleach-blonde cheerleader. Carl seemed entertained by my update. I got the feeling he missed home. Carl's college experience didn't appear to be going that well. He talked about his dorm, his new roommate, and the long walk to classes. Everything he mentioned seemed so negative, which was totally unlike him. I asked if he liked anything about school, and all he said was, "At least it is close to home." Then, he became quiet.

"Carl?" I stopped walking. "Why are you so quiet?"

He put his head down and I was sure it was going to be the moment; the dreaded moment that I had prepared for. The moment he was going to do just what I expected him to do. Granted, I knew it was only a week, but it was Carl who had a notorious reputation for straying.

Finally, he said, "I'm not going back."

"What?" I blurted. I was shocked and relieved at the same time. "What do you mean... not going back?"

His demeanor, suddenly melancholy, matched his white face as he pleaded his case: "I am not going back. It is that simple." He tried to make me understand by adding, "I hate it there. Anyway, I'm just a homebody. I don't go out drinking or go to bars or any of that stuff. You know?" He paused to check my reaction.

Carl bit his lip and then mentioned, "I like to be in my own bed, in my own house, and I don't know, I just... look- I know it's not for me. I honestly don't know what I was thinking. I should have just gone to community college or Glassboro State. I don't know what to do... I..." He was stuttering over his words, trying to justify his decision. I felt sorry for him because I knew that it wasn't my decision to make.

"Did you tell your parents?" I asked.

While shaking his head with frustration, he replied, "They know. I told them."

I just assumed he was homesick and when he got used to school, he would forget all about home. Part of me hoped that his decision wasn't based on me. I would hate to think that he would sacrifice his college experience for a two-month relationship.

"Carl, I have to ask you..." I cleared my throat hoping not to sound too presumptuous.

"Yeah?" he replied.

I looked from side to side, hoping it would come out right. "I mean, I hope that you're not doing this for me. I mean, not that I think you would, it's just that, like, I don't know. You really shouldn't do it for me." After I asked him that question, my face became red.

He looked at me sideways and then began to laugh. The statement made me feel like an idiot for assuming I had any influence over his college plans. He grinned and then became serious as he said, "Shannon, I mean, I'm not gonna deny that you had something to do with it... but..."

I never let him continue his sentence when I said, "Carl, no, no, no. Do it on your own. I mean, like, make that decision based on what you want- not me."

"Why? Why is that so bad?" he asked impatiently.

It was simple. The answer was simple. I would never come back home for a boy- *ever*. I felt a strange sense of guilt for even being a teeny, tiny part of his major decision to come home. I pleaded, "Well, it's not bad... but... I just want you to come back for you, not for me. I mean, I don't know. You know?"

Three days later, Carl's big locker was unpacked. I didn't know what to make of his arrival home. However, I was certain that when I left in three years, I was not coming back in one week.

when will I ever use algebra?

Sophomore year made me think- more than any other year. If that was even possible. I began dabbling into thoughts outside my head and started to focus on the world around me. There was so much to learn. In English class, we read The Scarlet Letter. After reading it, I was so pissed. There are so many injustices in the world. How many people (men and women) would have a giant A across their chest today? Of course, in History, we learned about all the World Wars and, with that information, I couldn't help but think we lived in a cruel, twisted, complicated world. Oh, and then there was Algebra. Seriously? Algebra? I could not even fathom one moment in my life when algebra would be remotely useful... ever.

In health class, we occasionally dabbled in social issues. By dabble, I mean watched a lame after-school special. The same typical educational crap they showed us every year. After twenty boring minutes of bad acting and equally bad music, it appeared all of life's problems were exposed and solved while wearing the same outfit. Afterwards, our teacher would ask, "Does anyone have any questions?" With the exception of Nancy Diener, who *always* had a question, the rest of us rubbed our eyes and thought- *you can't be serious.*

The issues that we discussed in school probably needed approval by the school board. The material was labeled 'delicate.' I really had no idea why it was so sensitive because every kid that I knew already knew all the stuff they were going to discuss- probably more. It was the mouthy mom, the overprotective mom, who objected to everything, obviously living in a world of denial, thinking that sexual education or drug awareness would somehow make their kid go out and have wild sex or do illegal drugs. I suppose those parents never went to high school because they were only kidding themselves if they thought that their teenage darlings didn't know that stuff already.

In health class, we watched two crappy videos from the early eighties. The subjects were predictably drugs/alcohol, peer pressure, and (gasp) sexual education. Sex education was never, ever sexy. It was just a bunch of adults telling us not to have sex or we would get pregnant or catch a disease. The storyline- typical. The outcome- predictable. My interest- nonexistent.

Typically, as in most of these health class skits, there was a helpless victim, hence, the poor, innocent, pimply freshman boy. The villain was the mean, bossy type who somehow had the world at his fingertips, but, in tragic fashion, was deeply insecure. The problem was normally a clash between two social worlds; worlds that battled in the high school cafeteria. The results were so expected. In the fabricated stories, truth, justice, and honor prevail. Hence, the villain is defeated by the victim and everyone in the story is all smiles and 'happily ever after.' The truth was blatantly ignored. High school is not that perfect- it is a sloppy mess.

The other film that our board of education agreed on was about peer pressure. The infamous two words that teachers and parents threw around like it meant something.

Peer pressure. I just got a kick out of those words. In the beginning of the movie, a b-list actor came out to give us a brief definition of the words. They were all sparkly smiles as they talked about the challenges of our nation's youth and bla-bla-bla. Then, the washed up actor smiled and then sternly warned, "Now, don't take my word for it. Let's see what peer pressure can do to Jessica as she struggles to find the strength to go against her friends. Watch Jessie as she faces her biggest fears."

I would sit lifeless in class and watch the film that revolved around little Jess that, once again, looked like a yard sale, washed up, old eighties video. I couldn't help but think: why was it so hard to understand? Why are they teaching us about this crap? I suppose watching a film about some stupid high school party or puffing on a joint was easier to swallow than acknowledging that some kids were just not happy. Why couldn't they understand that we weren't some poor, helpless kids? We had problems- big problems, adult problems. So, wondering if we fit in, contemplating puffing on a joint, or giving into "peer pressure" was just lame. We have issues that were way more complicated.

I didn't need a school official to tell me why we didn't learn about that stuff. I knew why. I suppose it was normal to believe that kids were moody, and then… *poof*…we're adults and we're happy. When most people heard the word "depression" or, even worse, "teen depression," they rolled their eyes and naively muttered, "Oh, everyone goes through bad times," or they would say, "You'll get over it." Or, "I know… I went through it, too." Teen depression was viewed as simple teenage angst or raging hormones.

As I watched the useless film, all I thought about was my brother. I couldn't help but believe that somehow, someway, he was cheated. He was cheated by the misinterpretation that his problem was with drugs, alcohol, or even heavy metal music. Not only was he cheated, but everyone who watched these brainwashed, useless movies would be cheated, too. I sat in the dark with my hands propping my head up. I became sad knowing that they were teaching us *issues* that weren't really our *issues*.

Not only was sitting through those movies difficult, but sophomore year was difficult. I spent a lot of my time in my room, writing sappy poems about Carl, war, my friends, and things that I didn't even understand. Every time I wrote something about Phillip, I would scribble it out or crumple it into a small paper ball. What was the use? It was the thing that I couldn't understand; the subject that tapped my back at night, the situation that fueled my angst, and the tragedy that I could not understand.

In tenth grade, I made the varsity field hockey team, started listening to *The Steve Miller Band,* and smoked (puffed) my first cigarette. The majority of my tenth grade year was spent hanging out with Lizzie, Shelly, and my wonderful and beautiful distraction, Carl. Most of the time, I was pretty happy. Some of the time, I became very, very low. It was a low that almost drew me back to the bathroom for another bout with a sharp razor, but I couldn't go back to that. I didn't like the shame of it all, and besides, it hurt like hell.

Sophomore year...

1. *I was madly in love.*
2. *In French class, my name was Monique and I was caught cheating on a test.*
3. *My zipper was wide open at a party and everyone laughed at me. (I laughed, too.)*
4. *I got bronchitis.*

5. *I (finally) got enough courage to move into my brother's old room because he had a huge closet. Big step for me.*
6. *I had two panic attacks, but had no idea what they were until much later.*
7. *That spring was boiling hot. We had no air conditioning in the school.*
8. *I had a wicked teacher named Mrs. Teal, who had long witch hair and a nasty pirate face. I learned more from her than any other teacher... ever.*
9. *I went to the gynecologist for the first time. (Hated it.)*
10. *Thought I saw Phillip in my closet staring at me. I couldn't sleep for days afterward.*

The day I turned sixteen, the thought occurred to me that I lived a life longer than my older brother. I outlived him by three months and nine days on that day. My friends bought me a huge array of Mylar balloons, each wishing me a "Happy Sweet 16!" Carl gave me a charm for my gold chain of a number ten. Mom and dad took me out to eat at Ponzios; I ordered fried shrimp. That day, the day I turned sixteen, was cold and rainy. That night, I sat with my knees up in my warm bed, listened to the soft rain tap against my window, and thought about him.

to thine own self be true

The summer before my junior year was, in one word, incredible. It was my first summer with a driver's license. That fabulous, tiny card that was tucked in my wallet granted me freedom to spend lazy days on the beach with Lizzie and Tiffany. They were perfect sunny days that were filled with gossip, sun, salt air, and grand aspirations about our senior year. That same summer, we upgraded to regular cigarettes, instead of the usual lights. We barely inhaled but still became lightheaded and triumphant for doing something rebellious. We started drinking beer instead of wine coolers on the weekends and told ourselves that, because we were going to be seniors, it was totally okay.

Carl and I celebrated our two-year anniversary, which in high school was basically a lifetime. It seemed our celebration, and the fact that we had been together so long, seemed more routine than eventful. Carl became increasingly jealous over stupid things and I believed that his jealousy was just his weird way of proving that he *really* loved me. Most times, I just ignored his blatant accusations, but, sometimes when I felt strong enough, I fought back. I hated fighting. I hated being mad at him. It was so hard to admit it, but I needed his affections so badly that I chose to let things slide.

Although we had our share of problems and insecurities, Carl and I did enjoy hanging out with each other. He knew me. He knew my favorite ice-cream. He knew what songs would make me happy. He knew what jokes would make me laugh. He knew my moods. He knew, he really did know, that there was something deeper lurking within me; something I chose to hide. He attempted to pry into that deep dark place, but I never gave in. He also knew that after my high school years were over that I would go far, far away.

On the fourth of July, Carl and I went to the shore with his parents. The time we spent together was refreshing; no fighting, no jealousy, and no worries. We watched the fireworks on the cold sand in Wildwood, took our picture in a tiny booth, ate funnel cake, and held hands as we strolled down the boardwalk. We were inseparable, perhaps, even invincible. We were young, and being young and in love meant forever. So, the trivial bullshit, the unwarranted accusations, and occasional breakups were just mere roadblocks. I was too weak, too in love, and too devoted to end it. Deep down, I knew it wasn't healthy, but I happily turned a blind eye.

That summer also brought about changes at home. Mom and I were starting to get along better. We went shopping together, sat and talked in the same room for more than ten minutes without fighting, and we even went to Valley Forge for a James Taylor concert. She and I still fought over trivial things, but it seemed to dissolve within a couple days, unlike our fights before. The fact that I had my license, friends to hang out with, and a devoted boyfriend who lived down the street all helped to keep Mom and me civil.

I started to receive letters from various colleges over the summer. The glossy pamphlets invited me to visit their campus or set up a meeting with the coach. Unfortunately, most of the letters I received were from local colleges in New Jersey, Pennsylvania, and a few from Connecticut. But, none of those schools remotely interested me. Just the thought of cold practices that required a turtleneck seemed like four more years of torture. Every letter that I received from a northern college was quickly tossed in the trash.

On my second day of my junior year, I had a meeting with my guidance counselor, who advised me that 11th grade was a crucial time for making decisions about college. Just the thought of going to college and exploring other things gave me an insatiable drive. I would do anything, take any test, fill out any form, and pay any amount of money to leave New Jersey. Shelly and I attended a college preparation seminar together. Basically, it gave us all the inside information about how to "find" the right college. At the one-hour training, the redheaded woman stood with composure at the podium and told us that junior year was simply preparation for our senior year. She claimed that we should have five schools picked out by the time we enter senior year. She rattled off information about; S.A.T.s, C.A.T.s, and G.P.A.s. There were so many acronyms written down in my notebook.

"What do they all mean?" I asked Shelly.

Shelly shrugged her shoulder and then proceeded to blow a big, pink bubble that popped so loud the redheaded lady glared toward us.

During the lecture about financial aid, my mind naturally wandered. Instead of absorbing the information, I wondered if the redheaded lady even went to college. Then, I became fascinated by her red hair. *What is it like to have red hair? Does she dye it?* Probably not- she had pale skin and freckles. When Shelly and I left the training session, I wrote four pages of notes, but all I could remember was her red hair and the slight lisp that came out whenever she said the word "applications."

In the fall, I experienced some major drama with my field hockey coach, Ms. Phillips. She stood at five feet and seven inches, had a short salt and pepper buzz cut, and wore a field hockey kilt all the time (even in January.) She was mean and she terrified me. Hockey is a misunderstood sport of sorts. Most who watch (including my dad) were often times frustrated by the referee's whistle that tweeted every four seconds and the constant shift in direction by the players. Ms. Phillips was exactly the type of coach a successful field hockey program needed. She was tough, controlling, strong, and sarcastic. I sometimes loved her and then, other times, I completely despised her.

She spoke with confidence and used vocabulary that was often witty and clever. She was an interesting mix of Saturday Night Live and CNN. She was quick with a comeback, sharp with details, and never wrong. Never. When she walked through the halls in school, everyone was aware of her presence. Football players liked her, scumbags liked her, and even the skanky cheerleaders liked her. Without speaking a single word, she naturally attracted a certain kind of respect that most adults worked their entire lives to attain. Ms. Phillips was a woman of substance and power, and I wondered if she was even aware of the power that she possessed.

During practice, Ms. Phillips never stopped yelling and, if she wasn't shouting like a military commander, she was blowing on her silver whistle. My hero quickly became my nemesis on a humid Friday afternoon. The game against Paulsboro was predicted to be a total blow-out. We crushed them every time we played them, beating them by at least seven. Paulsboro was also the grossest, smelliest, most disgusting place to play because of the factory that was close by. The warm September air intensified the lingering pungent smell coming from the Exxon Mobile plant just a few miles away. On the bright side, it was Friday night, we were going to slaughter them, and my friends and I were going to the football game later. During warm-ups, most of us fooled around and, by most of us, I guess that would include me, Lizzie, Tiffany, and our favorite senior class clown, Jenny. The only problem with that was out of the four of us, I was the only starter.

In our team huddle, I half-listened when Ms. Phillips rattled off the starting line-up; a line-up that did not include my name. I looked at Lizzie sideways, and her wincing eyes confirmed that I was not starting. Clearly, I had to play it off as if I didn't care. *Who the hell does she think she is anyway? Whatever! How dare she bench me?* I was fuming. So, instead of acting like it bothered me, I figured I would act like a total brat. Seeing my team start without me totally sucked, even if it was just Paulsboro. On the bench, I joked around with the other girls and laughed a little bit louder, so Ms. Phillips could hear me. She made her point, and now it was time to make mine. There was already one woman in my life who tried to control me and the last thing I needed was two.

I sat with my stick in my hand and my mouth guard tucked in my long, blue sock. Watching the girls score goal after goal made my head spin... *that should be me out there.* Seeing someone else in *my* position, a position that I earned, was beyond annoying. So, instead of admitting that I was wrong, I did what any 16 year old girl would do- I acted like it didn't bother me. She wanted me to sit there and take my punishment, but I wouldn't allow it. Ms. Phillips gave me the evil eye every so often, which actually made me feel victorious. I knew that my behavior bothered her and that was exactly what I wanted. I win. You lose.

During our half-time huddle, I refused to look up at her when she talked. I hated her. I really hated her for trying to make a point. At the start of the second half, I resumed my spot on the bench and watched each sub on the bench go into the game to replace a starter. By that point, I didn't even want to go in the game. It was humiliating. I stood my ground and still acted like it didn't matter. Ms. Phillips had no idea who she was messing with because I was a professional at pretending things didn't bother me. In my mind, she was just an amateur when it came to these types of mind games. I have spent the past three years in total denial, so I could handle a measly 90 minutes.

There was only fifteen minutes left in the game when Ms. Phillips finally called me over to end of the bench, so we could have a private conversation. I intentionally rose slowly, stretched my arms, gave a little giggle to the girls on the bench, and tried my best to piss her off. With my stick in my hand, I swaggered over and sat down on the cold metal bench. *Let the bitch session begin.*

"Shannon?" she calmly started, "Why are you sitting on the bench today?" She asked casually while keeping an eye on her team playing on the patchy field.

I knew why. Of course, I knew that I was fooling around during warm-ups. I also knew that her attempt to make me learn from it would ultimately backfire.

While twirling my hockey stick, I blurted out, "I don't know. I guess Paulsboro sucks, and you wanted to give the subs some time. I guess."

She placed her right hand on my stick to stop the twirling. I knew she wanted my full attention. "Did the starters go in first today?" she asked.

"Yeah."

"Then, why aren't you out there?" Her questions were so methodical, so calculated. All adults asked questions that way.

"Well, it's mostly just subs now," I sarcastically muttered.

She wasn't amused.

"And, so, why are *you* on the bench?"

"I don't know," I replied robotically.

But, I did know.

"You don't know, huh?" She cackled softly, as if she expected that response. "Well, you see Shannon, that is precisely part of your problem. This little attitude of yours is not very cute. In fact, it is quite annoying. And, I know..." She hesitated. "I know that you know exactly why you are sitting on your butt and not running out there." She pointed to the team and, with her two fingers pressed firmly in her mouth, she whistled for Jen Walker to mark a girl in the circle.

Attitude? What attitude? If she wanted attitude, I could give attitude. Who was she, anyway? My face began to turn red when her allegation began to set in, which made me feel completely misunderstood. *Of course, I'm going to have an attitude.* She benched me for most of the game. I scoffed, shook my head, and thought- *hey, I should be mad at her.*

"Look at me, Shannon!" she demanded.

Her sharp tone made me nervous. When I finally saw her face, my hard demeanor changed, and I really wanted to hear what she was going to say.

Her voice became soft, almost sympathetic, when she asked, "What is with you? I don't understand you. I really do not get you at all."

I looked away from her pale blue eyes and began to feel small tinges of guilt and humiliation.

"You know, what really gets me is that you are a tough competitor, a gamer, and I know you hate to lose. You worked your butt off to start, so why? Why do you act like you don't care? It is so difficult to watch you self-destruct. Yet, your behavior on the bench proves that you don't care." She stretched her muscular legs out and mentioned, "If it were me, you know, if I was the one on the bench, I'd make damn sure to behave, so I could go in. But, you..." She let out a deep breath to stress her next point. "You play games."

I really wasn't sure how to answer her, but I was aware that my chin was starting to quiver. Should I tell her the truth? Or should I lie? She had no clue what it was like to be me. She would never understand what it feels like to be so totally controlled by everyone that you just feel like you're going to bust. How could she even begin to understand?

"Why are you playing games with me, Shannon?"

I glanced sideways toward her and muttered, "Because then, you'd win."

She chuckled at my response and nodded her head as if she understood, but I wasn't really sure if she did. "Are we in some kind of competition?" she asked.

"No," I blankly stated.

"Then, why do you think it is a matter of win or lose between us?"

"I don't know. I just do." I looked in the other direction when I hissed, "You pissed me off."

Ms. Phillips placed her hand on my shoulder and said something that I never expected: "Shannon, I want to help you."

My chin was giving out. That was a crock- nobody wanted to help me. Nobody ever listened to me. My mom only cared about her dead son. My dad had no idea how royally screwed up I really was. My boyfriend constantly accused me of cheating on him. My coach bossed me around. I just felt so controlled.

"Hey." Her voice was soothing. "Shan, we cannot battle like this. It just isn't going to work. Believe me when I tell you that I want you to succeed."

I turned my head away from her and rolled my eyes.

"Well. Can we start over?" she asked.

"Yup."

She began to dispel some generic words of wisdom. She lectured me about being a role model for the underclassmen. She rambled on about facing challenges, being a winner, and finding my true self. When she spoke, I listened. I listened, but I didn't completely understand.

"Okay, it's time to go in." She rose from the bench, blew her whistle, and stuck me in the last ten minutes of the game.

On the bus ride home the girls giggled, told stories, and did funny imitations. I, however, was uncharacteristically quiet. *What does she mean by "find my true self?" What does that mean?*

That same night, I had a weird dream. It was the kind of dream that makes you question if it was real or fake. All I could remember was being in a movie theatre with Carl. He was so mean to me, so vicious. He kept yelling at me: "Where have you been? Where were you? You're cheating on me, aren't you?!" I wanted to defend myself, but I literally could not open my mouth.

Then, a huge majestic train came to the movie theatre. It was larger than any train I had ever seen or ever imagined. When it came to a hissing stop, I felt compelled to get on board. Carl was furious. He gave me an ultimatum: him or the train. I was hesitant at first, but somehow instinctively knew that I was supposed to go on that train. When I got on and sat down, I noticed that people were waving to me. They were so happy, so excited. Everyone hollered and jumped with joy. I knew they were waving to me- sending me away on a new journey.

When the train began to leave the theatre, I became uneasy. *Where am I going?* The train picked up speed and began floating in the sky. It was only when I was far away from the movie theatre that I noticed that everything and everyone I ever knew were all trapped in a big bubble. Or maybe it was a dome. Everything that I left behind seemed so small and insignificant. First, I saw my friends, then my school, and then the outline of New Jersey was visible. Finally, I could see The United States in that tiny bubble, slipping away. The scenery made me question if the world I knew was ever real.

I became very frightened. It was too much. I wanted to go back to the familiar. Somehow, the comfort of my tiny bubble made me feel good. After that thought passed, I was instantaneously back at the movie theatre. Carl was outside the tracks waiting for me. After I stepped off the high steps, he darted toward me and began his routine line of questions: "Where did you go? Why did you get on the train? How come you left me?" I simply could not respond.

When the train left, I almost ran after it but felt stupid and embarrassed for coming back. When I awoke, I tried to go back to sleep, so I could get back on the train. In my bed, I tossed and turned and became irritated for not staying on the train or sticking up for myself.

Things were going better for me and Ms. Phillips. Our relationship was on the mend and I thought we could be cool with each other, until the game against Woodbury High School and my fight with Carmen Miller. First, I should mention that I hated Woodbury and, second, I should mention that I can't stand Carmen.

For the first half of the game, she was all over me. Even when I didn't have the ball, or if I was about to receive the ball, Carmen was like a shadow on my back. She hacked at my stick, tripped me from behind, and intentionally hit my shins. After playing through for 45 minutes, I approached Ms. Phillips to complain and told her that she was hitting my shins on purpose. Ms. Phillips blew it off and strictly advised (warned) me to use my speed to get around her.

Twenty minutes into the second half, after two shoulder bumps from Carmen, I called her "an ugly bitch." Unfortunately, one of the officials heard me and gave me a warning. The skinny official told me that if she heard any foul language again, then I would receive a yellow card. A yellow card meant that I would sit for the rest of the game. A card from the official would have been much easier than any punishment from Ms. Phillips.

With a mere five minutes left in the game, I was beyond annoyed with all her shadowing. Carmen and I both went back and forth- hacking, lightly pushing, calling each other derogatory names under our breath. Then, she really pissed me off when she bumped me in the shoulder and knocked me out of the sidelines. The ref gave her an official warning. I had a free hit, so I picked up the ball and hit it in the circle. As I ran by Carmen, I pushed her down, and then playfully taunted, "Oooopppssss!"

She fell down on her stomach, but before she got up, she took her stick and tripped my right foot as I sprinted away. My body fell hard on the grass and it took me a moment to realize what had happened. *Dirty bitch!* Like me, Carmen ran past me and rubbed it in when she sarcastically squealed, "My bad!"

I knew the official was going to give us both a yellow card. With only about three minutes of play, I didn't care about sitting on the bench. She deserved it, and I was glad that I pushed her down. The look on Ms. Phillips' face was a clear indication that she was not at all impressed by my performance. She never acknowledged me when I sat down on the bench. My teammates congratulated me by giving me hidden high fives. They all agreed that I was right and she was wrong. I nodded along with them and felt slightly vindicated for my actions.

The team huddled up after the game and shook hands with the other team. Ms. Phillips made me stay close to her when we walked in a single file line to slap hands. After we had our team meeting about the game and upcoming practice, Ms. Phillips pointed at me and ordered me over to her. I put on my sweatshirt and flip-flops and then cautiously walked toward her. "Me?" I questioned, "Do you wanna see me?" I pointed at myself and looked behind me. It was my feeble attempt to act like I was surprised.

She blankly stared at the hockey field while crossing her arms. She didn't even look at me when she shouted, "You!"

As the rest of the team changed into their flip-flops and sweatpants, I stood next to my disappointed coach, biting my nails, and occasionally looking back to Lizzie for some support. Ms. Phillips continued to look out in the distance, arms crossed. Then, she flatly warned, "If you ever, ever pull another stunt like that, so help me, your ass will be riding pine. Do you hear me?" Without letting me answer her, she continued, "Am I clear?"

I knew it wasn't exactly sportsmanship-like to push someone down, but I was simply defending myself. Carmen had it coming. I tried to figure out a way to explain it, so Ms. Phillips would understand. With my hands in front of me, gesturing awkwardly, I said, "I was just, like, defending myself. I mean she was totally riding me the whole game. And I…"

"Did I ask you?" she retorted. "I have eyes, Shannon. I can see. You don't think I saw her?" She clicked her teeth and then scratched her head. "I told you to stay away from her and you deliberately disobeyed me." She let out a deep breath and then admitted, "You know I kept you in the game, thinking that maybe, maybe you would be the bigger person. You know? Maybe, just maybe, you would prove to me that you were above it."

I bowed my head.

She finally moved her body, so she could face me. I could practically see veins coming out of her neck. "You see, Ms. Bennet, you don't run the show here." She pointed to her chest with her pointer finger and declared, "I do! I'm the boss." She crouched over slightly to look me in the eyes and shouted, "Me!"

I stood next to my nemesis with my arms crossed and head down.

"I run this show, Shannon!" Before she walked away, she turned to me, scoffed, and stated, "It's such a disappointment. You'll never learn."

On the bus ride home, I sat next to Lizzie with my knees up against the back of the seat. Lizzie tried to make me feel better. "That girl was totally on you the entire game, and you know what? She deserved it. I'm glad you pushed her down. Big, hairy deal. So what. Right?" She blurted and then looked over to me. I half-listened to her words and blankly stared out the bus window.

Without turning to Lizzie, I focused on my propped knees and asked, "Lizzie, do you think I'm a bad person?" Part of me didn't even want her to respond because I knew she would tell me that I was a good. I just wanted to know the truth. Without letting her respond, I continued, "I mean, do you think I have, like, a bad attitude? Do you think I can be mean?"

Lizzie waited for me to finish. She always listened and I liked that. Sometimes I just wanted to say things aloud without any advice or any answers. I tried to clarify my opinion of myself by adding, "I mean, most of the time, my mom thinks I'm lazy or spoiled. Ms. Phillips thinks I have an attitude problem because I defended myself. And, I don't know, even my own boyfriend doesn't trust me. It's like nobody gets me." I stopped talking and had an immediate thought. Lizzie sat next to me, fidgeting with her Walkman, but still listening. I added, "Or, or maybe I just give off a bad vibe without even knowing it." I leaned my head against my window and whispered, "Whatever. I guess I'm just a loser."

I was ready for a response.

"Shannon, don't let it get to you." She popped in a homemade mixed tape, played with the buttons, and continued, "You're just really over thinking everything right now because you got in trouble. Anyway..." She looked at me and smirked, "Shan, she was totally on you the whole game and, so, you did something about it. I wouldn't have had the balls to do that." She shrugged her shoulder and said, "But, you did. So, whatever. Who cares what people think? Just don't worry about it."

"Yeah. I guess."

I smiled in agreement but knew the way I felt had little to do with pushing that girl down. It was the fact that I would never be understood.

I had the entire weekend to consider a new strategy to handle Ms. Phillips. My solution was simple. I was going to shut her, and everyone who made me feel bad, out. I would shut them out of my life. I mean, I didn't have to *like* my coach, so I would just shut up and do my job. On Monday, at practice, I tried my new approach. Instead of being my loud self, I would just ignore everyone. I would concentrate on getting through practice. It took a mere 40 minutes for me to break my promise. I went back to joking and fooling around. I couldn't help it.

Juniors were in charge of taking in equipment, so after practice, Shelly and I took in the huge Gatorade water jug. As we were walking out of the locker room, I heard my name being called several times. Shelly rolled her eyes, pointed at me, and then snickered. She silently mouthed the words, "Ooooohh, you're gonna get it!" I asked Shelly to tell my dad to wait for me in the car. My assistant coach, who looked like a shorter, plumper version of Larry Byrd, came out of the office, patted my back, and muttered, "Later, Bennet."

I entered her office ready and able to defend myself. Ms. Phillips oozed confidence by just sitting in her big office chair. She was thumbing through some papers, ignoring my presence until she was ready to begin. I was surprised when she politely asked me to go over to the sink that was directly to my left. With some apprehension, I faced the white ceramic sink and waited for more direction. She walked over and stood next to me. Her physical body next to me was a stark reminder that I was just an immature girl and she was the wise woman. Ms. Phillips placed the rubber drain stopper in the sink, and then turned to me.

"Fill it," she requested.

I shifted my cautious eyes toward her to verify, "Fill it? You want me to fill it with water?"

"Yes," she confirmed.

I filled the sink three quarters of the way.

"Now, roll up your sleeves and put your hands in the water."

"Umm, are you serious? Is this a joke?"

She smiled and then quickly stated, "Nope. No joke. Just do it."

I rolled my sleeves up and placed my pale, white fingers in the warm water.

"Now, move your fingers around…" She nodded her head as I moved my fingers to let me know that I was doing it the right way. She followed, "Yup. That's it. Move your little fingers around."

I felt like an idiot.

"What is the water doing?" she asked.

Duh. Dumb question. I quickly responded, "Uhh, it's, like, moving and splashing?" My answer sounded more like a question.

"Now, Shannon," she said as she reached for a brown paper towel and gently handed it to me. "Take your hands out."

I took the paper towel and stared at the still water.

"Look at the water now. What is it doing?"

I kept staring at the water and wondered if it was a trick question. "Uh, nothing. It's not doing anything. It's just, like, staying still." I looked to her for confirmation that I had answered her correctly.

Ms. Phillips smiled with agreement, walked back to her office chair, and then sat down. I dried my hands with the paper towel and waited for an explanation.

With her hands clasped together and her full attention on me, she began, "Shan, when you moved your fingers around, you had control over the water, right?"

"Yeah, I think so."

She put her pointer finger up to stop me from talking, "No, Shannon, you don't think so- you know so."

I was interested, very interested in where she was going with all this.

She continued, "That water sitting in the sink is just like your life, Shannon. Believe it or not, you have control over it."

After her statement, I scoffed and rolled my eyes. But, at the same time, I wondered if she could somehow read my mind. *Control.* Control was what I wanted most.

Ms. Phillips cracked a tiny smile. "You see, that is the beauty of life. It is the secret that nobody tells you until it's way too late. This grand idea that you, yes you, Shannon Bennet, can control and decide what your life will be like. When you moved your fingers around, it was you that moved that water."

I narrowed my eyes and hesitantly responded, "That's just water. My life is, is, kind of complicated. I just have a hard time figuring it out sometimes." I shrugged my shoulders and whispered, "Sometimes, I feel like I'm just a bad person."

"Why?"

"I just do. I feel like I should be nicer, smarter, or just better. I can't explain it."

She half-smiled and then looked at me with a sincerity that almost made me cry. It was a feeling of acknowledgement. Maybe, just maybe, she understood me.

"Shannon, you are what you think you are."

"Huh?"

She went on, "It's really simple. You have choices about your life, like what you'll wear, your friends, your music, interests, and even who *you* want to be."

It was making sense. "Uh-huh," I managed to whisper.

"So, my dear, the only question is: Who, exactly, do you want to be?" She never waited for me to respond when she said something I desperately needed and wanted to hear. "You are an amazing young lady who has unlimited potential. Shannon, you are smart, you are nice, and you are a great kid. I sometimes wonder if you know that."

I simply froze. My enemy, my nemesis was now my hero.

She asked, "Do you understand me?"

I nodded my head.

"Okay, then. See you at practice tomorrow."

I turned around to leave her office, but something made me stop. "Thanks," I whispered. Then, I left her office to meet my dad. "Thanks" was all I could say to her to her at that moment and, maybe, that was all she needed to hear.

Things got better. I really valued her advice and to show my gratitude, I became the athlete she wanted me to be. I guess I did the best that I could, but I still had bad days here and there. There were days when I wanted to change the world and, sometimes, I just wanted to escape it.

And then one day, my world did change. It happened on a boring Tuesday morning at precisely 7:56 a.m. The tragic, yet all too routine drama took place on my way into school. It was the day that I watched (hopefully, for the last time) Miles Donlon get his books thrown into the water.

Brian Brooks, or Big B., was a scrawny guy, which, I guess, was kind of ironic. He was cool. He was a senior. Brian was a hit with freshmen and sophomore girls, using his good looks, charm, and overall package to lure them in. He was the guy that our mothers warned us about. I didn't like Brian that much, but I didn't hate him either. We were sometimes cool with each other and occasionally partied together on weekends. So, the day he took a camouflage book bag from Miles and threw it in a dirty ravine was the day my world changed.

That morning was unseasonably warm, considering it was February. My mind was trying to recite the information needed for my killer history test in third period. So when I saw Brian steal Miles' book bag from his huge body, I almost didn't notice. Brian hollered and slapped other boys' high-fives after he tossed the book bag in a nearby shallow ravine. Miles tried to stop him, but ultimately gave up. Years of torture had taught Miles to "just let it go." I stopped with Lizzie beside me and watched the scene go down. After it was all over and Miles' book bag was wet, slimy, and beyond rescue, the crowd of kids just casually walked away. Brian and his faithful crew of skinny National Park skater rats cackled at the expense of Miles.

Brian taunted Miles by chanting, "Million pound Miles. Cheeseburgers make him smile!"

Everyone around laughed. It wasn't even that funny. It barely even rhymed. It was just mean and stupid.

"Hey!" Brian went on, "Hey, Miles! I bet you just burned about 30 calories getting your backpack out of there. So, basically, you owe me. I just did you a favor."

Miles didn't respond. He simply walked into school. Defeated.

In 1st period, I sat down and felt strange. My heart was racing, my palms were sweaty, and I could not think of anything but what Brian did to Miles. *Who does he think he is? Why didn't anyone help him? Why didn't I help him?* After sitting in class for twenty minutes and stewing over the situation, the old feelings came back. The familiar pangs of guilt, shame, and helplessness were all reminders; my body's way of telling me to do something. In 2nd period, I sat next to Jimmy Hummel. Jimmy was a close friend of Brian's.

"Jimmy?"

"Yo! What's up, Bennet?"

I was second guessing my request to find out where Brian was in third period. "Umm, do you know where Brian Brooks is third period?"

"Why?" He grinned and then, in typical fashion, said, "You wanna hook up with my man, Big B.?"

"Hardly. Maybe if I was a stupid freshman I would. You're man is nothing but a big baby. Did you see what he did to Miles this morning?"

Jimmy shrugged his shoulders. "Man, B. was just messin' with him. Dude, it was all a joke. Bennet, it's really not that big. B's cool."

"Really!" I said sharply. "Really? You really think he's cool for doing shit like that? Dude, what if that was your little brother who was being tortured? Huh? Still think he's cool?"

Jimmy laughed it off. "Shan, get over it. He's in woodshop third period."

After he gave me that information, he turned around and ignored me for the rest of the class.

When I entered my history class, all I could do was think about getting to Brian. The test sat in front of me, but it all seemed so insignificant. I wrestled with my thoughts. *Should I? What if everyone laughs at me or makes fun of me? I should. I really should give him hell.* He deserved it. If nobody else wanted to stick up for Miles- I would.

"Mr. Fisher? Can I get a pass for the bathroom?" I bravely asked.

"Shannon, you know I don't allow my students to leave during a test."

I put on a puppy dog face. "I'm sorry. Please don't make me tell you why, but I have to go so bad. It's an emergency." I winced. "Girl stuff." I have learned that whenever you tell a male teacher that it was "girl stuff," they basically leave you alone.

"Fine. Keep all your things here."

With my pass in my hand and possible scenarios swirling around my head, I headed to the woodshop room. I had never been in there before and had no idea what to expect. I cannot explain what happened in my mind that day. My entire body was shaking, my hands were sweaty, but something deep inside me needed to knock on that door.

When I walked in, I noticed the room was filled with rowdy boys. Some boys I knew, some looked a lot older, and most were delighted to see a girl walk in. I almost lost all nerve and ran out, but then, I saw Brian. He was making some kind of shelf with three other guys.

"Young lady! Yoo-hoo! You! Can I help you?" the burly, manly woodshop teacher called out.

I let out a deep sigh, a sigh that cleared all my emotional garbage. I had a job to do, a deed to finish, and it was go time. "Hi. I want to talk to Brian."

"Honey, this is woodshop, not social hour. Get his number and call him later."

When the teacher got up to lead me out the door, I bolted toward Brian. Brian looked amused by me. "I want to know why you did that to Miles?"

Brian inspected the guys in his class before he asked, "Huh? Bennet, what the hell are you talking about?"

I looked around the room as well. The teacher allowed me to continue. "Miles. Miles Donlon. You threw his backpack in the water... is it coming back to you?"

"Oh my God! That freak!" Brian scoffed. "What the hell do you care?" He looked around the room once again and his demeanor quickly changed. "Man, get out of here!"

"No." I crossed my arms and barked, "No! Tell me why you think you are so cool! I wanna know. Really. What is it that makes Big B. so cool?"

Brian shifted uneasily.

"Is it the fact that you pick on fat kids or call them names, or maybe it's because you use little 14 year old girls like garbage? Which one of those makes you so cool, Brian?"

Brian was totally caught off guard and I liked that. The kids in his class were curious, too. Brian retorted, "Man, F-off! Get out of here. You nosy bitch!"

After being called a "nosy bitch," something in me snapped. All the raw anger that I had for everyone who made fun of Phillip gave me super human strength. I shoved a table out of my way and lunged toward Brian.

I was inches away from him when I barked, "If you ever! If you ever pick on him again, so help me God, I will make your life a living hell!"

Brian backed up toward the wall. It looked as though he was somewhere between half shocked and half pissed. His teacher came over and placed his big hands on my shoulder.

He calmly said, "Young lady. You need to leave."

"Yeah," Brian chimed in. "Yeah, get outta here! You loser!"

"Loser!" I repeated, and then managed to shrug the teacher's hands off me. "You don't even have enough sense to even realize that someone who picks on innocent kids, who treats people like trash is a loser. In fact, you are just a little, insecure baby. If you were a real man, or anything like a real man, you would realize that."

Brian just glared at me. He never responded.

I added, "Leave him alone!"

"Or what?" he asked.

Before I could answer him, a kid from his class called out, "Dude, just leave Miles alone."

Another kid in the room shouted, "Really B., it's not cool. Just leave the kid alone."

Brian shook his head and scoffed, "Whatever, dude."

The woodshop teacher led me out of the classroom and stood next to me in the hallway. He looked at me and said, "You know, I should send you to the office for disturbing my class. I should reprimand you for threatening another student."

I didn't care. He could do whatever he wanted. I said what I needed to say.

Then, he winked at me and said, "But, I won't."

When I walked down the hallway, a weight had been lifted. I did it. I should have done that for Phillip a long time ago. I smiled when I walked away and told myself that *I* was in control- just like Ms. Phillips said.

in my mind I'm going to carolina

I figured that I could go anywhere I wanted when I left for college and there was no doubt that my destination would be south.

"I wanna go down south, like, I don't know. Deep south." I hesitated and thought about a perfect southern place. A place with porch swings, huge pillar houses, sweet jasmine, and visions of Rhett Butler lurking in every southern gentleman's eyes.

"Whatever," Lizzie muttered sarcastically. She rolled her eyes and added, "Just don't come back with a mullet." Lizzie looked over to me as she stood in front of her mirror applying her make-up. She warned, "Or a Rebel flag tattoo."

After Lizzie and I talked in great length about the mysterious people who actually have mullets, we turned our attention to the future.

I looked over to my best friend of ten years, admitting, "I have to go." I whispered. I wasn't sure if I was talking to her or if I was talking to myself. With confirmation in my voice, I said, "I can't stay here."

Lizzie nodded her head in agreement. "What about Carl? What's gonna happen with that?" she questioned.

To me, that situation was a no-brainer. I did not intend to stay home because of some guy, even if it was Carl. Carl made his choice to stay home and when he did, I feared that he might expect the same from me. I heard all the heartbreaking stories at the lunch table about the girl who graduated, then stayed home because of her loser boyfriend, only to break up three months later. It was disturbing.

I looked at Lizzie's reflection in the mirror and calmly answered, "I don't know. All I know is that I am going... to a galaxy far, far away. No matter what."

In a moment of uncomfortable sincerity that we hardly ever shared, she mentioned, "I really admire that about you." Lizzie looked back at the mirror and talked to her reflection, "I wish I knew what I wanted." She sighed and then winked at herself playfully.

The idea that she admired me made me blush. I wrinkled up my face with the thought.

Without even looking in her direction, I mumbled, "You'll figure it out. Everybody does, eventually." I got up to open the lip-gloss on her dresser, and as I applied the pink, gluey liquid, I remarked, "Everything happens for a reason."

Lizzie clicked her teeth. "Oh my God! You sound like Justine. Come on, Shan." She smiled and batted her lashes while placing her hands next to her heart. Lizzie began imitating an overly soft, feminine voice, declaring, "Just follow your heart." She placed her hand over her heart with an exaggerated sigh.

She was making fun of me or maybe Justine. Probably both.

True to form, Lizzie was always the practical one between us. I lived in two completely different worlds. In one world, I could easily pass as the girl next door, while in the other world, I could easily pass for insane. Nobody was privy to the secrets in my mind that were laced with dark thoughts, death, and "what ifs." I did develop some philosophies from my late night insanity. I knew that I was on the earth for a reason. I knew that because I had to believe that. I had to believe that everything wasn't just random. I could not walk though my life and just think... well, shit happens. That theory was too depressing.

I had a sense that there was more to life than just going through the motions. I often asked myself questions like: Why am I here? Why did all of this happen? Do other people think like I do? Am I crazy to assume that life was not accidental? I tried to figure it out by listening to teachers, coaches, friends, reading books, listening to music, but nothing could accurately pinpoint my purpose in life. I wanted someone to explain it to me. Instead, I settled with my own philosophy and held onto a belief that everything happened for a reason.

I believed in my cliché theory. It was hard to believe that others could buy into the concept that life was just living and dying.

"Lizzie, don't you think that things happen for a reason? That, maybe, you are the way you are because of everything around you. Or that all your experiences happen for a reason. Don't you think about that... ever?" I glanced toward her and wondered if she was going to indulge in my simple, yet, intricate questions.

Lizzie, clearly not convinced, shrugged her shoulders and mumbled, "No. It just happens. Life just happens... there is no, like, reason. It is what it is."

"I don't think so. I don't know. You can't just be born, live your life, and then just die. That is, like, so depressing. It is so meaningless. Don't you think there is a reason you were born?" I was aware that my secret thoughts were coming to the surface, but I didn't care. It felt good to share my ideas, even if they weren't accepted. I really didn't care if she agreed or disagreed.

Lizzie scoffed. "Shannon, you're getting way to serious right now. Come on? You're acting like one of those retards that paints their nails black and listens to The B'52s. Or, like, one of those dorks who sits near a tree writing poetry." She plopped herself on her bed, counting all the pictures of Herschel Walker on her wall. "Come on... everyone knows you just... just... have to live your life... and be a nice person." She began cracking up while using a manly, white voice, and cynically repeated, "Just live your life and be a nice person."

I never knew what people were referring to when they mentioned, "Be a nice person." On the rare occasion that my friends and I discussed religion, they often said that type of thing. What does nice mean? None of my friends were strict religious people, but they always believed that in order to get into heaven, you had to be nice or good. I was not an expert, but I had a feeling that God would accept you either way. I just couldn't accept that in order to win God's love and affection, you would *have* to behave a certain way or do certain things. It reminded me of a child who acted a certain way just to get what they wanted. I had to believe that God wanted more from us.

I bluntly asked, "Do you think we go to heaven when we die? Or do you think some people actually go to hell?"

Lizzie, now interested, stopped focusing on her wall scattered with Eagles and Phillies pictures. She was silent while she reflected upon my question. She cocked her head sideways and then answered, "Yeah, I guess. Hmm, uhh, yeah." She pointed her finger in the air, remembering something. "Yeah, like, sometimes at night I wonder what happens when we die and stuff like that." She sat up, looked over to me, and with new excitement in her voice, she stated, "I do believe in heaven. I do. I think that if we are good and, you know, don't break any of the Ten Commandments, well, the really serious of the Ten Commandments...'cause... God knows, I lie to my parents once in a while. I mean, we all do." She shook her head and let out a tiny chuckle. "Yeah, I am pretty sure that I will be in heaven. I am not so sure about the hell thing, though. I think it's something Catholics use against us if we are bad." Lizzie could say stuff like that because she was Catholic. I never debated her on her religion.

I was grateful that she was engaging in my conversation. I agreed with her. I wanted to talk about it more, so I mentioned, "I just have a feeling that everything we do is connected somehow. Once, I read that everyone you meet affects you in one way or another..."

"Obviously!" she retorted.

"No. It's like we are supposed to meet certain people. Even the ones we don't like are supposed to, like, teach us something." Lizzie's eyes grew wide with interest. I added, "My mom has this book and it says that whatever situations we run into in life, any situation... it's supposed to happen. I didn't really understand it, but, like, it's supposed to teach us something. And it said that everything happens for a reason, too."

Lizzie rolled her eyes. I went too far. She challenged me. "Number one... what the hell book are you reading? And number two... what reason exactly?" She perked up from her sitting position. "That's just a bunch of bullshit that people make up, so they can feel better when crappy stuff happens. It's like people can't accept that bad things happen, so they say it was supposed to happen."

She clicked her teeth and then snidely asked, "Why did Mike cheat on me?"

"That's a stupid question."

"According to that stupid book… it was supposed to happen. Why does my uncle have cerebral palsy? Oh yeah, it was supposed to happen." Lizzie continued with a sarcastic tone, laughing when she asked, "Why did my mom break her leg last year? Oh wait… don't tell me… it was supposed to happen. Give me a break!"

"You are, like, totally missing the point!" I cried. "It's, like, supposed to teach us something- bad or good. Didn't something bad ever happen to you and, like, then you realized it was a blessing in disguise? I mean, Mike was a jerk and him cheating on you was the best thing that ever happened 'cause he's a scumbag who hangs out with people who wears sweatpants and high tops! Now, you know better and…"

"Stop, Shannon!" She held up her hands, shaking her head seriously. "You honestly believe that Mike cheating on me was a good thing?"

"Yes. I do," I emphatically said.

She shook her head and narrowed her eyes with disbelief. "Why?" she asked.

I shouted, "I just told you… he was a jerk off and you couldn't see it! Don't you get it… you shouldn't have been with him."

We went back and forth debating cause and effect, and then, suddenly, Lizzie perked up with excitement. "Well!" She put up her finger again as she posed a new thought. "Here's an interesting question. What was the reason your brother killed himself?" Her look was challenging but not spiteful. She really wanted to prove that my theory was crap.

The problem was that I did not have an explanation for her. I tried to come up with several answers just for the sake of being answers, but nothing made sense.

I gave up. I whispered, "I don't know. I really don't know. I don't think I ever will."

She propped herself up, rose to her feet, and then remarked, "Well, there goes your theory. Things just happen... for no reason."

After my conversation with Lizzie, part of me wondered if I was *supposed* to have that talk. Lizzie made an interesting point. I walked home, trying to think of an answer to her question. I took the long way home that day, which was only about five minutes longer, so I could contemplate her simple question further.

First, I thought about Phillip's life, which only lasted fifteen years. Within those fifteen years, everything seemed so condensed. He managed to stir up so much emotion within a short period of time. I walked on the paved road and thought about all his weird episodes, his odd behavior, and the secrets he told me. I stopped on the corner of Oak Avenue and wondered why I didn't link his odd behavior to his ultimate demise. The cutting, the isolation, the constant trouble in school; it all made sense. Why didn't I see it? Then, I thought about the kids making fun of him because of his weight, the constant bullying from people he didn't even know, or his physical fights around town. Duh. What did I expect... someone normal?

I wanted to believe that there was one definitive reason why he killed himself. I needed one single reason. It was important for me to have a concrete, solid, ultimate reason why he walked into the woods with a shotgun. I realized, while thinking about the conversation with Lizzie, that it was fifteen years worth of reasons. I figured that all those reasons eventually added up and gave him the motivation to pull the trigger. Although my assumption regarding his reasons seemed solid, they would never take away the questions. Only one person knew why Phillip was dead and that person was Phillip.

The reason he killed himself didn't seem so mysterious to me anymore. I didn't live his life, although I observed it. I suppose killing myself seemed unimaginable or unthinkable or just plain crazy. However, I was not him and I didn't know how he felt inside. As I walked home, I thought some more about Lizzie's question. Instead of thinking about his death, maybe I had to shift my thoughts to his life. Why was he here? What could I learn from his short life?

senioritis

On a sticky September morning, I prepared for my last first day of high school. I dedicated my senior year mornings to The Beatles, affectionately naming it, "Breakfast with The Beatles." While all my friends were getting ready to *Rump Shaker*, I was happily singing the words to *Happiness is a Warm Gun*. In my long-view mirror, I held my head crooked and mouth wide open while I applied my four layers of jet-black mascara.

Shelly picked Lizzie and me up for school at 7:40 sharp. Shelly demanded punctuality. Lizzie and I were quite the opposite. Shelly and Thomas (yes, that Thomas) were hot and heavy since the middle of the summer. Thomas turned out to be quite the ladies' man. He seemed to enjoy the company of many girls. However, he always had a soft spot for Shelly, and she was just the heartbreaker to make him settle.

As we drove into the senior parking lot, we blasted *Baby Got Back.* How could you not love an anthem strictly promoting a big, round, juicy butt? *Oh my gosh -senior year!* I could not believe that I was a senior... finally. When I stepped out of Shelly's car, the first person I saw was Thomas. He grew up over the summer and surprisingly had the looks to back up his lady killer persona.

"Hey!" Thomas waved to Lizzie and me, but most of his attention was on Shelly. He looked at her like a puppy just itching for affection. As Thomas anxiously waited for Shelly to acknowledge him, I knew that he finally met his match. Sucker!

Shelly walked with Thomas hand in hand, whispering in each other's ears. Lizzie and I giggled behind them. Lizzie and I joked about the two lovebirds in front of us and swore that if we had to watch them make-out all year, then we would walk, ride our bikes, roller skate, or take public transportation to school. To begin our final year at Gateway, Lizzie and I entered the back doors while making fun of Shelly and her doting boyfriend.

Tiffany hurried to meet us at the doors and then proceeded to imitate Ralph Wiggum by reciting, "Me fail English? That's unpossible." I began cracking up with just the thought of the classic *Simpson* episode. Lizzie, however, was not into the whole *Simpson* phenomena, so she rolled her eyes as we laughed hysterically. Tiffany and I both shared a love for *The Simpson's*. We spent our free time calling each other on our answering machines reciting lines from Ned Flanders, Ralph, and, of course, Homer. I walked in the back hallway and thought: *The Beatles*, "*Baby Got Back*," and *The Simpson's* all before the first bell- it's going to be a great senior year.

I thought that I would be in a level III or level IV English class, but after entering room #103, I assumed that there must have been some sort of mix-up; a big mix-up, actually. I was officially entering "The Twilight Zone." After taking my first steps into the room, I immediately stopped and looked around for anyone who looked familiar. Instead, I saw glimpses of several mysterious strangers. It felt like I was in walking into an 80s John Hughes movie because of all the random stereotypical cliques. I looked at my schedule again to make sure I got the room number correct. I even walked outside the hallway to recheck the room number. Room #103- *yup, it was the right room.* After my inspection, I slowly entered the half-full room and tried to sit next to someone I knew. Thank God, I saw Chris Exerly frantically waving his arm, motioning for me to sit by him. Chris was on the basketball team and we hung out occasionally. He and I weren't exactly buddy-buddy, but I hung out with him at parties and he seemed pretty cool.

The seats began to fill up while Chris and I talked briefly about our summer vacation and the obvious bizarre mix of kids in our class. There were the gothic punks who dressed in black, disregarding the ninety degree weather. There were the vocational girls, who attended beauty school for half the day, who each had their long fingernails decorated with flowers and rainbows. Then there was the introverted group of nerds who kept to themselves and rarely went out to any school functions. The type of crowd that debated questions like "what is virtue?" on a Saturday night. They were the type of kids who would eventually rule the world. Of course, there were a couple of "druggies." I had to give them credit because they stuck with the standard mullets and black concert t-shirt. There were about five members of the football team who huddled in the back section of the room, holding a Sports Illustrated and debating whether Joe Montana should retire. Then, there was Chris and me. Maybe, just maybe, for once, we were the outcasts.

My senior English teacher, Mrs. Martin, taught at Gateway for nearly one-third of her life. She already looked tired on the first day of school. Her curly, red hair was a tangled mess that looked like a cross between Little Orphan Annie and Bette Midler. Judging by her wardrobe, it was evident that she gave up on keeping up appearances. Style or any current fashion was probably last on her list of priorities. In my world, looking sharp and put together was all that mattered. It was sad to see an educated woman wear such tragic clothing. She wore a button-up, short sleeve suit jacket and a long, black skirt that reached her big toe. Her shoes were flat, ugly, brown sandals and I would bet any amount of money that she wore them to the beach. I guess she made an effort to be somewhat glamorous by wearing a butterfly rhinestone pin on her jacket. After watching her for only 45 seconds, I guessed that she was the type of person who had many profound thoughts and clever words of wisdom. However, after several years of teaching lazy high school students, she neglected to mention any of her witty comments.

Chris leaned over while resting his chin on his elbow and asked, "Did you bomb English last year?"

I rolled my eyes, scoffed, and then factually stated, "No. Actually, it was my best class. I got three As, so I don't know what happened." I scanned the room, looked at Chris, and then shook my head.

Two minutes after my English teacher began taking our attendance, Ron Baduleese slowly strolled into the classroom. He was literally strutting toward the teacher wearing a half smile while carrying a tiny crumpled note. With the sight of Ron, she stopped calling out names, so she could study him further.

With slight sarcasm, Ron proudly announced, "Yeah, it's me- Ron B. I am here to grace you with my presence."

I was shocked. Ron? Ron Baduleese? I thought he dropped out of school two years ago.

She took his note from his hand by using only two fingers. Either she was a real slow reader or she read the note four times. Finally, she looked over to Ron, smiled pleasantly, gritted her teeth, and said, "Welcome. Please take a seat."

Ron bowed down to her.

I thought: *Am I in drama or English?*

After Ron lifted his head, he loudly proclaimed, "Your majesty… it would not only be my honor, it would be my privilege."

Oddly, Mrs. Martin appreciated his dramatic flair by returning his bow with a curtsy. The entire class howled out in laughter, enjoying Ron's show.

It *was* funny. Chris and I laughed with them. As he walked to his seat, I could not keep my eyes off him. Ron plopped down on the seat in front of me without any books, bags, or anything. It was just Ron with his effortless coolness. His presence mesmerized me, not because of his peculiar display, but because he used to be one of Phillip's best friends.

After taking a moment to scan the room, Mrs. Martin cleared her throat and announced that from now on everyone would remain in their permanent seats. She peeked from her attendance sheet and glanced into the sea of misfits. After assessing her classroom, she sighed. She knew. I could tell that she knew the class was going to be a challenge. I could tell that it was a challenge that she was not remotely thrilled about taking.

Mrs. Martin cleared her throat for the third time. Before she made an attempt to speak, she guzzled down a diet Pepsi that was sitting on her desk. She swallowed, nodded her head as if she was thinking to herself, and then cocked her head sideways. She began, "Okay… let's see. I do believe that this is our permanent seating chart…" She began scribbling on a piece of paper as we waited patiently. We were high school students and we could sniff out weakness within two minutes. She was looking pretty weak.

She then placed her pencil thin glasses on the tip of her nose. I cringed in my seat when she kept the glasses on the tip of her nose. I asked myself: why do teachers do that? Do they think it made them look smarter? It only makes them look old and senile. Everyone watched in anticipation (even the football players put away their precious Sports Illustrated) when she lifted her head to address the class.

With her shoulders back and head held high, she announced, "This is senior English. You are in room 103. If you are in the wrong room... please leave. My name is Mrs. Martin. And no... I am not related to Steve. I am not on this earth to baby-sit seniors. If you are late, then you will be written up. If you are disrespectful, then you will be dismissed. If you do not do your work, then your grades will suffer. If you are planning on passing this class, then pay attention." She looked us over, making sure we understood her firm position.

Hmmm... not weak at all. Surprise surprise.

Mrs. Martin continued, "There is no gum because you all look like a bunch of cows chewing your cud. There is no talking when I am speaking because I am the teacher and *I* am the one that gets paid to talk. If you need to speak, please raise your hand and extend those five fingers out, so I can see them clearly. I am not your mommy, so don't cry to me when I enforce the rules. I am not your daddy, so don't complain to me like little, whiny babies. Do I make myself clear? Do you have any questions?" With her right pointer finger, she slid her thin glasses back to her eyeballs.

Ron B. raised his hand with all five fingers strategically extended out. He said, "Yeah, Mrs. Martin..." He placed his hand to his chin, trying to look as if he was in deep thought. "If we have to go to the bathroom, should we put one finger up for a piss and two fingers up for a deuce?" As the entire class howled with laughter, Ron did not even crack a smile.

Mrs. Martin cocked her head sideways, rose from her chair, and appeared to stand about six feet tall.

She sarcastically responded, "Mr. Baduleese." She held up the white sheet with her seating order to make sure she had his name correct. "Do you think that you are somehow funny to me? If we are going to be a class of babies, then I shall treat you all like a class of babies. Ron, I will dismiss your foul question and request that you talk to me in a respectable manner; otherwise, I will have no problems telling you to take a hike. And I will give you just one finger... and you can guess which one it will be." She smiled and then began handing out our textbooks.

Touché. I was seriously impressed by her smart-ass comeback. Ron could not resist laughing and appeared equally impressed.

As she handed out the books, Ron turned to me, relaxing his arm on my desk, and then whispered, "Hey... pssst!"

I looked up from my class schedule and cautiously answered, "Yeah?"

"Do you remember me?" he asked.

Of course, I remembered Ron. He used to chase me around the neighborhood on his bike when I was in, like, fifth grade. Phillip and Ron used to hang out and play "Dungeon and Dragons" while I sat outside the door listening to their secret conversations of trolls and gargoyles. Ron used to dunk Lizzie and me in my pool. He demanded that we call him master. Ron would laugh as he pushed our heads in the water and ask, "Who's the master? Who's the master?"

I smiled recalling the memories. I quickly responded, "I remember that you used to beat me up in my pool and chase me around Heights."

Ron laughed. "Oh man! You remember that?"

I said, "Uh, yeah, I remember that Lizzie and I would run all the way to her house to get away from you and my brother."

Ron paused for a moment, so he could yell across the room to defend Randall Cunningham. He shouted to the jock football players, "You're all freakin' retards! Cunningham's the best quarterback in the entire land!" His debate over the Eagles game against the Cowboys ended in harsh words. Ron then focused his attention back to me.

He looked down at his hands when he spoke, perhaps trying to avoid the inevitable subject. He was calm and collected when he said, "So, yeah. I was really sorry about Phil. It's kind of weird to hear stories about him. Man, that seems like forever ago."

My heart began to pulsate rapidly with just the mention of my brother's name. I could not remember the last time I heard someone say it. Ron continued to fidget with his hands. "Phil was a cool guy. Man, it really sucks. He was a good friend. Man, I miss that dude." Ron smiled and then said, "Funny as hell. He was funny as hell."

I blurted out, "Yeah." As I nodded my head, I secretly hoped that he would say more about my brother.

Ron turned his entire body toward me, leaned in close, and whispered, "Did they ever... I mean, do you know why he did it?"

I honestly did not know how to answer his simple, yet extremely complicated question. So, I hesitated to collect my thoughts and tried to explain it the best way I could. I began, "Well, I guess, he was, like, extremely unhappy. I mean, that goes without saying. But, umm, I don't think there was one, like, single reason. I guess he just couldn't handle his life anymore. I don't know. It was a lot of stuff, but I couldn't say it was just one single reason."

He frowned. I could tell he wanted a better answer. Most people needed to have a definitive reason. He pressed, "Do you think it had anything to do with drugs?"

I shook my head, indicating that I didn't. "No, I mean, yeah, but he didn't overdose or anything. The toxicologist reported that there were no drugs or traces of drugs when they found him. Plus, he planned it for a while." I added, "But, during that time, he and his friends were doing a lot of drugs. That much we did know for sure."

Ron frowned again. I knew he still needed a concrete answer. Ron shook his head with confusion. He asked, "Well, do you think he would have done it if he was in Jersey?"

I looked him in the eye and very sternly stated, "Yes."

Before he could respond or even make a facial expression, the bell rang, signaling our next move. Lizzie met me in the hallway as we walked to gourmet cooking.

"How was English?" Lizzie inquired.

I rolled my eyes, smirked, and shook my head as I rattled off the names of the kids in my class. With disbelief, Lizzie repeated, "No! Really? No!"

I told her about the incident between Ron and Mrs. Martin.

She scoffed and then asked, "Isn't Ron, like, already... I mean, I thought he graduated or dropped out."

I answered, "I think he failed ninth grade, or maybe it was eighth grade... hmmm... not exactly sure, but he sits right in front of me."

"Ewww! Does he have like emphysema dragon breath from all the millions of cigarettes he smokes?"

Laughing at Lizzie's typical exaggerations, I tried to defend him, and I wasn't even sure why. "Nah, he's alright. Ron's an okay guy."

When the next class began, I kept thinking about the discussion with Ron about my brother. I liked talking about Phillip, probably because I never talked to anyone about him. Talking to Ron made me feel connected to my brother, instead of depressed. Maybe it was because I was talking to someone who knew him, who understood him. I laughed thinking about Ron's antics and thought: I bet Phillip would have been the same way.

Everything that ever happened during my senior year was heightened by the fact that we were seniors. Our chatter in class, during lunch, stretching at field hockey practice, and written in our notes that were passed along in the crowded hallways revolved around the word "senior." Our last year of high school represented the finality and uncertainty that allowed us to believe that we were entitled to buildup what we became... seniors. Everything, no matter how big or how small, had high expectations. For some reason, the thought process became: if we don't do it now, we never will. Every event was hyped because it was our last. Pep rallies, parties, football games, Friday night parties, whatever, it didn't matter. We had one more chance to do it up.

On Friday nights, we would all hang out in a place in Millville to drink beer and smoke cigars. I was never sure exactly where it was, but it looked like a bunch of drug up sand that had a large lake or something. There was a fire pit, broken glass, lots of sand, and plenty of alcohol. It was deep in the woods with a dirt road leading us back to privacy. I literally thought that, at any given moment, Jason from *Friday the 13th* was going to come out with a huge butcher knife and kill us. Most of the girls sat around on logs sipping each other's beer and taking slobbery puffs from a communal cigar. We laughed at the boys who tried to impress us with their manly drinking skills by taking beer bong hits. Every one of them cheered like rejects after they chugged an entire 12 ounces of Budweiser. I hollered with the rest of the girls, but I was not that impressed with scrawny boys acting like drinking beer was some kind of noble achievement.

Most of the time, I felt conflicted about going out with my friends. When I was with my friends, I thought about Carl. I just wanted to curl up next to him on the couch with a snuggly blanket and hang out. Part of me felt guilty because I knew that our time together would come to a bitter end very soon. On the other hand, when I was at home with Carl, the thought of all my friends having fun without me filled me with regret. I just could not win. What if I turned out to be that girl? I heard all about those stupid girls who hung out with their boyfriends all the time, then when she went away to college... poof... it was over. Goodbye, hometown honey.

Carl didn't make the decision easier on me either. He constantly reminded me that I was leaving soon and made me feel guilty for choosing my friends over him. Most times, the fact that he wanted me to choose made me furious. During the first two months of school, Carl broke up with me three times for choosing my friends over him, and I swore after the second time he dumped me that I would never go back out with him. Of course, by Friday night, I was ready to be his girlfriend again and he was ready to apologize for breaking up with me. I stopped telling my friends about our break-ups simply because they knew that Carl and I would eventually get back together by the weekend.

I swore many years ago that if a guy broke up with me, it was over. Unfortunately, that statement looked better on paper. Back then, when I made all those rules about having a boyfriend, I had no idea what it was really like. The truth was that after all the bullshit he put me through, I still loved him. In fact, I started to question who I was without him. I could not accept the idea of him being with another girl, so I would rather endure the on again-off again relationship. I spent most of my high school years with Carl and being without him felt weird. Even if things between us sucked, it was better than being without him.

if you asked me to

Senior year moved along. It was somehow different, yet remained the same. My life was all about the future as I began making plans to go to college in the fall. With every letter that came to my mailbox from a college, with every coach that called my house at night, with every college visit, the walls began crumbling down on my soon to be ex-boyfriend.

I could remember that it was very cold that night; the night *I* finally broke up with him.

I wasn't even sure how it started, but I knew how it was going to end.

While sitting up in my bed, I shouted into my phone: "You're ridiculous... you know that? So freaking ridiculous!"

I knew his next comment before he even said it. He dared, "Well, why don't you just break up with me then? Huh, just do it, 'cause you know when you go away... it's gonna happen anyway."

I winced, and then sarcastically asked, "Why is it always that? Why? It's like you want us to, like, breakup."

After going back and forth with immature accusations and assaults, he commented, "Shannon. I really don't understand why you can't see things my way? It's like, you're gonna leave in, like, five months and you just don't give a shit about me. Why would you want us to fight like this all the time?"

I replied, "Me?" I pointed to myself as if he could see me. "Me? I don't wanna fight! It's friggin' you! You get mad at, like, every single thing I do. I cannot even make a decision without feeling like you won't get mad. I can't do anything the way you want me to."

Carl sighed into the phone and then softly laughed. I knew he thought my allegations were totally random or distorted. I held the phone to my ear, grasping the plastic phone as it slipped from my sweaty hands. I was so ready. I was so ready to dump him for the first and last time. The words were on the tip of my tongue, but I did not have the courage to say them.

"All I ever..." Carl sighed again with exhaustion from repeating the same lines. "All I ever wanted was for us to be together. And it just seems like everything else, like your friends and stuff, are way more important. And you know what? I am tired of being second to you. I am tired of you picking your friends over me and I am tired of convincing you to hang out with me. I mean, I am your boyfriend, so why do you choose them?"

He and I were simply in two different worlds because I never put him second. After listening to him, I mean really listening to him for the first time, I felt sad and disappointed. His view of our relationship was much different than mine. It physically hurt my stomach with that realization. After all the time we were together, it was discouraging to hear that I somehow put him second. I knew it wasn't true and I wasn't willing to prove it anymore.

After several moments of silence that followed more petty accusations, followed by more silence- I gave up. I was just tired of fighting about the same stuff.

I shouted, "Carl, seriously, grow the f-up! You break up with me, like, every five seconds and I'm the one..." I laughed. "I'm the one who doesn't care... don't be an a-hole!" I laughed again. I added, "Oh my God! You are seriously delusional. You know what? You're not worth it."

I didn't know if he was hurt or angry. He yelled, "You know what?!"

"What?!" I shouted.

"I am so sick of fighting with you... I'm really just sick and tired of all this bull-shit!"

"Oh, and somehow, I'm not! It's your fault... not mine!"

Carl scoffed and sarcastically replied, "Right! You're right! You are always right!" He began imitating my voice, "Eww, my name is Shannon Bennet and I am soooo cooool. I am too cool to hang out with my boyfriend... and I am *always* right."

I shook my head as I reach for his picture that was pinned on my corkboard. I looked at the glossy picture and ripped it in half. Then, after ripping his face in two, I decided that it was time.

With newfound confidence, I whispered, "You know what, Carl? I don't need this. I don't need this aggravation. If I want to go out with my friends when I want, I will. If I want to go out, I will. If I want to be alone, I will. I'm tired of you calling all the shots! It's over. I'm done. Don't call me. Don't come by my house. Don't even tell people we ever went out." Impressed with my words, I raised my voice, and then shouted, "You know what? Why don't you forget you ever knew me?!" I was literally spitting into the receiver when I screamed, "Ya jerk!"

I slammed down the phone and threw it across my room.

With all my pent up anger, I had a new surge of energy. I jumped up from my bed and looked like some insane mental patient as I tore down all of his pictures from my walls. With my hands shaking, I tore them all into tiny, itty-bitty, little pieces. Then, I collected them in my hand, opened my window, and scattered them out into the cold air. After every shred of him was off my wall, I slammed the window down and whispered, "Asshole."

For the first time, I was empowered by making the decision. I had control and, for once, it filled me with pride. I stood in front of my long-view mirror and smiled, congratulating myself for having a spine. As the night progressed, I reminded myself that I was better off and that I deserved better. I looked in the mirror and tried to convince myself that I made the right decision.

In one word, the next five days were... rough. For the most part, I walked around school in a constant fog, dazed, and only slightly present. Among my friends, it was easy to pretend that I made the right decision, but when I sat alone in class or in my bedroom, I second-guessed my decision. People often told me that they thought I was a strong person, but the days after I broke up with him, I felt so weak and stupid. I didn't eat. I didn't sleep. I didn't know who I was if I wasn't Carl Kindsay's girlfriend. My identity was in question as I struggled to find out who I really was without my boyfriend.

At home, I tried to keep my mind off him by keeping busy, but every single thought I had revolved around Carl. I fooled myself into believing that he never cared about me because if he did, then he would be calling me or coming over to my house begging to have me back. However, Carl never called or came by and, with each passing day, the agony of officially breaking up hit me very hard; so hard, that I literally felt physical pain. In my head, I made up fake conversations between Carl and other girls. In every contrived conversation, Carl told the girls that he never loved me and that he wasted years on me.

Almost every attractive female was my sworn enemy, as I envisioned him happy and content with someone else. I no longer cared about my stupid rules of dating or if I was, in fact, that stupid girl. Inside, deep inside, I beat myself up for not being good enough, pretty enough, clever enough, smart enough, or worthy enough. With another passing week, I walked through the halls with my head down and with my pants practically falling off after losing seven pounds.

In my room, I listened to sappy, slow songs. I sat silently and felt sorry for myself. Patti LaBelle's *If You Asked Me To* played at least fifteen times every night. I hummed along, wondering if she wrote that song just for me.

I sighed as the words swirled in my head. I listened to Patti sing as I stared into open space. During the weepy hours of the morning when I should have been sleeping, I could hear that song. It reminded me, even subconsciously, that all Carl had to do was just "ask" to have me back. Old photo albums were scattered on my floor, stuffed animals, and old ticket stubs served as the tangible evidence that my summer fling was more than a fleeting moment, and I regretted the way it ended. It should have been different, I thought to myself. How could we go from telling each other we love each other to never speaking again? How could it end this way?

As I flipped through *Seventeen Magazine*, scoping out pretty prom dresses, I became depressed knowing that prom would just suck without Carl. For 21 days, I waited for him to show. For three weeks, I could barely function. During that time, I could only gain strength by knowing that I *could* get through it. I mean, if I could live through my brother shooting himself, then getting over Carl would be easy. But, still, prom would totally suck without him.

I gave serious thought to a 'perfect' boyfriend. I scribbled down all the characteristics that I longed for in my 'perfect' boyfriend:

1. *Must be cute and athletic (baseball player.)*
2. *Must not be hairy.*
3. *Must be nice to his mom.*
4. *Must not be a racist, sexist or any kind of "ist."*
5. *Must let me be myself... just let me be.*
6. *Must smell good.*

I reread my list several times and realized that Carl had four out of five of my characteristics, so I must have been on crack when I broke up with him.

With another lonely weekend coming up, I made plans with Lizzie. The plan was to fill any free time by cramming any activity into my forty-eight hours of freedom. On Friday night, we ordered Chinese food and played Trivial Pursuit with Jerry Howard and Chris German (two reject junior boys, who were just as immature as Lizzie and I.) As I read the sophisticated medical questions, I instantly thought about how lame I was for playing a board game on a Saturday night. After what seemed like five hundred hours of hard-core questions and pervy jokes, I ran home to my lonely room. The darkness still terrified me with the memory of "The Popcorn Man." After slamming Lizzie's back door, I bolted down the street and kept my head straight. It took forty-five seconds to get from her door to my door, but it seemed like an eternity. When I approached my front step, I nearly fainted when I saw a figure lurking in my bushes. I almost hyperventilated until I heard a familiar voice try to calm me down.

"It's only me."

Carl stepped out from the shadows, exposing his frozen body and pale face. Seeing him made me nervous because I knew I wasn't strong enough to face him, and I knew that deep down I wanted to be with him. I worried that he might tell me that I was right to break it off and that he was moving on without me. I was afraid he was happier without me.

"Shannon?" he began. He slowly approached me at the top of my driveway. He cautiously moved toward me, as if he needed permission. Of course, I tried to act like he was some kind of nuisance or that his presence was annoying. Seeing him hurt more than I thought it would, and I found it extremely difficult to look him in the eyes.

I snapped, "Yeah?"

We stared at each other for a while, neither one of us able to start the much needed conversation. There were so many thoughts running through my head, but I refused to look like a wussy idiot. I was afraid if I opened my mouth, the truth would come gushing out. With a puff of white air streaming from his mouth, he finally made the first move by asking, "How are you?"

It was impossible to look him in the eyes. Eyes will always tell the truth, so I could not look directly at him. How was I? Hmmm? After he asked that question, I felt nauseous. Truthfully, I was everything that I swore I would never be... a stupid girl.

I chewed my gum, blew a big bubble, and snapped, "Alright." Trying to play it cool and disinterested, I came off as bitchy (which was great.)

I demanded to know: "Well? What do you want?"

He responded by smiling. Then, he looked down my empty street and sarcastically replied, "Okay... alright... tough guy. I can see where this is going." He stepped back and then tried again. "I, uhh, was in the neighborhood. I, uhh, live just down the street and I was just taking a stroll and thought I would just stop by and see you." His attempt to loosen up the tense moment worked.

I missed his humor terribly, so, obviously, I had to act even bitchier. I simply raised my eyebrows, clicked my teeth, and checked my watch to make my point.

He added, "Well, I figured if you were out and I was out, then maybe, we could talk." His eyes met mine for the first time. "Will you talk to me?" he nervously asked.

I popped a bubble and muttered, "About what?"

"Us."

"What about *us*? There is no *us*."

Without thinking, I came toward him and pushed him as hard as I could, then shrieked, "You can't do this to me!" I pushed him again. He struggled to get his balance but was still able to face me. I began shouting again, "You can't do this... I won't let you this time!"

Carl pressed against me as he grabbed my hands and, with his face inches from mine, he asked, "What? You won't let me do what?"

He released me from his grip. I stepped away from him and cried, "I won't listen to your lies or how you're gonna change or how it's gonna be different this time! I am so tired of breaking up and then going back out with you and then breaking up again. I am so tired of it! I can't do it anymore. I just..."

"You think this is easy for me? Shannon, just let me talk and I promise that I will never bother you again. Please hear me out... okay?"

I never gave him consent, but my silence indicated that I was ready to listen. He sounded sincere. Carl laughed to himself as he placed his hands across his chest. "I'm sorry, Shannon. I am. I really, really am. If I could take back all the stupid stuff... I would." He backed away, looked up at the dark, cold sky, and pleaded, "I've had a lot of time to think- a lot, and I was wrong. And I know I have to change if you will ever take me back."

"Carl?" My voice was drawn and slow. "I know. I know that, right now, you are sorry. I do believe that you are sorry, but what's gonna happen in two days or two weeks or two months? Huh? It will just be the same stuff all over again. And honestly, I don't..."

Carl interrupted me by putting his finger over my mouth, so he could speak. "Don't say it," he insisted. "Just let me finish."

I wanted to hear him out. I wanted to believe him. I wanted him to change, but I could not endure that pain all over again.

Carl cringed, looked down my street, and then admitted, "This week, well the past two weeks, er, three weeks- whatever it is." He paused to get his thought back. "The past whatever days have been, honestly, the worst days of my life."

His admission filled me with relief. It felt so good to know that I was not alone in my misery. Hearing that he was completely lost made me feel that my agony wasn't in vain.

Still trying my best to play it cool, I retorted, "Why, Carl? Because I finally broke up with you or because you realized you were wrong. Which one?"

He shrugged his shoulders and sympathetically said, "Both."

Carl rubbed his hands together to warm them. Then he said, "I was wrong. I am wrong, but... I know that now. I do. I know what I have to do, and I can do it- if you just give me a chance."

I sighed. It was a sigh that let him know that I was ready to listen.

"Carl, I..." I was cut off as Carl came toward me and tightly held both of my shoulders.

"I don't want it to end like this. I want to be with you, and I need you to believe me."

"You don't understand," I began. "Carl, I really love you. The time alone made me realize that maybe I love you too much because I don't see all the bad stuff. I want to be with you, but it's just too hard."

"Why?"

"I don't believe you. I don't believe you anymore." I looked away. "You don't trust me. I don't think you ever have." I stood still and hugged myself in the cold air. "Carl, do you know what I want?"

He shook his head.

After taking a deep breath, I spoke very softly, "I want freedom. I want freedom. I want to have you, and only you, as my boyfriend, but I need to be free. Does that make sense?"

He quickly responded, "Yeah, I get it. You want me to back off, right?"

"Kind of. I want you to trust that when I am not right next you that I am not cheating on you. I want you to tell me to have a good time when I go out with my friends. I don't want you to ask me, like, ten million questions when I go out. I want you to trust me. Why don't you trust me?" I asked. I looked down at the gravel and whispered, "I just want to be free."

I almost cried after admitting to Carl what I really wanted in life. Carl was unaware that he could never give me the freedom that I craved. The freedom I longed for was freedom from guilt, shame, and the whole situation surrounding Phillip. Carl always served me best as a wonderful distraction, and I did love him, but he could never give me what I really wanted.

Carl looked down, too. He came within inches of me again. I could feel his warm breath on my neck as he whispered in my ear, "I do. I do trust you." Then we held onto each other tightly, keeping each other warm in the cold February air. Carl looked at me, held my chin up, and promised, "I will trust you and I will change. That is a promise… forever." Then he kissed me and I kissed him back.

Just like that, with one conversation, with one kiss, with one promise, we were back together and for some reason, I believed him. Perhaps I wanted to believe him; either way, I was happy because he was my boyfriend again.

My wonderful distraction was back in my arms-distracting me again.

forgiveness... the ultimate f-word

Being a senior did have its privileges, as well as its advantages. I felt I had permission to ease up on my schoolwork, but at the same time, the pressure to find the right college stressed me out. After four months in my delinquent English class, I adopted a totally new perspective for the freak show. I actually enjoyed walking into class because I never knew what craziness would erupt. I liked the misfits. I liked the punks. I even liked the vocational girls. The punks kept me entertained with their wild stories about South Street that seemed made up, but totally entertaining. They let me touch their spiky Mohawks, and they told me that the secret to getting it to stick in the air was Aqua Net hair gel and a blow dryer. The vocational girls gave me tips for hair and nail care and even did my nails one day before class.

Besides Ron, my favorite new freaky friend was Michael Storms. Mike was a guy that I never talked to in my entire life and probably would never talk to after graduation. English class would most likely be our only form of communication. Michael, Ron, and I sat next to each other and found very early on that we all loved the show *Cheers*. We came up with a game to play in class that revolved around *Cheers*. Someone recited a quote from the show and then the other two players had the challenge of figuring out who (in the show) said it. We had a point sheet and were very meticulous about our scores.

Michael never had a girlfriend that I was aware of, so when he came into class on a Monday with a gold necklace that read "taken," Ron and I almost fell out of our seats with delight. We both laughed at the idea that Mike would actually wear jewelry, or the fact that someone felt the need to stake their claim. We toyed with the idea that, perhaps, Mike went out and bought it himself.

When *Cheers* got old, Ron and I played "Where's Waldo?" We took turns hiding Waldo around the room and everyday, we had to find him before the bell rang. Sometimes, without asking, Ron would snag a Pepsi for me from the teachers' lounge. He drew pictures for me, usually consisting of *Eagles* helmets, The *Philadelphia Flyers* emblem, and, upon my request, a portrait of Darren Daulton. Ron hated drawing Darren Daulton; he always scoffed whenever I asked him to draw him. Every guy I knew hated my favorite Philly. They were all just jealous.

I do not recall any actual schoolwork that I did in English with the exception of writing haikus. Michael, Ron, and I rushed through our assignments, so we could spend the entire class writing our own haikus. Ron acted as if he was stretching his arms out as he dropped a folded, white-lined piece of paper on my desk.

"Chi" by Ron Baduleese:
Will you chi with me?
A six-pack will be offered.
Then, I will kick you out.

I laughed hysterically. The class of '93 adopted the word "chi" as a code word for sex. I tapped Ron on the back and requested another one. Ron smiled crookedly and proudly admitted, "Shit, I got a lot more where that came from... take it. You want me to write more? I am like the Shakespeare of haikus!" He dabbed the end of his pencil in his mouth, and turned around to write his new masterpiece.

"Hell yeah!" I quickly responded. "Make one up about Tiffany."

"Tiffany who?" he asked.

I cocked my head to look at him sideways. "You know, Tiffany Ledger... my friend. Duh, curly hair... hangs out with me all the time. She lives in Westville. Duh?"

Ron shook his head while admitting, "Shannon, all your friends look and act the same to me." He chuckled. "You know... I bet you guys all plan to wear the same outfits in school, don't ya?"

Somewhat offended, I retorted, "What's that supposed to mean?"

Ron put his hands up in a defensive position, and backed up from his seat. "Oh, well. Don't get all, like, offended and shit. It's just that all your friends are, you know..." He raised his eyebrow.

"No, I don't know... are what?" I insisted.

With a cynical tone, Ron cried, "Come on, Shan? You know you and you're whole crowd are known as, like, you know... stuck up. I mean, not you, but by association you are." Again, Ron put his hands out in front defending his accusations. "I mean, you have to know that, right?"

I did. I knew that everyone, no matter who you were, had some kind of label. I never thought anyone would actually say it to my face. His statement was weird because my perception of "snobby" was much different. I thought snobby girls lived in Haddonfield, wore Lacoste collar shirts, had perfectly straight, flat-ironed hair, belonged to country clubs, rode horses, had convertibles, and never gained a pound. So, my friends and I were not even close to being snobs. However, I was quite sure someone like Ron saw things completely differently.

I playfully pushed Ron, cocked my head, and shrieked, "We're not snobby. You guys just think we are. Actually…" I looked at him with a mysterious look and said, "We're a lot of fun. We like to have fun. Fun is our middle name. My name is actually Shannon "Fun" Bennet."

"Oh yeah? I bet! What do you guys do for fun?" He imitated us with a feminine voice: "Ohh, Buffy do you want to come over for tea and scrumpets? Maybe we can play croquette outside with the butler!"

I held in my side as I nearly fell to the floor in laugher. I giddily asked, "What the frig' is a scrumpet? And you've been to my house… duh… like I would have a butler? Dumbass!"

Ron couldn't resist laughing either. I turned to Mike, who was nodding his head with agreement. I looked at Mike and said, "What are you looking at me for? Aren't you taken?" Ron gave me a high five.

Ron persisted, "Well, Ms. Fun, what do you consider a fun Saturday night? Watching taped reruns of *Beverly Hills 90210*?" He imitated my voice again and said, "Ohh, it's Luke Perry… isn't he so dreamy? Too bad he is, like, forty seven years old and still in high school."

Just as Ron was finishing his imitation of me, the bell rang. I rose slowly from my seat, grabbed my book bag, and smirked. I playfully said, "We like to watch Cheers, go to Phillies games, eat cheese steaks at Jim's, and read perverted haikus."

Ron laughed as he went in another direction down the hall, and then shouted, "Yeah… but do you guys like to Chi?"

I shook my head at his typical remark and, under my breath, whispered, "Dirtbag!" Then, I giggled at his pervy comment and snickered as I repeated his haiku in my head.

Carl changed. After that cold winter night of promises, he kept his word. Although it was a nice to have a boyfriend who listened and tried to be what I wanted, I still wasn't satisfied. It wasn't Carl that could give me satisfaction; it was me.

Since Phillip's death, maybe even before he died, I felt guilty. Guilt was something that I developed over time, a long time. I was aware that other people would tell me that I was crazy to feel guilty because his death wasn't my fault. I wasn't dumb and I knew he pulled the trigger, but what could I do with all of the crap festering inside me? The crap. The garbage. The feelings that haunted me so much that I chose to ignore that they existed. Just as I told Carl on that February night, I just wanted to be free.

Freedom, my personal freedom, was something that I could only obtain myself. Freedom from anger. Freedom from guilt. Freedom from shame. Freedom from sorrow. Those feelings, those crappy feelings, could disappear if I allowed them. Still, I held onto the terrible feelings, knowing that they were like a disease that wreaked havoc on my body and soul. It almost gave me some comfort to believe that I was guilty or angry because then there would still be a connection to Phillip. I didn't know how to feel anything else *but* sorrow. To me, Phillip was the "tragic thing" that happened, instead of an actual human being that lost his life at a very early age.

He wasn't a thing. He wasn't a "tragic thing" at all. Over the years, I sat in class, thinking about what could have been, what should have been, and how I would do it so different. I toyed with the idea that, perhaps, I could have been his personal savior, instead of his prisoner. That is what it felt like... prison. Dealing with his suicide kept me isolated from my feelings, kept me angry, and, most of all, it kept me guilty. It was my own private prison without walls.

I was ready to break free. The only way I could break free, the only way I could get what I really wanted, was to forgive.

Forgive: Middle English, from Old English. To give up resentment. To grant relief from payment. To cease to feel resentment against. Stop blame and grant pardon.

The question or the unknown was how. *How?* How can I forgive myself? How does one learn how to release all the crap, all that stuff, all that negativity? Feeling bad about his death made me feel like I was holding onto him somehow. Letting go of that grief, letting go of that shame seemed like a betrayal. If I mourned him long enough, hard enough, and with enough conviction, then maybe I could win his affections. However, all that stuff wasn't true... I always knew that it wasn't true. I was ready to face the truth.

The truth was that there was nothing I could have done to prevent him from dying, and I was finally able to admit that. The truth was also painfully bitter because it reminded me that life was so precious, so easy to take for granted. I should have been nicer to him. I could have been nicer to him. It was a simple matter of being human... being kind.

I used to envy those who never had to deal with a death, and then I realized that everyone, at some point, had to deal with it. Death was universal. Fortunately or unfortunately, I was exposed to something traumatic at a young age. Phillip's death was out of my control, but for many years since he passed, I took on the responsibility of it. I had to choose- love or loss.

I chose love.

I chose to remember the relationship that was fun, instead of the painful. I wanted to remember his smile, instead of his tears. I tried very hard to remember that he was my brother, instead of a situation. I imagined us laughing at the lake, instead of fighting. I wanted to cherish the past memories, instead of the current reality. All I could do was love. All I could do was learn to love him all over again.

I vowed to spend a lifetime loving him… everyday.

no more pencils, no more books, no more teacher's dirty looks... well until august

Everything just fell into place for the remainder of my year. My last year of high school softball ended with a softball conference championship. My senior class went to Disney World for our senior trip. I ditched school on senior cut day. My black and white graduation picture was on our living room wall, adorned with a smile, and a fake diploma resting in my perfectly manicured fingers. I wore a bright fuchsia, sequined dress to the prom. I received my final yearbook, and my graduation gown hung in the closet with a thin, plastic cover to protect it. In a matter weeks, I was going to pack up my stuff and go south to Pfeiffer College in Misenheimer, North Carolina.

The graduation ceremonies were held outside on the most humid day of the entire year. My makeup practically melted off as I dripped off sweat in my seat with my white tank dress, pink lipstick, and my mother's pearls. My hair was down, neatly flat-ironed to give it the appearance that it was straight (which quickly turned to frizz after the National Anthem.) I tried to appear somewhat interested in the ceremony as I flipped my hair and slipped my little, white shoes off and on nervously waiting to grab my high school diploma.

Surprisingly, I received a couple of awards. Some academy gave me an award for most "poised" athlete. I stood up and heard the crowd clap for me and then sat back down and wondered what exactly "poised' meant. I was about to graduate and go off to college and I had no idea what "poised" meant. Lizzie received an award for perfect attendance in high school. She never missed one single day of school.

When the dean called my name, I quickly grabbed my diploma, faked a smile for a photo, and walked down the platform. I pranced back to my seat, sat down, and smiled. I thought my brother would be proud.

When summer came to an end, I packed and loaded all my belongings in our silver Honda Accord. The packing list that Pfeiffer sent to my house was in my fingertips. I mouthed the words on the list as I rechecked my belongings. I had everything on the list, a long list that included duck boots for the rain. I ran in and out of my bedroom, double and triple checking my dresser, my closet, and under my bed. On my wall, there was an 8x10 picture of Carl and me at the prom. I took it off the wall, caressed the glass, and wondered if I would still want to hang it up when I came home for Thanksgiving.

Carl walked to my house around 10:30 in the morning. He held a small, brown bag in his hand that was stuffed with homemade chocolate chip cookies. Immediately, I flashed back to New Year's Eve. The cookies made me laugh. It was all so ironic. I could not believe that Carl was standing in front of me, holding a bag of cookies after three long years. The moment was somewhat surreal and almost dreamlike. The day, the moment, was inevitable, but standing there and saying goodbye made me feel so detached from my life. Was I really leaving?

I took the cookies and smiled. Carl and I stood face to face in the middle of my street, perhaps for the last time.

I whispered in his ear, "I want you to know that I have to go, and saying goodbye to you is the hardest part. You're the only reason that I would ever stay..." I leaned over to hug him and softly said, "I love you."

Carl nodded his head and, in that one moment, for the first time, I think he understood why I had to go. He lightened the mood by joking, "Well, I guess I'm glad you let me call you that night." He sighed and went on, "Even if it means that, after all that time, all the great times... I have to let you go."

Dad shouted out the window to remind me that we were leaving in five minutes. I coolly nodded, trying to act like I was ready.

Carl rolled his eyes and exhaled, "Five minutes, huh? Wow. It's finally here, isn't it?" We both were silent as we faced each other.

"Shan..." His face became extremely serious when he said, "You are a good person, and you will do great things with your life." Carl exhaled again. "I know. I know this is your next step in life and I guess that makes it easier. I hope when you come back... I'm still the one you come home to."

My body became warm and my skin began to glow when he said those words to me. Hearing him say that I was a good person made me feel like everything mattered between us. I hugged him tight. I told him that he would be the first person I would visit.

I commented, "Carl, I will literally drive home, get out of my car, and knock on your door. I promise. Pinkie swear?" I put my pinkie up.

Just as we were locking pinkies, dad came out with his keys in hand, signifying that it was time to go.

"I gotta go."

"Hey! Hey Shannon!" Carl shouted as I walked away from him.

I turned around just before getting into the passenger seat to look his way.

Carl waved his hand and yelled, "Have a nice life."

I knew what he meant. I knew he was referring to the last episode of Cheers. The episode when Ted Danson and Shelly Long realized that love wasn't enough to save their relationship. The last episode when they finally said goodbye. Ted knew, Shelly knew, the audience knew, and Carl and I knew that you could never go back.

I never debated his final remark as I jumped in the car. I watched Carl slip away until he was no longer in the side view mirror. Dad and I drove away in silence. Then, dad reached over to touch my arm and, with a comforting voice, he assured, "Everything will be fine. You'll see."

A lot of stuff happened since the day I walked into eighth grade. My belief that my brother would be a distant memory, my belief that somehow the change of weather would make him better, or my belief that I could ignore the situation were just big lies that I told myself. On my way to North Carolina, I sat quietly in the car, watching the road signs become foreign and unfamiliar. There was plenty of time to think about everything during a traffic jam in Richmond.

Phillip's death forced me to re-evaluate life. His death wasn't as painful as I remembered, not as bitter. He taught me a lot about myself; unfortunately, the lesson came with a hefty price. I didn't want to live the rest of my life judging, criticizing, or blaming. My older brother was teaching me how to live my life from the grave, and I was grateful for that. He was a reminder that the words we use, the power of good or bad intentions, and the ability to love was the most important stuff in life.

After all the years of trying to figure out "the truth," I realized that the truth was always there. The truth, the God's honest truth, was that love will conquer all and love never dies. Love cannot be taken away, so even though I had not seen my brother in five years, I still loved him... actually... I loved him even more.

I read the sign: *You are entering North Carolina. The First in Flight State.*

I smiled.

I thought about what Carl said: "Have a nice life."

While gazing at the pines in the distance, I thought: *Yes, yes. I will have a nice life- after all.*

about the author

Janice Pettit-Brundage grew up in Woodbury Heights, New Jersey. After graduating from Gateway Regional High School, she attended Pfeiffer University in Misenhiemer, North Carolina. Janice played both softball and soccer during her four years at Pfeiffer. In 1997, she graduated with a major in sociology and a minor in criminal justice.

After graduation, Janice moved back to New Jersey and began her career working for The State of New Jersey Juvenile Justice Commission. During that time, she created her professional pitching instruction business- Pettits Pitchers. In 1999, Janice moved to Newburgh, New York, and began doing social work for The Astor Home for Children in Poughkeepsie, New York. After several years of working in the social work field with mentally disturbed children and teenagers, Janice switched careers and became a full time coach for the NCAA at Mount Saint Mary College in Newburgh, New York.

While facilitating her private business and coaching, Janice began to explore the literary world. In late 2006, she began writing her first book, Sweet Bird of Prey. It is a personal and beloved story that describes teen depression, bullying, and suicide.

Presently, Janice is a volunteer with The American Foundation for Suicide Prevention (AFSP). She is involved in the education department with the AFSP and serves as a group facilitator for teen survivors of suicide in the Hudson Valley, New York.

Janice lives in Wallkill, New York, with her husband, Frank, and her two daughters, Cassandra and Melanie.

published by sisu books

For more information on our small press please visit us on the web at www.sisubooks.com.

Sisu Books
P.O. Box 421
Sparrowbush, New York 12780

info@sisubooks.com

Attention schools and businesses:

Sisu Books Publishing books are available at quantity discounts with bulk purchase for educational, business, or sales promotional use. For information please contact sales@sisubooks.com.

CPSIA information can be obtained at www.ICGtesting.com
Printed in the USA
LVOW010727101111

254197LV00003B/43/P